# WEAPONSMASTER

WEAPONSMASTER SAGA

BOOK ONE

PHIL AERIX

Cover by Joolz & Jarling

Created with Vellum

**Want to always know when the next book comes out...and get another full-length novel for free?**

Join my newsletter to get the news on what's coming next and you'll also get Elf Queen for free.

Go to philaerix.com and click on the cover to join!

# CHAPTER ONE

"Sonofabitch!"

I swerved to keep from smashing into the back of some asshole in a Camaro after he'd cut me off. As if I wasn't already having a bad enough day, I needed to almost get into an accident?

I could only thank whatever god was out there that it was Friday, and I was heading home. Finally.

My phone rang through the delivery van's sound system. I checked the screen. It was the office.

"Shit!"

I cleared my throat and hit the button on the steering wheel to accept the call.

"This is Gar."

"Garfield, this is Stan."

I rolled my eyes and had to slam on the brakes to keep from plowing into the car in front of me as it stopped abruptly. On the freeway.

"Hey Stanley."

"It's Stan."

"Yeah, well, it's Gar. You call me by the right name and I'll do the same. What's up?"

My boss paused for a moment and I thought he might give me shit about my attitude. I mean, he wasn't *really* my boss, but he might as well have been. He scheduled my deliveries.

"I've got another delivery for you. Are you on your way back in?"

"I'm on my way home. I just did my last job. Stephanie is supposed to take any late deliveries."

"She clocked out early. Had a date."

*What the fuck*? "She had a date. That's all someone needs to leave work early?"

Silence. The fact of the matter was that Stephanie was hot and Stan had a hard-on for her. If he might get some action by doing her favors, he'd throw me and anyone else under the delivery van.

"Oh, and swap rides. Take van seven. Leave yours. It's going in for maintenance. I'll have your delivery waiting for you. Paperwork for a legal office."

"Great. I'm looking forward to it."

I punched the button on the steering wheel, accidentally honking the horn. Three other horns around me sounded, and one guy yelled curses out his window. Something about "asshole" and "eat a bag of dicks." At least there were no guns involved.

Welcome to paradise. Lovely Riverside, California.

Six o'clock on a Friday, and I was stuck with one more job. I usually liked my job as a courier. You know, other than the traffic. Being outside, even if I was in a van most of the time, wasn't a bad way to go. I'd had a bitch of a day, though, and wanted to go home and relax. I sighed. I'd have to do that after this one more delivery. I hoped it was local.

I pulled into the alley behind the office and jumped out of the van. After sprinting inside, snatching the paperwork from the counter, and nodding at Stanley, I made for van seven. Something triggered my peripheral vision and I spun, thinking it was either someone approaching to tell me how he needed money for gas, or one of the other couriers trying to sneak up and fuck with me.

Nothing there.

I rubbed my eyes. I really needed to get some sleep this weekend. When I did long hours for weeks at a time, I sometimes had that: shapes or flickers of movement at the edge of my vision. Whatever.

In the van, I checked the destination. "Fucking San Bernardino!" I cursed Stanley, Stephanie, and all their living relatives.

I made the trip—forty-five minutes because of afternoon traffic—and dropped off the paperwork with a paralegal who was almost gorgeous enough to make up for the whole thing. Almost.

I pulled out into traffic and a light at the corner of my vision snatched my attention. My anger spiked again. "Really? I mean, REALLY?" The low fuel light was lit and the needle was beneath the E. My fault for not looking at the gauge earlier, though it was really the fault of whichever asshole used the van last and didn't put gas in it. Probably Nick.

I knew the area just well enough to have a firm grasp on two things. First, I knew of two gas stations I could get to without running out of gas. Second, both were in shitty neighborhoods where I would typically not leave the windows down or the door unlocked as I drove through.

The day was getting better and better. I called dispatch and told them I'd delivered the paperwork and I was heading home, then I pulled into a sketchy gas station as the van sputtered and died. At least it rolled to the pump, so I didn't have to get out and push. I was going to kick Nick's ass for not filling the tank.

It had only been dark for half an hour or so, but the weakly lit street looked dimmer than it should have. Old streetlights, almost half of which were burned out, flickered and threatened to plunge the street into total darkness. I recognized the ambience. I'd grown up in places like this. Worse places, if I was being truthful.

I got out and took off the gas cap, swiping my card and getting ready to put a few gallons in so I could get the hell out of there and get home.

Another shadow moved far off to my right. I casually twisted and stretched, getting a better look that way.

Nothing.

Immediately, my peripheral vision picked up another bit of motion. I made a show of hitting the button on the pump so I could glance that way. A figure in dark clothes walked toward me. Dark beanie on his head, oversized jacket, pants that were either too large or were being worn too low. I knew the type. Guys like this were indigenous to this kind of neighborhood.

Yet another casual peek and I found a second person, dressed similarly, with the flash of metal under his jacket. Jewelry, chains, or something more nefarious? I turned to put the gas nozzle into the tank and saw a third person.

All three were slowly, nonchalantly making their way to me, one a little more quickly than the others.

"Hey, man," the first one I'd seen said.

*Fuck. Here we go...*

"Don't start no shit, won't be no shit," I said, hefting the gas nozzle and feeling its weight.

"Yo, you ain't need to be like that. I just has to ax you a question."

"Dude, it's Friday night, I just want to get some gas and get out of here. Whatever you want, believe me, you don't want it here."

I probably need to say a little bit about myself at this point. My name is Garfield Hailey, though I'll kick your ass if you call me anything but Gar. I won't go into my family life, or the lack of it, but one thing about my upbringing is pertinent (and yes, I do really talk like this): I spent most of my younger years trying to keep from getting my white ass whupped on the streets of Oakland.

Maybe you've heard of the city, or "the Town" as some of the locals call it. Near San Francisco in beautiful Northern California—NorCal—Oakland is one of the biggest shitholes in the country. I can say that. I grew up there. Say, for example, you were a white kid in an area like Coliseum or Fitchburg. If you happened to be in that situation, you had a choice of being one of two types of people: the fastest running motherfucker in the city, or a person who could not only take abuse, but give it. I'm the second kind.

I don't want to mislead you. I can run if I need to. But when you run, you eventually have to stop. When I stopped, I'd get my ass handed to me for no other reason than I existed. So, I started to fight back. A little at a time. I'd choose the battles, run if I had to. After a while I learned that I was pretty good. I mean, like prodigy good.

I'm not going to give you bullshit about how I'm some MMA fighter or special forces guy. Nope. I'm a street fighter, through and through. I fight to win—by any means necessary. I've been attacked with and, in turn, used about everything you can imagine as a weapon.

Case in point, my current situation.

Predictably, my new acquaintance rushed me. Stupidly, he did so with his fists. His friend to my left, who was circling around to what he thought was a blind spot behind me, took out a knife. That guy knew what he was doing. The guy on the right, he had a forty in his hand. I wasn't sure if he was going to drink it or use it as a weapon, but it didn't matter. I'd get to him. One thing at a time.

So, yeah, the first guy came at me, cocking his arm back like he was going to floor me with one punch. I took a step back, grabbed the hose part of the gas nozzle, and swung it hard in an overhand loop. The heavy brass nozzle cracked the motherfucker on the top of his head and he dropped like the sack of shit he was. I turned just in time to see knife guy lunging at me. Way too soon. I mean, come on, get some depth perception. I didn't need to do anything because I was a good three feet beyond his reach, even lunging forward to put himself off-balance as he was.

I clucked my tongue, choked up on the nozzle, pulled the emissions control sleeve up, and squeezed the trigger. A stream of gas sprayed into his face, getting in his eyes, mouth, and nose.

The moron brought his hands up to his face—still holding the knife—and almost cut himself as he screamed.

"Auuuuggghhh. It burns, it burns."

"Yeah, that's what happens when you try to drink gas, dumb shit."

I kicked him square in the face as he bent over to spit and whine. His nose crushed against my work boot and he flipped backward, landing on his back on the concrete. He may have hit his head on the curb. I don't know.

Don't care.

He sputtered a few times, but was pretty much out.

I turned to the third guy, holding his beer bottle like he was trying to decide what to do. I put the gas nozzle in the tank, started the gas flowing, and stepped toward him as he stood between two pumps about five feet away.

"You can leave if you want to," I said calmly. "I just want to get my gas and go home. You get to choose what happens here."

He chose wrong. Holding the bottle by its neck, he raised it—spilling beer all over himself like a fucking moron—and rushed me. I waited for him to get closer.

As the bottle came down, I stepped to the side, just enough for the "weapon" to pass by me. I caught his arm at the wrist as he tried to keep from falling over, twisted it and slammed my forearm into the back of his elbow. With a loud crack, his hand loosened around the bottle as his arm broke. He screamed like a little girl. I'd slid my hand up and took the neck of the container from him. As he let go, I pivoted to get into a better position and slammed it down on his head.

The bottle shattered, cutting my attacker's scalp, bringing another scream. He staggered, cradling one arm with the other as he tried to run away.

"Nuh-uhn. I gave you your chance."

I grabbed his broken arm and swung him around to slam him into the side of the gas pump. I eyed the window washing squeegee—I was surprised it was still there in this neighborhood—but decided against using it. Instead, as he bounced off the pump, I drilled him with a hard right hook. I think I felt his jaw crack as he rocketed back to the pump, bounced, and landed in a heap at my feet.

I eyed the three wannabe gangsters, making sure they were actually out and not playing dead. I had to wait another couple of minutes until the gas pump clicked off. I was already there, so I might as well fill the tank. I replaced the nozzle, screwed my gas cap back on, closed the fuel door, and went to get back in the van.

I rolled my eyes and dragged my first attacker out of the way so I didn't run his stupid ass over, then got in the van and started it up. I gave a little salute to the poor kid in the booth and shrugged an apology for the mess. Then I pulled out onto the dimly lit street and headed for home.

# CHAPTER TWO

As I drove, I sniffed, then heaved a sigh. Great. I'd kept any gas from getting on me, but the dude's beer had spilled on me. If my luck continued like it had been the rest of the day, I'd get pulled over next. That's all I needed, to have to explain to some cop why I smelled like alcohol. While driving a work van.

I hit the hands-free button on the steering wheel and spoke loudly, "Call Lucas Walker." The phone rang a couple of times and then picked up.

"Hey, Gar. What's up, man? You still working?"

"Hey, Lucas. I'm on my way back home after a shit day. What're you doing?"

"Imma get in my car and go home. I just got off work. What's shit about your day?"

I ran my fingers through my hair as I pulled onto the freeway. "What wasn't shit about it? Stanley thinks he's gonna get laid, so I had to do an extra delivery so Stephanie could take off early for a date. I had to go to San Berdoo to drop off paperwork."

"That's always fun."

"Yeah. Nick left the damn van on empty so I had to stop to get gas."

"In the 'hood?"

"You got it."

"Did you try to save someone from being mugged?"

"Very funny, asshole. I'm not in the mood for it. I'm not using up my energy only to get fucked for trying to be a good guy."

I could hear Lucas laughing, but at least he had the grace to pull the phone away from his face. "I know. So, getting gas..."

"I was just about to put the nozzle into the tank when three of the neighborhood welcome committee came to chat with me."

"Uh-oh."

"I clearly warned them."

"'Don't start no shit, won't be no shit?'"

"You got it." My mood lightened a bit. Lucas knew what was up.

"I think you look for places you can use that."

I grinned. He had me there. "Anyway, they made a run at me."

"Did you get your ass kicked?"

"Please. That hasn't happened since I was like ten. Before I even knew you."

"Yeah, yeah. I know. You didn't kill anyone, right? We've talked about this. These fools are amateurs. Don't risk your future taking them down like that."

"Yeah, yeah. I didn't kill anyone."

"You take 'em out with a tissue box or a used rubber you found on the ground?"

"Ugh, that's foul. No, it was the gas nozzle for one, a

face full of gas for another, and a forty the third guy tried to attack me with."

"Sounds right."

"They didn't consider the ramifications of what they were doing."

Lucas laughed right into the phone this time. "Rami-fuck-ations. Okay, professor. You couldn't say, 'they didn't think,' like a real damn person?"

I chuckled, but was interrupted by Lucas grunting in confusion.

"Again?" Lucas said. "Man, I need to get my eyes checked. Fucking boogeymen jumping out at me again."

"What?"

"Nothing. I keep seeing things out of the corner of my eye. It's probably one of those floating things people talk about in my eyeball. There's nothing there. I probably have a damn tumor in my eye."

*Seeing things out of the corner of his eye?* "You know your mom always told you if you kept jacking off, you'd go blind. I told you to stop that shit."

"Haha, fuck you. So, a little pool tonight? It's Friday. Wanna go over to Chico's and rack some up, see who's out?"

"Definitely. What, an hour or so good? I should be home in like twenty minutes. It'll give me a chance to change. And to wash the beer off me."

"Sure. I...what the fuck? There it is ag—"

The line went dead.

"Damn deadspots. If you can hear me, Lucas, I'll call you back when I get home. Talk to you later, brother."

After I got back to my apartment, I called twice more before finally giving up and heading to Chico's. They had a few pool tables and I liked the atmosphere. It wasn't a big place, which kept the crowd to a manageable level. I hated big bars and clubs that were wall to wall people, two or three hundred deep. Not for me.

On the way, I thought about Lucas. He was thirteen and I was twelve when I first met him. He was getting his ass beaten by Anfernee Tomkins, a punk-ass bully who'd learned a year before not to fuck with me. Who the hell calls their kid Anfernee? Jesus.

Anyway, being altruistic back then, I stood up for that short, skinny kid I'd never seen before. We immediately struck up a friendship. It only took a day of hanging out with him to start teaching him to fight. He was a big fan of martial arts movies and MMA. I didn't have any dreams of being Bruce Lee or Michael Jai White. I wanted to learn about everything, which is why he started calling me "professor." But fighting was more instinctual for me. And necessary. I was interested in how people did things in different parts of the world, sure, and watching kung fu movies was fun, but idolizing actors? Nah.

Though I taught him and sparred with him until he could hold his own, he never came close to my abilities. Maybe I wanted to be some kind of hero back then, but rough neighborhoods have a way of grinding that out of you.

When I was sixteen, I saw some asshole beating his girlfriend outside a Popeye's. I stopped him. Hard. I turned back to the woman to make sure she was all right and barely got out of the way in time to keep from getting a knife in the eye. She sliced my arm pretty good before I wrenched the blade out of her hand, and then I watched her coo at the man who had just given her a black eye, spitting and glaring at me while she did it.

I ran my finger over the soft ridge of the scar on my forearm. Thirty-two stitches.

There were other situations like that, along with one or two where the police got involved. You'd think I would have learned not to get involved. Nope.

I was living with Lucas after my mom passed—she caught a stray bullet in a drive-by, and his old man kicked him out of the house as soon as he turned eighteen. He signed the lease and allowed my underaged ass to move in with him. We both had shitty little jobs, but we were surviving. Neither of us had any goals other than getting out of Oakland, so we lived day to day, not thinking too much about the future.

Until that night.

I was sitting in my bed reading when someone emitted a horrible, screeching scream outside my apartment. By the time I made it to the front door, Lucas was there with me and someone was yelling "help me" amid the screams.

I looked at my buddy and we nodded at each other. I opened the door to the little courtyard and found one of my neighbors standing in a night gown, blood streaming down her head and onto her face, staining her previously white clothing red. Her husband or boyfriend or whatever was yelling at her.

"Fucking bitch. I told you not to talk back to me. Now you know." He still held the jagged remnants of a ceramic pot-style lamp.

I didn't like the situation to begin with, but I liked even less that he was stalking toward her, raising the shards of the lamp to hit her again.

No. Nuh-uhn. Not happening.

I ran past the screaming woman and caught the man's

arm as it came down. His eyes widened at my nerve, getting involved.

I elbowed him in the face.

The fucker's breath was something like ninety-seven percent alcohol, mixed with sour body odor and his cigarette breath. I didn't want to be anywhere near him and I definitely didn't want to punch him in the face. He'd probably give me HIV or herpes or some shit like that if I broke my knuckles on his teeth and some of his blood or saliva got into my cuts.

So, I did what any knowledgeable person trying to help would do: I punched him in the solar plexus hard enough that it almost knocked him out. As he bent forward, I snapped a kick to his jaw, which definitely knocked him out.

Lucas had been trying to help the woman, and other neighbors had gathered around them. At least seven people watched me over a hedge. When I walked over to the crowd, two women who lived in the complex, one of whom I'd seen in scrubs, were working to clean the woman's bleeding head. I jerked my chin at Lucas and we went back into our apartment.

The next day, a couple of cops were asking questions about what happened. The man and his girlfriend both were going to press charges against whoever had "attacked him." It was the same old shit. The woman was backing him up and people who tried to help were going to get the shit end of the deal.

Lucas and I didn't bother discussing it with anyone else. We put what little we had into his car—leaving the few pieces of shitty furniture we had—and we got the hell out of NorCal. South, to a place we could start over. Hopefully.

It worked out pretty well, so far. We weren't living the

lives of movie stars or anything, but things were better than they had been. We even got our own places, a luxury we never thought we'd be able to afford. Lucas was my brother in all the ways that mattered. Things were good.

Until I waited for him at the bar for an hour as he didn't answer the phone and didn't show up. No way he would leave me hanging like that and ignore me. Something had to have happened to him.

I got back into the delivery van and headed to where Lucas worked. Something was going on and I needed to find out what.

I spotted his car right away, a blue 2018 Toyota Corolla with a rear passenger side fender the color of Bondo. It made no sense. Why would he leave his car?

I searched the area, looking for signs he'd been attacked or something, though the neighborhood wasn't bad and unless it had been several people, he would have been fine. I knew exactly how well he could fight...and run. I'd taught him everything he knew.

Just to be sure, I went to his apartment also and banged on the door. One of his neighbors, a girl about the same age as me, or maybe Lucas's twenty-five, pulled up into her parking space and started unloading some groceries.

"Hey, Tasha. You seen Lucas this evening?"

"Hi, Gar. No. I've been gone for about half an hour, but I haven't seen him since yesterday. His car's not here."

"Yeah, I know. Here, let me help you with those." I picked up a few bags as she took them out and handed them to me, and then I carried them to her apartment a few doors down. I had no problem being polite and helpful; my problem was with trying to be a hero in situations where I knew I was going to get shit all over.

Tasha thanked me and said she'd have Lucas call me

when she saw him. I nodded and left, calling him another couple of times on the way home. It was looking more like a movie all the time. Mysterious disappearance, no contact and no trace. Next, people were going to start questioning that he ever existed.

Damn.

I waited around until nearly midnight, watching the news to see if anything happened that was strange enough to be reported. Maybe it wasn't just Lucas. There was no mention of any abductions, attacks, or unknown people ending up at the hospital with organs missing. I found myself dozing on the couch until a screech from outside my apartment woke me up with a start.

I blinked repeatedly, trying to focus my eyes and figure out where I was. I shook my head, trying to kickstart my mind. That sound I just heard, was it real or a memory of the scream that woman made back in Oakland? I pocketed my phone and went out to check it out. I still hadn't changed out of my work clothes.

Standing out in the parking lot, I looked around. No woman in a blood-soaked night gown showed up. That was good. But another loud sound pulled my eyes over to my left.

Two cats squared off, backs arched and fur standing up, tails as puffy as a bottle brush, near a bench in a grassy area. They howled and hissed at each other. It wasn't exactly what I'd heard, but close enough. I let out a sigh.

While I was standing there, I called Lucas again. As the phone rang, the shadows near one of the streetlamps twitched in the edge of my peripheral vision. *That damn thing again*. Those were the same words Lucas had used.

I turned and, by chance, looked right at a blob of shadow as it unfolded from a nearby bush. It extended into the shape of a man, if a man's shadow stretched at the edges to make it look like he had spikes on his arms, legs, and torso. I blinked, staring at the darkness and trying to figure out what it was.

Then I fell, the world spinning around me. My body didn't want to respond and all I could think of was my head hitting the concrete sidewalk.

Everything went dark.

# CHAPTER THREE

The world phased into existence slowly, the dimness brightening a little until the light hurt my eyes. I was sprawled out on something soft but scratchy, a strong scent of—I don't know, green—almost overpowering all my other senses. It kind of resembled the smell of cut grass, but not quite. Trampled bushes?

"Aaaarrggghhhh," I groaned. My body felt strange, lethargic. Weak.

A small motion grabbed my attention and I had to force my eyes to focus. It took way too long. When I could see halfway decently, I still disbelieved what I saw. That shadow thing, it was still here. Right in front of me. Worse, it was doing something to me.

It held its clawlike hand over me, like it was trying to pull on me with puppet strings or something. A faint mist, something halfway between condensed breath on a cold day and flat-out steam moved sluggishly from my body to the palm of that hand. Worse, I could feel it.

Something was being sucked out of me.

I freaked the fuck out. All I could think was that it was

eating my soul, or something like that. I moaned weakly and scrabbled my feet and hands to get away, but the thing's other arm, looped under me, held me tight.

Glowing yellow eyes met mine and the empty space where the thing's mouth should be seemed like it turned upward in an evil grin. I may have imagined that part, though.

Hell no. Dream or not, I was done. I gathered up what little strength I had in my right arm, and I punched the thing right in the face.

Amazingly, my fist struck something solid. The living shadow's head snapped back and the hand it held above me flailed. It lost its balance and we both fell to the ground. I rolled away, making it about two feet before I slammed into a hard object. I had to shake my head to clear my vision before I could see that it was wood...a fallen tree, complete with moss growing on it.

I kicked, landing another blow to the shadow's face, and heaved myself to my feet. I swayed, but didn't fall. Progress.

Whatever the fuck I was fighting smoothly flowed to its feet. In the diffused light—I was in the middle of a bunch of trees with ferns and other bushes around me—I finally was able to see the entire figure.

It was man-shaped and man-sized, probably just over six feet tall. All one color—black—it had sharp fingers and toes, basically claws, and those smears I'd seen before, they really were spikes. If they were solid like the rest of the thing's body felt.

That dark crevice of a mouth turned up again and the yellow eyes flared as it slowly closed the distance.

To be honest, I was cool with running away at this point. I didn't know where I was or what the thing was and

I wasn't feeling my best, but I wasn't too good to bounce. My legs shook from the task of holding me up, though, so running didn't seem like an option.

*Okay. I guess I'm going to fight.*

I sucked in a breath to calm myself and brought my hands up. Even as I did, my eyes scanned for a weapon. I'd long prided myself on being able to use anything as a weapon, but other than the fallen tree and some flimsy ferns, there wasn't much else available.

Ferns it was. I reached down and tore a large frond from the fern next to me and prepared to meet the shadow that was rapidly approaching me.

When the thing got close, it struck out with its arm, curving its sharp fingers into true claws to slash at me. Grabbing the frond with one hand on the base and the other at the other end, I caught the limb as I sidestepped the woefully telegraphed blow. The yellow eyes widened as I pivoted, twisted my arms to tighten the stem around its limb, and yanked as hard as my weakened body could manage.

I pulled the shadow body forcefully enough to wrench it around, throwing it off balance. I kicked down on its left knee, forcing it to kneel, and with a powerful twist of my hips, elbowed it as hard as I could in the back of its head.

The monster rocketed forward and face-planted on the soft forest soil. I quickly untangled my fern-stem weapon and looped it under the shadow's head with my arms crossed. Then I pulled up with everything I had to tighten the noose, hoping to hell the thing breathed. Otherwise, how could I strangle it?

It thrashed and tried to get loose, but I was holding it too tightly. The thing seemed to be slowing down, giving me a rush of energy. Maybe I could kill it after all.

Then the damn fern stem broke, not up to the task I required of it. With nothing else to do, I grabbed the monster's head on both sides and slammed it repeatedly into the ground as it continued to thrash.

Realizing the soil was too soft, I moved it in steps. Slam! Step. Slam! Step. It took me five cycles until I got close enough to the fallen tree, where I beat that motherfucker violently on the hard wood until the head I held onto felt mushy and misshapen. Then I slammed it into the log five more times.

Finally, I released the thing and let it fall. I collapsed, barely able to guide myself, so I landed hard on my ass on the fallen tree. I ran my hands through my hair after confirming that I didn't have blood or anything else from the creature on my hands. Well, that was good at least.

I watched it for several minutes for any signs of movement. There were none. As far as I could tell, it was dead.

I looked around. Trees and undergrowth and moss and dim light filtering through the canopy above for as far as I could see. No path, no sign of any other kind of life, nothing. There was also the corpse of the weird alien shadow monster.

Yeah, those parts were definitely *not* good.

*Where am I and what the hell am I going to do?*

I sat down on the fallen tree and glanced over at the body of the shadow creature I'd killed again. In death, it looked the same as in life, if it could be said that the thing was truly alive. I nudged it with my foot. It felt solid, but not quite as solid as a human body. It seemed different than before, a little more like a dark cloud rather than solid corpse.

The forest around me seemed endless, at least as far as I could see. Sunlight filtered in from above, but weak enough that the entire area had a gloomy quality, and I couldn't tell which direction the sun was in. Not only was that going to make finding a direction difficult, but I couldn't even tell if it was morning, noon, or afternoon.

The old rule about moss growing on the north side of trees didn't help me here, since the light was diminished enough that moss grew on all sides of the trunks around me. Hanging bearded moss told me the place got a lot of moisture, but the humidity in the air had already tipped me off on that point.

A mix of trees, some with straight trunks and needles and others that grew in a more twisted fashion, with a variety of leaf shapes, surrounded me. In between the boles were plants as well. Mostly ferns and some types of grasses. Moss, too, of course. Even a few mushrooms populated the darker areas. Nothing about any of that indicated which way I should go.

I couldn't very well stay in one spot. It wasn't like someone was searching for me and I could wait for rescue. The opposite was probably true. That shadow monster was obviously trying to kill me. What if there were more?

I pinched the bridge of my nose. *Okay, you need to think, Gar. What do we know?*

One thing I was pretty sure about was that I wasn't anywhere near Southern California anymore. There were no forests like this anywhere within a few hundred miles.

How did I get here? The last thing I remembered was seeing something out of the corner of my vision, and then I passed out. Or was knocked out. I didn't know how much time had passed from then until I woke up. I wasn't starving or dehydrated, so unless someone fed and gave me water as I slept, I'd bet I wasn't out for long.

I rolled my eyes and glanced down at my watch. It was an old-school, manually wound, analog watch called a Hamilton Khaki Field Mechanical Watch. Lucas had given it to me as a gift a few years back. It was almost identical to the one he wore, one I always said I was going to steal. That one had been his father's watch, passed onto him when his dad had been killed in action in Iraq. I'd memorized and thought about the inscription inside probably a lot more than necessary. *The only thing necessary for the triumph of evil is for good men to do nothing.*

It showed 2:37. With my lack of thirst and hunger, I doubted more than twelve hours had passed, even though afternoon made more sense with it being daylight out. It had to be early morning where I lived. Unless someone changed the time on my watch while I was out, I hadn't been unconscious long. Okay, one mystery solved.

Lucas. Where the hell was Lucas? He'd disappeared about six hours before me. Was he here? It sure sounded like he'd run into the same *kind* of shadow creatures. Maybe the same *one*. Was there more than one of them? What were the chances that he was taken and then I was taken? What was the purpose?

So many questions, with not one answer to be found.

My shoulders slumped. None of the emergency situations I'd imagined finding myself in were like this one. Not a plane crash or a shipwreck or getting lost while hiking. It was more like the portal fantasy stories I'd read, somehow transported to another place. Another world.

A spark of excitement fluttered in my chest. I'd always thought it would be cool to be sucked into another world or dimension or whatever. Like a video game, I'd start from scratch, learn magic, find treasure, and kick the shit out of any bad guys I came across. I looked at the shadow creature's corpse again. So, yeah, so much for that bullshit. This was *not* fun and exciting. At all.

But you know what, nobody knows how something really is without experiencing it firsthand. I'll admit, I was one of those assholes who would read a portal fantasy book and yell at the main character, "Why are you trying to get back to your own world? You're in a place where there's magic. This author sucks."

My apologies to every author I'd ever cursed at. I might be a few hundred miles away from home, several light years, or even in another dimension, but one thing was clear: not knowing what was going on and being all alone in an unknown place was *not* play time. I didn't know what the rules were. I had no idea if there was some kind of monster behind one of the many trees around me, waiting to make me its dinner. I had no idea what had happened to my cell phone, knew no one, and, to be honest, didn't know enough about how to survive in the wilderness to have good odds of making it.

Sure, it's easy to sit in your favorite chair and read a story and say, "I would take control and rule that fucking world." Right. At that moment, I needed to find water, food, and possibly shelter. If I couldn't do those simple things, I was going to die. Not from a mage's fireball, not from some exotic monster, but because I didn't know how to find food and water.

That was the reality.

What a downer. So much for being the great hero, eh?

I wasn't giving up. That would be stupid. But I did have a better appreciation for characters whose only thought was to get back to a place they were familiar with. A place where they knew how to get food. No matter how shitty you think your life is, it will always get worse if you suddenly can't get food.

I heaved myself to my feet and went over to the shadow thing. It didn't appear to have any pockets or other ways to carry anything, but I checked it over just in case. Not so much as a knife on it. Oh well.

Despite my thoughts on dying of thirst or hunger, I had some time. I needed to get moving, keep my eyes open, and do my best to keep from being killed by something stupid. I vowed that if I died in this place, wherever the hell I was, it was going to be from something cool. Like a dragon or other crazy monster. Not thirst. Not hunger. And goddamn it, not from dysentery.

One direction looked slightly less congested with undergrowth, so I plunged into the bushes, hoping like hell there weren't any poisonous plants or venomous bugs. It would be just my luck to be thrown somewhere like Australia where tiny creatures will poison and kill you in the blink of an eye. I tried not to think of funnel web spiders as I bashed through the foliage, glancing upward occasionally just to make sure.

Two and a half frustrating and sweaty hours it took me until the scenery changed. It was still daytime, so even if my watch was keeping time correctly for where I came from, it wasn't the same time as here. Or did this place have daylight all day long? How long was a day here? Shit. The questions kept piling up.

The change in terrain was a welcome one. The trees suddenly ended, and a dirt road spread off to my right and my left. What's more, I could see the sun, finally. After being in the dim forest for so long, I could hardly keep my sensitive eyes open. The sun was almost directly overhead, which meant the middle of the day regardless of whether it went from east to west or the reverse.

Actually, it could go from north to south, or the opposite, also. I didn't know enough yet to make a judgment on that.

I stood on the road, shading my eyes with my hand and scoping out both directions. To my left, the road went on for a distance before curving around a section of forest, with forest on the other side of it, too. It was like the road had been cut through the trees, separating them.

On my right, the road curved more subtly to the right, going around the forest I just emerged from. The opposite side of the road wasn't forested in that direction, but instead was rocky terrain. I thought the land might drop off, like those rock formations were cliffs, but it was hard to tell so far away.

I decided to go to the right.

This time, I didn't even walk for an hour before coming upon something different. In a small forest clearing off the side of the road stood a ragged solitary tent. It looked to be high quality, though its better days were in the past. Mostly faded tan, it had two drooping folds of blue-green canvas across the front that looked like someone had stolen the curtain from a theater. A fringe of gold-colored tassels hung down into the opening.

Large enough to sleep a dozen people, it showed no sign of anyone around or in it. Of course, I could only see a few feet into it, the rest of it shrouded in darkness. A few crates were visible just inside, and the dim silhouette of a table or other piece of furniture, but no people.

I narrowed my eyes, trying to pierce the darkness, and then I walked up toward it, scanning the surroundings for danger. If I were one of those shadow creatures, I'd probably choose a setup like this to live.

"Hello," I called out, wincing at how loud my voice sounded in the still forest.

"Come," someone said. The voice was female, which I was relieved about, until I thought of all the monsters that were female. Sirens, medusae, succubi, feminists. Okay, that second to the last one didn't seem too bad, but still. The point was, a feminine voice didn't necessarily mean safety.

I approached the opening slowly, peering inside but still not seeing the one who had spoken.

"Hello," I said again. "My name is Gar. Can you tell me where I am? I think I got turned around."

"Come in," she repeated.

I entered the tent. As soon as my foot passed the threshold, light flared from three different stand braziers, illuminating the entire space and showing me the one I'd been conversing with.

Not a monster—that I could tell—and not some old hag. What stood before me was one of the most beautiful women I'd ever seen.

Which didn't rule out her being a monster, now that I thought about it.

## CHAPTER
# FOUR

The woman stood near a table, looking at me expectantly. With the inside of the tent lit up, it was clear she was alone. I relaxed a little more. I couldn't help my body going into paranoid mode. There had always been dangers around growing up, and I treated every new situation as a possible risk. It had saved my ass more than once.

I met her light tan eyes, so bright they almost glowed in contrast with her long jet-black hair. Her skin had the creamy, milky color of someone who never went out in the sun, at least not without getting burned. The smooth expanse that was visible above her dress made me wonder how soft it felt.

She wore a loose and flowing dress that wouldn't have been out of place in some tropical resort, made of a very pale green—nearly an off-white—chiffon-type material. It allowed a good view of her slender yet curvy body. Seriously, I couldn't see how the thing sat so perfectly off her shoulders without falling off her completely. Her softly sloping left shoulder was fully visible, but her dark hair covered the right, spilling over it and reaching past her breasts. Though the dress extended down past her knees, the layered skirts allowed a good look at her smooth and perfectly toned leg. She had one of those bodies that hadn't been sculpted by exercise, but was shaped by nature and genes to be the perfect blend between softness and firm, solid body. Her lips, formed into an enticing moue, didn't reveal any emotion as she stared into my blue eyes.

"You are lost?" she said. She had the kind of voice a hypnotist or a therapist would be grateful to have. Soft, soothing, with just enough of a hint of an unknown accent and cadence to be unique and sexy. The way she inflected her last word was more than a question; it was almost a plea.

I shook my head. Hell, maybe she *was* a succubus. She'd sure snatched my attention completely. "I am. Can you tell me where I am?"

"You are in my tent."

"Oh, right. Sorry. I'm sorry if I'm being impolite. My name is Garfield Hailey." I'd already said it before I realized I'd already told her my name a moment ago.

"I am Qamara Enorana."

Damn. Even her name was sexy. It sounded Latin, maybe Italian. Now that I thought of it, that was what I'd heard in her voice: a mixture of Latin languages. Maybe the dead language itself.

"A pleasure to meet you. I found myself in the forest, but I'm confused about how I got here or where *here* is."

"This is the Ironwood Forest."

I'd never heard of it. "Okay. What state am I in?"

She tilted her head. "In a state of confusion, it appears."

I chuckled, but she didn't so much as smile. Her pouty

expression was certainly turning me on, but her lack of emotion was kind of freaking me out.

"Okay. I'm not still in California, am I?"

"I do not know that name. I am sorry."

"United States?"

She looked at me blankly.

"Earth?"

Nothing.

"Can you tell me what land we're in? Country, nation, kingdom?"

Something happened behind her eyes, just a flicker, but I couldn't interpret it. "No nation holds sovereignty here. The greater area is named the Zixuris Steppes."

I sighed. *What the hell. I might as well go for the big question.* "This may sound weird, but what world is this?"

"Valorae, of course."

"Valorae?"

"Yes. What world were you expecting?"

"I don't know. I'm from Earth. Have you heard of it?"

She shook her head and her long black hair moved, the firelight glinting off her soft waves. "I have not. How did you come here, Garfield Hailey?"

"Just Gar is fine. That's what everyone calls me."

She stood there, her soft tan eyes looking into mine, but she didn't say anything. *Okaaaaayyy.*

"I..." I rubbed the back of my neck. How the hell was I going to explain this? "I got attacked by some kind of shadow monster. I lost consciousness and then when I came to, I was in this forest, a few miles away, further into the trees. The monster was trying to suck out my soul or something."

An eyebrow quirked and I witnessed the first real expression on her gorgeous face. Curiosity. "A dark creature, the size and shape similar to yours, but of shadowy stuff? Perhaps with streaks or spikes along its edges?"

"Yes. Exactly."

"Umbrenix," she said. "A servant of....well, never mind that. It brought you here and began to drain your life force?"

"Yes. That's exactly what it felt like."

"How are you here?"

I scrunched my brow up at her. "I just told you. That... umbrenix brought me here and—"

"How are you still alive? Did a mage or a great hero rescue you, save you from the clutches of the umbrenix? If so, where were they?"

"What? No. No one saved me. It was draining me, like you say, and then I woke up. I fought with it and killed it. Its body is still in the forest."

Her face was really warming up now. Her eyes narrowed, her brow drew down, and her lips formed a crooked frown. "*You* killed it?"

"Yeah. It was tough, but once I broke its arm, half-strangled it, and then bashed its head in on a fallen log, it died."

Qamara stumbled back to sit in her chair. "Very... interesting."

"Qamara?"

She waved a slender hand in front of her face. "Umbrenix are *difficult* to kill without magic, yet I sense no magic within you." The way she inflected the word "difficult" might have been an accent thing, but it gave me the impression that "damn near impossible" would have been more accurate.

"Magic? That's a thing here?"

Again with the confused face. “All things are things here. I don’t understand.”

It didn’t escape my notice that she used a contraction for the first time. Not that she’d said a whole lot. Maybe she was loosening up. “I meant, is magic real here?”

“Magic is real everywhere.”

“Not in my world.”

“Truly?”

“Yep.”

“Strange, and fascinating. In Valorae, everyone has magic. Some are minor gifts while others are very powerful, but all have at least something. Yet you do not.”

“You can sense that about me?”

“Of course. I am alari.”

“Uh...”

“My race. You are human, correct?”

“Yes.”

“I am alari. My people are more powerful in magic than many. You have never heard of the alari?”

“Nope,” I said. “None of those on Earth, either.”

“Garfield, the umbrenix are travelers. They have an ability that allows them to go to other worlds. They cannot carry others away from here, but they can bring others back to their home. To Valorae.”

“You’re saying that shadow monster, that umbrenix, dragged me back here?”

“Yes. To drain the power from you and to create a power crystal from it.”

“It was going to drain my life and make a battery out of it?”

“I do not know that word within the context you use it.”

“Fine. I think I get it. So, it went to my world, snatched me, brought me back here to drain me and kill me, and instead I killed it. I think it took my friend, too. A few hours earlier than me. How can I find him?"

"I'm sorry, Garfield, but once an umbrenix drains a person, their physical form deteriorates. There is nothing left of it. Perhaps some bits of energy, some stray memories or thoughts, could persist for a time. If your friend was taken, he is gone."

"He would have fought. Where would he be if he killed the one that took him, assuming it was another one. Are there more than one of those things?"

"There are many. Or there were. If he escaped as you have, he might be anywhere. Like you, he would probably have tried to gain aid from others to find answers to his questions. He may not necessarily have entered our world in the same place as you."

"Well, shit." I put both hands up to squeeze my temples. "What do I do now?"

"Please, sit down. I thought you visited me so I could tell you your fortune."

"You're a fortune teller?"

"I am a prophetess, a seer. I do small readings of fortunes to earn a little money. There is not much gold in prophecy unless employed by a king or empress."

I snorted and took her invitation to sit.

"I assume you have no gold?" she asked.

"I don't. I have some paper money from my world, but I'm thinking that won't be worth anything here."

"You are correct. We have paper and it is not as precious as gold. I can tell you a little about this world without requiring payment."

"That would be great, thank you. The more information I can get, the better."

"Very well. I will gift you with basic information about the place in which you find yourself. Perhaps it will aid you.

"Traveling between worlds is not unknown, though it is far from common. Some great mages and deities have the power and the knowledge to accomplish it, but with the umbrenix it is different. The creatures are steeped in mystery, but some things are known. They were created specifically to cross to other worlds, and it is inherent in their nature to do so. As I said before, they cannot transport others away from Valorae, but they can bring them back. Such is the nature of their magic. I don't know what limitations they may have as to size or weight or if they can bring other items at all. You are not the first to have been taken and you will certainly not be the last.

"I have never heard of one surviving the process, not unless its master wills it. I know of no situations where this has occurred, however.

"Valorae is home to many races and species. You will have to discover them on your own. I am no academy instructor to teach you about such things. Suffice it to say there are a variety of people. Alari, elf, human, dwarf, goblin, many varieties of beastkin, and the list continues. Some have preferences or prejudices against other races, but humans are buffered from that more than most. They are universally tolerated, much as a useful slovenly imbecile is."

I didn't like the sound of that, but I didn't want to interrupt her to ask what she meant. It didn't seem she had a lot of respect for humans.

"As I said earlier, everyone has some type of magic, though it may be so minor as to be insignificant. Some have cleverly leveraged their abilities in commerce, trade, or for nefarious purposes. Thus, a piece of advice: do not look down on the simplest and most inconsequential of magical talent. It could be deadly to do so.

"There is no common currency, but most of the larger towns and all of the cities will trade or exchange currency from other places. The metals from which the coins are produced are what dictates the value. In general, copper is worth the least, then silver, then gold. You will likely not encounter platinum coins. Prices and weights of the coins vary wildly, but I doubt that is something unknown to you. I would expect most worlds are similar."

She tapped her temple, pausing to think. "Ah, the deities. A good manner of conduct is to avoid them."

"Deities?" I said. "You mean, like gods and goddesses?"

"Of course. Divine beings? All-powerful entities? Deities. For that matter, I would suggest you stay away from demi-gods as well. And powerful mages. You will live longer."

As she spoke, Qamara watched me. I kept eye contact with her, but her eyes flicked down to focus on different parts of my body. Arms, torso, my lower body, my legs, even my Doc Martin work boots. I'd been careful not to let my eyes wander, even though what she wore and the body she wore it on begged me to do so. I actually felt a little uncomfortable under the scrutiny.

"That is about as much as I can tell you of the general information of this place. The closest town is Stonefort, which is to the north. You will reach Fanning if you take this road back from where you came, to the east, though it curves into a northward direction after sweeping around a section of heavy forest fifteen miles from here. I would suggest you continue west, then take the smaller road north to Stonefort. Maybe you can find more answers there. It is less than twenty miles from where we are."

I noted that she used miles. The chances of that were pretty slim if this was another world. What language were we speaking? Was it English or did the whole magic thing translate our words allowing me to speak and understand whatever it was they spoke here?

What she'd said sounded like a dismissal to me, but her eyes still flicked over me. I wasn't sure what she was looking for. If her clothing was typical, then maybe she was trying to figure out my wardrobe. I wore dark blue Dickies, my work boots, and a blue button-up shirt with the company logo on it. Not what you would call medieval casual wear.

"Are there machines here?" I asked. "Steam engines, electricity, things like that?"

"Those terms are unknown to me. We have steam, of course, from boiling water or mage spells. Machines we have. Water wheels to power grinding stones, various tackles and such for lifting, ingenious levers in everything from moving heavy items to launching them in a catapult. I feel that those are not what you speak of, though."

Yep, definitely medieval. I figured as much seeing the things Qamara had in her tent. Well, shit.

"Okay," I said. "All that is helpful. Thank you for the information. Sorry to take up your time."

"It's nothing." Her eyes rested on my hands, folded in my lap as I sat. "May I...touch you?"

"Touch me?"

"Yes. I am fascinated by your lack of magic. I would like to see if I can feel any fluctuations, discover what is different about you."

Here's a pro tip. If a super-hot, gorgeous woman asks you if she can touch you, the answer is always, "Fuck yes!" Trying to be polite, I replied with a little less enthusiasm.

"Sure. What do you want me to do?"

"Allow me to take your hand?"

I held my hand out to her and she scooted her chair closer. Rubbing her own hands together, she took mine in both of hers. Her exquisitely unique eyes closed and she went perfectly still.

For about five minutes, I sat there, my palm producing a thin layer of perspiration, becoming clammy. With nothing else to do, I ran my eyes over Qamara's body. Leaning toward me and slightly hunched, she gave me a great view of the inner swell of her breasts, her softly curving shoulders, and her beautiful face. She had a touch of an overbite, but it looked sexy as hell.

So suddenly it startled me, her eyes snapped open. Her pupils contracted in response to the light, then dilated a bit to focus on me.

"Find out anything?" I asked.

"Thank you. I...would you like me to tell you your fortune?"

I blinked at her. Hadn't we already talked about this? "I still don't have any money."

"I would be willing to barter."

"I have no possessions except my wallet, with that worthless paper money I talked about, and my watch, which I'm not going to trade. It's precious to me."

"There is something I didn't mention earlier. Trading for items and services is done often in Valorae. In fact, some people make their living in providing services that are of an...intimate nature."

My eyebrows raised of their own volition. "Prostitution?"

"That is one type. There are many services dedicated to comfort and pleasure."

"Are you saying you'll tell my fortune if I provide intimate services for you?"

"Crudely put, that is essentially accurate. I simply want to continue what I just did, to try to learn what is different about you. I felt a resonance that fascinates me. I would like to learn more."

I met her stunning eyes and shrugged. "Sounds like a good deal to me. What do you want me to do?"

# CHAPTER FIVE

Qamara's light-colored eyes fixed on me as the prophetess considered me. "Perhaps starting slowly would be the way to proceed. Are you skilled in the way of pleasuring women?"

*To start with?* I coughed, unprepared for the question. "I've had some girlfriends. A few. They didn't last long because..." Her expressionless face had started me rambling. "Anyway, I think I can manage to start slowly. You just let me know if you want me to do something else, okay?"

She stood from her chair. With no answer, I assumed that meant she wanted me to go on ahead. I took up one of the hands she had so recently wrapped around mine and brought it up to my face. She wanted slow? I'd give her slow.

I hadn't noticed before, too surprised about her grabbing my hand, but her skin was so soft. I mean like silk would be embarrassed of itself in comparison. I kissed the back of it, like I figured gentlemen did in this crazy medieval type world. Dragging my lips across her hand felt really good. Maybe there was something to the whole chivalry thing.

Turning her hand over, I kissed her palm. Qamara's breath was steady and relaxed, almost to the point it sounded like she was purposely controlling it. When I kissed up her wrist, it hitched the tiniest bit, which was promising.

The woman was gorgeous and had a body to match her beauty. Her wispy dress made me think of what she'd look like standing out in a rainstorm in that getup. I was sure it would cling to her and become see-through. Damn, I wondered if we'd be lucky enough to get some rain soon.

As I kissed up her arm, I nipped occasionally. When I did, her breathing pattern definitely broke. I was glad because it was swirling sexy energies around my body as my lips made contact with her toned arms and then moved up to her shoulders. From there, I trailed my tongue up her neck to arrive at her face. Her chin was shaped perfectly for putting my lips around—a little angular at the end but curving gently rather than pointed. Not that I don't like pointed chins, but hers suited her perfectly. As did her lips.

When ours met, it was electric. Not in the sense that there was some kind of magical lightning, but the feel and the scent of the ravishing woman sent waves of pleasure down my body. I pictured that slight overbite in my mind and my arms went around her without my permission.

She let loose a little moan.

The prophetess's body felt so good in my arms. Her thin, barely-there clothing allowed me to feel her warm, silky skin as I pulled her close and kissed her. Our lips slid over each other. Her strong tongue and her taste dragged a moan from me, too. Her arms went around me and she adjusted her head slightly to increase the contact as our kisses got more and more passionate.

The prophetess tasted faintly of dry red wine, and as I sank into the kiss, I began to feel a little intoxicated.

She broke away momentarily, panting before she spoke. "You are doing well. I...uhhnnngg...am enjoying this. Does it please you?"

"You...uh, it does. Yes. Very much. Is it working, whatever it is you're trying to do?"

"Mmmmm." She pressed her lips to mine again and our tongues met.

I ran my hands up and down her back, daring to reach down and slide it across her pleasantly firm ass. She huffed in surprise, then hummed, sending energy directly to my crotch.

My lips attacked her neck, sucking softly on it for a second and nibbling her skin. Her head went back and her back arched, relying on me holding her to keep from falling backward. Breaths came in panting bursts that vibrated my middle and screamed at me to taste more of her spectacular body.

I had to remind myself to take it slow. Still, I kissed down past her collarbone to her upper chest, displayed spectacularly by her flimsy chiffon dress. She sighed when I kissed the tops of her breasts and worked down and inward to follow the swell of her cleavage.

She took a sudden inrush of air and pushed me away. I was left standing there, all heated up, wondering what the hell just happened.

"Yes," she said. "This will do nicely."

It took me aback for a moment, having her refer to it so clinically, but I wasn't going to complain. Her breasts were works of art and just having the privilege to put my mouth on them for a brief moment almost made everything that happened to me to get to this point worth it.

Almost.

"That was...most satisfactory," she said.

All I could do was to stand there, swaying and staring at the hot woman who I'd just met. Who'd offered to make out with me and then ended it abruptly. Queen of the blue balls.

"That was quite unexpected," she finally said after I sat down in a chair, facing her. "I had not expected to enjoy it so much. Of course, that was not the reason for what we did, but it was a welcome surprise."

I smiled at her, though I have to admit, I was a little let down by the sudden stop. Was cruel teasing the way people normally did things in this world? "You felt amazing. But what about the reason? You said you wanted to find out more about my lack of magic?"

"Yes. I will have to think upon it; dream upon it. I don't know what the things I felt and sensed mean. You have no magic, but our contact has energized me. No doubt I will have visions later, after my mind and my magic process what we just did. I am very pleased we decided to engage in such a way. It will no doubt—"

Qamara stumbled and fell back into the chair she'd been in before.

"Qamara, are you okay?"

"I...bed. Please, help me lie down. I am dizzy."

Rather than aid her in walking to the bed, I put one arm under her legs and my other under her back and picked her up, then moved over to set her down gently on the small bed in the corner of her tent. She closed her eyes and let out a long breath.

"A moment, please."

I stood there for a few minutes, but since she didn't move, I dragged a chair over and sat down next to her, watching and waiting. I took one of her hands, ostensibly to soothe her, but also because I wanted to feel her pulse. It was strong and steady, not racing, which I thought was a good sign. I continued to hold it as she wriggled occasionally grunting like she was having a bad dream. Her eyes moved underneath her lids, confirming that assumption.

More than fifteen minutes later, her eyes fluttered open and locked onto me.

"Garfield."

"Hi, Qamara. Are you all right?"

She glanced at my hands, still holding hers. I loosened my grip, but she didn't take her hand back right away. "Yes, I am fine. When I said you energized me, I spoke truly. Something triggered my abilities. Not a vision, unfortunately, but an intuition. I still owe you information, which I intend to give you, but this is perhaps more important. It concerns you."

"Your 'intuition' concerns me? So, you can read my fortune?"

She smiled. "To some extent, perhaps. I will sit up and tell you of it. Instead of seeing bits of pictures or experiences, what I received was a rush of words that came at me like someone had painted them out in solid form and cast them at me. Most curious."

Once she was sitting on the edge of the bed facing me, she told me what she'd seen. Or read.

"The message might not be accurately called prophecy, but I believe it to be truth. I cannot explain how, but know that in my work as a seer, I can distinguish between mere possibilities and pronouncements that are true. These are the latter. I will recite them word for word. My abilities include magic that will allow you to remember what I say to you now, more than normal experiences. Pay heed, for these warnings are no doubt important.

At the beginning, a companion will you find, one who knows what should not be known. This one will be necessary for you to succeed. Cleave to the one.

The parts are stronger together than ever they could be individually. Unite.

Dark things will haunt you and trace your steps. You shall not be free until the very source is destroyed.

A bright light will save your life after you have prevented it from going out.

Be wary of the symbol of the poison knife and spade. See beyond what your eyes tell you.

A shining warrior will aid you in your time of need as you must return aid.

Under the sign of the pike, the secret key may be found.

Strength of mind, strength of arm, and power to create will keep you from failing in your task.

There are secrets hidden where one would not think to investigate. Do not overlook the depths or the bowels, for within the roots, that which is desired may at last be found.

You will gain succor in the most unlikely places. Be vigilant, and accept aid where it is given in sincerity.

One from past ages grows in power and must be stopped or all will be forfeit.

When all seems lost, put your faith in knowledge

As the very world rebels, search out the one who searches and protect them from the searcher, to discover the prize for which you search.

Do not discount the little things in the world, for in them may lie the secret of your victory.

"I am sorry if these things are confusing. Such is the way with my gift. I have always believed it was the world's way of balancing out the power that might allow one to see the future clearly with the challenge of uncertainty so that those such as I cannot use our abilities to unfair advantage."

I went over what she'd said in my head. She was right about being able to remember it. It was almost like I could bring it up in front of me in written form so I could read it anytime I wanted to. I could have repeated the thing word for word, I had no doubt.

"Wow. All that for me?"

"Yes. Do not think yourself insignificant. In your first hour in this world, you accomplished two things I have never heard of: surviving being drained by an umbrenix and then killing the creature without any magical assistance. It would seem that despite you having no magic, great events are in your future."

I shrugged. "I don't want great events. I want to find Lucas, kick anyone's ass that had to do with bringing us here, and then figure out what we'll do. If, like you said, even those shadow guys can't take us back to our world, we're going to have to figure something else out."

"I would caution you, Garfield. The world is in flux at the moment. Things are changing, but I cannot identify in what way. Power is shifting and magic is fluctuating. That at least two from another world have been brought here by the umbrenix does not bode well for things, though you escaping from them is a good omen. I had not known any of the shadows still existed.

"The umbrenix will not be done with you. If you were important enough for them to stalk you in your own world and bring you here, you are important enough for them to continue to chase. To my knowledge, no one knows how the shadow people track their prey, but they are accounted extremely potent hunters. No doubt, you will see them again.

"I am afraid that I have no other information for you. Perhaps I will have more later, after I have had time to meditate and to receive visions. If so, I will tell you should I see you again. In the meantime, there is one more thing I can do for you, something I hope will aid you."

Qamara got up from her chair and paced over to a trunk in the corner of the tent. She dug through it for a moment before coming back with an item in her hand. She handed it to me.

I accepted it and held it up to inspect it. It was made mostly of wood, barely over a foot long, and about as thick as my index finger. Cylindrical with a diamond-shaped metal head, it didn't look like anything more than a short, fat arrow.

"Is that a siangham?" I asked.

Qamara's eyebrows raised. I got a little thrill. Every time I said or did something that made her display emotion, it made me feel like I'd accomplished something. "You know the weapon?"

"Not really." I snorted. "I met a guy when I was a kid. His family came from a place in my world called Malaysia. They had a martial art there—a fighting style. It was called kuntao. One of their weapons looked a lot like this."

"And this weapon was called a siangham?"

"Yes."

"Fascinating. It carries that name here, as well. It is

from the ancient Osgoth tongue, meaning *soul rod*, perhaps because of the legends of warriors who mastered it using the item to directly strike pressure points and mana meridians."

"Huh. The guy I knew never told me what it meant. I always thought it was kind of a stupid weapon. I mean, I could break an arrow in half and it would basically be the same thing."

"Perhaps," she said. "Nevertheless, it came into my possession years ago and something of the way you felt..." She actually blushed a little. Quite a change from her normal, emotionless self. "Something of your aura I sensed tells me that perhaps you may have some use for it. *Stupid weapon* or not." Her face displayed a wry smile at that.

*Yes. She does have a sense of humor.* She was suddenly twice as alluring as before, if that was possible.

"I'm afraid there is nothing else I can do for you, Garfield." Her eyes flicked upward. "No, perhaps that is not correct. I can give you a few coins. It may help you in your quest to find your friend. I can't spare much, but a few would be possible. After all, you did *help* me with my experiment."

I didn't like that the whole thing made me sound like some kind of gigolo, especially since I would have gladly done what we did for free. I mean, all we did was kiss, and I'd definitely do that again. And again and again.

"It's fine," I said. "I don't want to take any money from you."

"You will not be taking it from me. I will be giving it to you. Those are two different things."

I was going to argue, but I probably would need some money. Who knew how long it would take to find Lucas?

"Okay, but you're not giving it to me. You're loaning it

to me. I have a feeling we'll see each other again. I hope so, at least. I'll pay you back when I can. Fair enough?"

This time, she gave me a legitimate smile. "That sounds fair. I shall look forward to it, should fate deem it so."

She handed me a small purse, soft leather with a drawstring like it belonged to the Sheriff of Nottingham. It clinked when I tested its weight in my palm. I'd count the contents later. I put it in my pocket.

Qamara watched me as I stuffed the pouch away. "The weights of silver and gold coins are similar in most towns and cities regardless of where they are pressed, but as we discussed, prices of things and values of coins may differ. There are ten copper to a silver and ten silver to a gold. You will find the first two types in the purse."

"Thank you so much. I'm serious, I'm going to pay you back. Anything I can ever do to repay you for helping me, I'll do. Even the information you gave me might save my life."

"I certainly hope so. Fare well on your journey, Garfield Hailey. Keep yourself safe. I desire to see you again. I may even have more information from some visions for you."

"That would be great."

I stood there, not sure exactly what to do. I'd already thanked her to the point it was probably getting tiresome for her. I fidgeted and she sat in her chair, looking at me placidly.

"Okay, so I guess this is goodbye for now," I finally said. "Thank you again." *Damn it, so much for not saying it again.* "I...is it all right if I hug you goodbye?"

The smirk reappeared on her face. "I would like that." She got up and stepped over to me. "But not as much as I would like a kiss goodbye."

I grinned like an idiot and pulled her close to me so I

could kiss her properly. When we broke apart, I stroked her hair with one hand. "I can't wait to see you again."

"I feel that you will, though I know not when."

I left the prophetess's tent, taking a right to head to the west, according to what she'd told me. The road soon curved toward the north, around the edge of the forest. The closest town, Stonefort, was to the north on that road, twenty miles or so away. I could make it in a day if I had to, depending on how easy or hard the terrain was, but I doubt I'd push it. I was in good shape, but I didn't want to tire myself out too much. Just my luck if I pushed my body and exhausted myself, then got attacked by one of those damn shadow monsters.

Umbrenix.

I hadn't asked Qamara what other dangers were around. I stopped on the road, looking back toward the bend in the road I'd just passed. Should I go back and ask her? It was kind of important. I was only a few minutes out, so it wouldn't take much of my time.

My feet made the decision for me. When I followed the curve in the road and reached the little clearing off the side where her tent was, I found the area empty, not so much as a footprint to indicate that anyone had ever been there.

"Well, fuck," I said aloud. I guess I'd have to find out about the dangers of this world myself. I added the mystery of how the woman had packed up her tent and moved it in those few minutes' time to the list of impossible things I'd seen in this world already and headed to the north.

The dirt was packed down pretty solidly and there were few plants in the middle. Just tufts of grass occasionally. The only dirt roads I'd been on in my world were fire roads in areas I'd gone hiking, and the path under me was a lot better than those. There weren't even many ruts. It was hard to believe I hadn't seen anyone so far, with how well-trod it looked.

At one point, I left the road to cross over some terrain with scrub brush and grass on it. I soon reached the edge of a cliff and looked out over a vast ocean, with nothing west of me but waves. To the south, the cliff I was on arched back to the east. Did that mean I was in one corner of whatever land mass I was on? I instantly regretted something else I should have asked Qamara: what continent were we on, and how big was it? Hell, I had no idea if I was on some island I could cross in a few days or on something like Pangaea that I'd never find the limits of. Gravity felt the same, so this world had to be about the size of Earth, right?

I hiked back to the road again and continued on my way. I definitely wasn't going to make it to Stonefort before dark.

# CHAPTER SIX

With no tent, blanket, or even a bedroll, I didn't figure I'd be comfortable. My watch showed I'd been up for well over twenty-four hours—other than the unknown amount of time I was swaddled in blackness—so I didn't think I'd have trouble getting to sleep, even on the cold, hard ground, but I still didn't know if there were monsters or beasts around. Other than those damn shadow people.

I glanced down at the siangham I was carrying. How much good would that do against large animals like elephants or even bears? I muttered a curse, casting my eye to the west to where the sun was going down. At least that was the same as my world. It would be too weird if the sun went the other way.

I lucked onto a small spring close to the road. It burbled out of some rocks in a clearing that looked like it was probably used as a campsite for travelers, patted down so it was relatively flat with little vegetation growing there. I drank my fill, hoping I wouldn't get a disease or anything, then settled in to sleep near some other rocks. Nothing killed me as I slept, which is always nice.

The first thing I noticed about Stonefort the next day was the rocky plateau above the town, complete with ruins of some type of castle or fort with crumbling watchtowers. I guessed that was probably the reason for the town's name.

Medieval-looking stone walls surrounded the town itself, a clutter of structures that ranged from low, one-story buildings to a few that had three stories. From the high road, before it dipped down toward the main entrance, I saw the ocean and some boats and ships at a dock. I estimated four or five hundred residents, based on the hundred and something buildings spread out between the walls and the water.

I made my way down to the gate, my stomach complaining that it hadn't been filled for way too long. No guards were visible, so I walked through onto the streets of the town.

The first woman I saw made me stop and stare. She was young and pretty, dark brown hair spilling down her back and a simple but attractive dress draped over her lithe form. All that was great and all, but not enough for me to gape like a rube. What really drew my attention was her tail. A fucking tail! It was covered with fur the same color as her hair. That wasn't all, though. With her hair down, I couldn't tell if she had ears on the sides of her head, but I easily spotted the wedge-shaped ears on the top of her head. They were covered with fur, too, matching her tail and hair.

I blinked and looked at her face again. Nope, a perfectly normal human face. With cat ears tacked onto the top. The cat woman was the most exotic person I'd ever seen, discounting the people all over the internet who had modified themselves to simulate what this woman was.

The difference was that this woman looked legitimate, natural. Not manufactured. I suddenly saw the big draw for people who liked anime. Though she would have been pretty as a human, she was smoking hot as a beastkin. What kind of world was this?

As I wandered aimlessly, I passed more beastkin. I began to play a game, trying to figure out what kind they were. A man who I think was some kind of dog beastkin, another that might have been a raccoon beastkin, and a woman with the cute little ears of a weasel or a ferret.

I realized soon that as much as I was staring at everyone else, more than a few people were noticing me, too. While everyone I saw all wore time-appropriate clothing—or world-appropriate, I guess—I did not. With my blue Dickies and my button up shirt, I kind of stuck out.

The problem was, I didn't know what to do about it. There were some humans in town, so I didn't think it was my race. My clothes were too out of place. Maybe I could find a shop to buy some clothes so I could fit in a little better.

Food first, though. I was starving.

"Excuse me," I said to a human woman I passed. "Is there a place to get something to eat?" I almost asked for a restaurant, but didn't know if those were a thing. I hedged my bet and asked for something I thought might fit the medieval motif. "Maybe a tavern or something?"

She glanced at me, then did a double-take. Her eyes locked onto me, hard, and she smiled prettily. "Sure. Keep going down this street until you reach Sam's General Store, then go right down that street for a hundred paces or so. You'll find the Rustling Reed Inn and Tavern on the left."

"Thank you so much."

Her lips pursed. "You're welcome. Maybe I—"

"Are you coming, Melia?" a man called from up ahead. The woman flushed, turned toward the voice, and hurried toward him, sighing and giving me a hesitant wave.

I shrugged and started walking again according to her directions.

I tried my best not to gape as I walked down the street. The structures weren't what had me so interested. They were what I'd expect for the whole medieval vibe. Simple buildings built of timber, many with thatched roofs, though some did have wooden shingles or even slate.

What drew my attention was the variety of people. I saw a couple of short men with green skin and pointed ears that went out to the side, unlike fantasy elf ears—which resembled human ears, close to the head and angling upward, but pointed. Another man with a bushy beard, who was about as wide as he was tall, had to be an actual dwarf. One of the fantasy dwarves, I mean, not a human afflicted by dwarfism.

But the *beastkin*. I could probably have sat down at the edge of the street and watched them all day, trying to guess at what type they were.

The thing was, not only were there people with furry ears or tails, not to mention other exotic parts, but not all were like the cat beastkin woman I'd seen before. She was human looking but for the furry ears and a tail. Some of the people on the street had more animalistic faces. I saw a dog beastkin with a snout and a furry face, and a cat man with whiskers and all. That one even looked to have claws that retracted into paws that looked a lot more feline than a human hand.

Trying to be polite, I kept my eyes straight ahead as

much as I could. Still, I didn't miss how some of the towns-people seemed to find me interesting.

Especially the women.

I don't say that in an arrogant way. It could have been they thought I was good-looking, but I had a feeling it was more about my clothes. No one had pants and a shirt like mine. There were trousers, sure, and shirts with toggles and even oversized buttons, but it was obvious they were different than my polyester and cotton blend garments. I probably needed to see if I could get some clothes soon so I would fit in better.

That said, some women met my eyes and winked or gave me flirty smiles. That didn't have anything to do with my clothes. Sometimes people are attracted to anything different. Of course, none of that stopped me from looking at my reflection in a window as I passed a home, just to make sure I didn't have shadow slime or something all over my face. It was possible that I got the different reactions because they thought I was some kind of clown. My hair was kind of wild and I needed a shave, but otherwise, it was the same old Gar looking back at me. Without shadow slime or a booger hanging out of my nose. I waved or returned people's smiles and glued my gaze straight ahead to prevent getting into too much trouble.

Until I almost ran into a large statue in the middle of the road.

I stopped abruptly, looking around. The road bulged, almost like a roundabout, or traffic circle as some called it, with the stone monstrosity right in the middle. It was some dude with a stylized sword. The kind of weapon no one would actually use because it was too elaborate and gaudy. Weapons should be simple, like that crazy half-arrow siangham I got from Qamara. Okay, maybe not *that* simple, but still, I hoped to hell whatever hero the statue depicted didn't actually use such a crazy weapon. The blade was shaped strangely, with multiple hourglass curves in it, two hand guards stacked on top of each other, and what looked to have been a gem or something on the pommel.

He stood there, looking badass, holding his sword in a pose instead of taking some action, point down as he held the hilt. I shook my head, walked around the ten-foot tall hunk of stone, and kept moving.

I spotted the general store and, past it, the inn. The wooden sign, hanging by a couple lengths of chain from a horizontal iron pole attached to the building, had a picture carved into it and painted to show a group of cattails swaying in the breeze.

The Rustling Reed Inn and Tavern was a rugged two-story building with two large windows in the front and a wood-shingled roof. It wasn't new, by the faded look of the walls, but it was clean and I couldn't hear any noise of conflict within. Of course, it was only mid-morning, so that didn't tell me much.

I walked through the front door and into a decent-sized common room with a huge fireplace, a dozen or so tables, and only five people sitting at them; a couple and a trio. I headed to the counter that stretched nearly the entire length of one wall. About half of it had bar stools and the other half looked to be something like a check-in desk. A man stood in the exact center.

"Welcome to the Rustling Reed," he said. "What can I do for you this morning?"

I tried—and failed—to keep from blinking at him. The man had horns coming up out of his head. Not antlers or anything, but stubby little goat horns. Despite a thick five o'clock shadow, he didn't seem to be one of the furry, animalistic beastkin, but the horns kind of threw me.

I recovered, hopefully soon enough not to offend the man, and gave him my best smile.

"Good morning. I'd like something to eat and to ask a few questions, if you don't mind."

"We do serve breakfast, friend, so you're in luck. Would eggs, some ham, and toasted bread work?"

"That would be great."

"You want to grab a table or sit at the bar? Not many people, as you can see, so you can have your pick."

I glanced over at the barstools. "I'll sit at the bar. Less distance for you to go to bring the food out."

He tapped his temple with a finger. "I knew you were a smart one when I laid eyes on you, sir. It'll be three coppers." He turned his head toward the door to the kitchen, behind him, and shouted. "Ellie, one breakfast." He returned his attention to me to take the coins I held out. "The price includes ale, water, milk, or any combination of all three."

"Uh, how about some milk and water?"

"Yessir. Coming right up."

I found a seat and he brought me a pitcher of water, an empty glass, and a glass full of milk.

"You said you had questions?" the innkeeper said. I realized he hadn't given me his name.

It was just as well. He would expect mine in return and I wasn't sure if I wanted to be known. I still wasn't sure what the deal was with this world.

"Yes. I'm not from around here. In fact, I'm from very far away. I was in the Ironwood Forest but haven't seen much else. I'm looking for a friend of mine that I think may have come to the area. His name is Lucas Walker. He's...uh, human. Five foot eleven, black hair, brown eyes, his skin about as dark as your hair. He'd be wearing unusual clothes."

The man ran his eyes over me and I understood what he was thinking.

"Not exactly like mine, but maybe a little similar. Have you seen him around?"

"Skin that dark, and human? Is he from Teaphotria? Or from farther away like you are?"

"Oh, he—" A pretty woman, probably in her early thirties, brought a plate piled with eggs, ham, and what had to be about half a loaf of sliced bread, toasted unevenly and slathered with melting butter. She set it down, gave me a smile, then did a double-take. I actually saw the interest flare in her eyes.

I gave her a smile. "Thank you."

The innkeeper nudged her with his shoulder, setting her into motion to go back to the kitchen. She looked back over her shoulder at me twice before she disappeared.

"You were saying?" he said, a smirk on his face.

"He is not from around here either. I think he might be in some kind of trouble." I realized how that sounded and put my hands up. "I mean, I'm afraid he might be lost and in danger since he doesn't know the area."

"Like you."

"Yes, like me. But I can take care of myself."

"You do look to be able to. You a soldier of some kind? The way you move, it seems you've had some training."

"No, nothing like that. I lived in a rough place growing up and I learned to fight, that's all."

"Ah. Well, I'm sorry I can't help you. A man like that, he'd stick out here in the south. If he'd been around here, I'd have remembered. Are you going to stay around for a little while? If not, I can give him a message for you."

"I don't think I'll stay around long. I need to go search for him. If you do see him, tell him I'm looking for him. My name is Gar Hailey. I appreciate the help." I sighed. So much for not telling him my name.

"It's nothing. I hope you find him. Where will you look?"

I snuck in a few bites of my food between talking. Maybe I was starving since it'd been so long since I'd eaten, but damn, that food was great.

"I don't know. Any suggestions?"

He rubbed his chin. "If he has sense, he wouldn't go into the forest. I'd assume if he came upon a road, he'd follow it. There's only Stonefort and Fanning on the southern tip of the continent, so if he's not here, you might want to try Fanning. There are some other towns and villages, even a couple of cities in the Steppes, but I'd try Fanning first. Take the road going east and you'll run into it."

"I guess I'll head there, then," I said. "How far is it?"

"Close to sixty miles. You equipped for sleeping near the road?" His eyes ran over me again, no doubt recognizing I wasn't carrying anything.

"Not yet. I was going to head to the general store as soon as I finished eating. Would they have a pack and some supplies I could buy?"

"Oh, sure. Sam's got all kinds of stuff. He'll fix you up, don't you worry. If you stick mostly to the road, you should be fine. There are some wild animals that might get curious with you alone—coyotes, some mountain cats, possibly a bear—but most monsters and magical creatures don't go near the road so as to stay away from the hunters that stalk them for bounties. If you can fight a bit and you keep a fire going, you should be fine. Maybe see if Sam has a sword or a knife he's willing to let go for a good price."

"Thanks. I'll definitely talk to him. Thanks for the advice and the information. Uh, have you ever heard of an umbrenix?"

The innkeeper froze, his eyes drilling into me. "Where did you hear that word?"

"Someone said something about it. Some kind of shadow creatures? Do I need to worry about them?"

"Gods, you better hope not. I've heard a few rumors, but as far as I know, they haven't been around for hundreds of years. If it's true that they're back, that's a terrible thing.

"If I remember the old stories correctly, the shadows don't wander around like other monsters. They do things with a purpose. If they're in a place, it's because they're hunting. If that brings them to you, well, I'm afraid nothing I can say or do will help you. Two weeks ago, I'd have thought you were crazy for even mentioning them. Everyone thought they were all gone for good. Heard a couple of rumors lately though that sounds like they're back. I hope not."

I didn't have the heart to tell him I could confirm that they were back. "Got it. Thank you. Like I said, I don't know much about this area. I'll go to Fanning and look for my friend, camp near the road, and not mention that word to people. I appreciate your help."

The man's tension bled away and he nodded. "You're welcome. I'll let you finish your food in peace. Let me know if you have any more questions."

I finished wolfing down my food, waved at the innkeeper while he was busy with another patron, and I left the tavern. Next stop: Sam's General Store.

## CHAPTER
# SEVEN

I walked into the general store and took in the sight of the many shelves, chests, crates, and barrels with items scattered everywhere for my perusal. It reminded me of every army surplus store I'd ever been in. That is to say it was awesome, and the closest thing to feeling like I was back in my world as I'd felt since waking up with that damn monster sucking my life out of me.

That lasted exactly long enough for my thoughts to be interrupted by the proprietor of the store.

"Good morning! Welcome to my store. Looking for anything in particular?"

I turned toward the deep voice. It was easy to spot the man. He was huge. I mean, like NFL linebacker kind of huge. As if his size wasn't enough, he also had horns, but these were nothing like the stubby ones the innkeeper had. They were like bull's horns. No, bison. They were exactly like bison horns. His unblinking eyes were like that animal's, too, the deepest black you can imagine. Like you could fall into them and never hit bottom.

"I, uh, yeah," I said articulately. "I need to get some

supplies if you have them. A pack, some food, maybe flint and steel."

"Going on a trip, are you?"

"Already on it. For now, I'm heading toward Fanning, but it may be longer than that."

"I've got whatever you need, I guarantee it. I'm Sam."

"Hi, Sam. Pleased to meet you. I'm Gar."

"Like the fish?"

I chuckled. "Not really. My name is Garfield, but everyone calls me Gar."

"Garfield. Never heard the name before. Does it mean something?"

"Umm. Orange cat, maybe?"

Sam tilted his massive head at me. "You're not a cat beastkin, though. Human? Or alari?"

"Human. Never mind about the name. It doesn't matter. Actually, I'm looking for my friend. He's human, too. His name's Lucas and he has dark brown skin, brown eyes, and black hair that's...textured. Have you seen him?"

"I'm afraid not. Sorry. So, you said a pack, some food, flint and steel. Anything else?"

"Maybe a bedroll, blanket, a knife?"

"Certainly. Long knife? What type of use, for protection?"

"Utility."

"Got it. No weapons? The road is pretty safe from here to Fanning, but you never know what you might run into."

I thought of the money Qamara had given me. I didn't know how long it was going to have to last me. Technically, I did have a weapon: the siangham. I debated whether to see if I could get a bow or something else I could use to hunt with, but if I got some rations, I should be fine without that. I could use just about anything as a weapon, if I didn't want to rely on my own hands and feet.

"I should be fine. Just the other stuff."

Sam darted around the shop, moving his bulky body through the narrow aisles with more grace than I would have expected. In no time, he had all my stuff together.

"It'll all come to five silver," he said.

"Really? For all that stuff?"

"Yep. I don't believe in high prices. I'm not interested in getting rich by being unreasonable. A little coin for me and some good items for my customers, and it's all fine."

"Wow. Okay, great." I handed him five of the silver coins Qamara had given me. "Thanks. I appreciate it."

He handed over my stuff. Everything fit easily in the pack except for the bedroll, which I tied onto the outside. "Good doing business with you, Gar. Be careful traveling. I hope you find your friend."

I left the shop in a pretty good mood. The people in this place seemed to be pretty nice. It gave me hope that if Lucas had visited a town, he'd be fine. I still wanted to find him, of course, but it did alleviate some of my worry.

As I headed out of town, suffering through more scrutiny by the townspeople, I wondered if I should go back and buy some clothes. Just so I didn't stand out so much. I decided not to. With the prices I'd seen, the money Qamara gave me would last a while, but I didn't know how long it would take to find Lucas. Better to conserve my coin until I found him and figured out a way to get more money.

My eyes rose up to scan the plateau above the town. The walls and the towers in the ruins caught my interest. Looking up at the sun—it wasn't even midday yet—I decided to go and check them out. The medieval-style town was like living history, so how cool would it be to walk through a fort that was ancient to these people? It would be like seeing the ruins of the Roman Empire during the thirteenth century.

Besides, I might learn something about this world.

I headed up one of the roads going up the side of the plateau. It got my blood pumping, but it wasn't that tough. Ascending, I got some spectacular views of the ocean on the other side of the town, of the town itself, and of the road I'd be taking east. I was glad I'd decided to go up because following the road with my eyes helped me to visualize where I was going to go.

Once at the top, I wandered through the crumbling stone. The walls were in the worst shape. They might've been damaged before the fort was abandoned, because the tower and a few buildings within the embrace of the walls were still in decent shape.

As were the statues.

Four of the five statues were that same hero in different poses. Each one held that same stylized sword. It fascinated me. So many pieces of art made of him, but the weapon remained identical. That led me to believe his sword really looked that way. Who the hell was this guy, and why would he use such an ornate and flashy weapon? We he just a showoff, maybe a popular noble or ruler who lived for the spotlight?

I mean, from what I could tell on his weathered stone face, the guy was decent looking enough. The statues didn't agree on his body, though. Some showed him as a sleek, toned warrior, while in others he was a lot more muscular. They were obviously supposed to be the same hero, though. Maybe I'd ask the next person I met for his story. With this many statues in the only two places I'd visited, he had to be like Hercules or something like that.

This world's answer to a rock star, but medieval—or older—style.

The other statue I saw, the one that wasn't him? It was a woman. Her body was fit and toned as well, wearing clothing that was a lot skimpier than most Earth statues. Not flowing robes that allowed some choice views of her body sometimes, but modern-looking clothes that left no doubt what her body looked like. I wouldn't mind finding out about her, either. That story would be great. A hot, ancient heroine? I always had time to listen to that kind of story. Warrior women were...fascinating.

Shaking my head at myself, I took the road back down after I'd wandered around the ruins for a while. Qamara had woken up something in me, a desire or craving. Of course I'd want to hear a story about the stunning heroine whose statue I'd found. It was only natural, right? I was really looking forward to seeing the alari woman again. I hoped I would.

My exploration done for the moment, I hitched my pack and headed northeast on the road. I'd seen how it met up with another road at the northeastern corner of the Ironwood Forest. I didn't doubt that the other road was the same one I took to find Qamara's tent, just in the other direction. The path I would take looked to skirt the edge of the forest, so I'd see those trees again.

I wondered if I'd see any more umbrenix.

The road was mostly exposed, with the forest to the south of it and a combination of scrubland and grasses to the north. As I hiked along, I thought about finding Lucas and what he'd say when I found him. The brightness and mild temperature seemed to push thoughts of the shadow people away from me.

Continuing on near the edge of the forest, shadows

from the trees crowded the area in front of me. A chill ran up my spine. That monster I'd killed—even though Qamara hadn't believed it was possible for me to do so—had been in the middle of sucking the life out of me. Literally. What would have happened if I hadn't woken up in time? What would have happened if it had been able to knock me unconscious again?

I wasn't sure, because I had so little time to interact with the thing, but I thought it had probably physically hit me to knock me out before bringing me to this world. The headache I had afterward bore that out, as well as the sensitive spot on the back of my head. That was both good and bad. It was better than if it could use some magic to render me unconscious, but it also meant those things were probably experts at sneaking around and clocking someone from the shadows.

I continued, and I ran into more and more shadows. Of the ordinary, non-attacking variety. The road swung due east again, and eventually the late afternoon sun was blocked by the plateau at Stonefort. The landscape was becoming dim, shadows multiplying. I couldn't help but to think it was the monsters' playground.

I suddenly wasn't sure that, even if they might lead me to Lucas, I wanted to find another one of them. Not when it was dark. They'd have an advantage in that case. I was ignorant of the details of the creatures, and engaging them where they were more powerful was not the smart thing to do. Did the light affect them, or just make it easier to see them? There was too much I didn't know.

The sun became lost in the west, and darkness overtook me and the land through which I traveled. The moon made an appearance, not quite half full but plenty of its face reflecting light to allow me to see. I started to think about whether I would be better off continuing with my travels or hunkering down somewhere to sleep. I had my supplies, but I wasn't sure if a fire would repel the umbrenix or draw them to me like a beacon. I wished I'd gotten more information about them.

When I passed where the road coming up through the trees from the south connected with the one I was on, another forest—or a piece of the same Ironwood Forest—drew closer on the north side of the road. It didn't look as thick as what I'd crossed through right after I got to this world. Even by the light of the moon I could see well enough to distinguish the difference between the trees to the north and south, but the more important thing was that the edges of the fifteen-foot-wide road were moving inward, the undergrowth and trees hedging it in.

After debating while I walked for almost two hours after darkness fell, I decided to look for a small clearing off the road, preferably with rocks or something to block at least one side of my campsite. Just in case.

I plunged into the forest to the north of the road. It ended up being easier to move through than the Ironwood Forest to the south, for which I was grateful, but it took some time to find a suitable spot. Just when I chanced onto an area of sparser trees and a few boulders, I caught movement at the edge of my vision.

Movement that was eerily familiar.

Energy rushed through my body, the fight or flight mechanism I was so accustomed to. It might have been my nerves or residual thoughts from the day before when I had to fight for my life, but I didn't think so. I had the same feeling of being watched, the same sense that although my eyes didn't find anything solid when I thought I'd glimpsed movement, there was something there. I prepared myself for battle.

I didn't have to wait long.

A shadowy limb struck out at me, but I had been anticipating it. I ducked the blow, throwing a hand up to catch it if I could. That impact, too much give to be a real forearm, met my own arm, but I wasn't able to snatch it as I'd planned. It came back around and lines of fire burned on my skin. The claws—or the spikes on the creature's arms—felt solid enough.

It came in again and, lacking anything else handy, I drew out the siangham from where I had it shoved into a long side pocket of my pants and slashed out with the arrowhead-looking metal piece on the tip.

The umbrenix's arm jerked back. Though it didn't make any sound, I thought I probably had hurt it. I shuffled forward to press the attack just as something else tickled my peripheral vision from my other side. I rolled, a bit awkward because of the bedroll attached to my pack, and came to my feet a few paces away.

I strained my eyes and picked out two splotches darker than the shadows. Both were humanoid.

Shit. I'd attracted two of them. There might even be more.

I gripped my weapon and watched the darkness. It was so difficult to differentiate them from the surrounding night. Every little jerk or sway of encompassing vegetation caused me to anticipate, thinking they were attacking. Two flinches, and I could almost feel the monsters smiling. They literally had me jumping at shadows.

They rushed me together, their claws swiping at my face and torso. The thought went through my mind that they apparently couldn't use their draining attack unless they were close and I was not physically fighting with them. What I didn't know was whether one of them could hold me down long enough that the other could take my life force from me, weakening me until I succumbed to both of them.

I did not want to find out.

A claw landed and I got another cut—this one on my right shoulder—as I tried to evade both. I scored another hit with my weapon, though I wasn't sure where on them or if it did any good.

I was pretty much fucked. They had too many advantages in the current scenario. So I did what I'd rarely done in the last decade.

I turned and ran.

The monsters made no noise, but I could almost sense them near enough to reach out and slash me with their claws. I dodged through trees, hopped over obstacles like fallen logs or rocks, and got whipped in the face by small branches, but I kept going. I splashed through a stream that was too wide to jump over. Whatever magic the umbrenix had, it didn't keep me from hearing them as they ran through the water. That was somehow comforting.

They weren't quite close enough to strike, but they were right on my heels.

I looked desperately for something in the terrain to shift things into my favor but came up empty time and time again. So I ran, somehow keeping enough ahead that I wasn't cut down and killed. Not right away, in any case.

I'd completely lost my direction and had no idea if the monsters would ever tire, but a flash of something grabbed my attention ahead and to my right. Hoping it was something I could use, I angled toward it, my breath burning in my lungs and my legs hot with the exertion.

The thing I'd spotted grew bigger and I recognized it as the glow of a campfire. I'd never have spotted it in the thick forest of the Ironwood, but in the sparser trees, pieces of the flame glimmered like a promise of safety. With nothing else to do, I ran straight for it. Even if I could only use the people there as a distraction, I'd settle for that. I could take one of those monsters at a time, but two was too big an ask in the dark.

Before I reached the campsite where the fire burned, though, the sensation of the umbrenix watching me disappeared. It was so sudden, I stumbled, barely keeping control of my legs to slow down and stop. I turned toward where the shadows had been.

Siangham in my hand, I strained my eyes for any sign of living shadow. All I saw in the moonlight filtering through the trees was the foliage, standing before me as my rapid breathing slowed.

After five minutes of standing still and hoping not to feel an attack, I finally slumped. I wasn't sure why, but the shadow creatures had gone. Turning toward the fire, I wondered if I would be better off going around and leaving it behind.

# CHAPTER EIGHT

I sat down on the ground in the darkness and thought about it for a lot longer than I should have. My mind kept going back to why the umbrenix left. I was well out of the reach of the firelight, so it wasn't any kind of vulnerability to light. Besides, when I woke up and fought that first one, it was daylight out. Dim, diffused daylight in that heavy forest, but still light.

Which made me wonder if something else in the little camp had scared them away. What if it was full of horrible monsters that frightened even the shadow creatures? On the other hand, those ones in camp might be allies to the umbrenix, and they were kindly leaving me to be killed by them, as a gift. Unlikely, sure, but I was in another world, being hunted by shadow monsters, and there was magic here. "Unlikely" didn't have the same punch for me as it might have a couple of days ago.

In the end, it was curiosity that made me act, pure and simple. What kind of travelers were these? What if they'd seen Lucas? I couldn't pass up a chance to get more information about my friend.

Besides, I didn't think it was too late. While I stood and pondered, I heard voices and I saw movement even from where I sat in the darkness. Some—or all—of the people there were still awake. At least the speech pointed toward them being people, and not more monsters. I didn't know if monsters made campfires in this world. Or any world, for that matter.

I moved closer, going slowly so I wouldn't make too much noise. I wasn't a trained ninja or anything, but even as a kid that grew up in a city, I knew that moving slowly and deliberately was the key to avoiding the proverbial twig snap that would bring doom upon me.

Yeah, I'd probably read too many fantasy novels.

I settled maybe twenty-five yards from the edge of the camp. I was confident that I was hidden, but I could see the fire and those around it clearly.

Five people all together, three smaller and two larger. The difference in their sizes was pronounced, like toddlers compared to an adult. The more diminutive weren't toddlers, though. They were probably close to four feet tall, maybe a little bigger, based on the packs and other items scattered around them on the ground. The bigger ones were definitely taller than me, maybe seven or more feet tall, with hefty bodies easily in the vicinity of more than three hundred pounds.

One of the smaller ones shifted to face a companion and I realized it was not only a female, but that her skin was dark. Not just dark, though. If I was seeing color truly in the firelight, she was...green?

Tapping my familiarity with fantasy novels, that meant an orc or a goblin. If anything I knew even applied here. Definitely not an orc at that size. So she and the other two were goblins. What did that make the two bigger ones?

"I not like this," one of the hulking guys said. "Take too long get to town."

*Ogre*, I thought. *It's gotta be a fucking ogre. Unless it's a Tolkienian troll.*

I shook my head. I was really having an internal conversation about this. God damn it.

"Calm down, Brugg," one of the goblin males said in a scratchy voice I would have expected for his kind. The accent almost could've been from New York. "It took a little longer than we planned, but we got her. We'll have her delivered and sold soon and then we'll have some coin again."

"Tired of eating rabbit stew," the oaf said.

"Yeah, yeah," the female goblin answered. Her voice had the same quality as the other one, but at least she sounded feminine. More feminine, anyway. "We take her to Fanning or Windridge and sell her, then we'll have money to get you some...whatever you eat."

"We could eat her," the other ogre suggested. "Magic lady taste good. How that sound, Drimdor?"

The third goblin shook his head. "No, Urgath. We're not going to eat her. We hunted her down and captured her so we could sell her. If we eat her, then we won't get any money."

"But, but..."

"No. Eat your stew. In the morning, we'll head toward Fanning and after we sell her, you'll get your share so you can buy whatever food you want."

The ogre grumbled but turned his attention back to the bowl he held, scooping food into his mouth.

I listened to the five chatting as they ate, but none of it was important. I shifted, even moved forward a little, so I could get a better look at the camp. Eventually, I found an angle where I could use a tree near me to block most of the direct firelight so my eyes would adjust to the darkness better. It allowed me to see more of the camp.

Two animals—I think they were bulls or oxen—shifted nearby, placidly standing and nibbling at some of the plants at the edge of the campsite. There was also a wagon with a rectangular shape in its bed. It took more moving around to block out more of the firelight before I could see what it was.

A cage.

The goblins had only mentioned one person. A female. The cage didn't look big enough to hold a human, let alone something the size of one of those ogres. If this woman who was going to be sold as a slave was human-sized, she'd be cramped in that thing.

I clenched my fists. I didn't know anything about the situation other than what I'd heard, but hunting down someone to take them so they could be sold was not something I approved of. Not something good people did.

The piece of me that suffered from what Lucas liked to call my "hero complex" pricked me, urging me to action. I squashed it down like I typically did. I knew better than to engage in that shit. It had almost gotten me put in jail in my world, and I had no doubt it would kill me in this one. I didn't know who their prisoner was, but she was going to have to figure out her own deal. It was none of my business.

It was obvious I wasn't going to go and approach the camp to ask for directions or to see if they'd seen Lucas. The goblins didn't say anything about a "he" being their prisoner, so I doubted he was with them. Being slavers, I was pretty sure a lost individual stomping into their camp to ask for anything would result in capture and sale as a slave right alongside the woman.

*Sorry, honey*, I thought. *Nothing personal. Just the way the world works.*

Yet I didn't move. Even as the five finished their dinner and settled into sleep, I didn't move. Why?

Because I was a fucking idiot.

That was why I found myself sneaking into their darkened camp, the fire burned down to low embers, trying to keep from making any noise. Again, I was new in this world, but I couldn't understand why anyone would go to sleep out under the open sky without setting a watch.

Either they were supremely confident in their skills and their senses so they assumed they'd have time to react to any attacks by wild animals or whatever, or they were plain stupid. I was hoping for that last one, of course. There's no discounting the ubiquity of stupid people. Then again, maybe they knew something I didn't, and *I* was the stupid one. Not a comforting thought.

Having sat in the darkness for all that time, it wasn't a surprise that I could see well enough to keep from stepping on anything—or anyone. I tiptoed toward the wagon. One of the beasts snorted softly and when I looked over at it, the thing's big eyes were staring at me. I put a finger up to my lips, as if that would have meant anything to the creature. It continued to watch, but didn't make any other sounds or movements.

I got to the wagon without anything more than the broken snoring of one of the ogres as a reaction. I looked through the bars and found a pair of eyes locked onto me. They reflected the soft moonlight in a way that made it look like they glowed softly.

As I'd thought, the woman was bent over, curled up like she'd been stuffed painfully into the cage. It had to be as uncomfortable as hell. My anger flared and I swept my eyes across the sleeping forms. I was no stone-cold killer, but it would be so easy to bring out my knife and kill them all as they slept.

I immediately pushed that out of my mind. I was being stupid trying to help the woman as it was. Adding homicide to the mix was not something I was ready to do. I wanted to say something to the woman, who had kept silent so as not to give me away. I couldn't, though, not sure how lightly the slavers slept. Instead, I searched for a moment and found the door to the cage.

It didn't even have a legitimate lock on the door. Instead, a length of chain was wrapped around the door and the frame, with a padlock securing it closed. One of the clunky, huge, old timey padlocks. Great. Not only did I have to find a key, but even if I did and got the lock open without making noise, the chains would clink and rattle. It just got better and better.

The prisoner shifted slowly. The glow from the embers illuminated her face better and I stared for a minute. It was hard to tell in the dark, with all those shadows and angles, but she was very attractive. *Very*. Thoughts of what might happen to a beautiful woman with four males keeping her captive entered my mind, fueling my anger even more. Shit. I was already here, I needed to finish the job.

She moved her arm and pointed toward the one who'd commanded the ogres earlier. Drimdor, the ogre called him. I thought she was telling me he had the key. Of course he did. The little green fucker slept between the other two goblins, just on the other side of the fire from the ogres.

There really wasn't anything else I could do. I couldn't open the cage without the key, and now that I was here and saw the situation, I was not going to leave this woman to her fate. Fuck. Lucas would have been laughing his ass off.

I closed my eyes for a moment, wishing I was *anywhere* else. When I looked back in her direction, she put her hands up toward her throat, sweeping them out with her fingers together in the shape of an arch below her neck. I repeated her actions, mouthing "necklace" to her. She nodded. She had to have really good eyesight to see my lips, but the excitement in her eyes told me I'd understood.

With my attention drawn to her neck, I noticed that she had on some kind of collar. It was a couple of inches wide and fit loosely. It didn't look decorative, more like a dog collar, but of solid metal. A shackle. She saw me staring at it and made her gesture again, describing the necklace. Then she pointed toward the goblin. I nodded and put my hands up.

*Yeah, yeah, I got it. The key to the damn cage is on a necklace around the goblin's neck. Great.*

I slowly moved toward the green man, trying my hardest not to make any sound. Miraculously, I made it there without waking up the whole damn camp. I saw the shape of a key on a leather cord dangling outside the goblin's shirt. No, actually, there were two keys, one much smaller, but on the same leather strip. I guess it was good that it wasn't a chain. With the leather, I could cut and remove it without pulling it over the goblin's head.

I could feel the man's breath on me, the smell like rancid meat, as I took out my knife. My empty hand slid to the cord and picked it up in two fingers as my other hand brought the knife into position. Just as I slipped it under the leather, ready to cut it, the sound of a body shifting next to me caught my attention and made me freeze.

The female goblin mumbled, wriggling on her bedroll to get comfortable. I stayed completely still and waited, watching the woman. When I thought she was finished moving, her eyes fluttered.

*No. Don't open them. Fuck, don't open your...*

"What?" she yelled. "Assassin. Drimdor, th—"

A gasp from the direction of the cage barely made an impression on me.

I pulled up sharply with my knife to separate the leather cord and took both keys. I held the keys in my fist and punched the woman in the face. Hard. Her head snapped back and slammed onto the ground, sending her back into her slumber. I'm not proud of it, sucker punching a woman like that, but it was better than the alternative. I needed to get that cage open and get the hell out of there.

It was too late, though. Grimdor's hand came up to wrap around my arm as his other shoved a knife at me. So I wasn't going to get out of this mess by silently letting their prisoner out.

My knife met the goblin's and I easily overpowered him, deflecting his blade and cutting deeply into his forearm. His weapon dropped and he screamed in pain. Mine angled across him and the flesh on his throat opened up easily. He gurgled as I hopped to my feet, shoved the keys into my pocket, and prepared to defend myself as the rest of the slavers woke up.

# CHAPTER NINE

I jumped over the embers of the fire to evade a short sword the other male goblin swung at me. I'd made a shit show of the whole thing and now I was going to have to fight the three remaining conscious slavers. I doubted the goblin chick I punched was going to wake up anytime soon, but that left the surviving male goblin and those big-ass ogres, both of whom were lumbering to their feet while snatching up their weapons. Huge, lumpy clubs with knots on the surface that looked like they could probably crush rocks. Great.

Speaking of rocks, I found a few on the ground where I landed. They were small, less than palm-sized, but that didn't mean they weren't useful. I snatched three of them up and put two in my left hand with my knife. The third I hefted with my right hand, checking the position of my three enemies.

The goblin was wisely staying back from me, letting the ogres circle around the fire pit to sandwich me between them. I sighted, cocked back, and threw the rock with as much force as I could and keep my aim true. It nailed the goblin in the middle of his ugly green forehead. In the dim light of the embers, I saw his eyes roll up in his head. He leaned backward and slammed to the ground on his back. One down.

One of the ogres, only distinguishable to me by being even uglier than his companion and having a mole on the left side of his face, swung his club down at me, apparently thinking he'd crush me to paste.

I sidestepped and the weapon thudded to the ground. The impact made the ground tremble, actually disturbing my balance a little. The other club came around horizontally as his friend got to me and I ducked it. The stupid ass nearly clunked his companion in the head, only pulling his blow at the last minute.

It was a good news/bad news kind of thing. The bad was that I may have underestimated the ogres' heights. Both were a good seven and a half feet tall and I didn't even want to guess how heavy they were.

The good news was that they were both dumb as stumps. I could work with that.

I zipped toward the oxen and the bumbling oafs took a few seconds to chase after me. One of the stones found my right palm and I zinged it at old moleface. It cracked him on the temple with a sound like a tree falling. He blinked twice, put a hand up to his head, then narrowed his eyes at me. His hand came back bloody and I thought he might go down.

Nope.

He roared and took the shortest path to kill me. Right through the fire. Sparks shot through the air and a few flames flared from his bare feet, but I don't think he realized his skin was burning. His eyes frantic, he only had one thing on his mind: kill me.

I dodged around one of the oxen while the other ogre took a more sensible route to me. I threw the other stone at him, cutting his left cheek, but it didn't bother him any more than the temple shot did the other one.

I guessed I was going to have to get up close and personal. Too bad. I had hoped I could knock them out and not have to kill them. It was looking like that wouldn't be the solution.

Moleface did his best to play whack-a-mole with me—vaguely hilarious because of the name I'd been calling him in my head—slamming his club down repeatedly, hoping for a better outcome than every swing before. It wasn't too difficult to evade, but with both of them trying, only a small mistake on my part would probably mean instant death. The damn clubs were creating foot-deep divots in the hard ground every time they struck.

I spun to the side of moleface and lashed out at his side with my knife. It was mostly to see how thick his skin was and if I could hurt him with the small blade. He bellowed, surprising me with a backhand blow with his club that would have connected had I not thrown myself down onto my upper back.

I have to admit here that I'd seen some movies when I was a kid, ones where Bruce Lee did this cool thing where he got knocked back, landed on his upper back and shoulders, and flipped back up onto his feet instantly. I wasn't one of those guys who tried to be like the Kung Fu Theater fighters, but that one movement was fucking awesome. So I practiced it. A lot. I'd perfected it.

And at this particular moment, I used it.

The club whooshed by me horizontally as I went down and I popped up a second later to find my foe wound halfway around from the force of his swing. My previous slash had cut him, given him pain, but it wouldn't be enough. His eyes went wide as he desperately tried to arrest the force of his swing and bring the weapon back around to me. He'd be too late.

Before he could react, I pulled the siangham from the side pocket of my pants, slashed out with the knife in my left hand while I rammed the metal point of the strange weapon into moleface's eye. The flesh on his throat parted to my knife, but it didn't end up being necessary. I pulled the siangham from his eye with a squishy, slushing sound, and the ogre's body continued twisting the way it had been. He spun into the fire pit and slammed down, throwing stars everywhere and plunging the whole area into dark.

I dove to the side, having seen the other ogre swinging at me before the lights went out. He missed.

"It's not too late," I told the massive dude. "Run away and I'll let you live."

"You kill Brugg."

"I did, and I'll kill you, too, if you keep attacking me. I don't have anything against you. Go away and I won't kill you like I killed Brugg."

"No hunt Urgath down?"

"Nope. I don't care about you. I'll set the lady free and I'll leave. You can even come back later to...bury your friend." I had a feeling that he would come back to *eat* his friend, but I didn't want to get into that.

"Gretta," he said.

"I just knocked her out. I'll put her and the other one in the cage where they'll be safe. When you come back, you can let them out."

"Don't know. Drimdor boss."

"He's dead. I'll give you until I count to three. If you're still here, I'll kill you, just like Brugg. One..."

"I go." The ogre turned and ran into the night, his heavy footfalls fading as he ate up the distance.

"Shit," I said aloud. "I didn't think that would work."

I slumped, coming down from the adrenaline high. Then I remembered the woman and headed to the cage to free her. When I got there, she looked at me with wide eyes.

"Are you okay?" I asked.

"I...yes. I am unharmed."

I still wasn't sure exactly what she looked like, especially now that the fire was snuffed out, but damn, she sounded hot, and what little I'd seen, I was sticking to that assumption. She had a faint English accent and sounded like some kind of aristocrat or royalty or something. I wondered if she *was* royalty. Probably not. If she was, the goblins wouldn't have been selling her as a slave. They'd be holding her for ransom. But none of that mattered at the moment. What did was to get her free.

I pulled the larger of the two keys out and unlocked the padlock, then pulled the chains off the bars. When I opened the cage door she stared at me, like she was afraid to come out.

"I won't hurt you," I said.

She looked at the bodies around the campsite. To be fair, I didn't think I killed the goblin I'd thrown the rock at or the female I punched in the face, but yeah, the leader and the ogre weren't ever getting up from what I did to them.

"Pardon. The circumstances are surreal. I had not expected rescue."

"Yeah, well I hadn't expected to rescue anyone, but here we are. I'd like for you to get out of the cage so I can put the goblins in, like I told the...ogre?"

"What? Oh, yes. He is an ogre."

"Okay. So...?"

I put my hand out, just out of habit, and she took it as she squeezed her way through the cage opening. She climbed down from the wagon bed, but when her feet hit the ground, her knees buckled. I caught her in my arms and held her up until she could brace herself on the side of the wagon.

"Thank you. For that and for rescuing me. I am Brinawynn Tolsen. You have saved me from a dire fate."

"I'm Garfield Hailey. You can call me Gar. I'm glad I could help. I'm going to put those goblins in the cage now. Maybe you should see if there's anything you need. A pack, food, water, something to start a fire. Whatever. Maybe I should take a minute to start a fire, actually. It'd be easier to search the camp."

"Do you have the other key, the smaller one? It should have been on the leader's leather cord."

"Oh, right. Yeah. What's it for?" I pulled it out of my pocket and handed it to the woman.

She took it in both hands and let out a long breath, closing her eyes like she was praying over it. Then she felt around on the collar at her neck, located a hole, and put the key in. With a click, the collar swung open and she took it off her neck.

"Thank the moon goddess. I have never felt so powerless." She closed the collar with a click, then lifted her other hand in front of her, with the palm up.

A ball of light about the size of a baseball flared into being. It was soft and didn't hurt my eyes, through it did allow me to see not only around the camp, but more importantly, who it was I'd rescued.

My mouth dropped open.

"I...uh...thanks."

Okay, so yeah, maybe it wasn't the most articulate thing

I'd ever said, but you have to cut me some slack here. Not only did I just find out that the woman in front of me could use magic—something Qamara had already told me happened in this world—but it was more than that. Much more.

Despite just climbing out of a cage, clothes wrinkled and weak as a newborn kitten, the woman was dazzling. I mean it. I'm not just throwing words out there. I didn't know any other way to describe how stunning she was.

Long red hair that reached the middle of her back, bright green eyes that I imagined looked spectacular in the sunlight and that looked magical in the light she'd created, and a face that would make angels weep with jealousy, but even those weren't the most striking thing. She was blue. I mean, her skin, not her mood. It was actually tinted blue. Not like a Smurf, but more like in the movie *Avatar*, a powder-blue color that along with her hair and eyes and features squeezed the breath from me. Her lips, so shockingly red, had to be natural. I wouldn't think she'd just applied lipstick in that cage.

Her beauty was not limited to her face, though. I tried hard not to stare at her body, which was framed exceptionally well in the strange clothes she wore. It was a corset and miniskirt thing, sort of. The top of her blue garments—trimmed with a gold band all around it—was a corset top that left the top halves of her breasts to be kissed by the night air. Leather straps wrapped around her waist, snugging the clothes to her slender frame. A little miniskirt with the same gold banding barely covered her sumptuous thighs. Sturdy boots, stylish but functional, reached just above her knees.

A longer skirt, covering only the back side of her, was part of the dress and gave her an elegant look, like what she wore could be used for riding a horse or for dancing at a ball. As if I knew anything about ballroom dancing. Her arms, shoulders and upper chest were bare, with only some puffy cloth on her forearms, like some kind of flimsy decorative gauntlet.

I couldn't help but to stare, but to be fair, her eyes were searching me, too.

"That will be helpful," I said. "The light."

"I imagine it will. I shall look for supplies, unless you would like my help with the goblins?"

"No, I'm fine. I...I'm sorry. Where I come from, there is no magic, and there are definitely no women like you." I barely mumbled that last part, but a shy smile on her face told me she probably heard it.

"No magic? You must tell me about it. After we have finished our tasks."

I nodded and headed toward the extinguished fire to fetch the goblins.

# CHAPTER TEN

Brinawynn set her ball of light down on the rail of the wagon and walked over to the closest pack. One of the ogres had kicked it during the fight and as she picked it up, a puff of dust rose off it. She sneezed.

"Bless you," I said out of habit.

"Thank you. May you be blessed as well."

I chuckled under my breath.

The edge of the light she had made didn't quite reach the goblins, so I stood for a moment to let my eyes adjust before I picked the first one up. Brinawynn must have been watching me because the light suddenly got brighter, extending the illumination all the way to, and past, where the goblins lay.

"Thank you."

"You're welcome."

I was glad for the light because the blood from the leader goblin had spread before soaking into the dirt. I'd rather not step into bloody mud, thank you very much.

The male goblin I'd beaned with the rock was sprawled out on the ground in an awkward pose, almost like one of those chalk outlines of a murder victim. I checked his neck and found a pulse, which was good. I'd killed two people—something I was going to have to unpack later—but at least it wasn't three.

I picked him up easily, carried him to the cage, and laid him down in it. There was a lot more room in there for him than there had been for Brinawynn. I retrieved the female goblin, also alive, and placed her in the cage as well. Then I put the chain back in place and clicked the padlock closed. The key I set at the very edge of the wagon, far enough that the goblins couldn't get to it, but plainly visible for when the ogre returned.

If he returned. If he didn't, I didn't know what would happen to the goblins. I picked up a water skin lying nearby and put it next to the cage. If their companion didn't come back, it would only help them last a few days, but hopefully someone would find them and let them out before they died.

I was still thinking about how they could end up dying anyway, despite my best efforts, when I felt Brinawynn's gaze on me. I turned to find her standing a few paces away, considering me.

"What?" I asked.

"You are putting forth significant effort to ensure they do not expire."

"Yeah. If I wanted them dead, I would kill them. I don't agree with taking people as slaves, but it doesn't look like they abused you or harmed you. Maybe they deserve to die, but I'm not the one who should decide that. It's different in a fight. For those others, it was me or them. I have a choice now and I'd as soon not kill when I don't have to."

"You are not a warrior?"

I didn't like the way that sounded. To be honest, part of my mind translated it as, "*You're a pussy?*"

"It's not that," I snapped, then reined in my anger. I cleared my throat and started again, more calmly. "It's not that. Death is so...final. I'll fight, and kill if I have to, but I don't have to like it. I *don't* like it."

"My apologies. I intended no offense. The way you fought was impressive. You are obviously a skilled warrior. I have met few who are so skilled who would show such mercy. It is unusual."

"Oh. I don't know anything about all that. I just know that I'd rather not have to fight. I can do it, but I'd be happy not to ever need to fight to the death again."

She nodded. "An admirable quality. I agree and it gladdens me to hear that you have compassion."

I mumbled my agreement and went to check on the other two bodies. I was certain they were dead, but who the hell knew in this world. Maybe they could magically survive a slashed-out throat and a sharp weapon in the eye.

The two were indeed dead. It was mildly comforting to know that if I killed something, it stayed dead, even in this place. I checked their pockets carefully, trying to keep from getting their blood all over me, and found a folding knife, a few loose coins, and a purse on the goblin's belt with some other money. I pocketed them and turned to watch Brinawynn.

The blue woman—it still hadn't sunk in completely that her skin was really blue—made a careful search of the camp. She put all the packs in the bed of the wagon, checked the unconscious goblins through the bars of the cage, and rummaged around in the crates already in the wagon.

"Looking for something particular?" I asked.

"Yes. When I was captured, they took several items from me. There was another goblin with them at the time. He put my things in a sack and left to go sell them ahead of the group. The oxen do not travel quickly. From the discussions I heard, he was going to come back with the money and meet the rest. I was hoping one of the others had kept back a possession or two. Alas, I cannot find even one. All my things..."

"I'm sorry. They have some money. Maybe you can replace them."

She shook her head. "In time, perhaps. It took me years to collect them and it will take years again to get others. They...well, no matter. I am free of that cage, thanks to you, so I cannot complain overmuch."

"That's the spirit. Do you need me to help with anything?"

"No, thank you," she said. "All that remains is for us to determine what we want to take. You may go through everything and take what you like. I will choose from what remains."

"Nah, it's good. I'll split the food, water, and money with you. I don't need anything else. Someone helped me earlier and I bought what I need."

"Very well. I will take what is needful."

In a few minutes, Brinawynn had a pack full of things she wanted, a bedroll attached to it, and a short sword she'd taken from one of the goblins. Probably the leader. He'd never had a chance to reach for it.

"What will you do now, Garfield Hailey?"

"Please, call me Gar."

"Is your name not Garfield?"

I rubbed the back of my neck. "Yeah, it is, but I've never

been called that. Not unless I was in trouble with my mother. I prefer to shorten it to just Gar."

"I see. Then Gar it shall be."

"As for what I'll do now, I have to find my friend. Have you seen him? Dark-skinned guy with unusual clothes, similar to mine?"

"I am sorry, but I have not. I have been in that cage for almost three days and have seen no one but the goblins and ogres. Has some calamity befallen your friend?"

"I hope not," I said. "We're not from around here and I think he might be in the area. I need to find him."

"Then I shall help you. I am in your debt for rescuing me from these slavers and I would like to aid you in your pursuit. If you are not familiar with this place, my knowledge may assist you."

My blue eyes met Brinawynn's green. It would be nice to have someone who knew where we were. Besides, I kind of felt obligated to keep her safe, now that I'd rescued her. I didn't know if she could take care of herself. Besides, Qamara did tell me I'd find a companion that I should stick close to. Maybe I'd lucked out and found her already.

"Sounds good to me. I was heading for Fanning so I could ask about Lucas there."

"Splendid," she said. "I have business there as well. We will go together. Perhaps we should leave this place, travel a few miles and then rest. The ogre may return. I assume you have not slept this night?"

"You're right. I could use a nap. Do you know where we are, how to get to Fanning?"

"I do." She looked at the goblins in the cage. There didn't seem to be any malice there, but I don't know why. I was pissed off enough about them putting her in there for the both of us, but her calm, cool eyes didn't show any anger. "I will extinguish the light. It would not do to bring attention to ourselves."

"Are you going to be able to see well enough to lead us?" I asked.

Her ruby red lips turned up into a smile. "Of course. I am a moonwisp. I can see well in the dark."

*Moonwisp? What the hell is that?*

The light disappeared and everything went black. I tensed, wondering if I'd misunderstood and she was being kept in that cage because she was some kind of rampaging, murdering monster.

Something touched my hand and I almost attacked. Until I realized it was the same feeling I'd had when I helped Brinawynn down from the wagon. She grasped my hand in hers and tugged gently on it.

"Will you allow me to lead you until your eyes become more accustomed to the dark? We can wait here until they do, if you prefer."

I thought about it for a moment, but there was no need. If she could see as well as she said, we'd be fine. Besides, I kind of liked how her hand felt in mine. "We can go. Warn me if I'm about to trip over something though, okay?"

Her chuckle was the most welcome thing I'd heard all night. "I will not let you fall. Be assured."

Packs on our backs, hands clasped, we left the slavers' campsite. I'd met several people since I'd been in this world, even made out with one of them, but Brinawynn was fast becoming the most welcome presence. Soothing, calming. She gave me the feeling that together, we could make some progress on finding Lucas. I followed beside her, giving myself over to her direction in a strange show of instant trust.

Was she this companion Qamara had told me about?

What was it the prophetess said? The person she referred to would know something they shouldn't? I cast my mind back to what we'd talked about since I'd met the moonwisp less than an hour ago. She hadn't said anything that told me she had any kind of secret knowledge. I'd keep my ears open and see. Getting lucky enough to run into the person right away that Qamara told me about wasn't likely, but who knew? This world might have a goddess of luck or something. It wouldn't be the strangest thing I'd run into in the last couple of days.

After about ten minutes, I could see well enough to navigate, but I didn't mention it. Call me silly, but I liked the feel of Brinawynn's hand in mine. It wasn't even completely that she was gorgeous and it felt nice. Having a connection with another person in this world plain made me feel better.

"Have your eyes adjusted?" she asked me a few minutes later.

"I think so. I can see well enough not to fall down."

"Good. May I...keep hold of your hand for a time? I find it comforting, but I would not like to inconvenience you."

I squeezed hers softly. "It's fine. Your hand feels good in mine. It makes me feel better about not knowing anything about where we are."

"Thank you."

*No,* I thought. *Thank you.*

# CHAPTER ELEVEN

Brinawynn found us a spot several miles from the goblin campsite where we could lie down and sleep. As close as I could tell, it was maybe four or five hours from daylight. I glanced at my watch, the hands barely visible in the moonlight and starlight. Yeah, it was about five hours since it had gotten dark.

She didn't seem to worry about setting a watch and, to be honest, I was beat. I took her lead and laid down my bedroll, lowered my body, and pulled my blanket over me. That was the last thing I remembered until sunlight on my face woke me up.

I found my companion on her bedroll, pressed up against my side. I looked over at her, my first time seeing her in natural light.

Goddamn, she was exquisite. Her red hair was a bit wild at the moment, but that blue skin, her beautiful face, that body...she was a total knockout. My eyes ran over the lines of her form noting the perfection of every curve. Her clothes, while emphasizing her amazing body spectacularly, were interesting of their own accord. What kind of style was that, and what did it say about her? In most fantasy stories, clothing gave a good indication of what someone was. An archer? A warrior? An assassin? The clothes would make it clear. But what was Brinawynn? Her ensemble didn't seem to be protective, so she wasn't a fighter, or was she? She'd made that magical light ball, but was that something that her race—what the hell was a moonwisp, anyway?—could do or was it a spell?

I had so many questions.

"Good morning."

My head jerked up and I blinked. Where had I been looking when I had zoned out? Shit. Had I been staring at her chest, or her legs? I shifted my eyes to hers and my breath went right out of me.

With the morning light slanting over her face, those emerald orbs seemed to radiate power. I'd never seen eyes as beautiful as hers.

"Uh...good morning. Sleep well?"

She clasped her hands up above her head and stretched, releasing little happy moans. "I did. Sleeping in that cage was difficult, all cramped up like that. Thank you again for setting me free. It feels wonderful to be able to move about, and to stretch."

I still couldn't drag my eyes from hers and hadn't blinked since she said good morning. If I didn't get my shit together, I was going to freak the woman out. I shifted my head to scan our little campsite.

"Glad I could help."

We ate a quick breakfast of hard bread and some kind of meat jerky from the goblins' packs, then went on our way.

As we walked, we both kept mostly quiet. The questions swirling around in my mind needed answers, but everything that had happened to me so far in this world took my full attention. A few times, I thought maybe I was being rude, but Brinawynn didn't speak either, seeming content to walk alongside me as we headed east.

I'd planned on taking the road to Fanning, like the innkeeper suggested, but instead I found myself traveling through forest much like the one where I'd come upon the goblin camp. On second thought, it was probably the same forest, with the same types of trees, still sparser than the Ironwood where I'd woken up.

I caught some motion from the side of my vision and my internal alarm bells went off. It may have been a squirrel or some other small animal, but all my attention went to my peripheral vision, waiting to see if I'd spot some other motion.

I did, off to my left.

"Brinawynn," I said.

"Yes, Gar?"

"I think—"

That was all I got out before I dove to the side, evading a large shadowy figure hurtling at me, the familiar sharp claws swiping even as it passed me.

"Get back," I yelled at the blue woman, and turned to try to keep track of the monster. "It's an umbrenix."

The creature dove at me again. This time, I caught its wrist with one hand and punched it in the face with my other. The same feeling of its semi-firm flesh met my strike. I wondered if the shock absorption worked both ways. Did it feel my blows less because some of the force was dissipated into its cushioned skin? Probably. I needed to shift to something that wouldn't be lessened by that effect.

As it spun off from my blow, I drew the siangham from the long pocket in my pants. The shadow regained its balance and opened a mouth like it was yelling or hissing at me, though no sound came out. It charged again.

Brinawynn hadn't fled. I could see her off to my right, like she'd frozen in fear. I chanced a glance and saw that wasn't it at all. She was in a stable stance, hands stretched out toward the monster. What the hell was she doing?

The umbrenix veered from its course, like it had been body slammed by some invisible football player. It recovered quickly, rolling onto all fours and pausing for only half a second before taking off like it was in the starting blocks for a track meet.

Right toward Brinawynn. Shit.

I didn't think, just ran toward it on an intercept course as fast as I could. I met it a few feet from the woman. My body crashed into the shadow's and we both went flying. It recovered before me and leaped at me, claws slashing. One of them got a piece of my left shoulder and fiery hot pain exploded there. I screamed as I kicked its feet out from under it.

The shadow rolled, both trying to get away from me and trying to get to its feet. I chased it, looking for an opening to do some real damage. It regained its feet and turned to squarely face me. Good. At least it had given up on Brinawynn.

It lunged again, slashing with both claws, its mouth open to show the silhouette of sharp teeth. I wondered if they were solid enough to tear if it bit me. Better not to find out.

I dodged, slipping its blows like a boxer would. My left shoulder hurt like hell, but pain was nothing new. I put it out of my mind and focused on timing. I didn't know how smart the umbrenix were, but this one used the same tempo in its attacks as the others, not varying it to keep me from timing it. In half a minute, I had its rhythm down.

Two slashes of its claws and one elbow, trying to cut me with the spikes on its arm, and I sprang just before the next attack. I jammed the wide swing with my left arm—resulting in what felt like my shoulder tearing to shreds—rotated my hips and punched the tip of my siangham into the monster's upper chest. I didn't think it had a heart, or at least that it wasn't where it was on a human, but it obviously felt pain. That silent, dark mouth opened wide in a soundless scream.

I took advantage of the moment and punched it in the throat with the other end of my weapon, the hardened wood end. The monster went into a choking motion, which I thought was promising, but the strike had just been to distract it. My real strike happened immediately after.

With a simple pronation of my forearm, I rammed the point into the center of the monster's neck and pulled with all the strength I could muster. Black shadow flesh sprayed toward me and the umbrenix spun. I sidestepped, pushed a flailing arm out of the way with my left hand, and extended my right arm, levering the siangham into the top of the creature's head.

The weapon met more resistance than it had so far, like there was something thick like an actual skull in the monster's head, but continued down until it was half buried in the dark mass at the top of its body.

The softly glowing red eyes flashed for a moment, then dimmed, but I wasn't taking anything for granted. I swept the umbrenix's legs out from under it with a kick, following it to the ground, where I pulled out my weapon and stabbed it half a dozen times in the face.

I stood up and stomped down on its perforated head

and it squashed out into a parody of a crushed skull. It was eerie and fucking disgusting.

Taking a step back, I searched the area for another of the monsters, relatively sure it was alone or I would have been attacked from behind by now. I tried to remember if the eyes of the other ones I saw had been red. Or glowing. That seemed like a shitty thing to have when blending into the darkness.

Brinawynn hunched nearby, her hands on her knees, her eyes wide.

"You okay?" I asked. She didn't answer, only kept staring. "Brinawynn! Are. You. Okay?"

Those mesmerizing emerald eyes blinked and she nodded. "Yes. I am unharmed, only tired."

I kicked the umbrenix hard, but it didn't respond. "Is there a way to tell for sure if this thing is dead?"

The blue woman's mouth moved, but didn't make any sound. Finally, she managed a few words. "I did not know they could die."

*Well, fuck.*

"Do you mean they come back to life? The one I killed a couple of days ago, it might have revived and will come after me?" I looked down at the essentially headless shadow creature. "It could even be this one?"

"Y-you killed another one. Like this. An umbrenix."

"Yeah, though that fight was different. I didn't have a weapon with that one. I had to do it with my bare hands."

Brinawynn's legs gave out and she dropped to her knees on the forest floor. I gave one more look at the umbrenix—it still hadn't moved—and went to her.

"Come on. Let's find a place where you can sit down," I said. I slipped the siangham back into its pocket, then swept Brinawynn into my arms, picking her up and heading away from the body.

I only had to go a couple hundred yards until I found a few fallen trees that would do as places to sit. I gently set the blue woman down and handed her a waterskin.

"You sure you're all right? It didn't claw you or anything?"

"I am unharmed. I expended too much energy and the shock of...that was an umbrenix."

"Yeah, I know. Qamara told me that's what they were called."

"Qamara?"

"She's a prophetess. An alari? She told me a little about the shadow creatures. She's the one who gave me the siangham."

"Siangham?"

I took a good look at her. She was shocked, but said she was unharmed, so I'd take her at her word. Otherwise I wouldn't tease her like I was about to.

"Are you going to just keep repeating what I say?"

Her eyes widened, then narrowed. "Repeating?" A whisper of a smile played across her lips.

"Oh, ha ha." I was really starting to like this woman. "The siangham. My weapon." I pulled it out and the look she gave it almost made me laugh. By her expression, it seemed like a pretty shitty weapon to her, too. I probably just should have used my knife.

"May I see it?" she asked.

"Sure." I handed it over and she ran her fingers up the length of it. She closed her eyes and sat there for a moment. I had no idea what she was doing.

She opened them again and handed the weapon back to me. "It is not enchanted. I have no idea why it would have harmed the umbrenix. You say you killed one with your bare hands?"

"I softened it up with some punches, choked it with a fern, then beat its head on the ground and then on a fallen tree until it died."

"I don't understand. I thought only magically enchanted items could harm them. I felt no powerful magic in you when I held your hand. Perhaps we should rest here for a few minutes and discuss some things, Gar."

Thinking of what she'd done earlier, pushing the umbrenix out of the way like that without touching it, I had to agree.

"Yeah, I think we should. I have some questions, too, if you don't mind."

# CHAPTER TWELVE

Brinawynn's green eyes locked onto me. "You say where you come from has no magic?"

"That's right. I never saw magic until two days ago when I came to this world."

"To this world?"

"Are we going to go back to repeating everything again?"

She chuckled. "Sorry. What do you mean you 'came to this world?'"

"Just that. Here's the *Reader's Digest* version."

"Reader's...ah, never mind. Please continue."

"Here's the short version? The summary. I was in my world, living life and doing what I do. Then, Lucas disappeared, right in the middle of a conversation. He said something about seeing shadows out of the corner of his eye. Then, less than a day later, I had the same type of thing. I'd been seeing the things for a few days, always out of the corner of my eye, just shadows, but then it was like something hit me and I lost consciousness.

"When I woke up, one of those things was sucking the life out of me. I was able to fight back and I killed it. Then, I met Qamara, who gave me a little information about this place and the umbrenix. She's alari, a prophetess. She even told me a little bit of my future, though most of it doesn't make any sense. After I...uh, talked with her, I went to Stonefort asking about Lucas. He had to have been brought here, like I was, so I need to find him.

"No one I talked to here had seen him, so I bought some supplies with money Qamara lent me and I started toward Fanning. I happened to chance upon you and your captors, and you know the rest after that. Now I have a question for you."

"Yes?"

"What you did to that umbrenix, knocking it away like that. Was that magic?"

"Yes."

"So you can make light and you can knock people around."

"I can, and a few other things."

"Why didn't you do that to fight back or escape the goblins?"

"The collar," she said. "It's a null collar. It suppresses magic. Under its sway, I could do nothing magical. Until you gave me the key and I removed it, there was no magic I could utilize."

"So, you're a...?"

"Mage, but a poor one."

"What? Why do you say that?"

"Because it is true. Do you know of the moonwisps?"

I shook my head. "Never heard of them until you said it last night."

“A moonwisp is a special race, one created solely by the moon goddess, Auryana. It is restricted to her most important servants.”

“Are you some kind of priestess or something?”

She snorted. Delicately. “No. That is a different calling. I will tell you the complete story another time. For now, let me just say that I am a special servant, meant to do things the goddess requests and which take unusual talents.

“The goddess created you?”

“No, no. I was human, like you, but the goddess changed me. I became a moonwisp and gained abilities I had not had before. Unfortunately, a few years ago, my powers started waning. I sought the goddess to ask why, but I was not able to find her. My power comes partly from the moon itself, but most comes directly from the goddess. I believe something must have happened to her.

“I began to lose my powers. My most powerful spells failed early, then progressively more and more became unavailable. As if I didn’t have the mana or the ability to use it. Very few of my spells work any longer. I have spent the years since collecting items to help me. I am a mage still, and have the knowledge to use magic, but I need items to help me in utilizing raw magical power.”

“And those items were all taken by the goblins,” I said, connecting what she’d said after our search of the camp the night before.

“Yes. I have but a few spells now that I can utilize, and those take a toll on me. I used a significant amount of magical power, mana, to cast my Push spell. It fatigued me.” She sighed, but then her eyes found my torn shirt and the blood still dribbling down my arm. “Oh! Your injury. I can help you.”

"It's fine," I said. "The bleeding has mostly stopped. I don't think it was too deep. Those things don't have rabies or other diseases, do they?"

"I don't know. Please, let me help. It is the least I can do."

I figured she was going to bandage it for me. I shrugged, and then winced. Not a good thing to do with a torn shoulder. I took my shirt off, at her request, and pulled the sleeve of my undershirt up to expose the wound. Three horizontal cuts, and not clean ones. It looked more like my skin was torn rather than sliced.

Brinawynn put her hand out and a cooling sensation radiated through my shoulder, like I had an ice pack on. It lasted maybe five or six seconds and when it faded, the pain was gone. I looked over at my shoulder and my eyes bugged out.

"What the fuck?" I wiped off the residual blood and found the skin whole, with new skin slightly paler than the rest. In a pattern of three long lines. Not scars, just new skin. "How did you do that?"

She shrugged at me. "Magic, of course."

"Did you tire yourself out?"

"No. it doesn't take as much energy as the other spell. I'll be fine."

"Whoa, thank you. That's pretty handy."

"Better not to get injured, but it is nice when I can help others if they do get hurt."

"Definitely. So, we'll rest a little and then get back to it?"

"Yes."

"Thank you, Brinawynn. For the healing, and for helping me with the umbrenix."

"I am disappointed I could not do more to help, but I'm glad I could do *something*."

"We make a pretty good team, right?"

"We do, Gar. Perhaps good enough to find your friend."

"What about you, though? What were you doing when you were captured? Don't you have things you need to do?"

"I was, as ever, searching for magical items and for my goddess. It is my perpetual task. I can do those things as I help you find Lucas. Fear not that you are keeping me from my quest."

"Oh. That's good. Qamara said there's no way back to my world. I still haven't accepted that as absolute truth, but if it is, once we find Lucas, maybe we can help you with your 'quest.'"

"Your aid would be very welcome indeed. I cannot see being ambushed and taken by slavers with you at my side."

I laughed. "It's a deal then. We can help each other out and see what we can accomplish."

"I look forward to discovering what we can do together."

I thought about what I'd learned about this world as we picked our way through the forest. I hadn't really learned many individual things, but each was something big. Like there being magic here. Qamara had already told me, but something like that doesn't sink in right away. At least, it didn't with me. Seeing Brinawynn actually do it made it real for me.

"We will reach the road soon and then our travel will become more rapid," Brinawynn said. "When we leave the trees I should be able to determine where on the road we are, but I think we'll not reach Fanning this day. Another night under the open sky seems likely for us."

"That's fine. You mentioned earlier how together it'll be harder to fall into an ambush. Is that common here, to be ambushed? How dangerous is this world?"

The blue woman glanced at me, then turned her attention back to choosing a path. "It is not extremely dangerous. There are wild beasts, of course, and some monsters. There are also bandits and slavers, but those are not very common. I have spent my life traveling, most often alone, and have had little trouble. Even when my powers waned, I rarely encountered anything that would be considered truly dangerous. Being waylaid by the goblins was simply ill luck. Or perhaps not. But nevertheless, the world is generally safe overall. That the umbrenix have returned is concerning, though."

"I can understand that. Well, I'm glad it's not too dangerous. I'm not sure what position Lucas is in. I was pretty weak and disoriented when I got to this world. Fighting off that umbrenix wasn't easy. Lucas can fight, but he's not as good as I am at hurting things."

"It is disconcerting, being faced with one of the shadows while being in a weakened state. It still puzzles me that you did as well as you did."

"Really?" I asked. "I mean, it wasn't an easy battle, but it wasn't epic, either. Depending on how weakened Lucas is, he probably could have taken one of those things. Of course, when I ran into the ones last night, before I found the camp you were in, two of them were chasing me."

"Truly? I didn't know that."

"Yeah, I left it out of my story. I was having trouble fighting both of them in the dark like that, so I ran. When I got close to the camp, they went away. Which reminds me, are they afraid of fire or something?"

"No more than other creatures. I believe they did not pursue you because they are still in hiding. They probably did not want anyone in our camp to know they are skulking around. It troubles me that they were." Brinawynn pushed a slender branch to the side and held it for me so I could pass without getting swatted in the face. "Would you like me to tell you of the umbrenix?"

I blinked at her. Why I hadn't been peppering her with questions was a mystery. Maybe I was subconsciously enjoying just moving and having companionship. I needed to get my head in the game. "That would be fantastic. In fact, anything you want to tell me would be appreciated. About anything."

I liked the way her chortle sounded. "Very well, then. Umbrenix first. To learn about the shadows, you must first hear of their master and creator. Aeyr, the All-Engulfing-One, also called Aeyr the Ever-Hungering, is a powerful sorcerer. Some say a demigod. The titles he carries were not given carelessly. Above all else, Aeyr craves power. His goal has ever been to become so powerful that he transcends to godhood."

"So, wait. He wants to become a god?"

"He does. It is his fondest desire. He has tried many things, hatched many schemes since he rose in power over one thousand one hundred years ago. Of those I know, the umbrenix were the most diabolical.

"To gain the power he needs, Aeyr is not above stealing it. With dark magic—and I mean that both in purpose and in substance—he crafted and brought to life the umbrenix. They were created to capture life essence, power, from others and to deliver it unto their master.

"When first he sent out his minions, many fell to their

power, increasing Aeyr's. They targeted especially those with strong magical abilities, of course. Many a mage or witch was killed to feed his hunger. As it became clear what was happening, the nations and kingdoms of the world cooperated to create two grand weapons against the umbrenix.

"The first was a nearly unimaginably complex spell cast by dozens of powerful mages. It blanketed the world's magic with a ward against the umbrenix's power to drain life energy. Because it permeated all magic, down to each person's very being, the effect carried through so that each new person—and indeed, any creature—born thereafter retained the magical protection. That stopped the shadow people from taking the life force of anyone in Valorae, but the problem of the monsters existing still remained. They could still do harm, even if they could not drain the life from people.

"So were the Shadowstalkers created.

"Men and women of power and skill joined together, trained, and organized to hunt down the umbrenix. There were no legions, but merely handfuls of the heroes whose purpose was to scour the world of the dark minions of Aeyr. They did their job well, and within thirty years, it seemed that no umbrenix still lived. Some have postulated that Aeyr invested some of his own power into each of the shadows, which were linked to him. As they were destroyed, his own power was reduced.

"Time passed and no further attacks were reported. The Shadowstalkers, at their height, attempted to hunt down Aeyr himself, but were never able to locate and take down the sorcerer. As the heroes retired or died of old age, they were not replaced. Eventually, no Shadowstalker remained.

It has been nearly seven hundred years since the last walked the face of Valorae.

"The world's attention turned to other things, as is always the case. However, the last handful of years, perhaps as many as ten, there have been disturbing reports. Sightings of shadows moving where there was no body to cast them. Other stirrings in the world's magic. Disappearances of people occasionally. None of these things conclusively showed a catastrophe was growing, however. Such things could be explained easily through other means.

"Yet there is an uneasy feeling in the world. Sit in a tavern long enough and you will hear of absurd instances of unlikely events. Such as some coming from other worlds. A few magical researchers have studied the membrane surrounding our world, keeping it apart from others, and they have found evidence of temporary breaches.

"Over the years, mages of some renown have formed opinions that Aeyr is active again, that he modified his umbrenix in a way that allowed them to cross the membrane, to actually visit other worlds. What's more, at least one famous magical scholar believes that the shadows can bring things back from the other worlds. Things like people. So prevalent are the theories that many believe the monsters were *created* to visit other worlds, instead of the ability coming long after they were thought to have been eradicated. The umbrenix of old never demonstrated the ability, as far as I know.

"Most agree that they cannot take things with them *to* other worlds, though. I know not how they would have determined this, but cooperation between mages with different abilities, especially those who have powers of vision or prophecy, might make it possible. Personally, I believe that the theories are correct, that Aeyr has accomplished this, and that he has been sending his servants to other worlds to bring back people. When they arrive, the umbrenix drain them of their life essence to add to their master's power. I especially believe this now that you have told me your story."

*Damn.* My head spun at the ramifications. "I have two questions about that. First, why bring someone back and drain them instead of draining them in their own world and then bringing the power back? Second, and probably more importantly, if that's why they brought me here, how can that work, since I don't have magic they can drain?"

Brinawynn nodded at my questions. "The first is simple enough. It has ever been that when the umbrenix take energy, they use it to create a magical gem. They cannot store it in their bodies. Instead, they carry it and deliver it to Aeyr. The crystals of the gems hold the power and are easily assimilated by their master to utilize the power. Perhaps they cannot transport the gems between worlds. There is so much conjecture about the nature of life essence, I don't know if anyone truly knows how it works.

"As for your second question, you needn't have magic to be useful. The power the umbrenix take is pure, primal energy. It is the essence of life itself and though that is closely related to mana, or magical power, it is not the same thing. You do not have to have magic for your life essence to be siphoned out and used to create a gem. It is the power, the energy, of life itself."

"Which is why the victims die when they're drained by the umbrenix."

"Precisely."

"Well, shit," I said. "That all sounds pretty bad. Any chance the Shadowstalkers are going to be created again?"

"Unfortunately, I doubt it. Relations between different

governments are not conducive to such a thing at this time, and the magic for the spell and the Shadowstalkers largely came from the alari people, who have declined to a great degree. Simply put, the magic to repeat the feat no longer exists or is understood in this world. Whatever happens, we are on our own."

## CHAPTER
# THIRTEEN

We reached the road and, as Brinawynn said, our pace got a lot quicker. The hard-packed dirt was comforting in that it was familiar. It could have been the same section of road I'd been on going toward Stonefort, or leaving it. It actually *was* the same road I was on before my adventure with the nighttime umbrenix, though if it had a name, I didn't know it. Solid dirt, few wagon wheel ruts, and only wisp of grass or a weed every once in a while. I never thought I'd appreciate something so simple so much.

Despite that, my blue companion gave me a regrettable proclamation once she noted landmarks and knew where we were.

"We will not make it to Fanning today, not unless we want to finish the journey in the dark."

I thought about it for a moment. The moon wasn't going to be quite full when night rolled around, but it would be inching up on it. I'd bet it was going to be bright enough to see by, especially since we were moving out of the trees and into hilly country of dirt, rocks, and some scrub brush and grasses. But I didn't think showing up at a town in the middle of the night would do us any good.

"It's fine," I said. "We can spend another night outdoors and try to make it by midmorning."

"That was my thought as well."

I occupied myself checking out the softly rolling hills. Brinawynn kept up a constant conversation about the area and how Fanning was close to the shore of the Toreniol Ocean, on the edge of a large lake with waterways connecting it to rivers from the nearby mountains and to the ocean itself. I enjoyed chatting with her, telling her about the oceans I'd been to in my world. Half an hour before the sun went down, she led me to a place we could set up camp.

Throughout the day, she had glanced over at me, like she was studying me. I saw her in my peripheral vision without turning to indicate that I saw, but her furtive glances gave me the impression she was trying to figure something out about me, even as I was wondering about her. I almost asked her a few times, but didn't want to embarrass her. Maybe she was just checking me out. I'd snuck some glances at her myself. Her incredible beauty and impossible skin tone required it.

Once we settled in, sitting next to each other in front of a fire, she started asking questions.

"Gar, that weapon you carry, what did you say it was called?"

"It's a siangham. Qamara told me it has the same name here, from some old Osgoth term meaning 'soul rod.'"

"Truly? I have never heard of nor seen such a thing. It is an unusual weapon. The Osgoth lived in Valorae millennia ago."

I shrugged. "There's not much to it. Basically it's a stick

with an arrowhead attached. It's almost like someone broke a fat arrow in half and decided to use the pointy part for a weapon."

"May I...see it?"

"Sure. It hasn't changed since you looked at it before, though." I moved over to sit on the rock next to her so I could hand it to her.

"It puzzles me that a prophetess would give you such a thing."

"I think she had it lying around and decided to get rid of it. She didn't seem to have a specific reason."

Brinawynn took her lower lip in her teeth and worried it.

"What's wrong?"

She released her lip. "Nothing, sorry. I have found that seers and prophets rarely do anything that has no meaning. It could be she had it lying around, but I doubt it. Short of asking her, however, we may never know what her reason was."

"She did say I'd see her again."

"Did she?" The way she said it, absent-mindedly, made me shift my eyes from the fire to her. She was scrutinizing the weapon in her hand. "You said earlier that she told you your future? What did she say?"

I thought back to her words. It was as clear in my mind as when I first heard it. I wasn't sure about telling my new friend the whole thing, though. I mean, it seemed like I could trust her, but something held me back. "Just a lot of meaningless nonsense. She did say I'd meet someone who would be my companion, that would help me to be successful in whatever it was I needed to do." I didn't go into further detail, or mention I thought—even hoped—maybe it was referring to her.

"I see. Interpreting visions and prophecy is oftentimes difficult. The meaning of what she told you will become clear, as time passes."

"I hope so."

She held the siangham up. "I can still find no enchantments upon it, but the object itself is magical."

"It is?" I sat up straighter. "What does it do?"

"Whatever you choose to make it do. Perhaps I should explain something of the magic in Valorae. Here, something can be magical, or it may have or produce magical effects, or both. This weapon holds no enchantments and thus does not have inherent magical abilities and does not *do* anything magical. However, the wood and metal are magical materials, with the potential to be more than a common item."

I scratched my head. "Okay, so what does that mean? Does it mean it'll hold an enchantment better than if it was regular old wood and metal?"

"Yes. Had I my full power, I might be able to place an enchantment or two on it, though it would be far better to get a specialized artificer or enchanter to do the job. It could mean it is more durable than similar wood and steel that was not magical would be. I am no materials master. I apologize for not being able to tell you more."

"No worries. I hadn't expected it to be anything special, anyway. I'm pretty good at using whatever I find as a weapon, so I usually wouldn't carry anything. If it wasn't for it being a gift, I probably wouldn't haul it around at all."

"This Qamara, she is special to you?"

I jerked at the question. I purposely hadn't told Brinawynn what I'd done with Qamara. I didn't want her to think the first thing I did when I came to this world was to make out with the first hot alari I came across. Even if it was true. Still, as to her question, I didn't think Qamara was *that* special to me. I enjoyed what we'd done, but it wasn't like I was in love or anything. Though I did hope to see her again, maybe continue where we left off?

"It's a weird quirk about me," I said. "When someone gives me a gift, I cherish it. It's more than the object itself. It feels like disrespect not to. Like this." I held up my wrist and showed her the watch Lucas had given me. "My friend Lucas, the one we're looking for, has one just like it. It belonged to his father and it was his most prized possession. I always joked with him that I was going to steal it from him because I loved it so much.

"Well, he went out and found one that was almost identical and he gave it to me as a present. It's not only that it's a cool watch, but the thought, that he cared enough for me as a person to go through the trouble of finding it, makes it special. I would sooner cut off a finger than to give this away. Not because it's worth a lot of money, but because of what it means to me, sentimentally."

The smile on the blue woman took my breath away aimed at me like that. "I understand about the gift. But what is a watch?"

I barked a laugh so suddenly she jumped. "Oh, sorry. It's a device, a little machine that tells time. Like a...like an hourglass? It can quantify the passage of time."

"Such a small thing? How does it accomplish this? How does it fit all the sand?"

"A very delicate machine is inside, tiny little parts that if I opened it up and showed you, I'd probably break it. Here, you can see the second hand moving though, right?"

She oohed at the simple movement of the delicate hand.

"I need to set it to this world's time, then I can keep track of things better," I said.

"Your world is truly wondrous."

"Oh, you have no idea. The machines we have; we can talk to people thousands of miles away. We can ride in a carriage that flies up into the air, even to other places. My people have flown up to the moon and set foot on it. There are so many things I'd love to show you..." I rubbed my chin. "But we don't have magic. Not real magic. Your world is wondrous, too. And like I said before, there are no women to compare to you."

Her cheeks darkened slightly, not to a red but to a darker blue. I decided I loved that color.

She cleared her throat. "Ahem. Speaking of magic, it may be possible to commune with your...siangham."

"What's that? How would I commune with it?"

"It is mostly a mental exercise, but it may require magic. Because everyone in the world has magic, I am unsure if you could manage it. I believe it is a function of the materials from which it is made, not a specific enchantment. Essentially, you would connect with the magical nature of the item and it would be as if it were part of your body."

"Hmmmm. If a weapon is used correctly, it *is* part of your body."

She giggled and I decided I liked that, too. "You sound like the fencing master I had when I was young."

I shrugged. "It's a common enough concept. You don't really gain skill with a weapon until you treat it like an extension of yourself. So what would communing do?"

"I don't know. If it's possible, perhaps the item would be more effective? Maybe it could do more damage, especially if there is a magical affinity connected to it. All of this is speculation because without magic yourself, there is no telling if you can even commune with it to begin with.

"Which reminds me. May I be so bold as to ask you for an opportunity once again to feel your aura, or your lack thereof? It is a mystery to me how you live but have no magic. I felt...stirrings when my hand contacted yours, but I am unsure if it originates with you or within myself." Her eyes widened and her cheeks darkened again. "I mean, that is to say, I don't understand..."

I put my hand on hers, over the top of the siangham. "I understand. I must be an interesting freak, magicless like I am."

She put her other hand over mine, sandwiching it between hers. "No, no. I did not mean it like that. You are different and that excit...I mean, that interests me. As a mage, I tend to look at mysteries and puzzles as challenges. I desire to learn all I can, and what better way to learn than to try to solve the questions before you?"

I patted the top of her upper hand with my available one. "I get it. I'm the same way. What do you want me to do? I'm all for learning all I can about stuff. If it'll help me to commune with that stick, then all the better."

"It will be simple enough. Put your siangham away and hold my hands, let me feel any energy flowing through you?"

"Sounds awesome."

I spent the next hour holding hands with the most beautiful woman I'd ever met as the fire crackled happily in front of us. For a while, I watched her, her eyes closed in concentration. After a dozen minutes or so, I closed mine as well and dove deep into myself, trying to feel anything that was going on. Anything other than the warm, contented feeling of holding Brinawynn's hand.

A thought struck from out of the blue.

"Can I call you Brin?"

I felt her stiffen through her hands. It was something I had learned to do as a fighter. Wrestling, pushing, even punching in close quarters, I learned to translate small movements in the hands, arms, and shoulders into what my opponent was doing—or more importantly, going to do —with his body. It was clear to me from the small movements of her hands that her body had gone rigid.

I opened my eyes to meet her green orbs.

"What did you say?" she said.

"I asked if I could call you Brin. I love your name; it's beautiful. But Brin is gorgeous, too, and it's one-third as many sounds."

"Do your people shorten all names thus? Your name is Garfield, but you desire to be referred to as Gar. My name is Brinawynn and you ask permission to call me Brin?"

"Sorry. I didn't mean to offend you. It's no problem. I'll call you Brinawynn."

"I did not take offense. I merely asked to understand. Brin. I do like the sound of it, strange as it is to my ears. If you wish, you may call me by that name. I will look at it as a special gift, such as the watch you wear."

I smiled at her, warmth radiating from my chest to my hands, heating my palms up.

"Oh."

"What?" I asked.

"That was unusual. I felt a spike of warmth. Maybe I am too close to the fire."

"I felt it, too, but..." I took one of my hands back and held it up to her smooth cheek.

"Goddess. Your palm is warm. In truth, not figuratively. Please, leave it there for a moment. I want to try something." She closed her eyes, but put her free hand on top of mine on her cheek. I felt warmth in my own cheeks, but not the same type that was in my hands.

After a few minutes, her lids fluttered open.

"I feel strangely energized," she said. "The mana I expended last night had not refilled completely, but now it has. Somehow, though you cannot use magic, the warmth from within you has accelerated my recovery. I have never heard of such a thing."

"Don't look at me. I don't know anything about any of that stuff. I'm glad you feel more energized, though. I'm not feeling too bad myself." I chuckled weakly.

Our eyes locked and neither of us blinked for at least two minutes. Then, she looked away as if she was embarrassed.

"I will have to think on this. Perhaps we should sleep. When I puzzle it out, I hope I can teach you how to commune with your weapon."

"That sounds nice."

She removed her hands from mine and I instantly felt the loss of her heat. I pushed my palms out toward the fire to warm them back up. As I laid out my bedroll, I wondered if she had done something to me or if I had done something to her. I looked forward to solving that little mystery.

## CHAPTER
# FOURTEEN

For the second day in a row, I woke up with the inexpressibly gorgeous moonwisp nestled into my back. The warmth of her body reminded me of our hands clasping the night before and I let loose a little happy sigh.

"Good morning, Gar," she said sleepily.

"Good morning, Brin. Sleep well?"

"Mmmmmm." I felt her stretching, much of her body still in contact with mine. Through our clothes. "Even better than the night before. I believe you are spoiling me. I have never had such restful repose."

My mind shot off in many inappropriate directions after hearing that. I closed my eyes and took a breath, then went with a safe response.

"I'm glad I could help."

After gathering our things and burying the embers of the fire, we got back on the road and were at the mouth of a box canyon in which the town of Fanning was set within a couple of hours. I'd gotten used to the hills we passed through, but when we came around one and I spotted the town, I had to stop and take it all in.

To my left and to my right were cliffs. They formed what looked like huge parentheses, with each set of cliffs curved into an arc. The opening where I stood was maybe a couple or three miles wide, increasing as one went into the valley between them. Smack dab in the middle of the space sat Fanning, the road we stood on running through the center of it.

It looked more like a wild west town than a medieval one, but we were still some distance away. Some of the structures sat on the ground, but others were on stilts, support posts underneath with the main part of the building above and small shops, corrals, storage areas, or even open spaces below. I wondered if it was built that way because of flooding.

A wall of sorts cut the town in half, perpendicular to the road, and I couldn't for the life of me figure out why they had built it like that. Several buildings sat before the wall and the opening was so large, I was sure it would be hard to secure. I doubted the thing was defensive. Portable gates were stacked up to one side, almost like it was designed to channel livestock or something. I shrugged and set my feet into motion, following Brinawynn.

Once past the wall, the town spread out. There were corrals and fences holding horses, cows, pigs, and other livestock, but there were also craft areas. I picked out a smithy with the ringing anvil nestled within, a place with barrels in varying states of being put together by a couple of coopers, and caught the pungent scent of a tannery somewhere close. At the far end of the town, where the cliffs closed in again, the shimmering blue of the lake Brin had told me about reflected sunlight and dazzled the eye.

It was surreal walking through the town, and not only because of the old timey feel of it. I spotted short, green-skinned people, other folks with tails and furry ears, even some of what looked like animals that had learned to walk on two feet, though they still wore heavy coats of fur all over their bodies. Beastkin, goblins, elves, even one or two humans passed by me.

I tried to keep from gawking, but some of the residents didn't respond in kind. For whatever reason, be it my strange clothes or something else, eyes were drawn to me. I thought at first it must be the beautiful blue woman next to me, but nope. The eyes followed me, not her. Some of the watchers were men, but most were female. I had to look down to make sure I'd put clothes on that morning, and that my fly was closed. It felt like that common dream of going out in public naked. But I was appropriately covered up.

I glanced at Brinawynn and she gave me a smile, then pointed toward a building with several wagons in front and one of the largest corrals I'd seen beside it.

"Let's go this way. There's someone I wish to talk to."

As we passed a place that smelled wonderfully of something cooking, I noticed a smallish figure rummaging through a refuse pile. I stopped and stared for a moment. I blinked, then narrowed my eyes. The picture didn't change.

A man, or maybe a boy, picked through the trash. As I watched, he found something he liked and brought it to his mouth. Internally, my little voice was saying, *No, no, no. Don't put that in your mouth. Don't eat that. Ew.* He didn't hear it, of course, as he munched on God-knows-what.

Believe it or not, that wasn't even the most interesting part. The dude was maybe a little over four and a half feet tall, which wasn't too strange from what I'd already seen in this world. He was skinny as a rail, the skin on his bare torso clinging to his flesh as tightly as a speed addict's and proudly displaying his ribs. He was rocking an etched six pack, but not because he was muscular, but because he probably had something like two percent body fat. His clavicles stood out in sharp relief next to his surprisingly bulky and striated shoulders, but the toothpick arms beneath had me imagining they'd break if he fell down and tried to catch himself.

He wore only a fur thing on his lower body, bigger than a loin skin, but not by much. Below his spindly thighs were hairy lower legs with hoofs at the ends instead of feet. Oh yeah, and he had pointed ears and a couple of curved ram-type horns on his shaggy head.

I couldn't tear my gaze away from him, gaping impolitely. He noticed me looking and gave me an unexpectedly sincere smile, splitting half his face above his spotty goatee. I waved a hand, too shocked even to smile back.

Brin grabbed my hand and pulled me along. We passed around the front of the building—a restaurant, I figured—and she chuckled.

"Taranji. Satyr. I assume you do not have that race in your world?"

"Uhn-uh. I mean, we have myths about them, but they're not real. There's a famous story about one. He helps a group of kids to become heroes and rulers in his world, but he's a dapper guy, a little gentleman. Not someone picking through the trash to eat."

"Yes," she said sadly. "The taranji have a difficult life. Even doing what he's doing here, he is lucky. Many towns would beat him and throw him out of town."

"That sucks."

Brin raised an eyebrow at me.

"I mean, that's unfortunate," I clarified.

"Ah. Yes. Here we are. It won't take but a moment."

I looked up at a sign near the door. SONATIS TRADING COMPANY CARAVAN OFFICE.

"You planning on joining a caravan?"

"No. I am here for another purpose." The blue woman opened the door and strode into the office purposefully. I followed.

The caravan office was a small, simple room. Maybe a dozen feet to a side, it had a few chairs scattered about and a blocky desk at one end, placed near a door going out of the room, opposite where we came in.

A man with rounded ears like a ferret or weasel sat at the desk, the jowls of his overweight face conflicting with the image of a ferret beastkin in my mind. His hair and ears were sable, the former with a complete lack of style as it sat in stringy disarray on his head.

"Good morning. What can I do for..." As his head came up to take a good look at us, the color left his face. He swallowed hard. "Brinawynn. Umm, wonderful to see you again, my dear. How may I—"

"Stop," my companion said. Gone was the gentle and friendly tone I usually heard. It had been replaced completely with the aristocrat. The demanding noble's voice. "How much, Cedric?"

"I...I don't understand, Brinawynn. You wish to travel with the caravan?"

"How much, Cedric? How much did they pay you for the information to betray me?"

*Oh, shit.* This fat ferret guy had been the one to tip off the slavers. But how did she know? I thought again about what Qamara had told me, that I would meet a companion who knew what they should not. I'd already decided I'd stick with Brin. We could help each other, and I was already fond of her. This might just prove that she was who Qamara had told me about, though.

"Brinawynn?" Cedric said in a pleading tone. "Betray you? I would nev—"

"I said stop, Cedric." She lifted a hand and that ball of light appeared in it. It wasn't as menacing as crackling lightning or a fireball, but it was still magic, and still enough to cause the man to flinch. "The goblins spoke freely after they captured me, took all my possessions, and put me in a cage. They mentioned several times how they paid you too much. I will make this easy. You tell me how much they paid you, and if it's the same amount they told me, you will live for a while longer yet. Lie to me and your boss will find your body right about here." She pointed to a spot on the floor near the desk. "Now, how much?"

The man had started to sweat and his eyes darted around the room. They passed over me quickly and went to the door nearest him. I found myself cheering him on to come clean and not make a break for it. If this man took money to set Brin up to be sold as a slave, I'd kill him myself if he tried to flee.

"Fifty gold," he finally said, shoulders slumping as he slouched in the chair. "I—"

"I don't care. There is nothing you could say that would explain why you would sell me into a life of slavery, or into death, for all you knew. We were never friends, but I thought we had a working relationship. You disappoint me."

"Brinawynn..."

"Fifty gold, Cedric. You will give me the fifty gold you received, plus another fifty gold for my troubles. Did any of my belongings find their way to you?"

"N-no. Of course not. I'm not a thief."

"I believe that you are, and worse. You are a traitor and an accomplice to at least slavery, if not attempted murder. Give me my money and we will leave without giving you the thrashing you so desperately deserve. I want only to be rid of the sight of you."

"I don't have that much money with me. If you will allow me to—"

"No. You will deliver one hundred gold to my hand this instant or I will not only destroy everything in the staging yard behind you, but I will gift you with a long cut for each gold you are in deficit." Brin drew the short sword she'd taken from the goblins. "I will only waste magic if you are particularly displeasing to me, at which point you will feel pain such as you never thought existed. My gold. Now."

"But I don't carry that much. Please."

"I would suggest you borrow it from the box in the left side drawer in your desk, then. I will be kind and give you three seconds to comply. One. Two..."

The ferret man hopped up and threw the drawer open, scrambling for a box within. He slammed it on the desk and opened it, rapidly counting out coins.

Brinawynn glared at the man as he made a little pile of gold pieces. I wasn't sure how much that represented, but it seemed like a lot. When he finished, he put the box back in the drawer and dropped into his chair.

The blue woman counted out the coins and placed all but one in the purse she'd taken out. It was one we'd found on the goblins.

"You overcounted," she said, sliding the coin toward him on the desk. "Let it not be said I tried to cheat you or steal from you. You have bought the privilege of not having me harm you. This time. If I find that you have betrayed me in any other way, all the gold in the world will not save you from my wrath. Consider yourself fortunate I don't report your activities. The Sonatis family and the local constable would be interested in them, no doubt.

"Goodbye, Cedric. Pray that we do not meet again."

With that, Brinawynn swept out of the office, with me tailing her. I hadn't had to say a word. I glared at Cedric on the way out anyway, but he was caught up in his own self-pity. Or maybe the reality of what just happened was finally hitting him. It didn't matter. He should consider himself lucky. If someone had done to me what he did to Brinawynn, I wouldn't have let them off so easy.

I joined Brin outside the office and closed the door. Before my eyes, her body language softened and the harsh expression on her face turned to a soft neutral, her beautiful and friendly resting face. I blinked at the instantaneous change.

"We have some money now. We should go shopping. You mentioned new clothes and I will see if there are any useful items in the shops."

The striking moonwisp strode out toward the street. I paused, shaking my head for a few seconds before going after her.

CHAPTER

# FIFTEEN

I stopped again when I came around the caravan office to see the corrals. A few oxen were standing around, but no horses were visible. I wondered how much it would cost to buy a couple of mounts so we could cover more territory. I still hadn't counted how much money I had between what Qamara had given me and my share of the goblins' purses. I wasn't going to ask for any of Brin's newly obtained money. She'd more than paid for what she'd just gotten from Cedric.

While I contemplated, a voice from up ahead cut through the sound of the shifting animals and the soft background noise from buildings and people around me.

"Hey, foxy lady. Are you looking for me?" The voice was strangely high pitched and gravelly at the same time. I pictured a grizzled gnome or a young dwarf.

*What the fuck?*

Brinawynn's voice sounded next, apparently answering the first. "Pardon me, but I am not a fox beastkin. You are mistaken. I am a moonwisp."

"Yeah, yeah. What I meant was that you're a real hot

mama. That's a nice dress you have on. Can I talk you out of it?"

"Again, I believe you are in error. The temperature is mild and comfortable and I have no offspring. Perhaps you have mistaken me for another."

"There's no mistaking how sexy you are, baby. Come on over and take a ride. I promise you'll like it."

I rushed around the corner to find Brin staring at the satyr we'd seen earlier. He had a slimy look on his face and his eyebrows waggled at the blue woman.

"Hey," I said. "Don't talk to her like that. Go on, get the fuck out of here."

He dipped his head toward me. "Oh, that's your honey? Sorry. I would never have hit on her if I knew she was taken. I try not to unleash all this sexy where it will cause breakups. Plenty of other fish in the sea, am I right?"

I stared at the horned—and horny, apparently—little man, blinking as I tried to process what he said, and how he said it. By the time I was ready to speak again, he'd gone back to the trash he was digging in earlier.

I turned to Brin, my mouth open. The little fucker had been hitting on her hard, *while he was digging in the trash for food.* I mean, I knew some guys were fucking pigs, but damn. I'd never seen anything so brazen.

"You okay?" I asked Brin.

"Of course. We should ask about Lucas, check the shops, and perhaps eat something?"

"Yeah, that sounds..." I trailed off as shuffling and squeaking noises came from a few dozen feet away. I looked over to find four large rats waddling toward the trash where the satyr was. When I say large, I mean *large*, like rottweiler sized. Wasting no time at all, they charged the horned man, hissing and gnashing their teeth.

I stared wide-eyed at the spectacle. The little dude hopped around, mostly evading the oversized animals. He made similar sounds to the rats, little grunts, squeaks, and what could have been whimpers.

I laughed at the spectacle. It looked like a fucking cartoon.

Brinawynn swiveled her head from the fight to me and back again. "We should assist him. Those beasts will do him harm."

"Nah, he's fine." He kicked one of the rodents with his hoof, knocking the wind out of it. "See, he'll be all right. He looks like he can run fast. The rats are probably just there for the food."

Brin huffed and stalked over to where the scuffle had commenced. Her sword flashed out and one of the rats screamed. It immediately turned its attention to her, its beady eyes locking onto her and its claws coming up to slash at her.

"Oh, for fuck's sake," I said. I charged in, kicking one of the little monsters in the side and rolling it off its feet to slide in the trash. It popped back up, hunching down to attack, but caught the sight of Brin skewering one of its buddies. It lifted its head, sniffed at us, and took off running. Another of its companions did the same, leaving only one live rat left.

I stomped my foot hard on the ground and yelled at that rodent. It darted to the side, snatched up a greasy piece of something I didn't recognize, and followed its friends.

Brin cleaned her sword on some discarded clothing and slid it back into her scabbard.

"Thank you," the satyr said meekly. "I could have handled them, of course, but thanks for the help." He looked at Brinawynn and hunger flared in his eyes, but it disappeared a moment later. Apparently, he had forgotten for a moment that she was with me.

"You are welcome," she said to him. "Be careful. Beasts such as those often carry disease."

"Yeah, I know. I cook them well enough so I don't have to worry about it, though."

A little bit of bile backed up in my throat.

"Hey," I said. "What were you saying earlier?"

The satyr jerked at my voice. "Nothing. I told you, if I knew she was yours, I wouldn't have given her the opportunity to go a round or two with me, you know what I mean?"

There it was again. I hadn't met a lot of people in this new world, but none of them spoke like he did.

"So what's up with you?" the satyr continued. "Just chilling? I'm Tiporian Zethroban, at your service."

"Tiporian Zeth...how about I just call you Tip?"

"No way, man. That sounds like I'm the tip of, well, you know. The name is Tiporian or Mister Zethroban."

"Tell you what," I said. "I'll call you Tip or I'll call you Throb. Your choice."

His eyes narrowed at me, then they ran over my body. I wasn't huge like a bodybuilder, but I had a pretty good physique, definitely more muscular than him. And I was a lot bigger than him. "That's what I said. The name is Tip. Who are you?"

"I'm Gar and she's Brinawynn."

"A pleasure."

I scratched my head. The way this guy talked sounded so familiar.

"Gar," Brin said. "What you told me of the prophetess. She told you of a companion. Could this be him? If so, it would be a boon to—"

"Boon!" Tip yelled, a louder sound than I thought his body could make.

I spun toward him, startled and ready to strike out. "Jesus! What the fuck? What was that about?"

"Oh, sorry. I just have to do that. Can't stop, won't stop."

"Why?"

"You know. The universe requires it. Almost like 'Whoomp, there it is.' Like that." He shook his body in a little dance. "Boon! Boon-boon-boon-boon."

*Awwww, fuck.*

"Oh no. No, no, no, no. Where did that come from? In fact, where did *all* that stuff come from? You just used something like ten different bits of slang from my world. Old slang, but still."

"Slang?" Brin asked.

"It means informal language that's usually restricted to a certain group of people," Tip said without a pause.

*The companion will know what should not be known.*

"Really?" I said. "Really? No fucking way did a hot alari prophetess predict that I would find a companion that I need to stick to and that it would end up being...you."

"Dude," Tip said. "Relax, Jackson. If a prophetess told you you need to hang with me, it's all good. We can be besties." His eyes narrowed. "Did you say a hot prophetess?"

"Fucking hell. How do you know my world's slang from like three or four different decades?"

The satyr shrugged. "Things pop into my head. Stray bits of information, ideas, songs. You want me to sing some of them for you?"

"No!"

"'kay. Relax. It's my magic. Getting stuff in my mind. If

it was better, I might come up with cool new inventions or enlightening thoughts or great wisdom. Maybe winning numbers for a lottery, if we had lotteries. But no, I get *Saturday Night Live* skits and how to do to 'Gangnam Style' dance. What the fuck even is Gangnam Style?"

I put my head in my hands, feeling like for the first time in my life, I might actually openly weep.

"So, does that mean we're tight now? Umm, you got money for some food. This trash sucks big white donkey dicks."

I turned my head slowly to Brin, who was gaping at the little man. I shook my head sadly and glanced over at him. He smiled hugely and gave me two thumbs up.

"Fuck. I know I'm going to regret this."

"Gar," Brin said. "I have not understood much of what you two said. I know not what language you speak, but the words are familiar, though their use is not. Is this taranji the one of whom the prophetess spoke?"

"That reminds me," Tip said. "That prophetess, is she *really* hot? Does she like horny shorter men?" Those eyebrows were waggling again.

"Brin, can you do me a favor?"

"Of course, Gar. What is it?"

"Take out your sword and kill me right now."

"I do not understand. You would have me take your life?"

I sighed. "Tip, please tell me at least you've seen my friend Lucas. Dark-skinned guy, almost as tall as me, wearing clothes similar to mine?"

"He was wearing Dickies and a button up shirt? Are you guys appliance repair men or something?"

I grabbed two handfuls of hair and pulled hard. The pain helped to center me.

"Have you seen him?"

"Nope. Not a hint of him. I'll help you look, though, if you want. Maybe we can eat something first. Besides trash, I mean. I think I'm full as far as that goes. It doesn't fit well into the food pyramid, anyway."

I looked helplessly at Brin and she gave me a consoling smile. Well, at least this world had her. God knows, the rest of it was fucked up.

"Clean yourself up first, then we'll get some food. I think we have a lot to talk about."

"Awesome! I can't wait to get to know my two best friends better."

I definitely felt like an alari prophetess was sitting in a tent somewhere in this world. Laughing her ass off.

# CHAPTER SIXTEEN

Brin led us to a bath house half a block away from the tavern where we'd found Tip. Thankfully, the bathrooms were small, meant for only one person, and the women's were located on the other side of the building from the men's. It wouldn't do for Tip to try to peek at Brin and make me beat the shit out of him. Or cause her to stab him.

Once we were all clean, we headed over to eat. The tavern was set up basically like a restaurant, with wooden tables and chairs and a long bar where stools allowed patrons to sit and eat, or to drink and chat. We took a table and ordered some food.

"So, what's your deal?" I asked Tip. I'd gotten into a habit of trying not to be too colloquial because using slang tended to get me strange looks or at least confusion. With the satyr, I could speak like I normally did.

"I'm taranji," he said, as if that explained it all.

"Okay. Is that supposed to tell me anything? I don't know much about this world."

"What do you mean, 'this world?'"

"I mean, this world. Valorae. You know all that stuff about my home and you don't even know what world I'm from?"

The satyr leaned forward, stuffing a piece of bread in his mouth and chewing it while his brown eyes drilled into me. "You're from another world?"

"Yes. The world where you get all that information from. Earth."

"Huh. Now that you mention it, I do know what Earth is, but I didn't know you were from there. The things that come into my head aren't complete. And they come from several different worlds."

"Oh. Okay. The point is, I don't know anything about taranji. Will you tell me?"

"Sure, n-no problem, bud. Well, it's like this. My people are treated like shit. The end."

I glared at the satyr. "You have to do better than that."

"Oh, f-f-fine. The taranji were once a proud people. In fact, we were one of the founding races. Alari, elves, dwarves, and the taranji. Oh, and the osgoth, but they went extinct early on. Back then, there were no h-h-humans yet and the other races, the hybrids, did not exist. It was also before the monster races, like the goblins and the sirens, had elevated themselves from mindless monsters to real societies.

"In that time—we're talking thousands of years ago—the taranji were respected. Our thing was service. We helped others, and we did a d-d-damn fine job with whatever we did. Think public servants, but good ones—not the lazy fuckers people tell jokes about—and to the nth degree. That was us. We would rock the shit out of service. I mean, we had our groove and we—"

"Yeah, I get it," I interrupted. "You gave good service."

Tip's face broke into a wide smile. "You b-b-bet your milky white ass we did. In fact, I still—"

"Move on."

"R-r-right." The satyr's face twitched and he made a little *urk* sound. I wasn't sure what that was about, but I ignored it as he continued. "So we were doing our thing, the service thing, and loving it. As time went on, though, attitudes changed. With the big four—that's the four founding races, if you didn't catch it—things were always pretty kosher and mellow. I think it was when the humans showed up that everything started turning to shit.

"You see, humans fuck everything. I don't say that as a criticism. I myself am open to a wide variety of partners, so it is what it is." He jerked his chin at one of the serving wenches and winked at her. She scowled and looked like she was about to spit on the common room floor. "The thing is, a lot of the things they fucked got pregnant. With magic thrown in the mix, these new races started popping up. The beastkin."

"Wait," I said. "So you mean to tell me that the beastkin are the result not of some magical binding or spell, but from a human having sex with an animal?"

"Y-y-yep, for the most part."

I looked at Brinawynn."Squirrels, ferrets, rats? How the fuck...?" She nodded and gave me a shrug.

"I know, I know," Tip said. "I tell you from experience that fucking rodents is tough work. You need to be careful, have a small dick, and watch out for the claws and teeth."

I slapped my hand on my forehead. "Tip, don't ever speak of that shit again, okay? Can you finish your story?"

"Ack." That twitch was back. "I was trying to tell you but you keep interrupting. So, where was I? Ah. The humans, the b-b-beastkin, the monster races. They all started competing for everything. Food, sex, land, sex. You know, everything important in the world. Oh, and sex. Soon, the other three founding races joined the game. The taranji, though? We stayed true to our past and did our best to help others, even to our detriment.

"Of course, in a world where everyone is fighting—and fucking, too, don't forget that—those who live to help others are looked down upon. It's exactly what happened to us. Without competing for resources, we began to wane. Either through not having what we needed to being outright attacked and killed. Our communities, our society itself, came crashing down. Those remaining fled for their lives, their sacred service as well as their former homes abandoned.

"That's pretty much it. I don't know how many of my people still live. I've seen a few, but not many. We mostly try to survive now, which means settling for the most primitive of existences. People think we're thieves, beggars, and lazy lowlifes. The f-f-fact is, we're beaten down. We have a strong desire to serve, but circumstances don't allow it. If it weren't for you two, I'd have been kicked out of this place before I could sit down. Just look around you."

I did as the satyr asked and found several scowls pointed in Tip's direction. It kind of sucked. I mean, the little guy was a pain in the ass, but outright hatred like I saw in some of the eyes directed at him, that was too much. I felt a little bit sorry for him.

Until the woman brought our food and he pinched her ass.

He got a slap in the face for his trouble, which he totally deserved, but he still wore a smile.

"Worth it," he said, tearing a whole leg off the chicken in front of him.

I couldn't help it. I had to laugh. I knew guys like that back in my world. I didn't hang out with them, but I definitely knew them. Losers.

"Can I be honest with you?" he asked as he chewed the meat he'd shoved into his face.

"Uh, sure."

"I dream of doing something that will make people respect me, respect all taranji. We've put up with this shit for too long. I'm not asking to be made king or anything, but a little respect, maybe not being kicked in the ass by every teenage boy in the town, would be nice. I've had that dream so much, it might even be a vision. Or a prophecy. You said you knew a prophetess, right?"

"Yeah."

"Is she hot?"

*Fucking Tip.* "She was very lovely, and very kind. And she will be the death of you if you ever try to grab her ass or hit on her."

He put his hands up, one still holding the chicken leg. "Okay, okay. No problem, man. I won't try to get into your action. Lots of eligible partners out there, you know what I mean?"

I was afraid I did. He was looking for respect, yet still assaulting people, either verbally or physically.

"That sounds like a fine goal to have," Brinawynn said, sitting straight up with perfect posture. She cut a piece of chicken into bite-sized pieces and daintily nibbled at them. "To gain respect not only for yourself but for your people? A worthy thing to work toward."

"Yeah," he said. "It is. Thank you. Gods, you're beautiful. That blue skin is so gorgeous."

I tensed up, expecting to have to kick the satyr's ass.

"Thank you. It was a gift from Auryana."

"What? Are you a moonwisp?"

"I am."

"It's a great honor to meet you. I've never seen one of the goddess's servants. I hadn't heard they were so fucking ho...I mean, that they were so sublimely attractive that they befuddled a man's mind."

Brin gave him a smile. "You are a charmer, are you not, Tiporian?"

"Guilty as charged, baby. Um, I mean, Brinawynn."

I rolled my eyes and ate. A slimy little player was what he was. I could only hope Brinawynn was not so naïve that she fell for his bullshit.

We spent some time eating and conversing. I asked Tip more about his magic, but he didn't really know much about it. Turned out that there was a lot of that going around. The types of abilities were unlimited and according to both of my companions, some people never really got a handle on the extent of what they could do during their entire lives. There was no book, no expert, and no real way of finding out unless it involved gods or seers. All one could hope for was that they discovered the nuances or met someone who had a similar gift.

I noted that in addition to the dirty looks Tip was getting, I was grabbing my share of *flirty* looks. Women in the common room would meet my eyes and play the little games of staring at me, casting their eyes away from me and back, or softening their eyes and smiling seductively at me. I got a few nods or chin jerks from guys, too. I mean, the type a moderately successful sports star—or a guy with several hot women—would get if he was sitting in a restaurant. The whole thing confused the hell out of me.

I asked around about Lucas, starting with the pretty young woman whose ass Tip grabbed. I slapped his hand away as he tried again and I warned him to cool it, after which she was more than happy to listen to my questions about my friend. She didn't know anything, nor did the other serving women or the guy behind the long counter. I even wandered around the room asking people at individual tables. They were all polite, had no problem engaging me in conversation, but none of them had seen Lucas or anyone else with unusual clothes.

I sat back down at the table. "No luck. I'll keep asking as we visit the shops. Someone has to have seen him."

I hadn't even realized that I didn't discuss what Tip's plans were. With what Qamara had told me, I just assumed he'd stick with us. Thankfully, he brought it up so we didn't get into a position where we embarrassed the guy.

"Thank you both for the food. D-d-do you mind if I stick with you guys for a little while? It's nice to have someone to talk to. I mean, someone whose idea of conversation isn't, 'Get your skinny ass out of my trash, you fucker.'"

It had already been established that Brin was okay with it, so I answered the satyr. "Yeah, man. That'll be cool. Once we find Lucas, we can figure more out, but for now, you're welcome to hang with us. If you behave."

He crossed his heart with his finger and gave me a goofy grin.

With full bellies, we started the circuit, Brin leading us to different vendors. Looking at everything from clothes to general supplies, to weapons, we spent hours shopping. It was like a nightmare, a never-ending day at the mall. When we were done, we had some new items, but Brin had come up empty in finding those things that were stolen from her and I hadn't found anything out about Lucas.

I stuffed the new clothes I'd gotten into my pack. I wasn't ready to give up my Dickies just yet. If for no other reason than because I had that long side pocket that the siangham fit perfectly into, I'd probably keep wearing them for a while. I might change my shirt out, but for now I was fine.

We'd bought Tip a pair of pants to replace his ratty loin cloth thing. It was a vast improvement. He said he didn't need a shirt, and he didn't need shoes because he had those hoofs. The pants were short, barely covering past his knee, but since he had fur below that anyway, it worked out. We also got him a cheap shortsword, not even as good as the one Brin took from the goblins.

I did ask Brin about horses, but she said almost all of the ones in town belonged to the caravan company and that they wouldn't sell. It looked like we were going to be walking for a while.

Looking at the afternoon sun, a pang of guilt stabbed at me. We'd spent the whole day shopping and I still didn't know anything about Lucas. I didn't like it that I was wasting time when he might be injured or something.

"Brin, where do you think we should go next? I asked around in Stonefort, but there was no sign of Lucas there, and nothing here."

"We could head north, to Windridge. It's the largest city around, with a few little villages along the way. I would assume Lucas would want to find a place with people to get information."

"That sounds like it'll work. We can stay in town tonight, if they have an inn. Maybe we can..." A trio of women crossed our path, right in front of us, all of them staring at me. One tripped over her feet and almost fell, instantly blushing while the other two giggled. They hurried on their way, leaving me standing there in confusion. "Okay, what the fuck is going on? Brin, I've been getting this ever since I got to this world. People stare at me like they know me. The women flirt with me and even some of the men give me signs of respect. Why?"

Brin's cheeks darkened slightly. "You are very good looking, Gar."

"That wouldn't cause guys to give me respect. I mean, being with you, I could see men treating me in a way that expressed how lucky I am, but it happened before I met you, too. Is it my clothes? Do they know I'm from another world? What?"

"Kael," Tip said, picking at his teeth with a piece of straw he'd found somewhere.

"What?"

"Kael. Kael 'the Blur' Serus. You look like him. I mean, you look *a lot* like him."

"Who the hell is—"

"Goddess!" Brin said. "It's true. I was confused about why you looked so familiar."

"What are you two talking about?"

Brin held her hand out. "Come with me."

I took it, never needing an excuse to hold hands with the beautiful woman, and she pulled me along to a street we hadn't been to yet. When she stopped, we stood before another one of those damn statues. She pointed up to it.

"Yep," Tip said.

For the first time, I took a good look at the hero I'd been seeing statues of ever since I'd gotten to this world. In towns, in ruins, it was all the same guy. At least I thought so. Some of the ones I'd seen were bulkier than others, like the difference between a statue of some athlete and one of Arnold in his heyday. Some even had hair shorter or longer. But the face. Searching my memories, the face was similar. It was hard to tell with a weathered statue, but the one we looked at now was in decent shape.

"Huh. He does kind of look like me. A little bit."

"Not a little bit," Brin said. "That statue could have been sculpted today with you as the model. It's uncanny."

"So what does that mean?"

"It m-m-means," Tip said as he spit out his straw, "that you can probably get laid any time you want."

# CHAPTER SEVENTEEN

Brin and I shared a look, like *Whatchya gonna do?* I shrugged at her.

"First," I said to Tip, "that's not really what I was talking about. Second, maybe try to read the room, you little shit."

He had the good sense to at least look a bit abashed about it, glancing over at Brin sheepishly.

"What I meant," I continued, "was how does that fit into the bigger picture? Does that mean I am some long-dead hero reincarnated?"

"Nah. Reincarnation isn't a thing here. So what, you look like a guy who is depicted in statues, etchings, and paintings all over the world? It doesn't mean you will fight evil and save the world." He barked a laugh as if the thought of it was ridiculous. That didn't make me feel better. "It means you're the object of just about every woman's fantasy and all the dudes want to be you. They're probably too scared that you *are* Kael to even start shit with you. It's a good gig."

The conversation was getting out of hand again.

"Whatever. It's a coincidence. I'm sure people will get used to it."

"Yeah, right. Just like people get used to seeing sexy, hunky movie stars walking around. Keep dreaming."

"Not helping, Tip."

"Oh. I mean, yeah, I'm sure people will get used to an Adonis running around. They'll get bored fast. Yep."

I sighed. "It's getting late. Maybe we should get some sleep so we can start out early tomorrow."

"I think that is a grand idea," Brin said. "Rooms are not expensive. I will pay for them, considering my recent increase in funds."

"Thank you, Brin, but I don't want you paying for stuff all the time. We'll swap off. I have my part of the money we took from the goblins and you have items still to buy."

"If I can locate some," she said. "But I can agree with sharing the costs. There is no way to tell how long this money will have to last. If we do not find Lucas immediately, we will incur other expenses."

Tip sat, his head swiveling as we went back and forth. He sighed loudly, catching both our attention.

"I can work for what you spend. I find myself a little short of funds at the current time."

I laughed and slapped the satyr on the shoulder. "No worries, Tip. We've got you for now. No doubt you're going to save our asses or do something else to make up for it all."

"He he. S-s-sure, I'm going to save you from something you, a hero of ages, and the beautiful and magically deadly Brinawynn, can't handle."

"You never know, man. Which reminds me, can you fight?"

"Sure. I fight all the time. Yep, a great warrior, that's me."

"You seemed to have problems with those rats," Brin said.

I chuckled. "Well, we got you that weapon. I'll start teaching you some stuff as we travel tomorrow."

"Some stuff?"

"Yeah. How to fight. How to defend yourself, at least. The next bunch of rats that try to eat you, you'll kick their furry asses."

"Right on. Kicking furry asses. It's what we do." He put up a fist and I bumped it. Brin looked at us with one eyebrow raised.

"I'll tell you about it as we go to the inn," I said.

"It's an Earth thing," Tip added. "You wouldn't understand."

As promised, Brin got us three rooms, despite me telling her I was fine with us all sharing one. I was a little tired from all the emotional ups and downs of the day. I let loose with a jaw-cracking yawn as I thought of how much we'd crammed into the time since we got up that morning. Including the longest. Shopping. Day. Ever.

"I think I'm going to get right to sleep. Early breakfast in the common room and then head out?"

"You betcha," Tip said.

"That sounds like an efficient plan," Brin said. "I wonder if I might have a word or two, Gar? Privately, not in the common room."

"Uh, sure."

Tip's face reddened. Not from blushing, but because he'd clenched his mouth and appeared to be holding his breath. I glanced at him and he tensed up even more.

"Have something to say?" I asked.

"Nn-uhn."

"Okay, good. You should probably breathe, though.

I'm not carrying your ass up the stairs." He took my advice and sucked in a huge breath and I shook my head at him. "Don't do anything to get in trouble tonight. Don't, uh, insult any women—or anyone, really—and especially don't try to get under any woman's skirt. Clear?"

"Yessir."

I narrowed my eyes at him. I gave him maybe a fifty-fifty shot at not trying to grab the nearest woman's unmentionables.

Tip's room was the second to the last door in the hallway, with mine next to it and Brin's next to mine, all on the same side. We watched Tip enter his room and I heard the latch click.

"How about your room?" I asked.

"That will suffice."

I realized as I walked in the door that this was the first inn room I'd seen in this world. It was a simple thing, maybe a little bigger than ten feet on a side, with a table and chair, a bed, and not much else. Actually, there was a chamber pot on the floor and a basin on the table with a hand towel folded beside it. I eyed the bed. It had bumps and little pokey bits on the surface. I wondered how comfortable a straw-stuffed mattress was. Well, I'd find out tonight.

"I apologize if this is awkward," Brin said. "I do not feel comfortable speaking of it in front of Tiporian at this time."

"No worries." I wondered what she wanted to talk about that she didn't want the satyr to hear. I mean, part of me hoped it was something sexual, but I was pretty sure it wasn't. Brin seemed much too proper. I almost couldn't imagine her having sex. Almost. *I'd* definitely thought about it and a few fantasies had wriggled their way into my mind. But her? She was like a noble lady in the stories. I was *not* going to push and fuck this thing up.

"I am unsure if I want to share the information that my magic has waned and that I am trying to help you attune to your weapon."

*Attune to my weapon*? "Oh. The siangham."

"Yes, of course. Your knife is not constructed of magical materials, so I couldn't help you to commune with it."

I chuckled weakly. *Yeah, that's what I was thinking.* It suddenly felt a bit warm in the room.

She shifted her eyes away from me. "I must confess, however, that it is not only to aid you in working with your weapon that I asked you to speak with me. I find that I enjoy the process and it...energizes me."

I really wished she would stop saying "my weapon." My teenage mind translated that to mean things other than what she referred to.

"I like the process, too," I said. "I appreciate you helping me and I'm glad it's good for you, too." *Ouch.*

She kicked in her right knee and her cheeks took on a slightly darker blue than normal. "It is. We should get started so you may get your sleep. Come." She took my hand and sat down on her bed, dragging me over. Eyeing the chair, her mouth went to a straight line. "Would you mind terribly if we sit on the rug? The bed and the chair are different heights, and comfort is important in attaining complete relaxation."

"No, I don't mind at all." Her hand was still in mine and, to be honest, whatever she wanted me to do to keep it there, I would agree with.

We sat down with our legs crossed, knees touching. I looked into her gorgeous green eyes...and kind of forgot what we were doing.

"Perhaps you should hold your weapon?"

Ugh. There it was again.

"Ah, right." I drew out my siangham with my free hand.

"As before, I can guide you as you reach out to it with your mind and search its depths. Become intimately familiar with it, going inside, becoming part of it, filling it up."

Shit. Why did literally everything she say sound sexual to me? Maybe because my body was warm and vibrating like a heating wire that had been plucked like a guitar string?

I pushed the inadvertent innuendo out of my mind and did as she asked, getting familiar with my siangham. If I am to be honest, I have to say that holding her hand was affecting my concentration, but it also felt so good, so comforting, that it helped my body relax as well. Despite all the naughty thoughts trying to invade, my lower regions had not yet reacted. Basically what I'm trying to say is that though I was swirling in a blissful existence, I wasn't hard. Just that was strange to me.

I strained to focus. Which is the wrong thing to do in meditation.

"Are you well?" Brin asked, her hand squeezing mine. I reacted with a soft squeeze of hers.

"Yeah. It's the monkey mind, all those stray thoughts. I'm trying to empty them out. It might take a couple of minutes."

Her laughter sent jolts of pleasure through me. Not *that* kind of pleasure. The kind where you experience the perfect mix of relaxation, happiness, and companionship with someone dear to you. That in itself threatened to scatter my focus. Was she dear to me? Already?

I ruthlessly stomped those ideas and directed my mind

to the siangham. Like I was supposed to have already been doing.

I reached a state where it felt like my brain was separated from my head and in that perfect moment, something pinged in me. A flash of the weapon I held in my hand entered my mind and for a second, I understood what it was like to *be* it. I gasped and my eyes snapped open.

Brin's emerald orbs stared into mine from a foot away.

"What was it?" she asked.

"I...don't know. Something? I got a flash of inspiration. I felt like I *was* my siangham. Is that weird?"

She gave me a huge smile. "Not at all. It was what we were working toward. I didn't want to explain it to you beforehand because the expectation would have ruined your progress if I did. You would have been searching for it. But it is not something you can find by searching. Only by being receptive and letting it find you. I am proud of you. You managed that breakthrough quickly. It will be difficult to find again because your mind will argue with itself that it must search for it, but given time, it will become easier. When you can seek it out with your subconscious mind, you will be able to utilize it for other things. Things we will speak of when the time is right."

I grinned at her. "Thank you. It's exciting, almost like magic."

"It is not magic, I assure you. As you struggle to connect with your weapon, I have toiled to connect with you. I understand not what feeling you invoke in me, but it is not magic. On the contrary, it seems almost anti-magic, the reverse of magic."

"Oh. Is that possible?"

"It is not. As far as I know. And I have studied magic for many decades."

I laughed at that and her eyes narrowed. I'd never seen pupils dilate that closely before.

"What's wrong?" I asked.

"Why do you laugh?"

"Because you said you've studied magic for decades. Look at you. You have to be about the same age as I am."

"How old are you?"

"I'm twenty-two."

It was her turn to laugh. "I have passed seventy and six years upon Valorae."

My mouth dropped open. "No you haven't."

"I have. When I say that I have studied magic for decades, I tell it truthfully. It has been at least six decades."

"But you're so gorgeous and your body is perfect. Not a wrinkle or a grey hair to be found."

She colored. "I thank you. Moonwisps do not age as many races do. In fact, they may not age at all. I have never asked the goddess."

All I could think was that she was more than three times as old as me, as old as my grandmother. What would it be like to have a grandmother like her? Damn. All my friends would be hitting on her.

"My point was that you do not have magic. There is something, though. You energize me, as I have stated. I have difficulty trying to explain."

"It's fine. You just made me have a breakthrough. Now it's my turn to help you. Can I energize you more? I'd love to be able to do something for you."

She dropped her eyes to our hands, still clasped. I set my siangham down and put my other hand out to her. She took it with the cutest smile on her face. I had an urge to say "awwww."

She closed her eyes and began breathing deeply. I

watched her for a moment, taking in the sight of her, then I did likewise. It didn't take long to reach that half-dream feeling so common in meditation. The skin of her palms against mine, the firmness of her fingers interlaced with mine, I almost felt an electric charge. Or magnetism. Some force I might have called magic if she hadn't shot down that whole idea. Still, I sat there, breathing in sync with her—though inadvertently—and experiencing some force moving around and through me.

Eventually, she moved, her hands jerking and breaking me out of my trance. I opened my eyes to find hers trained on me, a wry smile on her face. She gently took one of her hands back, held it palm up, and took a breath.

"Avert your eyes," she said.

I did as she asked, shifting my gaze to the wall.

A burst of light like a flashbang had gone off making my eyes close up tight. Even with the lids down, it was bright enough that I was seeing purple spots in the dark of my closed eyes.

"What the fuck?"

The glare disappeared.

"You may open your eyes again. My apologies. I didn't realize it would be so bright."

"What was that?" I asked.

"The simple light spell you have seen before."

"I never saw it like that before."

"Yes, I know." I was having trouble seeing her clearly with all the spots dancing around, but I think she was smiling. Her voice had almost a giggle about it. "Now you see a fraction of the power I hold when I have the goddess's blessing. It has been years since I have felt so energized."

"Energized?"

"Yes. This is what you did for me, Gar. I know not how

or why, but you have helped me absorb more mana for my reserves. It replenishes slowly over the last years, but you helped to speed it up in some way. I thank you."

"Wow. That's...I don't know. Are you sure it was me?"

She chuckled pulled my hand up to her face, kissing it. "It was you. When I focused, I could feel my mana stores recharging. Thank you."

I sat, locked in place, my eyes fixed on hers. I leaned forward, just slightly. "You're welcome."

She squeezed my hand and got to her feet. "I should probably let you get some sleep. I would like to continue our work another time, if you don't mind. Maybe each day we can help each other? Me with your connecting to your weapon and you helping me replenish my magic?"

"Definitely. I would love that. Thank you for asking me to work with you. It's...a good thing."

"It is." She kissed my hand again and then released it. "Sleep well, Gar. I believe I will. In the morning, we will start our journey to Windridge. We must find your friend."

"Yes, we must."

I dragged my eyes from hers and slogged toward the door. I almost turned back around, but stopped myself. Plenty of time for that later. Like the lady said, we had a job to do. I sighed, closed her door behind me, and padded to my own room. I felt like I was going to fall asleep as soon as my head hit the pillow.

I knew what sight was going to greet me when I closed my eyes.

# CHAPTER EIGHTEEN

I was up early the next morning. I hadn't looked at my watch, but I didn't think I'd gotten more than maybe six hours of sleep. Yet I felt fantastic. I paused for a moment to wind my watch. People had told me I was stupid to wear one so old that it didn't even self-wind, but they could kiss my ass. I loved the timepiece. It was an unbreakable habit, winding it each morning, and inevitably, it made me think of Lucas. Was he winding his nearly identical watch right at the moment? Where the hell was he?

I opened my door at the same time I heard the one on my left. Tip and I stepped out into the hallway together. The satyr gave a little hop, like I'd startled him. He stared at me.

"Good morning," I said.

"Sure. Good morning."

"You okay?"

"I didn't expect you to be in your room."

I cocked my head. "What? Why not?"

"You know, because..." He jerked his chin toward Brin's door and waggled his eyebrows at me.

"Ugh. Please don't do that thing with your eyebrows. It kind of creeps me out. As for what you're insinuating, I came back to my room maybe an hour or so after you went to yours. Don't go jumping to conclusions."

"Fine, fine. All I know is that if I had the chance to go to the room of someone who looks like that, I'd definitely seal the deal."

"Listen, you little fucker. I don't—"

Brin's door opened up and she swept out into the hall. "Good morning. What are you talking about?"

"Nothing," I said. "Tip was just reminding me that I have to start training him in combat today. It's going to be rough. Probably painful. Definitely painful."

Tip gulped, but then stood up straighter and turned toward Brin. "You are looking lovely this morning, Brinawynn. Sleep well?"

"Oh, yes. Like I was slumbering on clouds."

My mood shifted instantaneously. "That's great. Ready for some breakfast before we head out?"

"I am. Shall we?"

I allowed Brin to go first, but put myself between her and the little goat bastard. He'd probably just try to look up her skirt if he was right behind her. True, with the long section toward the back, he'd never see anything, but even the thought of him running his eyes over her slim waist and her perfectly formed and exposed shoulders and upper back made me squirm.

Other than people staring at us, breakfast was quick, efficient, and enjoyable. We were soon on the road to Windridge. We'd gotten Tip a pack with a few supplies. He had his own flint and steel, some rations, a waterskin, a bit of rope, a long coat in case it got cold—even though he still wasn't wearing a shirt—and a bedroll strapped to the outside of the pack like ours.

I had to chuckle as he tried to get comfortable with the thing on his back. Apparently, he'd never owned one—or even enough stuff to put in one—so it was a new experience for him. His desire to go shirtless also meant the straps chafed his bare shoulders.

"Why do I have to wear this thing?" he whined. "It's uncomfortable. I've never needed one before."

"Well, I'm not carrying your shit. You'll be happy you have a bedroll, and even that coat, when it comes time to sleep and if the temperature drops."

"I've t-t-traveled all over and never needed any of this stuff."

"We bought it for you, it's useful stuff, so you're carrying it. Quit whining like a little girl and suck it up."

Brin giggled from beside me. I guess she found the exchanges between the little fucker and me humorous. I guess they were, though I usually felt bad after I said something to Tip. He had a way of getting on my last damn nerve, and I tended to be harsher with him than was probably merited. I tried again.

"Dude, I get it. It's uncomfortable. Still, you wanted to come along, so you'll need to bring your own stuff. I'm not sure how long we're going to have to travel before I find Lucas. So, just give it a try, okay? I know it's new and awkward, but try. I'm not used to all this, either. I'm not even from this world, remember? You have knowledge of cars. I've never walked so much in my life."

"He he. I get you, man." He rolled his shoulders. "I'll get used to it. Thanks. For buying me stuff. I've never owned this much."

Great, now I felt even worse about giving him a hard time.

The road going north from Fanning went through terrain unlike what I'd encountered in the few days I'd been in this world. It reminded me of parts of Arizona and New Mexico. I'd been through there once on a road trip with Lucas. Dirt and rocks, some cliffs and plateaus, and sparse low bushes scattered around. I looked hard but never spotted the roadrunner, or the coyote chasing him down with a rocket on his back.

I chuckled and Tip burst out laughing. "You thinking of Wile E. Coyote?"

I guffawed. "Hell yes. Exactly." I reached out and bumped fists with the satyr. Maybe he wasn't all *that* bad.

"What are you laughing about?" Brin asked, and I spent the next twenty minutes explaining what a cartoon was, what television was, and how my culture—and the planet, really—was obsessed with anthropomorphic animals. It didn't get past me that I was telling her all that with a straight face while sharing the world with beastkin. Strange times.

Around midday, as we were getting ready to take a break, I caught the unfortunately familiar shift of shadows out of the corner of my eye. We were in the shade of a long cliff and, though the area was still lit well, it was dimmer than the rest of our surroundings. My head snapped toward where I'd seen the movement and found what I'd expected. An umbrenix was in full charge toward me.

That was a good thing because I wasn't sure how well my companions could handle one of the monsters. Brin had magic, but she didn't seem to be able to hurt them much.

I, on the other hand, had killed two of the things already. This was going to make it three.

"Umbrenix," I yelled, and rushed toward the monster. We met in the middle of our charges, it with slashing claws and me with a hastily drawn siangham. I really needed to get a longer weapon.

I bent my knees and performed a slide any baseball fan would have appreciated, throwing up a cloud of dust as I scraped along. More importantly, I slid under the monster's claws and, as I passed by the umbrenix, which was going the other way, I slashed out with the sharp metal point of my weapon.

It still made me uncomfortable that that the damn things were so silent. I felt the resistance as I scraped the blade along its cushiony skin, so I know I did damage, but not a peep came from it.

I got back to my feet and turned. My eyes bugged out when I realized it was continuing on at nearly the same speed it had already been going. Heading straight for Brin.

"Brin!"

I sprinted to catch up to the thing and noted the moonwisp's eyes roll as she brought her hand up. A second later, the monster was coming back at me, but still facing Brin. She'd used one of her blasts to throw it back off its feet. I jerked to the side and rolled as the creature flew past me, managing to land on its feet, but barely.

"Ok, let's try this again." I lunged toward it and, as expected, met two slashing claws. I sidestepped, batted one away, put up a block for the other, and rammed my weapon into its face.

I don't think it liked that.

It went batshit crazy, arms flailing, feet kicking, and it even opened its mouth to come in for a bite. I calmly parried all its intended blows, hands with hands and feet with feet. When it so kindly opened its mouth to try to chomp me, I fed it my siangham.

While the weapon was too short to be practical for keeping an opponent away, it was perfect for close maneuvers. Especially things like ramming it up into the hard palate, near where it met the soft palate, of an open mouth. If the shadows had such things. It was just long enough that the point punched through the roof of the umbrenix's mouth and made it through the sinuses and to whatever pea-sized brain it had. If the shadow monsters had any of those things. It instantly dropped and didn't move again, so there was something important in there.

I looked down at it. "Huh. I'll have to remember that. Brain is vulnerable."

I had to order Tip to come over to the body when asking, cajoling, and pleading didn't work.

"This is one of those things that tried to suck my life out of me," I told him. "I believe they're what brought me over from my world. Lucas, too. So, we're probably going to see more. Until we can find some kind of magic weapon for you, you can't hurt one. That's my understanding. If we see one again, I'd appreciate it if you stay out of the way or hide so I can take care of it. Sometimes they come in pairs. I'm not sure if they hang out in larger numbers."

"You s-s-ay that like I'm not going to do that exact thing when we meet anything else dangerous."

"Sorry to tell you, but I'm going to teach to you fight things. Not these right now, but from what I understand, there are plenty of other dangerous creatures we may encounter. I want you to be able to defend yourself."

"Running has always worked for me."

"Did you see how fast that thing moved?" He didn't answer me. "Come on, let's go over there a little way and take a break. I can start talking you through what I'll be teaching you."

Fifteen minutes into working with Tip to see what his aptitude was, I couldn't help but to sigh. The satyr looked at me, a tentative smile on his face. No, a nervous one.

"Uh, good work."

The smile slipped. Damn. My tone must have given it away.

"We'll train you up, do some exercises when we can, starting without the weapon so you can get used to moving with your own body. How's your eyesight?"

"I can see fine."

"Have you ever used a bow?"

"I never held a bow. Wait, are you asking me if I ever put a bow in my hair?"

I sighed. "We'll get you one. Until you've trained more, it's probably better if you stay at a distance. Just promise me you won't shoot me in the ass by trying to hit an enemy close to me."

# CHAPTER NINETEEN

Drauger Trace was the smallest community I'd been to since I got to this world. A village, not a town. Wooden structures, most of them with thatched roofs, defined the crude, crooked streets and there was exactly one inn: the Dead Man Walking. It sported a sign with a picture that looked uncomfortably like someone had tried to carve a movie poster for a zombie flick onto a wooden plank.

We spent all of fifteen minutes checking the village's two shops. An all-purpose weapons store had a short bow and a quiver of arrows for Tip, so I bought them for four silvers. That was it, though. No magical weapons of any kind, no items that would help Brin to replace her lost possessions, nothing all that exciting.

If you didn't count Tip acting like a child at Christmas over the bow I got him.

"Maybe we can find the side of a building we can use as a target and I can practice," he said. He hadn't shut up since we left the shop where we bought it.

"No, Tip. These people don't want us putting arrow

holes in their walls. We'll find a place tomorrow on the way to Windridge so you can practice. Calm down."

The satyr gave me a look like a beaten dog. I almost felt sorry for him. If he'd kept his mouth shut, I might have. But his silence lasted about five minutes before he started in on me again.

As with pretty much everywhere I'd gone, I got more looks. It was the same old thing, mostly women. You'd think I wouldn't mind it, but it almost felt like something crawling underneath my skin. I didn't know whether to scratch at it gently or tear at my own flesh. Being a constant center of attention was not something I'd ever desired, and now that I was experiencing it, I liked it even less. This was the kind of bullshit attractive women dealt with all the time, though I could swing my knife to shoo my admirers away if I wanted to.

Not that I would. They weren't doing it to be irritating, but damn it was irritating.

"Good afternoon," the innkeeper said as we walked up to the counter in the Dead Man Walking. He did a double-take at me, but put on what I was coming to recognize as the "innkeeper's smile." "Are you looking for a room?"

"We are," I said. "What do you charge?"

"A silver a night. I will give you a deal for multiple days."

"How about multiple rooms for one day? We'd like three, but just for one night."

He glanced at Brin, then at me, confusion blossoming on his face. Then his eyes found Tip, standing there with his goofy smile. "How about two silver for three rooms, including breakfast."

"Throw in dinner and you've got a deal," I countered. I could have haggled more, but I didn't even have coppers left. What I offered him was a good deal, especially for a small village.

He glanced at Brin one more time, then let out a little sigh. "Agreed. Have you mounts to stable?"

"No, just us."

We stashed our stuff in our rooms and came back down for dinner just as things seemed to be picking up. The small common room soon boasted more than two dozen people and a lively buzz of conversation.

I chatted with my companions, but I also listened to conversations around us. It was something I'd always wanted to do, ever since the first fantasy book I'd read. Sitting at a tavern, listening for bits of news, maybe witnessing some guards from the evil ruler coming to try to capture me. Okay, maybe not that last part, but common rooms were the bread and butter—no pun intended—of many fantasy stories and it tickled me inside that I was living it.

Until I started to hear the conversations.

"Another one of those shadow things spotted," a man said.

"Kill anyone this time?" his companion asked.

"Don't think so. Before long, it's going to start affecting trade. No one wants to go outside a village or town. Some folks say it's the umbrenix come back to start killing again."

"Umbrenix," a woman with what sounded like an English accent said. More cockney than sophisticated like Brin's. "They was all killed, I thought. Did someone go and make more of them, then?"

The original man shrugged. "Dunno. You've heard that they haven't killed. Not this time, but who knows. The bodies disappear when they're killed by the shadows. Could be a lot of deaths we haven't heard of yet."

I traded looks with Brin. It wasn't more than a few minutes until I heard another conversation.

"They say most of the reports are from up near Greyveil," a large man said. "The shadowmen like it dim and gloomy. You couldn't pay me enough gold to go west. I'll stay here warm and comfortable, thank you very much."

An extremely thin woman, with a round face that made her look like a soup spoon, answered. "It won't help you. If it's true the shadows are back, they'll be feeding soon or late. If they can kill in Greyveil, what can we do here but hope they pass us by?"

"I guess we're on the right track," I said softly.

Brin took a drink, nodding as she looked around for anyone listening to us. "Yes. Windridge first, but then we'll head west toward Greyveil."

"What's the deal, there?"

"I know of no deal. They have shops, of course, but I sense that is not what you are referring to."

"Yeah, no. I meant what is the situation at Greyveil? What information is there about what to expect in the city?"

"I see. Forgive me. The city is surrounded by the Misty Wood. Being next to the bay, it is often foggy or misty there. Chilly, wet air. We would do well to purchase some cloaks to keep the chill off. There are beasts and some monsters inhabiting the forest, as well."

Tip nervously tapped his finger on the table. I looked over at him just as his face was displaying one of his tics: half his upper lip rose and he kinked his neck.

"You okay, Tip?"

"Ack. Are y-y-you talking about going *toward* Greyveil? After what you just heard?"

"Yep. We're looking for Lucas, and I believe they took

him from my world and brought him here. Can you think of a better way to look for him?"

"We could go the other way, to someplace where no one has rumors of those monsters."

A laugh escaped from my mouth. "We could, but we'd never find my friend then. Are you having second thoughts already?"

"Already? It's about the tenth time today. It's like the old saying, 'The tchitchit that enters the cave is the one that's eaten.'" He laughed, but it trailed off when he saw our lack of reaction. "Oh, shit. Never mind. Wrong world. Not an Earth saying. Or Valorae. Ahem. Sorry."

I leaned forward. "That was a saying from another world?"

"Yeah."

"How many worlds do you have thoughts or ideas from?"

"A lot. I never counted."

"It's all just random stuff?"

"Yes. I seem to have a lot from your world, from Earth, lately. I don't know why."

I snapped my fingers and Tip jumped. "Qamara. She told me that part of the thing with the umbrenix 'eating' people was that some of their residual thoughts or memories were left over. They escape and float around, she said. With your power, you can pick some of them up. Do you get them from this world, too, or only other worlds?"

The satyr shrugged. "I don't know. I guess maybe some from here, too. It's hard for me to keep them apart. Sometimes I remember things I've done, but then when I think really hard and analyze it, I realize I'd never experienced it. It was someone else's memory, but it was living in my head. I feel like I'm going insane at times."

"That must be very stressful," Brin said.

"Ack." A tremor went through the muscles of Tip's face and neck. The little guy was a nervous wreck. I wouldn't be surprised if he got panic attacks or had meltdowns. We may have gotten more than we bargained for when we let him join us.

"If you want to talk about it, even if to just tell us some of the things stuffed in your head so you can try to organize them, let us know," I told him. "Sometimes it helps to say things out loud when they're going around and around in your mind."

He looked at me and his eyes softened, almost like he was going to get teary-eyed. Then he blinked it away and a wry smile stole onto his face. "Maybe I'll share some of it. Thanks. I'll be sure to let you know if anything appears in my head that might help us."

"Awesome. Thanks, Tip." I put up a fist and he bumped it with his. "You two about ready to call it a night? Anything else you need to do in the village?"

"I do not believe anything remains to be done. Will you spend some time with me so that I may help you to better handle your weapon?"

I could feel my eyes flare even as I watched Tip's go wide. I put my hands up. "Okay, Tip, here's the deal." I pulled my siangham out and showed it to him. "Brin is a mage and she recognized this, my weapon, as being made of magical materials. It's not enchanted, but because of what it's made from, she has been teaching me how to commune with it. When I get better at being connected with it, she says I'll be able to use it more efficiently. So, when she says...well, what she said, she means what she does to help me to utilize the magic material in my weapon better. To fight. Better." I shook the siangham in his face to illustrate.

Tip's eyes turned sly and his full-on goofy smile splashed across his face. "I get it." He winked at me. "Hey, I don't judge. I'm not even jealous, not much. If you want the hot mage to help you handle your weapon, then by all means, get to it. Far be it from me to...ah, weapon-block you."

"Fuck you sideways."

"I wouldn't want you to wear out your weapon." He snickered, enjoying his un-humor.

"Why are you cursing at Tiporian, Gar?" Brin asked. "I do not think I understand."

"Don't worry about it. He's just being a dick." Brin put her hand to her mouth, the perfect picture of a lady who had been offended. "I'll explain it all to you later, okay? It's not how it sounds."

She nodded.

We finished the drinks we had, Tip giggling like a child for most of the time, and then we went up to our rooms. In the hallway, Brin opened her door, then looked over at me. "I will go to your room this evening. Give me a few moments and I will be there."

"Okay, cool." I eyed Tip. "What? Go on. Don't go sneaking out to get in trouble, either."

"I'd never think of it. Enjoy your—"

I lunged forward, stomping my foot on the floor. The satyr jumped, turned in midair, and darted through his own door. It was good to know he could move quickly when he had to. I went into my own room to wait for Brin.

# CHAPTER TWENTY

A soft knock at my door told me it was time for my gorgeous, blue-skinned companion to help me commune with my weapon. I opened the door to let her inside.

"Are you ready?" she asked.

"Yeah, still ready." I chuckled. "It's only been like ten minutes. All set and prepared."

We got right into it, sitting on the floor in our normal cross-legged positions. I set my siangham on the floor next to us, but we clasped hands first and breathed, getting ourselves ready. I wasn't certain it was necessary, but I wasn't going to turn down our little bit of closeness and contact.

Just about the time I sank into that half-waking state, the one that was ideal for all kinds of meditation or magical training—as far as I knew from the little exposure I'd had to it so far—another knock sounded on the door. It shattered my concentration and my eyes snapped open.

Brin's eyes fluttered open half a minute later, slowly and leisurely. Almost like she hadn't heard the knock but felt me looking at her. I opened my mouth to say something and the knock came again.

"For fuck's sake, Tip. The damn building better be on fire."

I rose to my feet and pulled the door open to find two extremely attractive women standing there, the blonde one with her hand up to knock again.

She was spectacularly beautiful, with long blonde hair and a body wrapped in a red dress that accentuated her curves wonderfully. Not that she needed it. The woman would have looked hot in a trash bag. I blinked at her, noting the rabbit ears coming out of the top of her head. My first thought was whether or not she had the little fluffy tail, too. Okay, maybe my second thought.

The woman next to her had dark brown hair, with some kind of...canine ears? A thick, fluffy tail swished behind her and revised my opinion. Fox. She had fox ears and a fox tail. And she was a total fox, her yellow dress, if anything, catching my eye even more than her friend's red dress.

"Oh," I said, trying to scrub the irritated look from my face. "Hi. Do you have the wrong room?"

The bunny girl looked me up and down. "Definitely not. This is where we were meant to be." She rubbed a hand up my arm. "You look like a hero. Wanna save a beautiful blonde damsel?"

"From what?" I asked. "Are you in trouble?"

"Mmmmm. I am. I'm so lonely and need affection right now."

I blinked at her, then looked at her friend.

"I'm just here to do anything you want me to do to you. Anything at all." She stepped forward, as if to push by me and go into my room. I stood my ground.

"Uh, I'm sorry. I'm not on hero duty right now, and I'm

kind of busy. Thanks for the offer, but I'm afraid I'll have to decline. Have a good night, ladies."

The bunny girl pouted so prettily, part of me tried to change my mind.

"We'll be down in the common room," she said. "If you change your mind, you'll be happy you did."

"Okay. Thanks. Goodnight."

The foxgirl blew me a kiss and the two of them headed down the hallway. They got two steps before the door to the room next door opened and a horned head popped out.

"Evening, fine ladies. Did I hear that someone needed a hero? Do you need to sit down? As long as I have a face, you'll have a place to sit."

I rolled my eyes.

"Don't talk to us, creepy little goat man," the bunny girl said. "If we wanted to pick up a disease, we'd be in the gutter having sex with the rats."

Ouch.

"I can fuck you like a rat, if that's what you're into," Tip said hopefully. I'd heard enough.

"Tip, go back in your room. Nothing is happening here."

The satyr grumbled but shut his door. The women stared at me for a moment. I gave them a wave and went back into my room and closed the door.

"If you would like to..." Brin said.

"No. Definitely not. Even if we weren't doing something important like me trying to learn more about my weapon, I still wouldn't take them up on it. I'm spending time with you, which is much more important."

She flashed a shy smile and patted the rug in front of her. "Thank you. Shall we try to get our focus back?"

"Yes."

After a few minutes, I was ready to try connecting to my

weapon. It was still difficult, but I finally started feeling something. Brin seemed to think I needed to progress a little faster.

As I sat with my eyes closed, a sensation like something stroking along one of my limbs entered my mind. It took a moment for me to realize it wasn't one of my physical limbs but the siangham itself. Once I came to that realization, the feeling intensified.

Another careful stroke up the entire length of it and my entire body shuddered.

"Ohoo."

I opened my eyes to find Brin running two fingers along my siangham. She had a strange look in her eyes. Almost like...pleasure.

"What was that?"

"Did you feel it?" she asked innocently.

Another tremble racked my body. "Hell yes. Did you use some kind of magic?"

She shrugged delicately, which pulled my eyes to her bare shoulders. "I just stroked it, like this." She dragged her fingers along the length of my weapon again and though my connection wasn't as strong as when I had my eyes closed, I still felt something. "Did you feel it?"

"Y-y-yes." I had to close my eyes. "Is it supposed to feel that good?"

Her shoulders raised again. She looked directly into my eyes as she did it. Was she fucking with me? I'd never had that kind of feeling or reaction to anyone casually touching me. I mean, she didn't even actually touch me. It was a piece of wood and metal.

"Now you understand a little more about what it means to attune to your weapon."

"Yeah, I do."

The hand that wasn't on my siangham was still holding one of my hands. I squeezed it and got the same in response. We sat, staring into each other's eyes for...some amount of time. I lost track of it. I did find, however, that we leaned in, closer and closer to each other.

I let the siangham fall to the floor and closed the last few inches, touching my lips to Brin's, then putting my hand up to brush her smooth blue cheek.

An explosion of sensations erupted in my body as we lingered, our lips moving ever-so-slightly, pressing into each other. I ran my hand along her jaw line, closed my eyes, and lingered in her space, the warmth of her breath washing over me.

I slipped my tongue tentatively toward hers and was thrilled to find it already on its way to me. Our lips stayed pressed together and my tongue orbited hers, then engaged more fully. The kiss was everything I thought it could be with Brin, and I reveled in the feel of her. I put my hand up to pull her into me.

She broke away abruptly.

"Oh. I...that's enough practice for tonight. Goodnight, Gar."

She hopped up, opened the door, and fled back to her room.

I sat, shaking my head and trying to figure out what had just happened. I'd thought it was a good thing, but apparently she didn't. I hopped to my feet and followed her. Standing in the hall, I knocked on her door softly.

"Brin? I'm sorry if that was too forward. Will you open the door so we can talk about it? Are you all right?"

"I'm fine, Gar. Thank you. Go to bed. I'll see you in the morning. Goodnight."

"I'm sorry if I freaked you out. Brin?"

"I'm fine. Goodnight Gar. We have traveling to do tomorrow. We should rest."

I didn't know what else to do. I shuffled back to my room, closed and latched the door, and fell into bed, hoping things would make sense in the morning.

I tossed and turned, never quite getting into the deep sleep I craved. I had a few snippets of dreams—nightmares, really—and it was enough that I left my bed in the morning feeling unrefreshed and dragging. I wished this new world had coffee.

The dreams were not about Brin, surprisingly. Most of them were about being snatched by the umbrenix and of Lucas being dragged to this world. I'd experienced it myself, so I know it didn't involve kicking and screaming, but that's what I saw. It left me in a less than cheerful mood.

I'd set my watch to the approximate time I guessed it was in this world and what it told me was that although I knew I wasn't going to get anymore sleep, it was too early to bother my traveling partners. But I hoped five-thirty wasn't too early to pester the cooks downstairs to make me some breakfast. At least that would help me pass the time.

I found two other people already in the common room, waiting for food. The couple wore the leathers of hunters. Not armor, really, but rugged clothing that I'd seen on some people in the towns I'd visited. They were no doubt heading out into the wilderness to ply their trade. I mumbled a good morning to them and got the same back in return.

When Brin and Tip came downstairs, I'd already finished eating and was sitting near the fire.

"Good morning," the blue woman said. "Did you sleep well?"

It didn't seem like anything was wrong, despite how it

was the night before. I answered with a lukewarm greeting and sat with them as they ate their own breakfast. Within minutes after they finished, we grabbed our stuff and headed out of town, padding down the road to the north.

Where I would see my first city in this world.

# CHAPTER TWENTY-ONE

Brin didn't seem any different than normal as we headed out to the road again. I kept looking toward her, trying to find something that said she was feeling bad about the night before, but it was like it had never happened. Weird.

"Are we gonna stop so I can practice shooting with my bow?" Tip asked. His voice was restrained, like he was acting cool, but his words were too controlled, unlike his usual banter. I smirked at him and how hard he was working to hide his excitement.

"If we find something that'll be a good target, maybe," I said. "We don't want to kill a tree and we don't want you breaking arrows."

Brinawynn turned to the satyr. "There are training yards in Windridge. They have archery targets. When we get there, maybe you can practice at one of them."

"Oh. Sure. Okay."

I laughed. "We'll hunt one down when we get there. Don't worry. We can still practice with your short sword on the way."

"Oh, yay." With the slow, emotionless way he said it, I laughed harder.

It took a whole day to get to the city. I could see it from miles away as we approached. Brin had explained what to look for and once I saw it, it took forever for us to get near.

The name of the city was fitting. Windridge had been built up on top of a plateau. It took up the entire top of the thing. At about three hundred feet from the ground, the plateau consisted of two "steps." The largest was completely surrounded by a wall, holding in most of the city. The other, twenty or thirty feet lower than the other platform, was mainly homes, some fields, and a surprising amount of forested area. That part didn't have a wall around it, but being so high off the ground, it wasn't like someone was going to sneakily climb up and do mischief.

"I've been there many times," Brin said, "though I haven't explored much of it. There are several inns, many shops, and other things—like the training yards—that smaller communities don't have. You can expect prices to be a little higher, too."

"While all that sounds exciting, my hope is that we can find out something about Lucas. I don't like it that no one we've asked has seen him. Especially because he stands out as different because of his skin color and his clothes."

Brin casually looked me over. "Speaking of which, are you going to replace your pants? You still stand out a little."

"Probably not. They're good pants. I like them. They're comfortable, and they have the long pocket that the siangham fits in perfectly."

"You can have a pair of pants made with pockets like that. People do it all the time."

"Yeah, but why pay to get some made when I already have these? Besides, my pants don't seem to stick out as much as I do. I'm pretty sure the attention I've gotten so far isn't because of my clothes. It's because of those damn statues."

Brin chortled at that. "I think you're right about that."

One of the drawbacks of the city being up high was that we had to get from the road up to the city. A wide swath had been cut into the hill, with gradual switchbacks so the incline wasn't too steep at any one point, but it was a slog. I'd glanced at my watch at the start and finish, and it took us almost two hours to go from the level of the road to the gates of Windridge.

The view was worth it, though. Looking back out over where we'd come from, I could almost pick out Drauger Trace along the road to the south. Several other hills and mesas surrounded the large plateau Windridge was on, but none of them had cities or villages on them, and none were as tall as where we stood.

The first thing we did was to follow Brin to an inn she had stayed at before. The place was nearer the edge of the city, so we didn't have to go far. That was good because with me and Tip gawking at every little thing, we traveled at a snail's pace. Brin was a good sport about it, even though we should have waited to gape at everything later.

The variety in building types was greater than any place I'd been to before in this world. A timber-built house might sit next to one made of stone block, with one of natural stones fitted together with mortar might be next to that. There were squarish buildings, ones with sharp roofs, even a round house or two. Then there were the people.

I spotted my first elf, a white-haired woman with a fancy dress who climbed into a carriage in front of a tailor's shop. Beastkin were everywhere, of lots of different types. I even saw a few dwarves and goblins. What I didn't see was anyone with blue skin like Brin, a satyr like Tip, or any humans. Those first two I could understand, because they were rare races.

"Why aren't there any humans?" I asked.

Brin looked around. "There are surely some here, but there will be few. Humans are not a populous race in most places except the Aesturith Kingdom and in some areas of Teaphotria. There are certainly more than there are of the taranji, but still few relative to other races."

"What about moonwisps?"

"You'll not see any of those. I believe I am the only one at the current time."

"Wait, what? You're the last of your kind?"

"Not in the way you seem to think. As I explained before, moonwisps are created by the goddess. I was born human but became as I am through the goddess's attention and power. There are ever very few of us. Ah, here we are. It has been some time since I stayed here."

The sign affixed to the wall next to the door read THE LUCKY DWARF, and carved on it was a pretty dwarf woman holding a shovel. In front of her was a hole with glowing gems and ore at the bottom.

We entered the busy common room and Brin led us to the other side where a short but stout woman stood on a little platform, her arms crossed beneath a pair of large breasts.

"Brinawynn Tolsen," she said, her voice deep but still feminine sounding, in a rough sort of way. "How are you, dearie? I haven't seen you in an age. Are ya here to visit me or are you on the goddess's business?"

Brin smiled at the woman and stepped up to give her a hug. "I'm always on the goddess's business. You know that." Her smile slipped a little bit. She'd explained the issues with the goddess and her power to me, though it seemed she didn't make it public information.

"I do, I do. Will you be staying with us?"

"We will. Shanna Oresearcher, this is Gar Hailey and our companion Tiporian Zethroban." She gestured at us as she named us. "Shanna here owns this inn with her husband. Where is Darrow?"

"Ah, he's about. Mostly likely getting into trouble. Tiporian the taranji. I've not seen one of your people for some time as well. Welcome to the Lucky Dwarf. "And you"— she turned toward me and looked me up and down — "you're the spitting image of Kael Serus, the Blur himself. Has anyone told you that?"

"Not in so many words, but I've been told I resemble the statues that are everywhere."

"Resemble. Ha! I'd bet good gold that his own mother couldn't tell you apart. Have you been hiding in a cave for a few millennia, now out to help us with all the problems in the world?"

"No, ma'am. Just looking for my friend. Maybe you've seen him? His name is Lucas, he's human, got darker skin than most, will probably talk a little differently, and he's got strange clothing on, kind of like my pants."

She shifted her eyes from me to Brin and back. "Someone like that would stick out in a crowd. I've not seen anyone like that, I'm afraid. How did you lose him?"

I opened my mouth to tell her about being snatched from my world, but Brin jumped in.

"They got separated near Ironwood Forest. They're not from around here and he thought maybe his friend wandered until he found a town. We checked Stonefort, Fanning, and Drauger Trace. There was no...trace of him."

Shanna slapped her thigh and barked a laugh. "No

trace. Ha. I'll ask the husband if I see his worthless hide soon, and I'll ask around to see if any of the caravans or merchants caught sight of him."

"Thank you," I said. "I'd really like to find him."

"You're a good friend, it seems. Not a hero, though? You're not here to do something about the shadows?"

I froze. "Shadows?"

"There are rumors about. The shadowmen are back, though not as bad as before. Yet."

"You've seen the umbrenix?" Brin asked.

"Personally, no. Plenty of talk about them, though. Attacks here and there, but mostly just people seeing them. It's been a while, but we remember. Made a shitshow of things back when Aeyr was trying to take over the world. Thought he died, but I guess not, not unless someone else learned how to make the shadows. You reckon he's after the same thing now?"

Brin shook her head. "I don't know. If he's gaining power again, then he must be working toward the same goal. Or worse, if that's possible."

"Aye. Well, seems to me we need a hero. Are you as good as you look, Gar?"

"I'm no hero. I'm just a guy looking for his friend, who may be in trouble."

"A shame," the dwarf said. "We could really use a hero in these times." She clapped her hands together. "So, how many rooms, Brinawynn?"

"Three, please."

"I have them. I'll give you my special rate for friends and relatives I like. Meals?"

"Yes, please."

"Great. We've got some goose with light gravy, fried potatoes, and vegetables fresh from our farm. You can eat anytime. Wenna started cooking for dinner an hour ago."

Brin glanced at Tip. "We'll eat a little later. Is there still a training yard down Thurdin Street?"

"There is. Looking for a little training to keep your skills sharp?"

"Tiporian is. He recently acquired a bow and he is eager to practice with it."

"They've got a good number of targets set up over there. Enjoy yourself."

Tip gave her a little bow. "Thank you, my dwarf lady. I will try my best."

I cocked my head at the satyr. *My dwarf lady*?

"Thank you, but I'm no lady. I appreciate the lie, though."

I gave Brin a few coins to cover half what the rooms cost and we dropped our things in the rooms before heading to the training grounds.

Despite Tip's excitement about trying out his weapon, it was a sad-faced satyr who sat on a bench an hour later.

"There's more to this shooting arrows thing than I thought," he said, rubbing his shoulder. "My left arm feels like a tree branch. It doesn't want to bend. The other one just wants to fall off to rest."

"Look at the positive side," I told him. "Your aim is a lot better than when you started. You can even hit the target more than half the time. Sure, it's the edge of the target, several feet away from where you're aiming, but it's better than missing completely. Let me just repeat that I don't want you trying to hit anything that I'm fighting with. I don't want an arrow in me, least of all from you."

"Yeah, yeah. After I practice a little more, I'll be good. You'll see. All I need is some practice."

I patted the satyr's shoulder. "I know. Remember Sherlock Holmes."

"Huh?"

"The violin."

"Oh. Ha. Hahaha. Right, the violin."

Brin watched us as she normally did, with either curiosity on her face or with her eyes rolling. "Sherlock... violin?"

"It's something from my world," I said. "There was this guy who solved crimes. He was super smart, could figure out things others couldn't, was a skilled martial artist, and basically did everything at an expert level. Except the violin. He was constantly angry and throwing tantrums because he couldn't play it like a professional from the first time he picked it up. That he had to actually practice it to get better irritated him. He was so used to doing everything perfectly from the start."

"Oh. So you were reminding Tip that things take practice and he shouldn't expect to master a weapon in a single hour."

"Exactly."

She nodded. "I agree. It would be wonderful to be able to do so, but unless there is magic involved, such a thing is rare. Though, I did hear stories about Kael that he was born to fight and wield weapons. He could pick up an object and use it to defend himself or to kill as if he'd trained with it all his life. I believe I have seen someone like that." She raised an eyebrow at me.

I changed the subject. "Are you finished for now, Tip? We can train a little with your sword—"

"Dinner," he interrupted. "I'm hungry. Aren't you? Let's go eat so I can replace the energy I used up. Yeah. Back to the inn." He snatched up his bow and walked so quickly, the arrows in his quiver rattled.

We had to rush to catch up to the satyr. Dinner did sound good. We'd have the whole next day to explore the city and to ask about Lucas. Maybe we'd even do a little shopping.

# CHAPTER TWENTY-TWO

During dinner and when we sat talking after the food was gone, I waited for Brin to ask about helping me commune with my siangham.

She didn't.

I couldn't feel truly downhearted while sitting next to her and talking, but when we went to our rooms, the disappointment I'd been pushing away the entire day came back with a vengeance. She hadn't acted any differently than she normally did, but I was afraid I'd ruined something by kissing her the night before. I almost asked to talk to her privately a few times, but ended up deciding that I should leave it alone and see what happened. There was no reason to make things messy by putting her into an awkward conversation.

After breakfast the next morning, we started scouring the city for news and for shops that might have something we needed. The information I was looking for was anything about Lucas, but we heard more than one rumor of what the umbrenix had been up to. Of course, we had to take everything with a strong dose of suspicion. One woman swore the shadow creatures had returned so they could steal eggs from within women of a particular age, keeping them from becoming pregnant. I had to put a hand over Tip's mouth on that one, before he offered his services for free. As if he could solve a shortage of eggs.

It wasn't until something like the eighth or ninth shop we went into that our day changed. It was a small establishment, in a poorer part of the city than most we'd visited. The buildings weren't exactly in disrepair, but they looked like they'd been well used, with peeling paint, doors that hung slightly askew, and windows that weren't quite square from settling.

The sign on the shop was gorgeous, a work of art, and depicted a stylized sword and shield that looked so realistic, I could have sworn I saw the blade glinting in the sunlight. Turned out that it was, but the reflection had been created along with the image, with something to reflect the sunlight. A piece of metal or glass or something embedded into it.

The place was called Simply Dangerous and if the sign was accurate, it was a weapon shop.

We stepped in and the scent of metal and honing oil smacked me in the face, followed closely by a hint of leather. From the back, a bit of a smoke smell wafted over. Not all of firewood, but of coal as well. There must have been a forge in the back. A hammer ringing out a second later confirmed it.

A grizzled dwarf stood near the counter, his shaggy head covered in reddish hair, though it was shot through with grey. He stood solidly, the typical dwarven physique apparent as his short, thick legs planted him like a concrete highway divider.

"Good day to you," he said, a hint of a brogue on his tongue. "I'm Dorva Stouthammer. What can I do for you?"

"We are looking around town for suitable weapons," Brin said. "We are not sure which type, but will know when we see them."

"Aye, that's the way of it. Have a look-see. Any questions, let me know."

"Thank you," I told him, and walked over to an open-topped wooden barrel of swords. Other blades were mounted on the wall nearby, with some others on shelves.

"I see the way you move there, lad. Even if you didn't look like the twin of Kael the Blur himself, I can tell those in the barrel are not for you. They're serviceable enough, but the balance won't be what you're looking for."

I raised an eyebrow at him. *The way I move?* "Okay. Thanks."

I really wasn't sure what we were looking for. I wasn't used to carrying a weapon around. Just my knife and my siangham were enough for me. Most of the time, I preferred to fight with my bare hands. They couldn't take a weapon away from me that way. Brin had her short sword, as did Tip, and the satyr had his bow as well. It seemed like a waste of time to—

"Ooh. May I see that bracelet?" Brin asked the dwarf.

"You may. It's something I picked up a few days ago. I usually don't get things like that, but I thought the missus would like it. It's a pretty thing, would go well with your skin color. Alas, she wasn't interested in it."

I walked over just as Brin picked up a bracelet and held it to the light. It was pretty enough, sections of what looked like steel wire forming eight circular sections all strung together to hold a ninth section. That last one was bigger and the wire made a design that reminded me of Celtic knots. But those were just little embellishments, because together they held a blue gem bigger than my thumbnail. A pulsing blue light emitted from it.

"How much?" Brin asked as soon as she lifted it up and took a good look at it.

"I'll take twenty-five gold for it. I know enough to recognize it's not just a pretty bauble. I can also spot the way you look at it. This is not the first time you've seen it, or something like it, I'll wager."

"You are very astute Master Stouthammer. You are correct. I am well acquainted with this item. Would you happen to have any of the other items the one who sold it to you had?"

"No, I'm sorry. It's the only one he offered and the only one I bought. He had more, did he?"

"When he and his ruffian friends took me captive and stole all my items, yes. He did."

"I'm very sorry to hear that..."

"Not to worry. I do not blame you and I will pay your asking price. Here you are." She handed him the gold without blinking.

"Now that the transaction is complete and it's yours again, will you tell me what it does? It's clear it has some magical effects."

"It does," she said. "It is called the Lunar Light Bracelet and it allows me to cast the spell Lunar Light. I needn't get into the details, but few can use the item. Only those who have Auryana's blessing can do so, and as a moonwisp it practically calls to me."

"Thank you. I've learned something today. I'd like to give you some information in turn, if you have questions I can answer. It's how I live my life, trade for trade, whether currency or barter."

Brin looked at me and I nodded. "I'm looking for my friend..."

After an explanation, probably including more detail than I needed to provide, the dwarf shook his great shaggy head.

"I'm afraid I haven't seen your friend, but you mention the shadows. I do know that the attacks seem to concentrate over to the west, near Greyveil. In fact, I have my suspicions that Arinthalas over there might have his hands in it. Can't trust the light elves. If you or your friend are tangled up in what the shadow creatures are doing, might be you can find answers over there. Be warned, though: you might find your death instead. Unless you can fight like Kael as well as look like him, I'd advise you to stay clear. There's more than those walking shadows in the Misty Wood."

"Greyveil," I repeated, "and Misty Wood. Got it. What is this about Arinthalas?"

"He's a light elf, and like most of them, he's only interested in power and money. He has himself a manor over on an island inside the bay. I'm not sure what he he's about, but that type would sell their mother for a handful of silver. What with all the shadows congregating around there, he's probably involved."

"Your information is very much appreciated," Brin said. "I thank you for it. I shall remember your establishment if I find myself in Windridge and need weapons in the future."

"I appreciate that. If I see that goblin again, I'll see if he has any of your things left. I don't have a problem picking them up and holding them for you. Nor with picking *him* up and shaking him to see what comes loose."

"Thank you. I will pay you a fair price for them." She turned to Tip, who had been very quiet the entire time we were in the shop. He stood there, almost like he was dazed. "Did anything strike your fancy, Tiporian?"

"Huh? What? Oh, no. Can we eat something? I'm a little hungry." As if to emphasize it, his stomach growled. That must have been why he was lethargic. Probably low blood sugar or something.

I tossed him a piece of jerky from the little belt pouch I'd been wearing, courtesy of the goblins. Thinking further on it, I tossed him an apple, too. "We'll go eat lunch right now. Thank you, Dorva. I'll be sure to see you again if I need a weapon."

"I look forward to it. You be careful if you go west. I hear those shadows can't be killed."

Tip swallowed the meat he was chewing and blurted out, "Oh, don't worry about it. Gar has already killed three or four of them."

I couldn't decide if I wanted to smack my forehead, or Tip's.

"Is that true?" the dwarf asked.

"Yeah, it was mostly luck."

"Some prophetess gave him a magic stick with a point on it and that can kill them," Tip happily added.

"A wooden stick, you say?" The dwarf leaned forward, more interested than he'd been with anything so far.

"Uh, that's not true. I killed my first one before I got the siangham. It is made of magical materials, though, so maybe it can hurt them. I don't know."

The dwarf rubbed his bearded chin. "I'll keep my ears open for tales about you. Gar, was it?"

"Yes, sir. Gar Hailey. Don't bother listening. Once I find Lucas, I'll disappear before anyone can even say my name."

"Aye? Well, we'll see won't we. You sure you don't want

a weapon? I might even give you one if I can tell folks how it's my weapon you're using."

"No thanks." I chuckled at his offer of sponsorship. I wondered if they normally did that in this world or if he was a marketing genius. "We better get going. We have other places to look and other people to ask about Lucas. Thank you for your help. Have a good day."

"Aye, and you three as well. Stop by and say hello if you're back in the area. To check and see if I got any more of Lady Moonwisp's possessions, you know."

We bade the dwarf farewell and went on the hunt for a place to get some food. In the meantime, I was going to make it clear to the shortest member of our party to keep his fucking mouth shut.

# CHAPTER TWENTY-THREE

Brin led us down a street we hadn't been to yet, no doubt knowing where we could get some food. As we walked, I decided to have a little conversation with Tip.

"Oh, Tip."

"Anything really," the satyr said, scanning the street ahead. I assumed it was for food. "I'm not picky."

"Tip."

"Yeah?" He turned to look at me and the satisfied smile on his face dropped off.

"We need to discuss how to keep your mouth shut. The way I see it, you can manage it yourself, or I can shut it for you. That second way will involve some pain. A lot of it, probably."

He gulped. "What did I do?"

The sincere look of confusion on his face cooled my anger, at least a bit. The little fucker wasn't *trying* to be an asshole. He just came by it naturally.

"Listen, Tip. A lot of what's going on shouldn't be talked about with others besides the three of us. They're not strictly super-secret, but unless I bring up a subject around someone else, why don't you assume I don't want it talked about. Got it?"

"Sure, Gar. I've got it. I didn't mean to...do whatever I did."

"I know you didn't mean to say something that would get you in trouble. The thing is, I don't think you're reliable as a decision maker on what you should or shouldn't say. So to make it easy, don't say anything that involves me or Brin, okay? Or about anything that happens to us when we're all three together."

The satyr hung his head. "Okay."

Brin looked at the dejected expression on the horned man's face and had to try and make him feel better. "Tip, there are very dangerous people and things we're dealing with. The umbrenix, this Arinthalas, the situation with Gar's arrival in this world, and the disappearance of Lucas. There are many people who would use any of that information against us.

"For example, someone might think they could gain favor from Arinthalas if they go and tell him we might be looking for him. If someone found Aeyr and told him how Gar killed some of his minions, well, that would not bode well. These things can draw the attention of people we don't want attention from. Do you understand?"

"Yeah, I get it. I wasn't thinking. I'll pay more attention. I won't let you down. You'll see."

"Splendid."

I eyed Tip suspiciously, then decided I'd let him get away with it this time. "Just make sure you think. You can't use that excuse more than once. Your loose lips could cause us to be attacked, even killed. Worse, it could make things happen that might prevent me from getting to Lucas in time. I fully intend to kill whatever and whoever is necessary to make sure my friend is safe."

I left that veiled threat hanging in the air as Brin stopped in front of a little stand where a man with dog ears and a tail stood. I hadn't been paying attention, but now that I noticed where we were, my eyes ran over the man and his setup with interest. A slight change in the breeze filled my nostrils with the most delicious smell.

The medieval equivalent to an outdoor grill dominated the covered portion of the stand. On it were long sticks with bits of food, sizzling over a fire. I guess kebabs were a thing in this world, too.

"Hungry?" I asked Tip, though I didn't need to. He was leaning over, close to drooling. I laughed. I turned to the man. "Can we get six? What are they, anyway?"

"Sand worm, desert fruit, onion, and small potatoes," he said. "Marinated for half a day in a solution of spices that would make the gods weep for not needing to eat."

"Sand worm, eh?" I looked to Brin, and she smiled. Fine, I guess I was going to eat sand worm. It probably tasted like chicken, anyway.

"Does it have spice?" Tip asked, then chuckled at his own cleverness.

That man, having no idea that Tip was trying to be funny, answered as best he could. "They are flavorful, but not spicy in the manner of food that requires you to drink to cool your tongue."

Tip sighed, until he looked over at me and I jerked my chin to him. "*Dune*?"

"Yeah, man."

"Nice."

That seemed to cheer him up a little bit.

I paid the man—getting some copper coins in return—

and handed two of the kebabs to Tip. Despite how hot they were, he tore into them like he hadn't eaten in a week. Steam jetted out when he bit into a chunk of the meat and he let out a slow groan of pleasure.

"Let's sit here and eat," I said, pointing to some benches nearby. "We may have to get more before we leave."

With my first bite, I completely understood Tip's actions. I devoured my food only to find Tip staring at the empty sticks. I ended up getting him two more, and buying another for me. I gave a wave to the seller and followed Brin to our next stop.

"Where are we going?" I asked her.

"There's a very large shop I have heard about but never visited. They specialize in items for those living an adventurous life. Explorers, hunters, others such as these. Perhaps they have something that would interest us. Maybe they will even have more of my stolen possessions."

"Oh, cool. Let's see what they've got."

We found the place and stood outside taking in the view. From the looks of it, the shop was at least four or five times bigger than any other place we'd gone. It was a bit rough and ramshackle on the outside, but that didn't necessarily mean anything. The name—Scar's—didn't have a picture on the sign like most places did. Just the one word. It sounded like a tavern or something, not a store.

I opened the double doors and let Brin and Tip go in ahead of me. The change from the bright sunlight to the dim inside took a moment before my eyes adjusted. When I could see well, I looked around with interest. This place, like the general store in Stonefort, had an army surplus store vibe, which was cool. Not only did it make me feel a little more at home, but it also made me think of necessary gear at good prices. I hoped I wasn't disappointed.

No one greeted us, but the store was so big, maybe the owner didn't know we were there. I didn't hear a bell or anything when we walked in. Instead of calling out, I decided to walk through some of the aisles.

As I expected, there was camping gear and adventuring stuff like ropes and containers and skins. The weapons were probably nearer the counter, and magic items were most likely locked away. There was one type of thing that was easy to find in many parts of the store, though. All along the walls, hunting trophies were mounted. Most of them were heads of animals and large creatures—some I had never seen before—but there were whole bodies of smaller creatures on the wall, too. I still didn't know enough to differentiate between monsters and beasts.

I stared at one particularly ugly animal. It was some kind of reptile that reminded me of the gorn on the original *Star Trek* TV show. At first I thought it might be a Halloween mask, but nope, closer inspection showed it to have actual scales, some of which were flaking off.

Damn. This guy must be a real hunting fanatic. Or at least a fanatic that purchased stuff other people hunted.

"I told you, Vonni," a man yelled in a deep voice on the other side of the shop. "I don't pay you to casually laze your way through the day. When I tell you to do something, I mean right now."

I stepped into the center aisle just in time to see a large beastkin man kicking a smaller one. The smaller, who was normal sized for a man in this world, about five-foot-seven or so, stumbled and cried out as the larger's foot landed squarely on his ass.

I gritted my teeth. I had to remind myself that I didn't know what was going on, though it seemed to be pretty clear. It was none of my business. I couldn't go jumping into everyone's affairs. I'd learned that the hard way. I took a breath and waited to see what would happen. As I did, I considered the two men.

The smaller one was bald, but more than that, his face was kind of turtlish. As I looked, I realized that was exactly it. Some loose skin at the neck, an oddly shaped mouth, almost a sharp beak, and the stub of a little fleshy tail where he'd been kicked, this guy *was* a turtle. A turtle beastkin. Without a shell. The other man's comments made sense now. Turtles were known for being slow, right?

Brin came up next to me, already raising her finger. I took her hand and shushed her before she got us involved.

The larger man had the look of someone who had been muscular once, but age had melted it into fat. Not that he was obese or anything. He still looked like he was strong, but his best days were definitely behind him. His dark-orange hair sported a couple of cat ears, the left one torn, the top split into two sections. A tail lazily waved behind him, striped like a tiger's. I had a feeling now that I knew where the name for the shop came from.

The tiger beastkin raised a hand to the turtle guy, even though he was too far to strike the other man, and his eyes shifted to me.

"What're you gawking at?"

"Nothing," I said. Not apologetically, not timidly, but with a bit of an attitude. "Looking for gear."

"Well, find what you want. You expect me to hold your hand?"

"Nope." I met eyes with the turtle, who was rubbing his butt and wincing. I decided to make quick work of going through the other aisles, talking as little as possible with this dude, but found Tip standing a few paces away, trembling.

I followed his eyes and found the reason. On the wall behind the counter, there were more trophies. Including three that had very human faces were it not for the horns that came out of the top of their skull. Two men—both with spotty beards—and a not-very-attractive woman, all with those goat horns.

Satyrs.

It was about that time that the tiger guy spotted Tip. His face split into a predatory smile.

"Ah, did you bring that one for me? I pay good gold. Who told you about my policy?"

He was talking to me. I glared at him. "What the fuck are you talking about?"

"I'm Scar Tillet," he said, as if that explained anything. "I hunt everything, but these are my favorite. They're shit when it comes to fighting, most of them, but boy can they run. When I can't find them outside of the city, hiding in some trash pit or hole in the ground, I pay to have them captured and bring them to my land outside the city. I set 'em loose, give 'em a head start, and hunt them. Good sport. Better trophies." He pointed to the wall and grinned.

"Fuck you," I said. "You're a sick bastard."

"So you didn't bring him here for me?" He rubbed his hands together. "All the better. He's fair game then."

That's about the time when Tip's eyes rolled up in his head and he fell to the shop floor. I blinked at the prone form of the satyr. *He fucking fainted.*

"Ah ha ha," Scar said. "One of the fainters. Does he scream, too? Some of them do. Closer to goats than people. Well, this is quite a day. All I have to do it pick him up."

He headed for Tip's unconscious form and I stepped in between them.

"Nuh-uhn. One, you're a fucking asshole. Hunting

people? Jesus. Two, Tip is my friend, and if you don't back your fat ass up, I will have no choice other than to kick it. Don't start no shit, won't be no shit."

The turtle guy scrambled out of the general vicinity, making a point to put Brin between himself and me.

"You don't know who you're messing with, boy," Scar said. "Do us all a favor and step aside before things get—"

I closed the distance in a heartbeat and drilled a straight punch into the tiger's gut. He huffed and bent forward. I met his chin coming down with an elbow going up. His teeth clacked together satisfyingly and he levered backward. It was like he did it in slow motion. The back of his head slammed into the wood floor and bounced.

I stood, waiting to see what would happen. Did he have minions or friends who would shoot me with a crossbow, someone who would rush in with a sword?

Nothing. The man rolled over, groaning, then dragged himself to his feet with apparent difficulty. He reached up to feel his teeth, then looked at the blood on his fingers.

"That was a mistake, boy."

"You try to touch my friend again, I'll kill you. To think I'm kidding is a mistake."

"Perhaps we should go?" Brin said. She hadn't moved and there was no fear in her voice. Just good advice. We didn't need to deal with me murdering a citizen and shop owner in the city.

"Yeah," I said. "We probably should." I picked Tip up and threw him over my shoulder like he was a bag of mulch. "I don't like how it smells in here."

I motioned for Brin to head out the door before me, then did the same for the turtle guy. I doubted he wanted to be in the shop with Scar feeling butt hurt about having his ass kicked. He scurried out behind the moonwisp. I glanced over at Scar, still fuming and clenching his fists as his mouth dripped blood. Seeing he wasn't going to do anything, I left.

"You made a mistake not killing me," the cat called out as I crossed the threshold. "I won't make the same mistake. I'll take you out, then I'll make the hunt extra painful for the goat. The blue women will get the best of me."

I turned in time to see him putting a hand on his crotch.

I set Tip down gently and took one step toward the beastkin before Brin's hand wrapped around my arm.

"No, Gar. Leave it. It's talk, nothing more. Let us depart. It is not worth the trouble your actions will cause. Please."

That last part got me. I wanted to beat that fucker to within an inch of his life so badly, but that was my anger talking. He'd threatened Tip—and Brin—but he hadn't actually done anything. I didn't even know if he'd killed those satyrs or if that was some story he made up to act big for his customers. I looked into Brin's green eyes and let out a breath.

"You're right. He's not worth it. Thanks."

I picked Tip up, closed the door, and headed toward the inn.

"I don't feel like shopping anymore today."

## CHAPTER
# TWENTY-FOUR

Tip revived halfway back to the inn.

"What? Who dat? Where is me?" The satyr sputtered, then stopped speaking when he realized he was slumped over my shoulder.

"You fainted," I told him, swinging him down so he could stand on his own feet. "Does that happen a lot?"

Tip's brow furrowed. "It depends on what you call a lot. It happens on occasion."

"Always when you're in the middle of something scary?"

"Not always. It's a common condition among the taranji."

"Wonderful. Not a great survival instinct. Instead of fight or flight, you have faint or grovel."

He shrugged apologetically. "We don't grovel. Much. I can't help it. I've thought about it and maybe if I become used to being threatened, it won't happen as much. Or at all."

"I'm afraid you may end up getting used to it. This

world seems determined to try to kill me and the ones around me."

He glanced at Brin, then back at me. "So. What happened?"

"That mangy cat asshole said you were fair game and went to try to grab you so he could take you somewhere and then hunt you down to kill you. I disagreed with him."

"Did you...kill him?"

"No."

"He'll probably try again, huh?"

"Yeah, I think he will. It doesn't matter, though. I think we're done here. If we didn't find anyone yet who could help us with Lucas already, we probably won't. We've already checked out the shops that interested us, so we can leave. We'll have a nice dinner, get some sleep, and leave in the morning."

"Do you not think Scar will try to snatch Tip before we leave?" Brin asked.

"Maybe."

"You're not going to let Tigger get me, are you?" Tip asked.

Brin's nose scrunched. "Tigger?"

"Something from my world," I said. "Though Tigger was adorable and Scar is absolutely not. Anyway, there's not much daylight left. Do you really want to leave and travel in the dark, only to make camp to sleep a few hours from now? I kind of like sleeping in a bed instead of on the ground."

"It is preferable. I agree."

"Good, then let's go with my plan. We'll get an early start tomorrow. We should be able to get to another village or town by tomorrow evening if we leave early in the morning, right?"

"Yes. Greyveil is too far to travel in one day, but there is a village called Edgewood where the road intersects with another. They have a single inn, if I remember correctly."

"And enough people that we can ask about Lucas, maybe get more news about what the umbrenix are up to?"

"Precisely."

"Great. Let's go back to the inn, eat and relax, and get ready for an early departure tomorrow."

AFTER A DELICIOUS MEAL, we sat in the common room for another two hours. Besides talking on several different subjects—Tip didn't speak about our more confidential topics even once—we listened to some of the chatter around us. There were a few reports we hadn't heard yet about umbrenix encounters, but overall, it was the same old stuff. Crazy murderous shadows weren't the only thing in the world, and we heard a fair bit about farming, the weather, and politics of places I'd never heard of.

When we finally went to our separate rooms, I practiced trying to commune with my weapon. I still hadn't talked to Brin about helping me again, but it seemed like I was progressing at least a little. Slowly. I soon grew bored of it, though.

I checked my watch and it was still a bit early to go to bed, so I headed out of my room and the inn to get some fresh air. Sure, I could have opened my window, but I wanted to stand under the sky, maybe see some stars. Lanterns lit the streets, but dimly, and they didn't generate enough background light to obscure the view of the night sky too much. Without pollution in the air, the millions of tiny points of light were clear and beautiful.

Especially in the area where the Lucky Dwarf was, it was calm and quiet. Soft murmurings of the conversations from the common room leaked out, but a few steps into the alley left me in almost total silence. I wondered what the more popular areas of the city were like at the moment. In a few minutes of standing and enjoying the cool night air, I only saw two people walking down the street, both unhurried and unafraid.

That part was new to me. I'd grown up always checking my surroundings, always wary of being jumped. I'd been targeted so many times, I couldn't begin to count, so even when I moved down to Southern California, I still kept my eyes moving all the time when outside and especially in the dark, paranoid that someone might try to get a piece of me. It was nice to relax, breathe fresh air, and watch the star-filled sky for comets.

Something in the corner of my vision caught my attention. I sighed. *Really? Fucking umbrenix again?* I realized I'd left both my knife and my siangham on the table in my room. Great.

No attack from shadow monsters came. Instead, footsteps approached. Heavy ones. I turned and found a short man walking toward me. I thought at first it might be Shanna the innkeeper, or her husband who I hadn't seen yet, but though I recognized this guy as a dwarf, he looked younger than the burly woman, with hair and beard not quite wild enough for him to be older. I doubted she'd have married someone so much younger than her.

The man came straight for me. When he was four or five paces away, he brought out a large club. Like a Fred Flintstone club. All gnarled and knotty and a little longer than a baseball bat, but much thicker.

My peripheral vision was working overtime, my senses

heightened by the thought I was about to be robbed. A shadow flitted up higher on the inn. Someone climbing up or coming down from a rendezvous they wanted kept secret?

The dwarf's eyes locked onto mine and I could see in them what any street kid from a bad area would recognize as a predator look. Actually, "bully look" is probably a better way to describe that. The other word was loaded with baggage in modern times. As if "bully" wasn't.

"Don't start no shit, won't be no shit," I told the dwarf. He looked at me in confusion. Well, maybe it didn't translate into this world. "Back the fuck off, is what I'm trying to say."

A few other shadows resolved into people. A couple of cat beastkin, one with a short sword and the other with double daggers, slinked along the edge of the alley. Another figure emerged. With the dozens of quills on his body, he had to be a porcupine beastkin, if that was a thing. The last was a very large man with bull horns on his head, holding a huge two-handed axe. Yeah, all beastkin, except for the dwarf.

I scanned the alley for a weapon to use, cursing myself for leaving mine in the room. All there was, besides me and the people ready to attack me, were a few pieces of trash and the occasional stone or loose cobble. Damn.

"Do you really want to do this?" I asked. Rhetorically, of course. I didn't think any of them were going to answer me or have a nice chat with me.

Sure enough, the cat beastkin with the sword and the dwarf rushed in to attack. So much for negotiation.

I analyzed the two attackers and the ones who had yet to come in. If those cat beastkin took traits from their animal side, they'd be fast and flexible and extremely agile.

The dwarf would be strong. I needed to mark their rhythm and skills fast to take on all five. Luckily, the alley wasn't all that big, a definite advantage for me because I was at my best in close quarters.

The dwarf swung his club downward like he was trying to break rock while the cat lunged in to stab at me. As if I'd stand there and let his telegraphing ass simply poke a blade into me.

The short sword was fairly broad, single-edged, with a beefy round hand guard. I slapped it on the flat of the blade to deflect it and sidestepped to follow it, evading the clumsy downward swing of the club. That put me in a perfect position.

I snapped out a roundhouse kick, my instep slamming into the dwarf's face as he overextended with his club. As soon as I dropped my leg, I shouldered the cat to the left before he could bring his weapon back around. I felt the huff of air as my shoulder rammed his midsection and knocked the wind out of him.

Thankfully, the bull man hung back. With his massive two-handed axe, he would have a hard time swinging the weapon in the tight alley, and there was no way he could do it now without hurting his companions.

The porcupine, on the other hand, shuffled toward me, no doubt to get within range to use one or both of his short-swords on me. I took the lull in attacks to pick up a stone near me. It was flat and nearly the size of my palm, probably a broken cobble. It wasn't much, but it would have to do.

The porcupine lunged in, slashing at me with both swords. He was competent with wielding the weapons simultaneously. At least, he didn't cut himself, which was a problem with using both hands independently. When I say competent, though, I don't mean he was particularly skilled. He started slashing at me way too early and by the time I backed up a couple of steps, his flurry was petering out.

As soon as he paused to catch his breath, I surged forward and punched him square in the throat. What I hadn't counted on were those fucking quills.

They were apparently not just for show.

As I pummeled his neck, several of them swung up to bite me. Three or four punctured my hand and forearm. The damage wasn't serious, but it hurt like a bitch. I spun off to the side, dodging both him and his friends, who had recovered and were coming back at me.

The cat slashed downward with his sword while the dwarf—who had recovered from my kick—swung his club like a baseball bat, meaning to pulverize my ribs. Or maybe my legs. He was pretty short, after all.

I gauged the distance and trajectory of the sword. Luckily, though the cat was agile, he didn't seem strong enough to move the weapon fast. I took a chance and slammed the stone into the moving blade. Sparks jumped off from the collision and the sword deflected with a loud *ting* so hard the cat stumbled a little.

That didn't stop the other cat, this one with two daggers, from launching himself into the fray. When I say launch, I mean *launch*. The dude was airborne, with Michael Jordan level hang time. I had just enough time to finish my kick to the dwarf's forearm, jamming his attack and possibly cracking a bone or tearing a ligament in the man's arm.

My movement put me just far enough away from the incoming cat that by the time he landed, he could only roll and get back to his feet to try again.

As for the cat that I'd imbalanced, I had something for him, too. I spun and delivered a beautiful high roundhouse kick to the back of his neck, slamming him face-first onto the cobbles.

I continued my spin and hucked the rock I'd been holding like it was a damn discus. My aim was perfect and it bounced off the porcupine's head with a loud crack. He dropped as well, but I didn't know if he was just unconscious or dead. At this point, it didn't matter. He was out of the fight.

I reached down and snatched the sword from the cat I'd kicked, swinging it immediately at the other cat, who had regained his feet and charged me. He mostly evaded my powerful slash, but threw a dagger up to deflect it just in case. The force of my weapon backed him up a step. It gave me just enough time to ram the blade into its original owner as he struggled to get up. The sword point went down at an angle, bypassing the ribs and entering the chest cavity. The cat's limbs went limp and he slammed face-first to the ground for a second, and last, time.

The dagger cat was there again, knives slashing at me. I juked to the left, sidestepped to the right, and lashed out at the cat's right forearm. The cut I laid down didn't cause him to drop the weapon, but his grip on it slackened enough that I didn't worry as much about that one anymore. I whipped the sword around in a downward strike meant to do only one thing. The cat fell for it and tried a hard block with the dagger. His whole arm was forced downward from the power of my strike, leaving me the opportunity to finish him.

I pronated my sword hand, cut up vertically to open up the cat's chest, then brought the weapon around in a tight arc to slam the point into his throat.

Spinning, I tore the weapon out of the cat's neck just as the dwarf got around his companion. He rushed me, swinging the club in a figure eight configuration, trying to find an opening to crush my skull. As the weapon came down from my left to my right, I stepped to the side and licked out with my blade, cutting deeply into the dwarf's shoulder.

He shifted his grip and swung at me again, slower with his shoulder injured. I easily evaded the blow with a step to my right and then one forward. Now that I was inside the dwarf's guard, I had a multitude of options. I chose one that was less lethal. Rotating my hips, I slammed the pommel of my sword into the back of the man's thick neck and he tumbled bonelessly to the ground, where most of the rest of his friends were.

During all that, the huge bull beastkin had been bouncing on his toes, his axe held at the ready, but he hadn't had a chance to come at me with everything so crowded. He looked at his buddies now, all on the ground.

I looked him in the eye. "You don't have to do this. It's over. I don't want to have to kill you, but I will if you force me."

"If I don't try," he said in a deep voice, "Scar will kill me."

It suddenly clicked. *Oh, shit.*

I picked up one of the cat's daggers and threw it at the bull man. He shifted the haft of his axe enough that it deflected from where I'd aimed—his chest—and bounced off his shoulder, tearing his clothing and the skin underneath.

By the time he recovered, I'd already run into the inn.

# CHAPTER TWENTY-FIVE

*Shit, shit, shit!*

I couldn't believe I didn't see it earlier. Of course those guys in the alley weren't some random thugs looking to rob me. I should have seen that they were the distraction. Well, maybe that was not what they were meant to be. After all, Scar was pretty pissed off at me for kicking his ass. Still, that shadow I'd seen earlier, climbing up the inn? That had to be someone meaning to get Tip.

The one thing I could count on was that they wouldn't kill the satyr. Probably not even harm him too much. Scar wanted him whole and alive so he could hunt him, and probably torture him to punish me.

But that didn't mean they wouldn't kill Brin.

Then I remembered what else Scar had threatened. Whoever he sent after Tip probably wouldn't kill her either because Scar had other plans for her. I pumped my legs harder, sprinting through the common room, dodging people drinking and eating there, and rocketed up the stairs.

My heart dropped into my stomach when I saw Tip's

door open, and even more so because there were people in the hallway in front of it. A beastkin with furry weasel ears and tail held a crossbow up while a guy with what looked like bear ears stood by. He was about the same size as the bull guy I left in the alley, so I'm guessing he was in fact a bear beastkin. I wasn't sure I'd ever get used to all these animal mixes.

Brin had just interrupted the men, it seemed. She had her shortsword out and stalked toward them. I was happy to see that the weasel beastkin hadn't leveled his crossbow at her, confirming what I'd thought earlier. On the bad news side of things, though, once he saw me, he had no compunction about swinging it over and targeting me.

While he tried to find the perfect angle to punch a quarrel through me, the weasel shouted toward the room. Another one of those damn cats popped out into the hallway, making the odds three to two. With a crossbow half a second from launching a bolt into me, I would say they had the advantage. Those missiles flew way too fast and powerfully to be deflected or snatched out of the air.

It looked like dodging was going to have to do. I lowered my center of gravity and prepared for the ultimate dodge ball competition.

A wave of pressure passed down the hallway and for a second, I thought maybe I'd missed an enemy. A magical one. But nope, the beastkin were pushed back, hard enough that the two smaller men looked like they'd been hit with an invisible tackle from an NFL player. The bear was rocked back on his heels, but not tossed as powerfully.

The best part? Brin had used her spell just as the weasel fired the crossbow. The wave of force pushed the missile off course and it stuck in the wall near me. There was no way that fucker was going to get another one loaded before I got to him.

I charged in.

Just before I reached my enemies, I glanced in Tip's room to find another cat doing his best to get the satyr under control. Again confirming what I'd thought, Scar's minion wasn't attacking Tip with his knives, but using them to try to get the satyr's sword from him so he could carry him off.

Brin and I reached the three in the hall together. The bear recovered first, swinging his massive double-bladed axe at me. Monstrous axes seemed popular among Scar's minions. The swing was ponderous, coming straight down like judgment from the heavens. I deftly sidestepped as I continued to run. Though the man tried to adjust his swing, he was already committed and I passed the blade unharmed. As I came up even with the man, I lashed out with my stolen sword and cut deeply into his throat. I was a few feet past him before he dropped his weapon and reached up to his throat, as if he could hold all his blood in.

Brin attacked the weasel with her sword before he had a chance to drop his crossbow and unsheathe his own short-sword. That left the cat in the hall for me. With my blade still in motion from my drive-by slashing of the bear, I adjusted its path and swung down to cleave the cat's skull.

He crossed his knives and caught my blade, barely restraining the powerful strike. But that left his hands up at about shoulder level, far too high to provide an adequate defense or check. I transferred my forward momentum by stomping down with my left foot while bringing the right up into a front kick, plunging the ball of my foot into his solar plexus.

As expected, air rushed from him as he slammed

against the wall of the hallway. He did well to not only retain consciousness against the jumble of nerve signals from his solar plexus, but to keep hold of his knives as well. Good on him.

Of course with no breath and his head rattled, he was in no position to block the short slashes I made by pulling my hand back toward myself and dropping the blade vertically, gashing his right forearm. A twist of the hips and a torque of my shoulders and the blade had reversed and slashed upwards, cutting into the brachial artery in the left arm. I must have taken out some nerves, too, because that hand released the knife it held and the weapon clattered to the floor.

With my empty left hand, I slammed my fist into his right shoulder to keep the knife away from me for another second or two, then angled my blade and thrust it downward, point toward the floor and edge toward the cat. The sword sawed downward exactly where I'd aimed it, deep in the inner thigh where the femoral artery was. I spun away to reassess and found Brin backing off as well, her sword still embedded in the weasel's face.

She jerked her chin toward the cat, as if to ask me why I was backing off.

"He's done. I just cut two major arteries. He'll be dead in a minute."

She raised an eyebrow.

"I read a lot. When I was fighting for my life when I was a kid, I learned a lot about anatomy. It can come in handy. You know, if you want to kill someone or hurt them very badly."

Without a word, she turned toward the open door and the two struggling figures inside. Tip didn't notice us, too busy trying to wrestle his sword under control, swinging ineffectively at the cat who almost lazily deflected the larger weapon.

The cat beastkin did notice us, though, his eyes going wide when the blue woman and I both strode toward the door. He slammed a knife against Tip's sword, glanced at the bodies of his companions, and leaped out the window.

I rushed to see where the cat was. We were on the second floor. I doubted his beastkin traits were good enough to make him indestructible to falls like regular cats were. Sure enough, he'd grabbed part of the window, used the one on the floor below as a jump-off point, and bounded across the alley to grab onto the trim on a window over there. A second later, he was on the ground and running for his life.

"He'll be going back to report to Scar, no doubt," I said. "Are you two okay?"

Tip swayed on his feet. I snatched the sword from him so he wouldn't fall on it, and guided him to sit on the bed. "He didn't try to kill me. Even though he blocked everything I threw at him, he didn't try to kill me."

"Yeah. Most likely, Scar told them not to hurt you. If they did, he'd either have to nurse you back to health before hunting you or to be cheated out of his recreation." I narrowed my eyes at him. "Good job not fainting."

He screamed. Not one of those scared screams, not even what someone would use when they were in pain. It was simply a *very* loud outlet of nervous energy that left my ears ringing.

"Fucking *hell*, Tip. Don't tell me, that happens occasionally, too. Screaming for no apparent reason."

He looked at me sheepishly and I shook my head. *Fucking goat traits.*

"What about you, Brin? You okay? Did you get hurt?"

"No. I am fine. Thank you for returning when you did. I hadn't known you were gone."

"Yeah. I went outside to get some fresh air and to look at the stars. There were five more there."

"Five more what?"

"Five more of Scar's men. They attacked me."

She inspected me, eyes going to the sword in my hand. "Why are you not using your siangham?"

I shifted my eyes to the ceiling. "I...kind of left it in my room."

"You defeated five armed men without any weapons?"

I held up the bloody short sword stupidly. "I found one. This nice cat had it and offered it to me. Point first, of course, but still. I couldn't turn down a gift like that. So timely."

Tip began to cackle maniacally and I looked at the pommel of the sword I held. *Maybe just a tap on the noggin...?* I shook the thought loose as inappropriate.

"We should depart," Brin said.

"What? We're going to leave in the morning. We can all stay in one room. They won't try again tonight, but even if they do, we'll be ready for them."

"And you would stay in the room and sleep?" she asked. "You would not wait for us to slumber so you could go after Scar?"

*Aww, fuck.* "Probably not?"

She chuckled and it was like the bubble of pressure that surrounded us popped. "I think not, Garfield Hailey. We must leave. I do not trust that Scar Tillet will refrain from sending yet more people to die by our hand this night. I also do not want to test the limits of your anger or your wariness. It is reasonable and logical to want to eliminate a dangerous enemy, especially one who has just launched an attack against you. However, we have other things to occupy ourselves. Scar will not chase us across the world. Once we leave here, we will not be troubled by him again. If we are, we can finish things then."

The way Brin spoke, so formally and politely, sometimes I forgot that she was a badass. I hadn't asked a lot about her past, but at more than three times my age, she had to have seen some shit. The way she explained that we would snuff out Scar if he caused us trouble again reminded me that she was probably at her weakest in more than half a century, but she still could take care of business. It was comforting, in a way.

"Fine. Let's get our stuff together. We might as well hit the road. Maybe we can take a nap during the daytime or something. I'm assuming it'll be easier to avoid umbrenix and other dangers that way. You up to getting the hell out of here, Tip?"

"Can we eat something first?"

# CHAPTER TWENTY-SIX

Though there were still patrons in the common room, I wasn't about to sit down and eat a meal. If Scar sent others after us, we'd only cause a bigger mess. I explained to the innkeeper that we were attacked, apologized for the mess, and put a few coins in her hand for her troubles. I added a few more for some food we could take with us when we left. We ended up with some fruit, cheese, and not-quite-day-old bread.

After gathering up our stuff, we headed out the front of the town and spent a couple of hours hiking back down the switchbacks to the road.

"Nothing to do but head northwest, eh?" I said.

"Yes," Brin answered. "We follow the road until we see Edgewood. The town sits to one side of the road, nestled up against the trees of the forest."

Tip snacked as we traveled. The little man could put some food away, that was certain. I wondered how he looked like skin and bones if he ate that much and realized that he was probably making up for years of not eating. Maybe he'd gain a little weight, get stronger.

I needed to teach him how to fight better. His showing was pathetic with that cat beastkin. If the minion hadn't been under orders not to harm the satyr, he'd have slashed Tip's throat without a problem within seconds of encountering him.

It made me think about Scar. That son of a bitch. If I ever saw him again, the world would have one less tomcat strutting around.

Brin must have noticed my face in the moonlight. We were within a few days of a full moon, so the landscape was almost as well lit as a rainy day. "You must let it go, Gar."

"Yeah, I know. The problem is, that fucker sent his men after me to kill me, and more men not only to capture Tip, but to either kill or take you captive so he could make good on his threat. That's not something I can forget easily."

"But you must. For now. If we encounter him again, such as if he stupidly comes after us, then you can call him to account. I very much doubt he will take that action, however. He might send more of his lackeys, but he will not leave the safety and comfort of the city and his shop."

"Okay, I get it. No use worrying about things we can't—"

A flicker of movement behind Brin sent my heartbeat into overdrive and flooded my body with adrenaline. She watched my eyes flare and shifted to look at my hands, now gripping both my knife and my siangham ready for action. She drew her own sword.

Tip didn't seem to notice that the two of us had stopped walking and had our weapons out. I really needed to sit him down and explain some things to him. Later.

More shadows moved. "There are at least two," I said.

"Prepare yourself. Cover your eyes when I tell you to."

That brought Tip's head up from staring at the road we trod. "What do you mean we sh—"

"Now," Brin shouted.

I closed my eyes and covered them with the back of my hand for good measure. Still, the bright flash of light made its way through my eyelids, though weakly. It quickly dimmed to a little brighter than the moonlight and I looked around. Two of the shadow creatures were right where I'd seen pieces of them. One swayed like it was partially dazed.

Brin ran at one as I sprinted toward the other. Hers was the one that looked dazed, but I still didn't know what the hell she was doing. I was going to yell at her to stop, but it would have done nothing but distract her. As far as I knew, she couldn't hurt the creatures with her sword so she was putting herself in danger. I'd have to finish mine off first and go help her.

The umbrenix I confronted moved awkwardly. They didn't have any eyes I could see, but I got the sense that it was blinking from the light flare. It was slow to react to my knife lashing out, but as my blade cut it, it reacted more quickly, swinging its claws. I ducked under its swipe and rammed my siangham into its chest.

The monster moved just enough that my lethal blow ended up being deflected. A minor injury, but still an injury. It swiped at me again, using both claws. The left came across to slash me horizontally as the right scooped up like an uppercut but with claws spread to tear.

I timed the blows and threw my right arm up to block the wrist of its left hand, keeping the claws away from me. At the same time, I stepped inside its guard, slashing downward with my knife to reach the claw coming upward. The umbrenix adjusted to keep me from cutting its hand off, but not quite enough. Parts of two fingers sheared off as the momentum from its strike brought its hand up toward my blade.

I adjusted my siangham and stabbed it down into the shadow's neck, right next to the clavicle, as I brought my knife back around and punched it upward underneath its jaw.

One thing I liked about the umbrenix was that they didn't bleed all over me when I killed them. This one's body jerked as life fled it, managing to tear at my shoulder with its left hand before I could spin clear. The claws were sharp, but the wound felt like the monster had torn my skin rather than cut it. It was going to leave a hell of a scar.

I didn't have time to worry about the pain or how I looked, though. I needed to help Brin. I turned, ready to sprint, and almost ran into Tip, who was standing there looking confused.

"Outta the fucking way," I shouted, which only made him jump. At least he didn't faint. I guess that was a good thing. Still, it was an extra couple of steps to go around him even as he danced to try to get away but only placed himself right in my path. I ended up shouldering him aside to get to where Brin was fighting the umbrenix with her sword. He was so light, he went flying.

She was good with that weapon, but through some quirk, she couldn't damage the shadow creature seriously with it. I didn't know why she wasn't casting. Her little globe of light lay nearby, its weak light illuminating the area just enough for us to fight. Could she only have one spell active at a time? I'd talk to her later about it. I needed to know the capabilities of my companions. It was obvious we'd be seeing more combat.

I reached the two combatants as the shadow man slashed at Brin again. She dove at the ground and rolled away impressively, leaving the umbrenix to me. It was no contest. Mid-slash, off balance in its rush to tear into Brin, it hadn't been expecting me. I slammed into it, leading with both my knife and my siangham, the first punching into the center of its chest and the second going through where the eye would have been if I could see more than dark shadow stuff.

It went down without a sound. I'd been running so fast, I slid for a few feet before stopping, having dragged the monster with me.

I yanked my weapons out of the shadow corpse, my eyes scanning the area for more enemies.

"I see no others," Brin said. "Here, let me increase the light slightly."

She didn't make a movement, but the ball of light got brighter, enough to illuminate about fifteen feet around it. We watched for any signs of more umbrenix while Tip grumbled and climbed to his feet. The three of us stood there, looking, for at least two minutes.

"I don't think there are any others," I said.

"I agree."

"We barely got back on the road. It was like they were waiting here for us."

Brin nodded. "Does that surprise you? Whoever sent these creatures obviously knows others have been destroyed. If I were that person, I would want to find the enemy who accomplished that."

"Yeah, I guess you're right. That means he—I'm assuming it's that Arinthalas guy—knows about us and is trying to eliminate us."

"It would appear so."

"I wonder if he's got Lucas."

Brin gave me a look almost like she'd bitten into something sour. I was going to ask about it, but Tip decided to make his presence known.

"Why'd you knock me down?"

"Because, you little fucker. Not only did you do zero to help in the fight, but you stood in my way, even moved into my path when I tried to get by you to help Brin. You know she can't harm those things, right?"

"I didn't do it on purpose." The little pouty face he displayed gave me the urge to slap his horned head.

Instead, I took a breath, let it out. Then another. "I know, Tip. I wasn't trying to punish you or anything. You were in my way, Brin was in danger, so I moved you. I'm sorry if it was rough, but we're talking Brin's safety here. Know that I will *always* push your ass out of the way if it means keeping her from being hurt or killed. Fair enough?"

He shrugged. "I guess. I'd knock me on my ass to save her, too."

"Good, man. You okay? I didn't hurt you?"

"Nah. I'm kinda scrappy."

"You wish. More like Scooby."

"Huh?"

"Nothing, buddy."

"Oh, hehe. I get it. *Rokay raggy*."

Better late than never, I guess. At least he got the reference. No one else in this world would, except for Lucas.

"We just need to get you trained up so you don't freeze, you don't faint, and you don't dance into my path. Maybe even get you a magic weapon. You said magic should hurt the umbrenix, right Brin?"

"That is correct, as far as I know."

"Good deal. Speaking of magic, though, why the hell did you go after that thing with your sword if you knew you weren't going to hurt it? Why didn't you cast a spell or something? Can you only have one spell active at a time?"

She gave me a look that made me feel like she was repeating loudly in her head, *Idiot!*

"Why would you think that? What kind of world would this be if one could only cast a single spell?"

"I don't know. I'm not from this world, remember? I have no magic."

"Ah, yes. I suppose that is understandable. The reason is that my mana stores are very low. We have discussed how since the goddess has been absent, I have lost much of my power? Well, that is the reason. I have a dozen spells I cannot hope to cast until Auryana helps me regain my reservoir. It regenerates far too slowly. I used nearly all of what was left to cast my light spell. To make it that bright takes more power."

"But..." I was going to bring up that night, how I helped her recover more of her mana than she could naturally, but I didn't want to say anything about it in front of Tip. "Oh. Okay, I've got it. We really need to do something about that situation, don't you think?"

"Hmmmm." It wasn't really an answer, but I'd let it go for the time being. We had other things to worry about.

I checked my watch. "It's less than two hours until dawn. Let's keep moving. Hopefully it was only those two who were waiting for us. Keep your eyes open, though. Can you bring that light with us and gradually lower it until you make it disappear? That way, we won't have to sit around letting our eyes adjust to the dark and we won't have to walk blindly on the road."

Brin did as I asked, and we didn't have any further encounters with umbrenix. As the sun rose in the east, I blinked my gritty eyes at it.

"How about we take a nap? One of us can stand watch while the other two sleep for a couple of hours. Then we'll swap."

Tip, probably feeling bad about not doing a damn thing in our fight with the shadow creatures, volunteered to stand watch first. Because Brin seemed to be pretty worn out from using her magic and fighting, I told her she was the lucky one who could sleep the entire four hours while I took the second watch.

With a little salute to Tip, I laid down on my bedroll and went right to sleep.

# CHAPTER TWENTY-SEVEN

My muzzy mind reached out for whatever had brought me to sudden consciousness. I lay there for a moment, wondering what had done it. A sound? A feeling of danger? What?

Something crunched near my head, loud enough to make me flinch. My eyes snapped open and I looked around, a little disoriented, just as a pebble landed next to where my head had been. It bounced with the same sound I'd just heard, though not nearly as loud since it wasn't right next to my ear.

I blinked at Tip. What was the little asshole up to now? He held another pebble, which he dropped as he looked toward the sky, whistling.

"What the fuck, dude?" I said. "Throwing rocks at me so you don't have to get off your lazy ass to wake me up?"

"It's not like that," he said, jerking his chin toward his right side.

Without my conscious approval, my head leaned to the side, like I was a dog trying to figure out what his master had just said. When I looked at where he was indicating, bright colors snatched my attention.

A—shit, I didn't know what it was—stood there. Looking a helluva lot like a plucked chicken that had gotten into hormones to make it grow to like three times its rightful size. Double-checking, I revised that description. Like it had gotten into radioactive sludge.

For all intents and purposes, the thing looked and moved like a giant, fucked-up chicken. It also had arms. It was a conglomeration of scales, leathery skin, and...something I didn't recognize the texture of. Like a mix between fur and feathers. Its beak, pink-tinted grey as wide as its head, sat close to its face, except in the middle where it protruded like a sparrow's. The center part gradually faded into the blue-green of the rest of its face. The rest of the creature's body was a mixture of greens, yellows, and even some pinkish red fluff radiating out from its skull in a strangely Einsteinian way. The two eyes fixed on me were bright, with orange sclera, but they seemed to operate independently like a lizard's, even though they were set in its face and not on the side of its head. The scales covering its arms, legs and chest were large and knobby, like cobblestones had been glued onto it.

It sat on its haunches with two skinny arms propping it up. As my eyes found the thing, it...clucked, but from the throat, not the beak. Tip threw a piece of bread at it, which bounced off the little monster's head. It scrambled after the morsel and scarfed it down. Tip threw a second one and it caught the damn thing in midair. With its beak, like a chicken would, not with a long tongue as would be the case with a lizard.

"What the hell is that?" I asked without taking my eyes

off it. The furry, feathery stuff above the ridges of its brow made it kind of look like one of those troll dolls with the multi-colored hair. Yeah, exactly like that. It was actually kind of cute, in a disturbing and freaky way.

"Dunno," Tip said. "I caught it trying to steal my pack. I didn't know how dangerous it was, so I didn't want to go after it with my sword, so I threw what I had in my hand at it."

"Don't tell me, you were snacking and what you had in your hand was food."

"Got it in one. See, that's why I disagree with Brin. I told her you could definitely think your way out of a paper bag. Definitely. Given some time."

"Ha. Ha. So you fed it."

"I don't know that I would really call it 'feeding.' I may have gotten a little carried away. Once he started snatching stuff out of the air, I was having too much fun to stop."

I slapped my palm to my forehead. "Okay, so you fed an unknown monster, thinking that was the way to handle the situation. What's the deal with throwing rocks at me?"

"I wasn't going to throw food at you. He might have attacked you going for it."

"He?"

"Yeah. He's got a, you know. He must not be all lizard because I think those keep their junk inside their bodies. Until it's time to use it. He's got a—"

"You know what, it doesn't matter. I don't know how you even know that, or if it's true, but I don't care. Now that you fed him, he's going to make a nuisance of himself. We'll constantly have to watch our packs or he'll tear them apart to get the food."

"Nah. You wouldn't do that, would, you Cock?"

"Wait. You named him?"

"Of course. It's rude not to address someone by name."

"And you named him Cock?"

"He kind of does look like a chicken."

"No. Nuh-uhn. One, he's not coming with us. Two, you are not naming him Cock."

"I'm not married to it. How about Cock Gobbler. Get it? It's a double entendre."

"How the fuck do you know what a double...you know what, never mind about that, too. No on Cock Gobbler."

Even as he frowned, he chuckled at the name. I had to keep my thirteen-year-old mind from laughing with him.

"Just Gobbler."

"Not after you already put Cock Gobbler in my mind. That can't be unheard."

"Scrappy?"

"Better, but no."

"Tor. I can teach him to rap. Then he'd be Rap-Tor."

I audibly groaned at that one. "Nope."

"Pterry, with a P on the front. You know, like a *puh*-terodactyl."

"No."

"Trex, like T-rex put together."

I sighed.

"Fine. Just Rex. That's a solid name. It harkens back to his dinosaur heritage, but not so blatantly as T-rex, and people call their dogs and other creatures Rex. Well?"

"Harkens?"

"I know shit. That includes words. It's my superpower. Or at least my magical power. So, Rex?"

I suddenly realized what the horned little prick did to me. I was so busy arguing about what name to call the monster, I'd given tacit approval for him to stay around. I narrowed my eyes at the satyr. Did he just play me?

"Get some sleep. You have two hours and then we're on the road again. I'll chase this monster away from us, so don't worry about names or anything else."

Tip tossed what was left of the bread to the lizard chicken thing. It expertly grabbed it from the air with his beak and choked it down.

Choked. Chicken. I had to hide the smile that was forming on my lips. God, Tip was worse than Lucas at putting my mind exactly where it shouldn't be.

I picked up one of the pebbles on the ground near me and hucked it at the monster. It squawked and dodged the missile. I almost thought it was going to eat the rock, thinking it was bread. Three more followed, the last one pelting it on its scaly body. It complained more loudly, gave a look to Tip like it had been betrayed, and wobbled off behind some rocks, using all four limbs instead of just the two like a chicken.

"There, job done. You have *less* than two hours now."

Tip kicked the dirt with his hoof and grumbled all the way to his bedroll. He laid down, pulled the blanket over his head and said, "You don't have to be a dick about it" before he settled down to sleep.

I looked over toward where the creature went. I hadn't thrown the rocks hard. I'm sure it didn't hurt him, though I did feel a bit bad. He was a stupid creature. Whatever he did, it wasn't malicious. He was a lot like Tip. Just wanting some food and companionship.

Yeah, sure. That's how it always is until you wake up one night with the bastard chewing on your neck. I was not in this world to start an animal shelter. I needed to find Lucas, make sure he was safe, and then we'd figure out what we could do. Assuming that Qamara was right and we couldn't go home. The last thing I needed was to get a pet.

I sat down on the rock Tip had been on, putting my elbows on my knees and my chin in my palms. I glared at Tip's back. Such a pain in the ass. Well, I had two more hours without dealing with his bullshit. I settled in and let my mind wander about all the things we needed to get done.

Before I knew it, Brin was up. I took a minute to wind my watch for the day and then went over and nudged Tip with my boot. Hard. Yeah, probably harder than was necessary, but better than throwing rocks at his head. Part of it was probably frustration over Tip himself, but I wasn't going to fool myself. Anytime I wound my watch, I thought of Lucas, which sent my mind off into a dozen different directions, all of them unpleasant.

"Get up, you little fucker. We need to get moving."

More grumbling and stalling ensued, until I gestured forward to Brin and started walking. Tip gathered his stuff and the clop-clop-clop of his hoofs told me he was catching up.

We made it to Edgewood without being attacked by monsters, without being chased down by umbrenix, and without killing each other. A total win. The sun was close to setting as we walked into the village.

As Brin had described to me, the intersection of the road we were on and the one crossing it at what had to be a perfect ninety-degree angle afforded a good look at the surrounding forest. If we kept going northwest, the road wound around and through Misty Wood. Going toward the southwest, the other road was bordered by the forest on the right and some grassland on the left. To our right, close to due east, sat the village and the smaller section of forest the road had carved off from Misty Wood.

The quaint community boasted a single inn and a general store. The rest of the buildings, other than a town hall type building, seemed to be homes. All rough wood with slat siding and thatched roofs. With only a couple hours of sleep in the last day, I only had eyes for the inn.

I dragged my feet, following behind Brin who, I assumed, knew where she was going. The village wasn't that big, so sooner than I expected, we were standing in front of the most glorious sight I'd ever seen. I wondered if it would look so miraculous when I'd had some sleep and eaten a full meal.

The sign swaying from a little pole attached to the building had a picture of a dragon's head, a smile on its draconic face and a dreamy look in its eyes. There wasn't really anything to tell me it was so, but I thought it was a female dragon. The name carved into the wood was MISTY EYED DRAGON INN. People really leaned into the mist theme around here.

We slogged into the common room and headed immediately for the bar, where an attractive deer beastkin woman stood. She looked to be somewhere in her thirties, with a curvy figure and small horns on her head. They were fuzzy, like new-growth antlers, and I wondered how they felt. I blinked, forcing myself to focus. So. Tired.

"No," she said after I'd missed what Brin had told her. "I'm sorry, but I only have two rooms available."

"Not a problem," I said. "Tip and I can share. We'll take them."

"Dinner for you? You lot look like you could use some food."

"Yes, please. That would be great."

"We've got whole chicken or some nice cuts of roasted beef." She eyed me, inspecting me from my feet up to my face. "How about I give you a big helping of everything we've got and you can all share it."

I smiled and my lips felt like they were attached to weights. "Perfect. Thank you."

She pursed her lips, her brown eyes drilling into me. "Has anyone ever told you that you look exactly like the statues of Kael the Blur?"

I sighed. That again. "A few. Just my luck."

"Mmmmm. I'm feeling lucky right now."

"Food," Brin said, then cleared her throat. "I mean, we shall sit down and wait for our food. Thank you, Carmilla."

I wasn't sure how Brin knew the woman's name, whether she knew her before or if I'd missed more of the conversation than I thought. I nodded at the woman and the three of us found an empty table next to one wall.

The food was amazing and between that, the wine and water I drank, and the energy in the common room, I perked up a little. My head felt clearer as the ravenous eating I'd been doing slowed down to enjoyable nibbling. I leaned back against the wall and entered an almost meditative state.

Tip didn't speak much, shoveling food into the bottomless pit that was his belly. Brin watched me, something going on behind her eyes. I was going to ask what she was thinking, but then caught something someone else nearby was saying.

"Two of them, in different places," a man's voice said. "One was in the Aesturith Kingdom and the other all the way over in Olliaran. Both powerful mages. One was weakened so much he almost died and the other was found by one of her servants, passed out but not harmed. The investigators scanned them with their equipment and found both had been drained of their life energy, but not enough to kill them. Turns out they were found before it ended them."

"We all know the shadows are back, even here locally," another man asked. "Do you think it was them?"

"No way. These were two powerful mages. They could have destroyed umbrenix. No, it was something stronger."

"You mean?"

"Yes. My grandfather told me how it was back then. Back when Aeyr was killing and growing in power. It's no coincidence the shadows are back. Who but Aeyr could attack someone powerful like that and steal their energy? It's what he does."

"Vaure—" a third voice started.

"No, no. None of that. We've enough to worry about with the shadows and Aeyr the Ever Hungering. Let's not bring your fancies into the conversation."

One of the men saw how I leaned forward, watching them, and he said something in a low voice to his companions. One of them looked back at me over his shoulder, then replied softly to his friend. After that, I couldn't hear what they were talking about.

Aeyr. Brin had told me about the guy. He was the one who created the umbrenix. So he wasn't just relying on his minions, but was taking part himself. Did he directly have something to do with Lucas? I hoped not. He sounded powerful.

Brin finished off the wine in her cup and let out a long breath. "I don't know about you two, but I'm ready to get some sleep. Shall we retire?"

Tip nodded. Even he was at the point where need for sleep overcame his hunger. Of course, there was nothing left on the platters and plates in front of us. We, and I mean *he*, had done a good job in eliminating all the food that had been brought.

"I'm ready," I said. "I could use a good ten or fifteen hours of sleep."

# CHAPTER TWENTY-EIGHT

I found myself giddy at the prospect of lying down in bed and going right to sleep. I'd stayed up much longer without sleep before in my life, but for some reason, the combination of fighting, then fleeing, then fighting some more, then getting a little taste of sleep had my body craving rest more powerfully than ever. Thus the giddiness. I actually let loose with a chuckle on the way to the room.

Then that fucking Tip ruined everything.

To be fair, the little pain in the ass didn't do it on purpose, but that hardly meant anything to me as I lay there, eyes wide open and staring at the ceiling as the satyr generated an impossible amount of noise with snores that would have belonged better coming out of a damn rock giant.

The room was nice, if simple, with two beds so we could each have our space without needing to sleep on the floor or anything. The temperature was good, too, just a little chilly, which was perfect for sleeping.

But the satyr. Ugh.

I hadn't noticed his snoring as much when we camped, but we'd only done it the one time and it was just a couple of hours. He hadn't made anywhere near as much noise. With the small room and the silence around us, the racket was magnified. Long, sustained sputtering pops, almost like cars with performance mufflers on them, rattled my head as he cycled through his breaths. That was just on the inhale. The exhale sounded like a thirty-foot bear with a sore throat.

Fucking taranji asshole.

I shook him, causing him to sputter but not come completely awake. I even grabbed his horns and twisted back and forth like he was a calf I was wrestling to tie up in a rodeo. I eyed the basin, half full of water, even reached toward it. But I didn't douse him. Even if it did wake him up, he'd go back to sleep and continue his noises.

I debated evil things I could do to stop the sounds. When I got to the point I was considering smothering him with a pillow, I knew it was time to take a step back and breathe. I grumbled—probably more loudly than I should have, subconsciously hoping it would wake him up—and stepped out into the hall in my bare feet. I closed the door behind me, leaned against the wall, and reveled in how much the wood deadened the sound.

I looked up and down the short hallway. There were only maybe ten rooms at the inn. I wondered if I'd piss anyone off by sleeping in the hall. While I pondered my decision, the door into the room next door opened and a familiar gorgeous, blue-skinned face with red hair framing it appeared.

"Would you like to come in out of the hallway?" Brin said.

"I would," I said gratefully. "Thank you."

I stepped in and closed the door behind me. Her room was identical to mine, except with one bed, so there was a little more room to move around. Brin was wearing her sleeping clothes, tiny tanga-cut panties that left half of her perfect, firm cheeks exposed and a simple cloth, like a tube top, snuggling her chest tightly. Both were red.

"Did his snoring keep you up, too?" I asked. "It wasn't me grumbling and cursing while I tried to wake him up, was it? If so, I'm really sorry."

"No. It was neither of those things. Have you experienced being too tired to sleep? I know, it sounds ridiculous and contradictory, but it happens."

I laughed. "Once or twice, though I usually fall asleep quickly."

"There is another reason, as well. I have been wrestling with something in my mind. It has me preoccupied. My brain will not let me relax."

"Oh, sure. *That* I've felt before. I even tried meditation. It helps. I'm not that good at it, though. It wasn't something that people did, that people talked about, where I grew up. Even mentioning it could get you beat up."

Brin sat on her bed. "Then why did you partake of the practice?"

I shrugged, sitting down in the one chair in the room. "I'll try just about anything once. Especially if it helps me to not get beat up."

"You speak of being beaten up often. Was your life so difficult that you were attacked frequently?"

"Oh, yeah. I was...different than others around me. I'm not sure if it's the same over here, but where I come from, your physical attributes can prompt others to attack you. Verbally, financially, physically, in all different ways. You, with your skin, would probably be attacked often. Maybe not, though, since you're so gorgeous. Of course, other women would do their passive aggressive bullshit because you would be more beautiful than them. Maybe even be aggressive."

I shook my head. "Anyway, what I was saying is that my skin color was different than everyone else's in the neighborhood I lived in. I talked about how Lucas was a lot darker than me. Well, everyone there was. I was the only light-skinned kid."

"And for this, you were accosted?"

"Yep. Simple enough. Not everyone. I mean, Lucas is my best friend, like a brother to me. But there were enough. A lot of kids wanted to hurt me because I wasn't like them. To be fair, though, there was more than enough violence to go around, so it wasn't just me. Lucas had his share of people going after him, too."

"How did you tolerate such treatment?"

A smile curved my lips. "I learned how to fight. Not the smooth, pretty fighting people do in movies—uh, stage plays—but vicious, ruthless action taken to hurt as much as possible with as little effort as possible. I still got attacked occasionally, but it was by a group. No single person wanted to take a chance at me.

"But all that doesn't matter. You asked why I tried meditation. I will do anything to improve myself, to allow me to better handle whatever life will throw at me. It's why I am grateful you helped me with communing with my siangham. I haven't seen any powerful changes yet, but I can see that it might help. So, thanks for that."

"Ah. You...are welcome. But you have either inadvertently or cleverly brought us back to what I spoke of before. I am afraid I have been unfair to you, Gar, and I apologize."

"Unfair? How?"

"The last time we practiced, helping you to try to attune your weapon, I acted rashly and inconsiderately. Inappropriately."

"No, it's fine, though I have been meaning to ask you. I'm sorry if I made you uncomfortable when I kissed you, Brin. If I'd known it would cause problems, I never would have tried."

"No. It wasn't that. I..." She heaved a sigh. "A moment, please, for me to arrange my thoughts so I do not cause further problems." She closed her eyes, her breathing shifting to slow and controlled.

I took the opportunity to look at her, though part of me balked. I wasn't a hardcore voyeur or anything, but I did enjoy looking at the moonwisp. I'd thought, before, that we were getting closer, that maybe we'd...I don't know. The kiss felt good, but it was obvious she didn't see me in that way. It was a shame.

Brin's eyes popped open and her green eyes found mine.

"I would tell you a story. I ask that you listen and not ask me questions. The purpose will be clear when I am finished. It will help me to explain something."

"Okay. I'll keep quiet."

"Thank you. There are myths in this world of a demigod. His name is Vauregar. He is a particularly insidious evil, one that strikes fear in those who believe he is not just legend, but reality. Though I have seen no direct evidence of his existence, just the possibility of him is frightening.

"Vauregar is described as being charismatic and likeable. He would associate with others, primarily women, and they would draw close to him. Whether from raw magnetism or through magic, I am not sure anyone knows.

But when his victims feel affection for him, that is when he is at his deadliest.

"His unique magic is that he can entice others into a kind of euphoria, or at least numbness. When they are distracted by their joyful feelings, he subtly drains the life force from their bodies. He feeds as his victims slowly slip into unconsciousness and death, never knowing that they were truly in danger. Some few who were spared because of Vauregar being interrupted apparently said they felt more powerful, though they were on the edge of death.

"It was Vauregar whom Aeyr based his research and experiments on. The ones that led him to create the umbrenix. He developed powerful spells and items to accomplish things similar to what Vauregar did, though his magical talent isn't naturally powerful enough to accomplish it himself without aid."

Brin paused, maintaining eye contact. "When I felt the empowering effects of being in close proximity to you, I panicked. Especially that kiss, which not only made me feel euphoric but also increased the mana I held in my body significantly. I began to wonder..."

"If I was this mythical demigod," I finished for her. "I mean, I get it. Even his name, Vaure*GAR*. I can understand your caution."

"It is more than that," she said. "More than a similar name and my confusion as to what was happening with me. You are from another world. I have not much knowledge of what that means. How are people transported from one world to another? Are they physically brought over as one entity? Are they simply recreated here with a similar body? Are they perhaps susceptible to a portion of them being replaced?"

“Possession. You’re afraid that I might be inhabited by Vauregar somehow.”

“Not as such. Tell me, is your form as it is in your world?”

“My form?”

“Yes. Your body, your face, all there is about you.”

“I think so. I’ve seen my reflection a few times since I’ve been here. My body is the same, too, even down to a few scars I got when I was younger. Hell, I even have a small blister I got on my foot a week ago when there was a little rock in my shoe and it rubbed enough to form the blister after a long day at work.”

“That is comforting. With your uncanny resemblance to the hero Kael, I thought perhaps you absorbed the essence of more than one person.”

“I can understand all that, Brin. I’m not going to say it’s logical because nothing in this world is because of the magic and all that, but I do understand. Where does that leave us? How can I prove to you that I’m not some ancient guy trying to get close enough to suck the life out of you?”

“I don’t believe you are.”

I stared at her and blinked. “You don’t? Then what the f—?”

“Not anymore. In truth, I did not fully believe it before, either. There was only that shadow of the thought within me. Enough to cause me distress. I have observed you and interacted with you, seen what your actions convey about who you are. I find no part of you that would try to convince me you were a friend to take advantage of me.”

“Unless I was really good at it,” I said before mentally kicking myself. That wasn’t helping my cause any.

She smiled at me. “No one is that good. Besides, there is the matter of my mana. No story I ever heard stated that

Vauregar's power actually benefited his victims despite what the one victim believed. You are...something else."

"I'm just human, Brin. Maybe you enjoyed the kiss and your body relaxed enough that it recuperated on its own."

"I think not, but that is a nice sentiment."

"Okay, so what does all of this mean?"

"I means I am very sorry for pushing you away. I apologize for taking time to try to settle my mind. And my heart. It means that if you would still like me to help you connect to your weapon, I would be willing to do so. It also means that I would be open—if you would like—to experience being close to you once again. Perhaps even a kiss?"

"Yes," I said. "Yes to all of that. I know I've been traveling with you all this time, but I miss you, Brin. I miss our training. I miss being close to you. I miss kissing you. As long as you're sure I'm not some kind of monster, I would love to remedy all those things. I have also noted that you used a lot of mana in our last fight. That could have been disastrous. I'll make you the offer right now that anytime you want me to help you to recover your magic, I'm definitely open to that."

I watched her plump lips as she smiled at me. "I would gladly accept any help you can provide in that sense. Gladly."

I got out of the chair and moved closer to her. "Let's see if we can figure this stuff out."

# CHAPTER TWENTY-NINE

I sat down on the bed next to Brin and ran my fingers through her red hair. The color clashed with her turquoise skin, but in such a fantastic way it drew the breath from my lungs. She lifted her chin and her eyes slitted as I stroked her tresses.

"I really, really missed you," I told her again. "I've been trying to figure out a way to talk to you and ask you what's wrong without pushing you too much. I'm glad we could have this talk. Maybe I won't kick Tip's ass for keeping me awake."

"Oh." Her eyes opened fully. "You have not slept. I didn't have to take a watch earlier and was able to rest more. You should probably—"

I leaned in and put my lips on hers, stalling out her speech. Her body tensed, but relaxed a few seconds later. The change from all her muscles tightening to her body loosening to mold to me was like the difference between drinking tepid water and drinking directly from a pure spring of ice-cold water on a hot day.

"Mmmmmm," she hummed.

I leaned back a little to look into her eyes. I wanted to make sure she was okay with what was happening.

"I could stay up all night if it meant holding and kissing you," I told her.

"Perhaps we can compromise? A little kissing, a little holding, then you get some sleep?"

"That sounds perfect." I dove in for another kiss and she welcomed it warmly this time.

We spent some time exploring the venerable art of tongue wrestling, Brin taking my lead and developing our own unique style. She didn't seem to have a lot of experience—something I'd ask about later—but once we'd broken that ice, she was warm and wonderful and I never wanted it to end.

I held her in various configurations, trying to find one that made her feel most comfortable, but like all new relationships, it would take some time. My hands twitched, wanting to explore her body and caress her in every way and location possible, but I held back. I would not rush this thing and risk making her nervous again. She knew I wasn't some ancient evil demigod now, but I had to prove I wasn't a wolf, too. Or a pig.

We did our fair share of nuzzling and though I still needed sleep, I felt great. I could definitely get used to this woman in my arms.

"Oh," she said suddenly. "My mana has recovered more than it should have in several days of waiting. Are you sure you don't have magic, Gar?"

"Just the magic of how much I care about you." It sounded corny as I said it, but she snuggled against my chest and hummed happily. Okay, I'd have to remember that one.

"You have made me feel wonderful and you have gifted

me with magical power," she said. "Somehow. Now I will stop being selfish. You must sleep. I cannot abide being the reason you are deprived of proper slumber."

I was going to argue, but part of my mind kept going to another way she could deprive me of sleep. I had to remind myself to take it easy and slow with her. She was timid with affection and I had to respect that.

"You're probably right. It's not you who kept me up, though. It was Tip's snoring that made me go out in the hallway. If you don't mind, I'll curl up on the floor and take a little nap."

"Nonsense. The bed is not large, but it will suffice for two, if we huddle close."

"Are you sure?"

"Yes. I am not inviting you to partake of all my charms, but I would like to feel your body against mine as we slumber. If that is something you desire."

I kissed her again, pulling her so hard against me the air huffed out of her. "That is definitely something I desire. Thank you. Thank you so much."

We curled up together and my fatigue took over. In seconds, I was out.

I WOKE with a start and a snort, not remembering where I was, but noting the sunlight coming in through the window curtains. The pleasantly soft and warm body next to me reminded me and put a grin on my face. I turned my head and crooked my neck so I could see Brin. The woman looked like an angel as she slept, as she did in waking. A blue angel.

I watched her for a time, her beautiful face, gorgeous

hair, and her spectacular body. Especially with her slow breaths expanding and contracting her chest, I could have continued to spectate for the entire day.

Her eyes fluttered open and focused on me. A sexy—and somehow still innocent-looking—smile graced her lips.

"Good morning."

"Good morning to you. God, you're gorgeous."

Her cheeks darkened. "Thank you. You are as handsome as a famous hero."

I laughed at that. "Touché." I didn't have my watch on, since I'd taken it off before trying to go to sleep the night before in my own room. "I'm not sure what time it is, but what do you think about getting some breakfast?"

"That is a fine idea. Allow me time to get dressed. Perhaps you should go back to your room and wake the snoring taranji?"

"Yeah." I snorted. "Good idea. I'm sure he's ready to eat again. Knock on my door when you're ready to go?"

"I shall."

I gave her a quick peck on the lips and hopped out of bed. I wasn't sure how much I'd slept, but I felt fantastic. Making out with a hot woman and falling asleep while snugging with her will do that to you.

During breakfast, Tip kept throwing looks at me and Brin, his eyes suspicious. Thankfully, he didn't ask any questions. He'd still been asleep when I got back to the room, but he'd probably woken up during the night and had seen I wasn't there. Whatever. If he asked, I'd tell him the truth. If not, then he could continue to wonder. I didn't care. Brin and I had resolved our little misunderstanding and things were only looking up.

At least as far as the stunning moonwisp was

concerned. I still had Lucas to find, the umbrenix to worry about, and a nagging little spot in my mind that Scar and his bigoted ass would no doubt be planning to get me back eventually.

We hadn't slept in too late, as it turned out. After a quick look at the general store and asking around for any information on Lucas, we left the village of Edgewood to head into the thick of the Misty Wood to get to Greyveil. Two steps past the last building, I stopped to blink at what I saw.

Across the road, catty-cornered from the village, was a tent I recognized.

"Huh."

"What is it?" Brin asked.

"That tent. Was it there when we got here yesterday evening?"

"No."

"I didn't think so. Come on, we need to go check it out. I recognize..." A familiar figure waddled out from behind a nearby rock. "Shit. Tip!"

Brin looked at me with confusion.

"It wasn't me," the satyr said. "I mean, it was, but I didn't do anything after you chased him away and I went to sleep. Honest."

The little chicken lizard creature stood there, his huge, orange eyes reflecting the morning sun.

"Well, shit." I threw my hands up. "Deal with it, Tip."

"Him. Rex is a him."

"Rex?" Brin asked.

"Yeah. Our friend here decided to feed that monster over there. I didn't find out until it was too late. We'll have to kill the damn thing to keep it from following us now."

"Him," Tip reminded me.

"Yeah, yeah. Kill *him*."

"No, you mustn't kill a furcan. They are considered fortunate, a good omen."

"But Brin," I said, "we don't have time to deal with a pet. Even a...what is it? A furcan. Like a fur can?"

Tip laughed, but Brin didn't seem to get the humor.

"His species is *furcanis*, but they are commonly called furcan. I'm sure he will be no trouble. I have heard they are intelligent and can be trained to do many things."

"Can we train him to find Lucas and kill umbrenix?"

"I think not. They are not powerful in combat. As for finding Lucas, perhaps."

"Fine. Tip, don't you make me regret this."

"No way, man. Never gonna happen." He turned to the little monster. "Hiya Rex, how's it hangin'?"

I rolled my eyes and walked across the road to the tent. It looked exactly as I'd seen it last, down to the chairs and the table within. I felt a wave of warmth looking at that chair. The last time I'd seen it...well, it was a fond memory. As was the woman who walked from the shadows deeper in the tent into the sunlight slanting in to illuminate it.

"Garfield. It is my pleasure to see you again."

Qamara looked as amazing as when I'd last seen her. The wispy, airy material of her dress cradled her magnificent body in such an enticing way, I could swear she actually looked better than when we'd parted. With her body language—a sexy, provocative pose with hips cocked, one hand on her waist and her shoulders back—I expected a smirk on her luscious lips. Instead, her mouth wore the familiar neutral expression. I pictured her mouth parted and her eyes half lidded, as I'd seen her last.

"Qamara. I turned back and went to tell you something

else when I left your tent last time, but you, your tent, and everything else had disappeared. Like magic."

"As we discussed, magic abounds in Valorae. In everything and in everyone, except for you. I have thought much about you in the last week and a half."

I'd thought of her a fair amount also, though mainly before I met up with Brin. Whether it was because of all the danger and excitement since then or because Brin had been dominating my thoughts, I wasn't sure. I wasn't going to get into a discussion about it now. Internal or external. I decided to hedge.

"Good things I hope?"

She did smile then. "Mmmmmm."

"Uh, Qamara Enorana, this is Brinawynn Tolsen and Tip. Oh, and I guess Rex."

"Hey there," Tip said, his tone slimy enough to make me shudder. He didn't seem to mind I didn't give her his full name. "So you're the super hot prophetess Gar told us about. With your magic, you must already know how I could rock your world and make your toes curl. How about we go into your tent and—"

"Tip!" I said firmly. "For fuck's sake. Stop trying to get into my friends' pants. Uh, dress. She's off limits."

Tip scowled. "How is that fair? You can't take all the beautiful women."

The prophetess ignored us and spoke to Brin. "A moonwisp. I had heard one of the goddess's special servants existed currently, but I didn't think I would meet her. Not until my vision a few days ago. It is a pleasure and an honor, Brinawynn Tolsen."

"Your vision? You saw something of me?"

"I did. Come around to the back of the tent and we will sit and discuss it."

## CHAPTER THIRTY

Qamara led us around to the back of her tent. As she did, Tip's eyes roamed over her form so intensely, it made *me* feel creepy. He grinned at me and gave me a double thumbs-up. I dragged my finger across my throat and glared at him. His eyes went back to the stunning prophetess, though in a less focused way.

Four chairs were set out in the space behind the tent, gathered around a small table with a pitcher and four glasses. Beads of condensation dribbled down the outside of the pitcher.

"Please, sit. Have some fruit juice."

We accepted her offer. I noted that Rex had followed us, poking his chickeny head around the edge of the tent cautiously.

"You saw me?" Brin asked as she accepted a cup that Qamara filled for her. "In a vision?"

The prophetess filled the other cups and offered them to me and Tip, then took one for herself. "I did. It was brief, and unexpected. I saw you with Garfield. There was also a flash of an image. Jewelry. A bangle. I believe that is what a rigid bracelet to be worn on the upper arm is called? Simple but beautiful, shining even without light to reflect, with a large gem of swirling color, green and blue? It felt like it belonged to you and that you had been looking for it?"

"My Bangle of Spell Capture. You know where it is?"

"I do. It is in Forgehaven."

Brin bounced excitedly in her chair. "Forgehaven. Perhaps we should go there first and recover it?" She glanced at me and the excitement bled from her. She cleared her throat. "I mean, after we finish what we're doing, maybe we should go to Forgehaven."

"Thanks, Brin," I said. "You know how important it is for me to find Lucas. He may be in Forgehaven, but... Qamara, did you have any visions about that? Did you see Lucas or where he is?"

"I am sorry, Garfield, but no. I still have not seen your friend, though it was not from lack of trying. I am at the whim of my power, I'm afraid."

"That's okay. Right now, our plan is to go to Greyveil to look for Lucas. The umbrenix seem to be centered there and we think maybe some guy named Arinthalas over there is the one sending them out."

"Though I have not seen it in vision, I know that Arinthalas has dealings with the umbrenix. Perhaps he commands them. Some have said that he is a follower of Aeyr. It would not surprise me. Do you know of the elves?"

"Not really. Is this Arinthalas an elf?"

"He is. Arinthalas the Collector is a light elf."

"Oh. That's a good thing, right? I mean, usually in fantasy stories, anyone that has "light" in their name is a good guy."

Qamara looked at me like I was a moron. She even

swung her gaze to Brin as if she was asking her to confirm it. Thankfully, Brin sipped her drink and didn't comment.

"No. Light elves are simply of a lighter color than the dark elves. Whereas dark elves have skin much as yours—tanned instead of pale—and dark hair, the light elves are fairer in complexion and have light-colored hair. Often white, as is the case with Arinthalas.

"You must understand that the dark elves are concerned mostly about how their environment, how nature, is balanced. That's not the way with light elves. The pale elves generally care only about money or power, most usually both. They engage in business and often do well. Their society is built around titles and possessions."

"That's Arinthalas, eh?"

"Yes. They call him the Collector. It is because he is obsessed with owning things no other has. Pets, art, exotic weapons, anything that is unique catches his eye. But that is simply his hobby. His life's work is to gain the power he seeks. It's reasonable that he would make a deal with someone like Aeyr, providing his services for the rewards and a bit more power than he would otherwise obtain."

I swept some of the condensation off my cup with my fingers and wiped it on my forehead. All this thought of evil masterminds and power trips was making me sweat. Considering Lucas being involved in all this was not doing wonders for my anger.

"That sounds about right," I said. "A megalomaniacal, power-hungry asshole hurting other people so he can get more stuff."

"Yes. I have learned something else as well. Aeyr created the umbrenix; you know this. The Hungerer will use them, but he will also provide them to his minions to use. Arinthalas will not be the only one. The shadows will help to bring in power, but they can also perform other tasks. In addition, Aeyr is using some of his own power, though I know not for what specific purposes. He was more selfish in the past with the shadowmen, all of them working directly for him.

"He is keeping himself well-hidden this time, not wanting to risk the world uniting against him once more, but he still acts. There are reports of mighty ones who are being attacked. Some have died, but a few have lived. Drained of their life energy, of their magic, much like what the umbrenix do with those from other worlds. Some think Aeyr might have the power to take energy from demigods or perhaps even minor gods. Or will soon."

Brin's eyes grew wide at that. I knew exactly what she was thinking. Her goddess was missing. Could Aeyr be responsible?

"Hold on," Tip said, shattering the tension between the two women. "You're saying that this Aeyr guy sucked the life out of powerful people, here in this world? I thought that was why he sent the umbrenix to other worlds, because the spell the alari cast kept them from doing it here. He's that powerful?"

"Perhaps," Qamara said again. "Much of this information is cloudy, but it will become clearer. You have wandered into deadly territory, Garfield Hailey. Are you sure you wish to continue? Many would take this opportunity to travel far away and be satisfied with surviving one attack by Aeyr's minions."

"It's up to something like five now," I said bitterly.

"Pardon me?"

"I've killed a few more of those umbrenix since I saw you last, so it's more than once I survived. We just killed two more of them a couple of days ago. None of that matters, though. They took my best friend from our world and dragged him here. I don't know where he is, but I'm getting him back."

"And if they killed him?" the prophetess asked. "I ask not to be insensitive, but you told me he can't fight as well as you. What if he didn't survive?"

"That better not be the case. Anyway, until I know, I'm not going to stop looking for him. I don't care if it's a fucking god we're fighting."

Tip raised his hand. "I do," he said weakly.

"Well, no one else needs to go with me. I told both of you I'd help you with your own concerns, but not at the expense of my own. If you want to sit this one out, I'll do it myself. When I'm done, Lucas and I would be happy to help you with whatever you want. You've proven to be my friends." I looked at Tip and frowned. "Some more useful than others, but still, I don't abandon my friends."

"I will go with you, of course," Brin said. "With what Qamara just told us, it seems our goals are intertwined in any case."

"Thank you. A lot of this is just conjecture. We'll find out more about it, but I still think our best bet right now is to go to Greyveil and ask around about Lucas. While we're there, we'll try to dig up some dirt on Arinthalas, too. If that fucker is calling the shots with the umbrenix that snatched my friend, he and I are going to meet sooner or later.

"What about you, Qamara? What's your part in all of this?"

The prophetess gave me a knowing smile. "That is an interesting question. I told you I've been thinking about you lately. It's not solely because you are handsome and have lodged yourself in my mind. I've thought much on what we did, and the effects of those actions."

My eyes flicked to Brin. I wasn't sure if my cheeks were reddening, but the air around me seemed to be warming up quite a bit. "Uh."

"It took me some time and analysis, but I think I understand now. When you...soothed me, I experienced an increase in magic. In fact, the very vision I told you about was a result of that burst of magical energy, in addition to the words I gave you before. I told you when I met you that I sensed no magic within you, something I have never encountered before. The explanation that you are from a world without magic made sense, but it still troubled me.

"After much thought, my theory is that you are insulated from the magic of this world in a way I can hardly comprehend. Whenever magical effects occur, it's more than one person or thing applying their abilities or qualities on another. My people have long believed that what happens is that the magic of the projector and that of the receiver interact. So, instead of the caster of a magic spell using her power to harm another, her spell is mostly using the magic inherent in the receiver to produce the effects. Mostly, but not fully."

"What does that mean?" Tip asked.

I narrowed my eyes at the prophetess. "I think she's saying that if I truly don't have any magic, I might be immune to effects from other people?"

"No. It could be that some magic does not affect you as much, but it would be too much to say you were *completely* insulated. There is still much we don't know. I only bring the subject up to explain my theory further.

"But it reminds me of another thing I have pondered, more relevant now that you tell me you have defeated others of the shadows. Are you aware of how the umbrenix operate? How they engage in combat with others?"

I shrugged. “They pretty much just attack. They don’t really defend because they’re used to nothing being able to hit them. That’s what it seems like, anyway.”

“Yes, but I speak of the mechanism of their attacks and their defenses. We have discussed how the umbrenix are able to absorb power, the very life source within people. That is a conscious action. Another thing they do, innately, is to utilize the magic of others. When one of the shadows attacks, they siphon off a small amount of magic from their opponents. This fuels them, but more importantly, it uses the particular magic from the person to power their ability to become ethereal. Thus, one cannot contact them to harm them.

“If, however, a powerful magic is used, such as an enchantment on an item, it overloads the umbrenix’s ability to allow that object to pass through them, so they may be struck.”

“Does that mean that some enchantments might be too weak to hit them?”

“It is possible, but I do not know the answer to that question. More important is this: you have no magic.”

“Yeah, yeah. I know, it puts me at a disadvantage.”

“Not at all,” she said. “In fact, I believe that is the reason you are able to touch them with your hands, or with whatever weapon you wield. They are unable to siphon any magic from you to power their phasing ability, and so you can strike them directly. It’s another quirk of your state of being without magic. A positive one, when it comes to engaging in combat with the umbrenix.”

“Hmmm.” I scratched my head. “Okay, yeah, that does seem like a good thing. If I actually had magic, I probably would have been killed right away by that first umbrenix, huh?”

"I believe so. Unless you found a magic weapon capable of harming it."

"What about other items? Let's say Tip shoots an arrow at one of them? Without him being close enough for them to use his magic, wouldn't it hit them?"

"I don't know for sure, but I believe that statement is false. Many have tried to hurt the shadowmen, undoubtedly from a distance as well as up close. If I were to hazard a guess, I would say their interaction with the slight residual magic inherent in all things in this world is sufficient for them to be out of phase with the projectile. I know of no tests performed on umbrenix, however. A frustrating characteristic of the body of knowledge about them, to be sure."

"Hmmm. Lucas is from my world, too. He wouldn't have magic, so it should work the same with him. He could have fought back against the umbrenix that brought him here."

"Just so. As to the theory I spoke of, here are my thoughts. Without magic of your own, you have no need for any that you might absorb from your surroundings. There is magic of all types accessible, but most cannot use all the different kinds. It passes through all things, people included, but unusable variations pass out again with no effect. You, however, not needing any of it, might be able to absorb a certain amount, though you can't use it. As it passes through you, it changes. Purifies.

"I believe that you might take in many different types of magic and cleanse them of impurities, combine them together, and have the ability to pass it on. Perhaps not consciously, but through proximity and contact."

Brin gasped. "He thereby can infuse raw neutral mana itself into others."

"That is my assumption. It's the only thing that I can

think of that would explain my...ah, someone, gaining an increase in magic immediately after contact."

Brin's eyes narrowed at me. Then she turned back to Qamara. "If he were to, maybe, kiss someone, would that possibly increase the mana in their internal reservoir?"

"That is exactly the result I am speaking of. Have you... experienced something like that?"

Brin's flushing face was enough for even Tip to understand. I wondered if all moonwisps, or people from wherever Brin was originally from, were so bashful about intimate things. Qamara wasn't. We'd made out less than fifteen minutes after she met me, though she did stop it from going further. The only reason I could see why she was dancing around the subject was so she didn't embarrass Brin any more than she had. She earned points for that.

"So, what does all this mean?" I wanted to get my blue-skinned companion out of the hot seat and move the conversation along.

Qamara fixed me with an intense gaze, her light tan-colored eyes drilling into me. "It means that you might be a power source for magic that could greatly aid those with whom you wish to share it. Will you spend some time with me and allow me to gather evidence to that effect?"

I wasn't positive, but I was pretty sure she was asking me to pick up where we left off. My body and mind screamed, *YES!* I had to play it cool, though. Looking over at Brin, I faltered.

I shrugged. "Why don't we talk about exactly what you want me to do?"

# CHAPTER THIRTY-ONE

Brinawynn watched the interaction between the prophetess and Gar. Part of her felt like she was intruding on something private, that she didn't belong there in the small area behind the tent with the other two. She fidgeted in her chair.

"We can come to some accommodation," Qamara said to Gar. "In exchange for your assistance in my research, I can possibly provide you with some small boon."

"BOON!" Tip shouted for some reason. Then he started to sing, though the beat was unfamiliar. "Boon, boon, boon, boon, boon." He rose from his seat and began moving similarly to how Rex did, like a rooster strutting across a barnyard. The awkward man was...dancing?

Gar glared at the satyr. "Tip, why don't you go play fetch with Rex or teach him some tricks or something?"

Tip deflated, then shrugged. "Come on, Rex. We'll see if you can jump and catch food in the air." He tramped around the tent and out of sight. Gar's eyes didn't leave him until he disappeared.

"Now then," Qamara said, "about repeating our interaction from a few days ago? Escalating it?"

Brin didn't like the way the alari woman looked at Gar. It had been decades since she had last had close interactions with other people, but she could still recognize the hunger in Qamara's eyes. Gar glanced over at the moonwisp, as if he had a question for her.

"Brin," he said. "I don't want this to cause any problems. I..."

"It is fine. I will excuse myself and take a walk. Yes, a walk."

"No. That's not necessary. I mean, I'm not asking you to watch or anything. I don't want to make things awkward."

"I appreciate your concern, Gar. It will be better for me to remove myself from the area."

"If I may?" Qamara interjected. "It might be a more reasonable option for us to remove ourselves and go inside the tent so you can remain here to relax instead of you going off to walk in a dangerous part of the woods."

Brin nodded. "Yes. Yes, of course. That would be acceptable. Thank you."

The prophetess looked to Gar, who kept studying Brin's face. She did like his attention, but at the current moment it felt a little uncomfortable. He finally let out a breath and stood.

"Okay. Qamara, let's go into your tent so I can help you. With your research."

The alari woman rose gracefully and led Gar around to opening of the tent. With a whisper of canvas, the front flaps dropped, followed by the sound of the leather straps being tied to keep the tent closed. She sighed.

The moonwisp slumped in her chair, aware of the proximity of the two on the other side of the canvas wall and of

Tip and Rex as the two interacted, the satyr calling out to the furcan as he attempted to train the little monster.

Brinawynn Tolsen had never been comfortable around people. Not truly. Born into the royal family of the kingdom of Iseldar, she was trained from youth to interact with others, but it was rarely pleasurable for her. With an older brother and an older sister, it was clear to her from a young age that she would not ascend to the throne. The plan her parents had always held out to her? To marry into a noble family, take care of her estates, and raise children.

It never really appealed to her.

When pressure grew to the point where she could stand it no longer, her parents pushing for her to wed, she decided to take another path. She began to travel the world. She'd been trained in combat and had worked to develop her magic, her ability to cast spells as a mage. It was not a unique talent, but still a useful one.

Her abilities, as well as her interests, aligned well with adventuring, exploring new places and doing what she could to help those in need. During her travels, she chanced upon a temple of the moon. While she meditated within, the goddess Auryana touched her mind and invited her to become the goddess's servant. Not clergy, but a special retainer, one who did the goddess's will in ways other than service in a temple. Traveling, aiding others, and demonstrating Auryana's will through her own actions. It was what she had been doing, anyway.

She accepted. The goddess transformed Brinawynn from a human to a moonwisp. It took some getting used to, her appearance changing like it did. Really, it was only the coloration of her skin, but at times that seemed drastic enough. What it did to her within was even more pronounced.

The princess was suddenly more powerful, magically. Her mana pool deepened, the power of her spells increased, and she even gained many new spells that were apparently created by the goddess specifically for her moonwisp servants. Her lifespan increased, her aging slowing considerably, and special communication with her goddess, mind-to-mind, was also granted to her.

One of the tradeoffs was that her desire for carnal pleasures was cushioned somewhat. Not that she had been particularly hungry for such things before. She had only been in the middle part of her third decade when she had been transformed, and because of her generally shy nature when it came to social interactions, she'd not had much experience with intimacy. The tradeoff seemed fair and she threw herself into her service.

For five decades, she pursued the tasks her goddess gave her, sometimes working on specific things for Auryana and sometimes taking opportunities that presented themselves. It was a comfortable existence, with new things to learn and experience often.

But then her powers started to wane for some reason. As time went on, communication with the goddess faltered. Many things had changed in the last few years. One of those was that she felt something missing in her life. Her family had died in a war that ravaged their small kingdom of Iseldar, so there would be no visiting them. She hadn't been back to see the area, a remote location in the southwestern part of the Teaphotria region.

Then she was captured by the goblins. It had been her own recklessness, distracted by her strange thoughts. In that cage, she had come face to face with a future of slavery, of potential abuse, of powerlessness in her own life.

Until Gar charged in and killed the goblins and ogres.

She recognized immediately his heroic bearing and, later, his similarity to the great hero Kael, whose statues adorned every city she'd ever been in. There had been dozens of statues to the Blur on the grounds of the castle she grew up in. It was surreal, having the hero step right out of legend and free her when all hope had been lost. It was unlike anything she'd ever experienced, or expected.

She had never been a romantic girl when younger. While her sister and her friends had dreamed of romance, Brinawynn only thought of exploration and adventure. She wasn't about to give in to girlish fancies now as an adult, having lived as long as a grandmother. Seventy-six years were many for a human.

But Gar had grown on her, with his single-minded dedication to his friend and his fierce warrior's spirit. When he had gotten close to her and she felt the power he had inadvertently gifted her with, she'd been confused. As she thought about it, she had an inkling of what was happening, but things did not fall completely into place until Qamara explained her theory. It was suddenly clear what happened to Brinawynn internally, magically, when Gar had kissed her.

She still hadn't come to grips with it, but she saw it as a good thing. A very good thing. Not only was it enjoyable, but his strange non-magic body was able to recharge her own, at the easy cost of "suffering" through the pleasure he provided for her with his very touch.

The moonwisp wished she could talk to the goddess, could ask Auryana what to do, why she felt the way she did. She was not completely naïve in the ways of affection, but the pull of it was frightening. Those days after he had kissed her, when she thought he might be Vauregar come to life, were pure torture. It had turned to pure bliss only the night before.

And now this. With Qamara.

The two in the tent tried to be polite, keeping their voices—and their noises—low so as not to be inconsiderate to others, but goddess, Brinawynn could still hear them. She'd guessed they had been intimate, though Gar had never come right out and said so, but to find out for a certainty was a shock.

How did she feel about it? As the sounds of their interaction, the slow moans and whispers reached her keen ears, her emotions were jumbled. Excitement, arousal, longing. Jealousy? Maybe not that last one, for some reason. She understood Gar did not belong to her, and even if he did, she saw nothing wrong with him helping Qamara out with her research and the two of them enjoying the process.

She pondered that, hoping she had not missed her opportunity to explore further this strange dynamic between herself and the man from the other world whose fate seemed tied to hers. At least for the short term.

Brinawynn brought herself up to sit straighter in her chair. Whatever would happen, there were things to address. More important things than chasing after pleasure. Powerful currents were flowing through the world and Gar seemed to gravitate toward them, or draw them to him. They would travel together, find Lucas, track down her items, and solve the mystery of her goddess's disappearance. If she happened to find pleasure along the way, well, that was the way of things sometimes.

"They left you out here all alone?" Tip said, interrupting her musings.

"They had 'research' to perform." She didn't like how her voice inflected the word.

The satyr strutted over and sat in another of the chairs. "You know, I can help you to do some re—"

"No." She cut him off quickly. She tempered her razor-edged voice and continued. "No. Thank you, but it's fine. Have you taught your furcan some tricks?"

"Damn straight. Wanna see?"

"Yes, please. That would be lovely."

## CHAPTER
# THIRTY-TWO

I felt bad leaving Brin sitting by herself as Qamara and I went into the tent. I think she understood what the prophetess was referring to, but she may have been acquiescing just to be polite. The moonwisp and I had gotten close in the time we'd been together, especially the night before when we finally discussed the awkwardness hanging over us. Still, I didn't know how she felt. Not really. I almost turned back to discuss it with her further.

"She will be fine," Qamara told me, closing up the tent flaps and tying down the leather strips to keep the wind from blowing them open again. "You care for her?"

"We've grown accustomed to each other and she is my friend."

"You care for her?" she repeated.

I sighed. "Yes. I'm not sure to what extent she cares for me, though. We trust each other and rely on each other, but I'm not sure how much further it goes for her."

"You would like it to go further?"

"I...yes. Of course. I've kissed her and thought about doing more. She said she felt that energizing you're talking about. I don't want that to convince her to do things she's not comfortable with, though. What if what we do hurts her feelings?"

"Do you love me?" That question came out of nowhere.

I knew instinctually that was a tough question to answer, though it *seemed* simple enough. Search my feelings, then tell the truth. But there were so many implications, so many ramifications. If you said no to someone who asked you, it could cause issues, but if you said yes, it might even be worse. Especially since the definition of love was such a hard thing to pin down. My bullshit detector went off as I pondered.

As with any other question I got, I decided to be honest, though still couch my response. Maybe even deflect a little.

"I don't really know you, Qamara. If you're asking if I desire you, the answer is a definite yes. But love? I met you one other time, spent half an hour with you, and didn't see you again until just now. Everything I've seen—and felt—with you is wonderful and I want to get to know you more, but to talk about love after so little time, I would be unreasonable, or just a liar, to say yes."

She smiled at me. "Then you have emphasized my point. There is no reason for her to fear what you do with me. It's merely physical pleasure and experimentation for research. If what we did stole away your feelings for her, then she might have cause to be upset. When you leave this room, even if your desire to be with me physically again is stronger, it will not diminish your wish to be closer with her. Correct?"

"Sure. I don't know. I feel like I'm already committed to her. Maybe that's it."

"Then when we finish, why don't you tell her that?"

She had me there. "That's a good idea. We did have a nice talk last night. We can have another one."

"Very well. Would it be too flagrant of me to suggest we engage in...research now? I've been looking forward to it for some time. Since right after you left my tent last time, to be honest."

I finally released my tension about Brin and what she would think as I looked over the super-sexy prophetess. I'd thought about her, too. It had taken a spectacularly gorgeous moonwisp to keep the thoughts of Qamara at bay.

They all came crashing back now.

I stepped closer and put my arms around her. "What do you have in mind this time?"

"Nothing specific. Would you like to improvise?"

Enough talk. I pulled her into a kiss and reveled in the feel of her lips and in her red wine scent. The wispy material she wore had almost no weight, but I didn't like that it interfered with feeling her soft, warm skin. I pulled the top of her dress off her shoulders so it fell down to her hips. She released a happy moan as her bare breasts pressed against my chest while I stroked her back.

My hands drifted down, ruffling through the airy skirts covering her tight ass. Her skin was so soft, I was embarrassed of my rough fingers. The traveling, camping, and fighting I'd done in the last week had left them dry and it almost felt like an insult to run them along such perfection.

"I enjoy the feel of your strong hands on my bare skin," she said, as if she'd read my mind. "But I would feel more of your skin."

She kissed me more as she unbuttoned my shirt and dropped it to the rug, then pulled my t-shirt over my head. When she brought her lips down to tease my nipples, pleasant jolts, like weak electrical current, ran down my body. Moving up to kiss me again, she smeared her chest across mine, nipples to nipples.

"You feel so good, Qamara. You smell good, too."

She chuckled and worked on the clasp on my pants as if she was on a treasure hunt. I hoped she was searching for a great snake because her actions already had me hard enough to hammer nails with my cock.

Not to be outdone, I pulled the rest of her dress down, fully revealing her spectacular body. I stopped and stared for a moment. "How old did you say you were?"

"One hundred seventy-two years."

I hissed. *Jesus*! "You are so fantastically sexy."

She finally got my pants off and dropped them, and then my underwear, to the floor. "Words. Can you *show* me how much you like my body?"

I smirked. It almost sounded like a challenge.

My hands ran up both sides of her, along her hips and up to under her arms. She shivered and goosebumps pebbled her shoulders and upper chest. My dick may or may not have twitched violently at that. *Hint: it did.*

I kissed her skin, licking the raised flesh until it was smooth and flushed. Qamara dropped her head back and sighed.

"Uhhhhhhnnnng. Your lips feel good on me."

I kissed down until I could take her nipple in my mouth, applying pressure with my teeth and sucking hard. Her arms wrapped around me and pulled me into her as her body wriggled.

The chair she'd fallen into the last time I was in the tent sat a few feet away. I almost guided her into it, but then spotted a small couch, maybe more of a divan. I kissed her other breast, flicking the nipple with my tongue, and then her toned tummy. With both hands on her pretty ass,

I lifted her and carried her over to the new piece of furniture.

"Ooooh. What is it you intend?"

"To taste you until you wash your juices over me. Is that okay?"

"It would be a good experiment."

"Yes?"

"Mmmm. A *very* good experiment."

I set her down and she leaned back against the side rest, her arms out in surrender. My finger trailed along her neck, tickling her ear before I dragged it back down over her breasts and belly, stopping to circle her navel. I bent over her and kissed her, my tongue aggressively attacking hers and drawing a soft moan from her. Then my tongue retraced where my finger had been, flicking it inside her navel rather than just going around it.

"I would really like to spend a few hours with you," I told her. "Exploring every part of your body and seeing what I could do for you. With your experiment, though, I'm afraid I'll have to restrict it to one orgasm. Will you let me make it up to you another time?"

"Mmmmm. I shall look forward to it. There are things I have thought about that I would like to try. Several things. Many."

I grinned into the skin below her navel and dragged my tongue down and to my right. When I reached the very top of her thigh, I kissed her, feeling the warmth on the side of my face from her junction and smelling her scent, stronger than I'd experienced before.

As I licked and kissed her from the outside of her hip toward the inside and down, she grabbed one of my hands and brought it up to her chest, pushing it onto her breast. The hardened nipple pressed into my palm and I pinched it.

"Uhhhhnnnng. More of that, please. I...ooooooh."

I'd reached the inside of her thigh with my tongue. Using my shoulder and my other hand, I spread her legs open so I could get further in. Her unique dry red wine scent wafted over me and I sighed. Saliva flooded my mouth as my body prepared my tongue for a sumptuous meal.

I stared at her beautiful pussy for a moment, the pale pink set of lips like a perfect flower with its buds waiting for my tongue to slide over them. I squeezed her tit and licked slowly up her inner thigh, stopping just as I reached her lips. They glistened in the brazier light, tantalizing in their simple flawlessness.

I flicked my tongue out to tease them and Qamara's body tensed.

"You like that?"

"Lick me, Garfield."

I licked her. From the bottom of her slit to the top, I pressed the point of my tongue through the exact center of her opening, flattening the rest of my tongue to slide up like I was licking an ice cream cone. When I reached the top, I skimmed from side to side to tease the clit that was barely peeking out of its hood.

"Ooooooh. Yes, yes. *Cresanto pedale emi.*"

I ran my tongue around her lips, circling her entire slit. "Do you want me to go slow? Should I take my time and tease you until you beg me to finish you?"

She muttered something else unintelligible until I leaned back and took my tongue off her. Only then did she speak so I could understand her, and that was in between panting breaths.

"One day...for now...I want to climax right now. Please. Put your tongue inside me."

I felt a keen sense of loss. I had been so looking forward to bringing her to a world-shaking orgasm, which only came with a long build-up. But she was the boss. It was her experiment. I dove back in.

Exactly two revolutions around her lips, a deep plunge with my tongue, and some mild sucking on her clit as I put a finger up inside and slowly made the "come hither" motion and Qamara screamed out.

"Garfield. Aaahhhh. *Schomalte. Securum. Sena, sena, forisen eschoma mea*. Oooooh. Aauuuuugghhh."

I wasn't sure what she was saying, but the sound of it thrummed me like a guitar string. She bucked and writhed but between my hand clamped tightly on one of her heavenly breasts and one shoulder pressing down on her leg, I was able to keep my face in contact as I fingered her to orgasm.

When her muscles gave out and she lay there twitching, I replaced my finger with my tongue and lapped up her nectar, each lick causing new tremors in her body. The taste was as before, but the wine was joined by a sharp metallic tang, almost vinegary, and a dash of salty bitterness.

For a minute or two, she lay there panting, then it was like she'd been shocked with a defibrillator. She pushed me away, got to her feet, and wrestled me with surprising strength so I slammed onto the little couch on my back. In a snap, she was positioned, with her hands around my diamond hard shaft and her mouth opened and half an inch above my head.

She flashed an evil grin at me. "The experiment must be complete. I need to know if it is simply close contact and my pleasure that allows magic to seep into me or if your pleasure is also a factor."

"Oh," I said. "That's a good id...oh, God!"

The prophetess's tongue shot out and licked the tip of my dick, putting the perfect amount of pressure on the opening. I didn't know the tip was that big an erogenous zone. I guess I was ignorant.

She proceeded to demonstrate an amazing talent for putting her tongue in exactly the right place and angle to reduce me to a shivering mass in less than half a minute. She expertly wrapped her tongue around the head and teased the frenulum before taking the top into her mouth and sucking so lightly, I had to hold my breath to feel the nuance.

Her hands got into the picture, too. She smeared them on the creamy, thick liquid she continued to produce, then spread it on my shaft. Along with a few well-placed drips of saliva. Her palms and fingers slid over my shaft, spinning around and up and down until I had to close my eyes because they were so crossed I was getting light-headed.

She didn't go far down on the shaft. She didn't need to. The way she focused on the head—and a little below it—and used her hands, my hips kept juddering and thrusting without my permission, almost like my body was preparing for launch. *Three, two, one...*

My back arched without my consent and rammed my shaft farther into Qamara's mouth. She kept it under control with her hands and only took half my length, but I wasn't complaining. Whatever the hell she was doing with my head, it was the best fucking thing I'd ever felt.

All my muscles fired and cum rocketed out of my dick. The gurgles of the sexy prophetess sucking down my semen were hot enough that I'd be reliving that sound and feeling for years to come. No pun intended.

My body finally allowed me to take control of it again

and I collapsed into the cushioned couch. "Holy shit, Qamara. Is that some kind of magic you have?"

Her mouth curved into a smile around my dick as she finished cleaning me off. She pulled off with a pop. "No. Just visualization within my mind and a keen desire to pleasure you to the best of my ability."

"Fuck. That was amazing. You're amazing."

"Then my part of the experiment meets with your approval?"

I laughed for half a minute. Like I had the giggles. "You could definitely say that."

"Then I am pleased."

"So am I, Qamara. Damn. So am I."

# CHAPTER THIRTY-THREE

The prophetess and I got dressed and joined the others behind the tent. Tip was tossing a stick, which Rex chased after, either catching it in the air or grabbing it as it bounced after landing. Either way, he ate it. Tip grabbed another from a small pile next to him.

"No, Rex. Don't be stupid. It's fetch, not eat. You're gonna need to get those two straight. If I ask you to steal something for me, I don't want you eating it. I won't want to wait until it passes through you to get it."

The furcan cocked his head at Tip, then bounced on his feet, waiting for another stick. I wouldn't have been surprised if the little monster had his tongue hanging out. Sometimes he was positively dog-like.

"I have confirmed my belief," Qamara said without so much as an acknowledgement that Tip existed. "Close physical contact does indeed allow magic to transfer into the recipient of Garfield's attention."

*Jesus. Read the room, Qamara.* Brin's expression didn't change, but I saw a frown in her eyes. The worst part was that I didn't know what to say. I dragged up what I could.

"Uh, to answer one of the questions from before, I didn't get anything out of it." *Oh, shit.* "No, I mean, that's not what I meant. As far as me getting any energy or magic or anything like that, it didn't happen. Of course, I got out of it what the activity is meant to...umm, I think I'll shut up now."

Tip grinned like a maniac. "So, you—"

"That is not a polite question, Tiporian," Brin said. "Thank you, Qamara, for your research and for allowing us to learn what we supposed was indeed fact. As we were not expecting this delay, we should likely be on our way toward Greyveil."

I slumped. I really screwed up. Brin's voice was too perfectly controlled, too even. She was pissed off, big time.

"Qamara, would you join us in our travels?" the moonwisp said.

I turned to her, putting a finger in my ear and wiggling it to make sure my hearing was working. "Wait, what?"

"She is a prophetess, and has much more experience with magic and even living than any of us. Her help will be invaluable and if she were to accompany us, our chance of success would increase dramatically."

My head swung to Qamara, then back to Brin, and finally to Tip, who was still showing all his teeth and was now nodding emphatically.

"That is kind of you to offer, Brinawynn," Qamara said. "But I'm afraid I must refuse. There are tasks I still must accomplish, though I do desire to associate with your group further. I will see you again, when I am able. I will gather as much information as I can to aid you in your quests. Not only finding Lucas, but also the particular goals that you, Brinawynn, and even you, Tiporian, have adopted as your own."

I wasn't exactly sure what I was feeling at the moment. Why would Brin ask Qamara to join us? I'd thought about it but knew better than to float that idea. As for the prophetess's answer, that was complex, too. It disappointed me, but it was also probably better. I'd need to discuss everything with Brin first. I didn't want to alienate her or hurt her feelings. Aside from not wanting to make her sad simply because she was a wonderful person, I didn't want to step all over the feelings of one of the three people I knew in this world.

"I guess we should get going then, huh?" I said.

Qamara nodded. "You should. Do not tarry in the forest. Stay on the road and try to reach Greyveil before dark. The things within Misty Wood become more active when darkness falls."

That was all I needed to hear. We bade goodbye to the alari woman—with hugs from both myself and Brin, but not from Tip—and started walking to the northwest, following the same road we'd been on.

Within a few hundred yards, the road narrowed, the forest on both sides closing in and making me feel claustrophobic. Qamara had talked about things getting worse when it got dark, but it almost felt like the sun had gone down already. The trees towered above us, boughs often hanging over onto the road, keeping the whole thing shaded. If the light was that dim on the road, how was it between the trees in the forest itself? There were even little wisps of fog or mist traveling across the ground near the edges of the forest. Already.

"Have either of you two been to Greyveil before?" I asked, mainly to distract myself. I didn't like the feeling of the forest, kind of like wet, cold tendrils were tickling my back underneath my clothes.

"I have been there," Brin said.

Tip kicked at a stone on the road. "Nope. Don't really want to go *this* time."

I ignored Tip. "What's it like, Brin?"

"Misty. It is not only the wood that bears that quality. Greyveil is a bay town, surrounded on three sides by the Misty Wood and also bordering the Axor Ocean. It is shrouded in mist most of the time, or a denser fog, and the gloomy atmosphere has given birth to a particular personality of the place. Most of the people I have met in the city are serious and hardworking. They tend not to be frivolous or jocular." She looked at Tip.

"I hate jocks," the satyr said.

"That is not what—"

"It's fine, Brin," I told her. "He knows. He's just *trying* to be funny. Ignore him."

"I see. Those are the primary things you need to know about Greyveil. Being so close to the danger of the forest, they are a distrustful lot, especially of strangers. Do not take offense at their attitudes, for they are the result of living a harsh reality. I will speak for us, if you desire. I am accustomed to their quirks."

"We'll see how it goes. I don't care if they're rude, as long as I can get information about Lucas."

The day grew darker. Some was the trees blocking the sun, but part of it was the mist that gradually increased as we progressed. It reminded me of the old horror movies, especially ones about werewolves or vampires. Strands of vapor crawled across the ground, slithering like ethereal snakes. It was kind of cool. Nostalgic.

Until one particular wisp of the stuff solidified in front of me.

"Back," Brin shouted and thrust her hand out in what I was starting to recognize as that force spell she used.

Not surprisingly, the long section of mist blew back from her. But it didn't disperse like it was blown by the wind. Instead, it was like a solid, physical thing. When it stopped a few paces away, it solidified even more, with a recognizable body and head.

"Mist serpent," Brin said and it finally clicked.

It was a fucking snake that could take the form of the mist, or mist that could take the more solid form of a serpent.

I drew my knife and my siangham even as I heard Brin's sword leave the scabbard. Belatedly, the ring of another sword came from behind me where Tip was. A gurgling, growling sound came out of Rex.

Not knowing what the proper response to the snake was, I waited to see what it would do. As I watched, it became fully solid. The thing had to be ten or twelve feet long, nearly as thick as my thigh. The color of its scales was close to the washed out appearance of mist, but had slight blues and greens mixed in. When it stopped moving, I could hardly tell where it ended, it faded into the fog so perfectly.

The monster's head looked more like that of a dragon, with a huge maw holding dozens of sharp teeth. Stringers of something—flesh or scales—swept back from its deep red eyes and its mouth, appearing to blow in a breeze that didn't exist. They reminded me of fine tentacles on monster illustrations.

By far, the strangest thing was that its body was made up of two trunks, like there were two snakes attached to each other, Siamese twin style. Toward the end of its body, though, the body split completely so it had two tails, though I had no idea how that could benefit the creature.

Maybe I'd ask it. After I killed it. It seemed to have the same idea, its head—almost as big as my torso—swaying while its eyes stayed fixed on me. It was either trying to hypnotize me or it was working out the exact timing for when it would strike.

"Do they have venom?" I asked.

"Some do. The ones with more green in their color tend to be the most venomous."

"Great."

Like a flash of lightning, the thing's head shot toward me. I don't know if it was as fast as a regular snake's strike because with the size, it was hard to compare. I barely twisted my body and jerked to the side as it came for me. It wasn't trying to latch onto me; it was trying to tear off a large chunk of me.

Its head retreated and I managed a slash with my knife. I didn't like being so close to it in case it twisted to attack against without resetting. I wished I had a sword or something longer that wouldn't require me to be so close.

Brin made another motion toward the monster, like she was throwing something. What looked like a sharp chunk of ice appeared and punched into the snake's side. The monster's scales must have been tough because the missile only caused a small wound, though it bent the snake almost in half with the force.

The serpent hissed and swung its head toward Brin, opening its mouth and rearing back to strike again. I took the opportunity and lunged in, drilling the tip of my siangham into the side of the snake's head. In addition to a hiss, it screeched at my attack.

When it turned to me, Brin slashed at the monster with her sword. For a moment, it was caught in indecision, wavering between me and Brin. Then it struck out at me again.

This time, I was more ready for it. I cut it very close, dodging only enough that it missed me by barely an inch. As it came even with me, I slashed upward with my knife and downward with my other weapon. The siangham punctured the scales nicely as the knife drew across the other side of its head.

The ferocity with which the snake swung its head around threatened to tear both my weapons from my hands, but I maintained my grip. I still hadn't hit anything vital, apparently. I'd need to keep trying.

Brin thrust her sword into its body several feet away from the snake's head, but her attack definitely got its attention. As it swung its head once more to strike at Brin, I attacked again. My aim was perfect. I rammed the siangham into its eye with all my strength and, holding it still with that weapon, swung my knife around and punched its point into the other eye. Between the two, I figured I'd hit the brain in there somewhere.

The snake's body started gyrating, faster and more chaotically than before. The sheer size of the thing had me whipping around with it, almost losing my feet completely. I twisted and wiggled the weapons, then pulled both out so I could roll away from the thrashing beast.

Brin had retreated already and Tip, still holding his sword, hadn't moved since the beginning of the fight. It took a few minutes for the snake to wind down and finally stop jumping. It twitched a few more times, then lay there on the ground.

"Did it bite you?" I asked.

Brin shook her head. "No. You?"

"Nah. It didn't ever make contact. Is this...normal?"

"It is, though this one was smaller than some I've seen. They occasionally come onto the road, but not frequently."

"Well that's good. Wait, did you say this one was smaller than others?"

"Yes. I have seen mist snakes more than twice as large as this one."

"Damn. I hope they stick to their normal habit of not coming onto the road. I'd as soon not see another one."

"I cannot guarantee that," Brin said.

I scoffed. "Yeah, I know. Tip, what's going on? Did you freeze up?"

"I d-d-didn't know what to do. I'm sorry."

"No worries, man. We'll get you there. Some more training and you visualizing what you'll do in case of another emergency and...oh, shit. Duck, Tip!"

Thankfully, the satyr dropped to the ground. It probably saved his life.

# CHAPTER THIRTY-FOUR

A shadowy claw swept through the air where Tip's head had been a second before. Before the umbrenix recovered from its missed strike, my knife was already in the air, on its way to the monster.

"Get out of there, Tip," I shouted as I sprinted toward the shadow creature. My knife missed, the umbrenix slithering out of the way, but it delayed the creature from going after Tip for another second or two, time he used to roll away and clamber to his feet. Instead of turning to run, though, the satyr fumbled with his sword, holding it in front of him.

*Of all the times to find his bravery*. There was no way he was going to hurt that thing with a regular shortsword.

A squawk from Brin snatched my attention, but I couldn't turn to see what was going on just yet. I reached the umbrenix with my siangham already out. I wondered if I made a mistake in not throwing that weapon, too. The damn thing did look like a chopped-off arrow.

The shadow man hissed at me, something I hadn't experienced before, but I didn't let it distract me. I lunged with the siangham, slashing at the monster like my weapon was a knife instead of a stick with a small metal tip at the top of it.

The umbrenix, being what it was, whirled and twisted, evading my strike. It lashed out with its claws and I sidestepped. The cloth of my shirt tore easily under the sharp nails, but I didn't feel any pain. I slammed my open left palm on the arm, right at the elbow, as I pulled my other hand toward me, trapping its wrist with my forearm. The cushiony feeling of it, with more solid structure at its core resisting my opposing forces, was strange. The resistance suddenly disappeared. Good to know that I could break the things' arms like I could with a regular person.

I spun along with the momentum of my strike, skimming the shadow's back, and snapped my arm out in a reverse grip strike with the siangham. The point punched into the side of the umbrenix's head. It made a gurgling sound and collapsed to the ground. I didn't know a lot about the shadow creatures' anatomy, but I'd found that a solid head shot worked well. For me, anyway. The guy without magic they could harness to avoid injury.

I turned to locate Brin and, sure enough, another one of the shadows was trying its hardest to shred her with its claws. Her sword did no good, sometimes striking it with no damage and sometimes traveling through it as it turned ethereal. It pushed her back, slashing, and she held her left hand up, palm forward.

A muffled *whoof* accompanied the monster being thrown back a few feet, but that was only a delaying maneuver. Magic affected the monsters, but her spells were pretty weak since she hadn't been getting power from her goddess.

"Hold on, Brin." I pumped my legs to get to her in time.

Just before I reached the pair, Brin used another spell. This time, it was her light ball, which she cast into the monster's face as it charged her. I guessed she didn't have the mana left for her water spike spell. That one took more out of her.

The umbrenix swatted in front of it, trying to make contact with Brin, but the light had done its job, blinding it temporarily. It was enough. I swung my siangham while still at a dead sprint, aiming for the shadow's head, but it gyrated and ruined my aim. Instead, my weapon struck it near the base of its neck. Not even a fatal blow.

"Goddamn it."

I kicked the monster's legs out from under it and it wheeled its arms as it fell. I pounced on it and gave it the old sewing machine attack, plunging my siangham into its face and chest five times in rapid succession. The last one, into one of its eyes, finally did the trick and its body went slack.

I stood up, breathing hard.

"Thank you," Brin said, looking me over. "You're injured. Allow me to..."

A cool, welcome sensation passed through my body as she put her hand on me. For a moment, it highlighted the several cuts I'd received that my adrenaline had let me ignore. Then they were gone.

Brin slumped and I caught her before she fell.

"You should have left them," I told her. "You're pushing yourself too hard, using too much magic." I swept a lock of her red hair from her face with a finger. "Come over here and rest." I picked her up and carried her to a patch of grass at the side of the road, scanning for more of the monsters.

"Those are the only two," Tip said. He walked up tentatively, his eyes on the ground.

"Thanks, buddy. Good job in dropping when I told you, and in getting your sword up to fight. Until we get you some kind of magic blade, though, you should probably just stay out of it when the umbrenix are concerned. You won't be able to hurt them. You saw how it was with Brin."

His eyes darted up to meet mine briefly, then flicked away. "You're gonna get me a magic sword?"

"Of course. I'm not going to train you to be a badass and then not give you the tools to kill these fuckers. What kind of asshole would I be then?"

"Dunno. Probably just the regular kind of asshole. It's not like you're special or anything." He looked at me again, a little longer this time, as a smirk stole onto his face.

"Don't I know it." I met eyes with Brin. "Thanks for healing me, though I wish you hadn't wasted the mana for minor cuts. How are you?"

"I will be fine. The physical fatigue will pass quickly, though my magical reservoir is almost empty."

I nodded. "So, I understand what you and Qamara were talking about before, how the umbrenix aren't able to use my magic—because I don't have any—to make themselves stronger or to switch back and forth from intangible to solid, but what about my knife?"

"Your knife?"

"Yes. I don't know if you saw, but I threw my knife at it. It didn't phase out so the knife would pass through it. The umbrenix dodged it. Does that mean I can hit it from a distance? What if it's near enough to someone else so that it can take some of their magic to make it intangible or invulnerable? Would I still be able to hurt them?"

"I know not. Even what we discussed was merely conjecture. No one but Aeyr truly knows how the umbrenix operate or what they can do. If the shadow dodged your knife, it is a good sign. I could not see it doing such if it knew it could allow the blade to pass through. Or it could have been a coincidence. We will have to try new methods, observe, and come to conclusions as we engage with them in the future.

"These did not seem to be random, but to be stalking us. I have no doubt there will be more to test our hypotheses upon."

"Yeah, I'm with you there. Rest for a little while. I need to go and find my knife. Tip, will you keep watch with her? If there were two, there may be more. We're not even close to Greyveil yet."

Tip gave me a salute and I went to dig through the brush for my blade.

It took damn near half an hour for me to find the weapon. It had bounced a few times and skittered away through the underbrush to the point I had almost given up looking for it, but I continued out of sheer stubbornness and spite.

I don't know why. I'd always prided myself on being able to use anything as a weapon. Maybe I was getting soft and sentimental.

I crashed through the vegetation to get back to Brin and Tip. "Found it. How are you feeling, Brin?"

"I am fine, ready to continue. My magic is low, but I can fight with my weapon. Anything but the umbrenix."

I didn't like the sound of that. It was bad enough that Tip was vulnerable. I didn't want to have to worry about Brin as well.

"The items you've already found, they won't help you?"

"Not for that. The nullification collar keeps the one wearing it from using magic and the Lunar Light Bracelet will allow me to cast the spell to see hidden objects. While the bracelet would allow me to do so with less mana than casting without it, the spell will not aid us in combat. And even if I were to put the collar on one of the umbrenix, I do not believe it would work. Their magic is different than a person's specific magical gifts."

"Well, that sucks big white donkey dicks," Tip said. Brin glared at him and I looked at him, shaking my head. "What? It does."

I squatted down in front of Brin, where she was sitting on a convenient rock. "Brin, let me help you. Let me give you back some of your magic?"

Her eyes darted to Tip, then back to me. "I..."

I put my hands up. "I don't mean the whole, complete thing with...I mean, just let me hold you for a little while. That should do something, right?"

She bit her bottom lip so cutely I wanted to hug her right there, but I knew what was making her hesitate.

"Tip, I think you missed out on some of the conversations we've had. Qamara and Brin have figured out that I am somehow able to recharge some of their magic when they expend it by casting spells. It kind of happens automatically. With close contact. The closer it is, the more magic, it seems."

"Oh, of course," the satyr huffed, throwing up his arms. "It's not bad enough you look like the most famous hero ever, but you have a thing that requires women to get close to you. 'The closer the better.' What a total crock of shit. What do I get? I learn stupid things from other worlds that make me even less likely to get laid when I speak them."

His eyes went wide and he put a hand over his mouth. "I mean..."

"I get it," I told him. "I'm sorry, Tip. It's not like I have any control over any of this. The reason I brought it up is that it's what Brin and I are talking about and I wanted you to understand it's not just me trying to, you know."

"Trying to make time with your lady, trying to make out when we should be walking, trying to get a little piece of—"

"Hey! Watch it. Don't you dare. Brin is our friend. Don't you drag her name through the gutter where you live."

The satyr at least had the decency to look ashamed. "Sorry, Brin. I didn't mean anything by it."

The moonwisp gave him a confused look. I wasn't sure how much of that she understood. "It is fine, Tiporian. I take no offense. Gar, I would...appreciate your help, though it makes me uncomfortable to pursue actions such as these for public display."

"Hey, no problem," Tip said. "I'll go over there a little way and work with Rex. He...hey, where's Rex? Rexy, here boy. Where are you?"

The little pest poked his head out of a bush nearby, swinging it back and forth, checking for danger. I hadn't seen him since before the umbrenix attacked. It appeared he had the good sense to run like hell when danger appeared. Good chicken lizard dinosaur thing.

Tip did as he said and I sat next to Brin.

"We don't have to do this if you don't want to. I won't lie to you, I do like to be close to you, but it's up to you. I think it would help, even if it weren't so pleasurable."

Her eyes met mine. God, the woman was gorgeous. "I do not object, and the actions do not bother me. I enjoy them. I am unaccustomed to doing things such as this in public where anyone can see me. I'm sorry."

I took her hand. "There's no reason for you to be sorry. I understand. It's up to you. I am at your disposal." I brought her hand up and kissed it. She fidgeted. "I could sit here and kiss your hand, if you like. It'll take longer to return some of your magic to you, but that's fine."

"No. We must reach Greyveil before dark or the road will become more dangerous. Perhaps if you kissed me?"

She didn't have to ask twice. I leaned in and pressed my lips to hers. It took her less time to relax and sink into it this time. Progress. We soon graduated to holding each other and kissing, even stroking each other's faces or hair. I kind of lost track of time, but she finally broke away from our current kiss.

"I feel that I have recovered an adequate amount of my magic," she said. "Perhaps we should continue on our journey?"

"Sure." I put my hand on her cheek, looking into her beautiful green eyes. I had to blink a couple of times to recover my composure. "Ah, sure. Let's get going."

I got up and put my hand out to her to help her up. She took it with a slight blush on her face. "Thank you."

"Hey, do you mind if I hold your hand as we walk? It won't do as much as kissing you, but the contact might help you to gain a little more magic back while we continue."

She narrowed her eyes at me suspiciously, then shrugged. "That sounds like an efficient way of traveling. As long as it does not put us at risk in reacting to threats, I am willing."

"We'll be fine. If something threatens us, all we have to do is let go." I turned to the satyr, a few dozen paces away. "Come on, Tip. Let's get going. Daylight's burning."

The satyr muttered something and hurried toward us with his distinctive goat-leg gait.

# CHAPTER THIRTY-FIVE

I didn't know who was more uncomfortable with me holding Brin's hand: Brin or Tip. Though I occasionally squeezed the moonwisp's hand, hers sat there in my grip like it belonged to a corpse. I cast my glance toward her occasionally as I was scanning the road ahead and she had a completely neutral expression on her face. Too neutral. I almost let go of her, but couldn't quite bring myself to do it.

I started to feel like an asshole, like I'd pressured her into holding my hand. Then I stopped and mentally kicked myself in the ass. It was holding hands, not forcing myself on her. She was a grown woman. If she wanted to let my hand go, she could do it. This was for her benefit, to help her recover her magic. So I kept reminding myself.

The mist increased as we got further into the forest. I knew that each step took us closer to the ocean as well, so it wasn't too unusual. Was it?

"How bad does the fog get?" I asked.

"Fog get aboud it," Tip intoned in a New York accent,

then chuckled as he did every time he tried to tell a joke. He nailed the accent, enough so I had to laugh, but Brin had no idea what was so funny.

She answered me instead. "It depends. Sometimes it is as thick as this closer to Edgewood and sometimes it is very light in our present location. I have never heard of an explanation as to how it acts as it does."

I could understand that. Meteorology wasn't an exact science in my world, either. Just ask a TV weatherman who got shit all the time for not getting his predictions right.

Even as we discussed it, we stepped into a pocket of visibility. It was eerie, like something had scooped out the mist to leave a nice hole for us to enjoy. Motion to my right prompted me to release Brin's hand.

It didn't drop free. The woman took this particular time to hold onto me.

I shook my hand, but she wasn't getting the hint. While I tried to wriggle loose, I turned at the exact right time to see what was in my peripheral vision. I forgot all about my hand and stood like a moron, staring with my mouth open.

"What the fuck is that?"

Brin stepped to the side so she could see—still holding my hand. "Oh, that's an ergol."

"Ergol."

"Yes. They are not too rare in the forests around Valorae."

"Did I do that?" Tip said in a high-pitched voice. I was too tense to laugh at the sitcom reference.

I didn't understand why Brin was so calm. My first instinct was to run, possibly dart behind a bush or something. My second thought was that freezing might be the best option, since it didn't seem the thing had seen us yet.

The ergol was massive. Like, twenty-five or thirty-feet-tall kind of massive. Apartment building size. I could only see the silhouette of the monster, but it looked approximately humanoid, if huge, with two long arms that reached the ground as it stood. It was fuzzy, bushy, like it was made from small plants, though the six sharp fingers on each hand appeared to be more like tree branches. If the branches were each the size of a man. Its blocky head held a mouth that split the bottom third of its face, the teeth in which looked to be easily able to impale an elephant. Orange glowing eyes the size of three or four human heads filled out its frightening appearance.

"Do not be alarmed," Brin continued. "The ergol, while powerful physically, are not typically aggressive. If provoked, they will destroy everything around them, but if you do not anger them, they are harmless enough."

"Harmless? That thing could accidentally step on a carriage and crush it, along with all the passengers and the horses."

"They rarely go onto roads. They seem not to like them. We have nothing to fear. Not unless you wish to attack it."

"No, no. I definitely do *not* wish to attack it."

"Very well. Then enjoy the sight. They are reclusive and seeing them is not common."

I looked over at Tip, who was showing the appropriate amount of tension, unlike Brin. He smiled weakly and gave me a thumbs-up. His hand shook. Rex was nowhere in sight.

We watched the colossal monster as it picked its way along whatever path it was making through the trees. Then it was swallowed up by the mist and soon after, even the heavy footfalls that had shaken the ground and rumbled around us disappeared. I shook my head. What other kinds of creatures did they have in this place? I couldn't wait to find Lucas and see if we could get the hell out of here.

We resumed our trek, my hand firmly attached to Brin's. She seemed to have come to grips—no pun intended—with the situation and would squeeze my hand occasionally even as I did to hers.

"So, the spell you were talking about," I said. "Lunar Light. It helps you to see things that are hidden?"

"Yes. The bracelet allows me to cast the spell for a small amount of mana. In fact, holding your hand as I am doing, I can regain my magical energy approximately as fast as the spell uses it if I keep it active."

"Oh. It's an ongoing thing?"

"It can be. I can control if I want it to continue or if I want the spell to end. It has been useful in the past, if I was looking for something specific, such as a hidden door to some underground complex."

I thought about that. She sounded so badass, like she was some kind of Gandalf mixed with Lara Croft, and even hotter than the tomb raider. "So you can leave it 'on' for a period of time?"

"I can. In fact, perhaps I will cast the spell and maintain it. I am interested in if it will use up the magic you are helping me attain or if perhaps it will increase the rate at which I get the magic from you so there is a net gain."

"Huh. Yeah, go ahead and do that. Let me know if you see anything, okay?"

"I will."

"What about your other spells? I know about Soothe. That's the healing one, right?"

"Yes. It lets me heal a small amount of physical damage. It does not cure ailments or the effects of things such as poisoning. The mana cost for it is happily small as well. I have demonstrated my light spell many times, as well as Push, the spell I use to force things away from me. The only one remaining is Water Spike. It allows me to generate and thrust forward at great velocity small projectiles of water, approaching the hardness of ice. They do not do a great amount of damage individually, but I can create many small ones or a single larger variety. Unfortunately, that spell requires a moderate amount of my magical power to cast, which is why combat with the umbrenix drains my resources so quickly. It is the primary spell I have that can damage them."

"That's too bad, but I'm glad you have something to hurt them. I'll do my best to help you regain your mana when you have to use it. Maybe when we find more of your items, you'll have other weapons against them."

"That is my hope as well. It seems that you attract the shadows, so we will encounter more, I am sure." She smiled at me, but what she'd said was no laughing matter. She was totally right: being near me was dangerous.

We had to be getting closer to Greyveil. It was nearly dark, but I didn't know if that was because the fog had gotten so much thicker or if the day was ending. We needed to make it to the city.

A sharp squeeze of Brin's hand, almost to the point where it hurt, energized all my senses. I hadn't known the moonwisp had such a strong grip. I opened my mouth to speak, but she shook her head emphatically, then jerked her chin to my right. One more sharp squeeze and her grip relaxed completely.

I let go as well, allowing her hand to drop away. With my right hand, I got ready to draw my siangham from the long pocket on my thigh. My eyes darted, trying to pick up any sign of something in the mist, but I couldn't spot anything. I did see Tip, closing the gap between us and drifting over to Brin's side.

There wasn't much warning, just a shift of the darkness I wouldn't even have noticed had I not been looking for it. A darker spot of mist launched itself toward me. I twisted, ducked, drew and rammed my siangham into the umbrenix that tried to get the drop on me. My aim was good and I followed its body down to the ground, drawing and slamming my knife into its head, close to where I'd already skewered it with my first weapon.

Brin spun as I got to my feet, throwing her hand out as a bright ball of light flashed, illuminating another shadow man. I put my hands up in front of my eyes, but it was too late. All I saw were purple spots. The distinctive sound of those hardened water missiles Brin could cast passed by me and thumped into something. A hissing, wheezing noise followed, the closest thing the umbrenix got to screaming or moaning.

"Brin?" I said, blinking rapidly to get my vision back.

"It has fled. I apologize for not warning you, but I do not know how much the umbrenix understand our language. I did not want to tip it off."

"Huh?" Tip asked.

"No, Tiporian, not you."

"Oh, cool."

In a few minutes, I could see spot-free again.

"I tried to balance between blinding the monster and not permanently injuring you. Ah, pardon me. Let me..." I felt the soft, comforting power of her healing spell wash over me and any residual issues with my vision disappeared.

"Thanks. Good thinking, both with letting me know

about them and with the light. You saved our asses on that one."

She gave me a wry smile. "Thank you for returning some of my mana for me, or I would not have been able to do so. Alas, I have used a significant amount, though I am still in a better position than when we finished our fight with the other pair."

I grinned. "You know I'll help you whenever I can."

"I do. We will continue our hand contact. I think we are getting close to the city. There are few signs because the monsters like to destroy them, but I think I recognize where we are. It may be better to push on quickly. The umbrenix that fled will be reporting to its master. It is clear they are hunting us."

"Yeah, I was thinking the same thing. All right, let's go. You good, Tip?"

"Cool as a cucumber."

I chuckled. Hearing things from my world was somehow hilarious when the source was a little dude with goat horns and hoofs.

Sure enough, less than an hour later, we came upon what had to be Greyveil.

The city looked like something out of an old horror movie, like Dracula's home or something. From a small rise, rooftops were visible in the last rays of the setting sun, as well as the dull yellow ball at the edge of the world trying its hardest to push more rays through the insistent fog. And failing.

A castle or some other large building, complete with high towers and what I thought might be a wall, told me this wasn't a small town but a legitimate city. Other roofs scattered around, some with spires themselves, confirmed that. I could barely make out the road as it wound downward and through thick stands of trees. I didn't get the impression they were the forest, but tamer groups within the civilized area. The ocean wasn't visible through all the fog, but the slight tang of salt scented the air.

"We have made it," Brin said. "Welcome to Greyveil, where perhaps we may find your friend at last."

# CHAPTER THIRTY-SIX

As we walked down the street in Greyveil, mist swirled around at our feet. We couldn't see more than twenty or thirty feet ahead of us. People strolled about, doing things that people normally did in their towns or cities: buying, selling, chatting, doing all types of work. They didn't seem to notice the fog. Or they didn't care about it.

"I will take us to an inn I have stayed at before," Brin said. "It will be dark soon. We should get rooms, eat, and sleep. We can explore the city tomorrow."

"I can ask around about Lucas at the inn," I pointed out. "If someone has seen him, we'll get a head start on tomorrow."

"Just so."

"Can Rex come with me into the room?" Tip asked. "He's not used to cities and I'm afraid someone might try to hurt him."

I eyed the little pest. The chicken-lizard, not Tip. I had no idea if they let pets in the rooms in this world. "Uh..."

"It will be fine," Brin answered. "Make sure he does not damage anything or hurt anyone and there will be no problems."

"Yayuh!"

The inn we ended up at was called the Ogre's Tooth. It was approximately three times the size of the Lucky Dwarf, but the common room still seemed warm and cheery, in stark contrast with the city outside. People chatted, ate, and drank. Brin led us up to the innkeeper.

The man's name was Polto Gerin, and I think he was the first pig beastkin I'd ever seen. Not a boar beastkin, which I guessed was similar, but an actual *pig* beastkin. The man was huge, a rounded belly that gave him the same physique as Santa Claus in the off-season, when he wasn't burning calories by humping toys around the world. His chubby face was porcine, with the hint of a snout to his oddly round-shaped nose. I was afraid to check behind him to see if he had a little curly tail. He seemed nice enough, despite his unusual—to me—appearance.

"Of course we have three rooms. How long will you be staying with us?" As usual, Brin was setting up our arrangements.

"Perhaps two days?" she said. "We are not sure. Gar here is looking for a friend with whom he has lost contact. Much will depend upon how long it takes to find him."

The innkeeper's smiling face turned to me. "A lost friend?"

"Yes. His name's Lucas and he's a few inches shorter than me, has dark skin, about the color of your counter there, and he might be wearing unusual clothes and saying things occasionally that don't quite make sense. Expressions and such."

"I'm sorry, but I haven't seen anyone like that. Is he a beastkin?"

"No, he's human, like me."

"I can't remember the last time I saw a human with darker skin. They are common in the north, but humans are not plentiful in any variety here south of the Aesturith Kingdom. Have you asked the city guard?"

My heart sank. I had to remind myself that just because the first person I asked hadn't seen Lucas, it didn't mean he hadn't come to Greyveil.

"No. We just barely got here before dark, after traveling from Edgewood. I'll go check with them in the morning. Thank you."

"Of course, young sir. I will keep my ears and eyes open and inform you if I find any information on him."

Brin paid for the rooms. I added an item to my mental notes to talk with her about finances. I still owed Qamara some money—though she didn't mention it when I'd seen her—and what we got from the goblins who captured Brin wasn't going to last much longer. We were going to need to get our hands on some more, even with what she got from Cedric. I doubted Lucas had any local currency. One more thing to deal with.

We ate dinner and listened to gossip and news from people in the common room, but nothing we heard was new to us. What was new was what Brin did as we sat next to each other. Whether I was conversing with my companions or we were listening to a snippet of someone else, the moonwisp fiddled with my hand.

Sometimes under the level of the table and sometimes with our forearms on the table's surface, Brin touched my hand, interlaced her fingers in mine, or gave me little pats or strokes. And she didn't even seem to realize she was doing it. I looked at our hands a few times, especially when she was outright holding mine with our fingers entwined together. Only once did she follow my eyes and then react in any way. She pulled hers away, looked flustered for a moment, then her hand was back on mine as soon as the conversation resumed.

Tip raised an eyebrow at me within the first few minutes, but thankfully, he didn't say anything.

I wasn't going to complain. I liked Brin, liked to look at her, and her hand felt like it belonged in mine. She was probably simply getting into the habit so her magic would refill faster, but that was okay.

All three of us decided to turn in early and we headed to our individual rooms. Brin—still holding my hand—peeled off first and said a quiet goodnight, and Tip and I continued to the second door, which was mine. By the time we got there, the moonwisp's door was closed.

Tip whirled to face me. "What the hell is going on?"

"What?"

"You know what. Did you two sneak off and play 'hide the salami' when I wasn't looking?"

I snorted. "No. You were there when we talked about it. She recovers her magic faster with contact with me. I guess she's making a habit of holding my hand as much as possible to help her magic."

"Why don't you just fuck? If holding hands helps, something with a lot more contact should do more, right?"

"Be careful, Tip. You're talking about our friend, not some street whore."

"Dude. Do her. Please do her. I'd hit that right away if I was in your shoes."

"Then it's a good thing you're not, besides the fact that they'd be too big for your hooves. Brin is our friend first, a super hot and sexy woman second. Or maybe first and a half. The point is that I want to help her, not exploit her."

"Yeah, yeah. Well, you're touching her, at least. That's more than I—"

"Don't even say it. And don't you ever try it. You push the boundaries with her and I'll kick the shit out of you."

The satyr put his hand up. "Okay, okay. Don't worry. Like you said, she's our friend. I'm not going to ruin that. I like Brin, and for more than her amazing t...uh, appearance."

"Good. Now go to bed. We need to find Lucas tomorrow. It's going to be a big day."

Tip gave me an inscrutable look. "Goodnight. Thanks, Gar. You know, for getting me stuff and saving my life and all that. I keep wondering when the bill is going to come due. No one has ever been this kind to me."

"That sucks. I mean, yeah, you can be irritating, but never having anyone treat you with normal kindness, that doesn't say much about this world."

"Would I do any better in yours?"

I didn't have to think long about it. "No, not really. Good point. Goodnight. I'll see you in the morning."

I went into my room and closed the door. Tip's door closed a minute later. I thought about what he'd said. Unfortunately, our two worlds were alike in many important things. I wondered if there was anywhere people didn't have to deal with the bullshit, punishing ones who weren't the same as others, weren't "normal." I doubted it. Anywhere people existed, some were going to try to lord it over others.

I settled into the chair in my room, taking some deep breaths to relax my body and my mind. I held the siangham, resting it in my lap, and reached out with my mind to try to connect with those magical materials it was made of.

I'd only been at it for a few minutes when a soft knocking interrupted me. Not from the door, but from the wall. The wall my room shared with Brin's. I paused, waiting to see if it was actual knocking or if she was moving around and banging on it accidentally.

*Knock, knock, knock. Knock, knock, knock.*

I lightly tapped the wall with my knuckles, in the same pattern, then waited.

*Knock, knock, knock. Knock, knock, knock.*

The whole thing was strange. I was pretty sure she was trying to get my attention, but what I wasn't sure about was what I was supposed to do. Did she want me to knock on the wall unintelligibly for the entire night?

Unsure what it was about, I slipped out of my room and went to her door, knocking on it three times. It opened up to a smirking Brin, who promptly grabbed my shirt and pulled me into her room.

"Brin?" I said.

"Did I interrupt you? You weren't sleeping, were you?"

"No. What's going on?"

"I thought we should prepare for our search tomorrow. We don't know what will happen."

"Okay. I'm not following you. It's not like we have a lot of stuff. We're prepared already."

"I thought I might do well with a little more magic within me. Just in case we encounter trouble."

Ah. I got it now. "That sounds like a great idea. What were you thinking?"

She grabbed my hand in hers. "Nothing too different. Maybe we can sit and talk, maintaining contact with our hands."

I rolled my eyes mentally. Her idea of a wild night was holding hands. "Sure."

"Maybe you can hold me. Kiss me?"

Now she was talking. "Yes. That would fill your magic more quickly."

Her green eyes locked onto mine, but she waited for me to make a move. I was more than happy to do so. I led her over to her bed and sat down, pulling her down beside me. I gently drew her closer and put my arms around her.

"You're not used to this type of stuff, are you?" I asked.

"I am not. I have not had much close contact with others. With us, it serves a utilitarian purpose. Furthermore, I have found that I enjoy it."

"You do?" I swept some hair from her face and took the opportunity to caress her cheek.

"Yes. Is that...acceptable?"

I tickled her ear and delighted in the cute shrug she did in response. I filed away that her earlobe was ticklish.

"It is. I enjoy it, too. It also has the side benefit of helping you regain some of your magic, at least temporarily."

"Yes. I'm not sure that anything short of the goddess infusing me with her power again will fix my magical disability permanently, but at least our activities help me to regain some as I use it."

"And kissing gives you more than just holding hands does?"

"Yes," she said. "It surprised me at first, but it makes sense. More skin contact and the heightened rate my heart beats should provide more magic."

I leaned in and kissed her along her jaw line. Her eyes closed and she shifted her head back so I could reach more of her neck. "It does make sense. Do you think even more contact will be more powerful?"

Her eyes fluttered open. "I think it will, but I..." She squirmed in my arms.

"Shhhh." I kissed her ear, then her cheek. "Don't worry. We'll do whatever you want. If you want me to hold you and to kiss you, and that's it, then it's fine. I do love to kiss you."

She turned her head, trying to look me in the eyes, but only succeeded in putting her lips exactly where I needed them. I had only to move half an inch and they met.

We moved tenuously, taking our time and kissing while I caressed her back and neck. Things went slow. Like, really slow, but that was okay with me. I enjoyed every second of it, squirming around on Brin's bed and exploring how many different ways we could kiss.

I think as a society, my world didn't put nearly enough emphasis on kissing. Don't get me wrong, sex is great and I would never say no to sex with the woman I was making out with at that very moment, but if she was nervous and unfamiliar with the heavier stuff, then kissing would be fine. I wasn't in this world to get laid by every woman I could—even though I did have amazing sex with Qamara. My purpose was to save my friend. Kissing the blue-skinned beauty who had become my first real friend in this world was icing on the cake.

Did I want to do her? Absolutely. But that could wait. If she never got to that point, well, it would be a shame, but didn't make what we were doing now any less fantastic.

I kissed and held Brin for quite a while, cuddling with the moonwisp until I started dozing. Lying on my side and facing her in the bed, I felt like I was home for the first time in a long, long time.

"I should probably go back to my room," I said finally, drowsy enough to slur my words slightly.

"No. Will you stay with me, hold me? I can use the extra magic and I do not desire to let you go at the moment."

"Well, if you put it that way..." I pulled up the blankets and settled in, the gorgeous blue woman in my arms.

# CHAPTER
# THIRTY-SEVEN

The morning light in Greyveil wasn't much different than the dim evening light had been the day before. It may have been a little brighter, but at the same time, the fog was thicker. For some reason, I thought of a Jack the Ripper movie I'd seen years ago, a classic in black and white where most of the scenes were shrouded in mist. I hoped it wasn't prophetic.

After breakfast, we visited several taverns, more market stalls and shops than I could count, and even resorted to stopping people on the street who Brin thought might know something. Sailors, merchants, messengers, pretty much anyone we could find who would have news of what was going on or who might come in contact with a stranger in the city. Especially a stranger whose appearance was less typical in Greyveil than in other parts of the world.

Besides what was going on in other cities I'd never heard of, we found out two things.

One was that there was a general lack of rumor about umbrenix. A few people brought them up, with tales of the shadow people doing things in other places, but none of them mentioned the monsters locally. I asked a few people directly if they'd had trouble or seen the shadows, but no one we talked to had. When I told them they had been spotted near Edgewood and in the Misty Wood, they shrugged and said that there were many dangerous things in the woods.

The other thing we found out was that no one had seen Lucas. I mean, no one. Even without the strange clothing, it seemed that it had been a very long time since anyone with dark skin like my friend's was seen in Greyveil. I didn't get a sense that it was a prejudice thing, just that the people with that appearance were tightly concentrated into only a few locations, all of them up north.

What was worse, none of Brin's items were anywhere to be found. Whatever path the goblin who took her possessions to be sold used, it seemed he didn't go to Greyveil. There weren't even any other decent items for sale. I scoured every shop we visited for some kind of magic sword or knife or other weapon for Tip, but came up short. For the immediate future, the satyr was going to have to stay out of any fights with the umbrenix.

After a day of traipsing around in the fog, evening was approaching and we were heading back toward the inn from near the waterfront when I heard a group of men conversing.

"Aye, Master Arinthalas, we'll have it for you within three days. The ship is due any time now. Yes sir, they found it, sent a pigeon back to tell us it was coming."

I traded looks with Brin and we slinked along the wall of a warehouse to get a better look at who was speaking. A tall, slender man in rich clothes stood next to an elaborate carriage, the door open and waiting for him to enter. Around him, several men in rough clothes—the same type we'd seen dock workers wearing earlier—stood timidly, one of them with his head down subserviently and his hat crumpled in his hands.

The man, no doubt this Arinthalas we'd been hearing about, had long white hair, lying free down his back, swept behind pointed ears. His pale skin gave him an almost ghostly appearance. Gold and gems twinkled even in the dim light, from jewelry and attached to his clothing. This was definitely what I'd pictured a rich prick in this world would look like.

"That's Arinthalas?" I whispered to Brin.

"I have never seen him, but he meets the descriptions I have heard."

I took a step toward the group, but Brin grabbed my arm.

"You cannot. The way those men are treating him, they will not stand for us to accost him. We will have the city guard after us, even if more of the workers do not attack us. Would you kill innocent men because they try to defend an important noble?"

I growled low in my throat. She was right, damn it, but we couldn't just let him go. I wanted to ask him straight out about Lucas. "Look, he's getting back in his carriage. Let's follow him."

"Follow him and do what?" Tip asked.

I wished he had brought his bow when we'd left the inn. I wasn't a crack shot with one, but I could try and nail the pasty bastard through the carriage window.

"Hope he goes through an area where there aren't many people. Then I can ask him really nicely if he took my friend and if he's responsible for those shadow fuckers bringing me here from my world."

The look Tip gave me was like he'd seen a ghost.

"You don't have to come, Tip. In fact, it might be better if you don't. With your hoofs, they'll hear us even above the rattle of the carriage wheels."

I didn't give him time to decide. The wagon lurched into motion as the dock workers dispersed. I skirted them and started to jog after the carriage, Brin a few steps behind.

Luckily, the vehicle traveled slowly down the misty road so it wasn't a problem for me to keep up. We passed several warehouse areas, all of them pretty sparse with people. Three times, I sped up to confront the elf, but each time small groups of people appeared out of the fog and ruined my plan. Then we entered an area where there had been a fire. Blackened timbers lined the road, with pockets of construction to rebuild what looked like more warehouses dotting the destruction. If the work was currently ongoing, it seemed the workers had gone home for the day.

This was my chance. I sprinted up ahead of the carriage and placed myself in front of the single horse drawing it. With my hands up, I called out.

"Stop."

The driver pulled the reins and stopped the carriage. He was one of the few humans I'd seen since I got to Valorae, dressed in what was undoubtedly livery. Rich blues and black accents made him look very official, even if not comfortable. He glared at me in a way that only a haughty mid-level servant to a powerful noble could.

"Move out of the way, rabble," he said to me in a dry, emotionless voice.

"Arinthalas," I called out, ignoring the driver completely.

The carriage door swung open, which surprised me. I figured a big muckety muck like this guy would have shouted at his manservant through the window rather than bothering himself to open the door. When he stepped out, my shock was probably evident on my face.

"Patok, what is the meaning of...oh. I see. You have saved me a great deal of trouble by coming to me, though you have caused even more already by your actions." He swung his head, checking the area, barely pausing when he saw Brin and Tip running to catch up to me. "It is the last mistake you will make."

Arinthalas waved his hand, the ruff at his cuff swaying with the motion. A shadow detached itself from the darkness under the carriage.

*Really? After all the umbrenix I've killed already, he's going to sic one of them on me?*

"Take him," Arinthalas ordered. "Then drain him. The other two you can kill. They are of no use to me."

He climbed back in his carriage but didn't order the driver to move. I could see his white hair in the recess of the cabin. He was not disinterested, just trying to make a point. Fine, he'd get a point all right.

The shadow glided toward me, faster than a sprinting person, claws raised as if I'd stand there and let it tear me to shreds. I drew my knife and my siangham. When I did, a soft chuckle emitted from the carriage.

*Think it's funny, motherfucker?*

The shadow creature slashed at me in the same way all the others had. I wondered if they trained the monsters to fight. They seemed to use the same movements, but I got the impression that Arinthalas believed the relative invulnerability the umbrenix had was enough.

I ducked one swipe, twisted to evade the other, slashed the monster in the chest with my knife, and punched my siangham into its head. As all the others had, it dropped to the ground soundlessly. I looked toward that carriage as Arinthalas let loose a small gasp.

"That's what you send at me? How many of these do I have to kill before you figure out they can't take me? Now, I want to talk about my friend, Lucas Walker. Your monsters took him a few hours before me. Where is he?"

The white-haired elf stepped out of the carriage again. His head jerked to his right, where two more of the umbrenix glided toward us. I guess he only kept one near him, but there were others close. I turned to face the two new arrivals, but they rushed toward Brin instead.

"See if you are flippant when fighting me." Arinthalas pulled a scabbarded sword from the carriage, drew the blade, and tossed the scabbard back into the cabin. The weapon was slender, with just the hint of a curve, single-edged with a substantial hand guard. He swiped it a few times in the air and bounced, preparing.

It was fine with me. If I had to cut the secret out of him, so be it. I stalked toward him while a short distance away, Brin created a ball of light to delay one of the umbrenix while both she and Tip readied their weapons.

I was going to have to make it quick with Arinthalas. My companions' weapons were useless against the shadow men and Brin's magic—as it was—wouldn't last long against them. She had more magical juice than she did the last time she faced an umbrenix, but the spells she had were better for stalling the monsters than killing them.

The elf lunged in, more quickly than I'd expected from his thin, weak-looking form. With his pale skin, he almost looked sickly. I tapped the slash with my knife and a dull *ting* died immediately in the foggy air. He brought the sword up and back around quickly, but I'd already backed out of range.

Arinthalas smiled. The curve of his lips told me he enjoyed a challenge, but he didn't think I was too great an encounter. I'd have to show him how wrong he was.

He came in again and I parried with my knife. I wasn't sure how tough the siangham was, even though it was made out of magical materials, and didn't want to risk using it to deflect sharp steel. That was a good way to lose a weapon and get cut.

This time, as I parried, I closed the distance and got inside his guard, jabbing at him with the weapon in my right hand. He slipped the strike like a boxer would a jab, dropped his shoulder, and rotated to his left. That brought his sword up at an awkward angle, catching me by surprise and touching a piece of my shoulder with his blade before my knife got into position to stop it.

I kicked at the elf's knee, making contact, but he rolled it to mitigate the force instead of it buckling. I hopped back as the sword came at me again, horizontally this time. A quick, sloppy parry that consisted of me slamming my knife downward to deflect the blade saved me from another cut. Barely.

The smile on the bastard's face was bigger now. He was enjoying himself and thought he'd finish me easily. I growled and waited for his next attack. It was too dangerous for me to lunge in with his longer range.

Arinthalas raised his sword, shifting his feet. His hips cocked the slightest amount and I knew he was going to come at me again. Then voices sounded around us.

"I heard something over here," a man said. "Just past the burned warehouse."

Other voices joined him. Shit. If they caught me fighting with their local lord, it would not go well for me. I wasn't sure what the presence of the umbrenix would do for the situation, but it wouldn't look good.

Arinthalas tossed his sword into the carriage and made a motion with his hand that prompted the umbrenix to flee into the mist. I put my siangham and knife away just as six men came into view from the fog.

"Pardon, Master Arinthalas," one of them said. "We thought we heard metal striking metal. Is everything well here?"

"It is, thank you. I heard it as well, and stopped my carriage to investigate, but found only these three." He waved his hand toward us. "Nothing seems amiss. Thank you for your concern. I will continue to the dock."

"We'll go with you, just to be sure nothing's afoot."

"Very well." He turned to me and gave me a smile. "You are fortunate. I—or my pets—will be seeing you again. If you were wise, you would flee to some corner of the world. Perhaps it would allow you to live a bit longer before your life is drained for the use of your betters." He paused, looking me over. "Or you can come see me anytime you like, if you are foolhardy enough. I promise I will make your death quick. More or less."

He climbed into the carriage, closed the door, and shouted out the window for his driver to continue. The men looked at me quizzically as they passed, following the carriage, but didn't say anything.

Brin and Tip joined me, watching them leave.

"Are you two all right?" I asked.

Brin nodded. "I was able to keep the shadows back so we were not injured."

"Good. Let's go back to the inn. We need to talk about how we're going to go after Arinthalas. This time, I'll cut all the information out of him by the time we're finished."

# CHAPTER THIRTY-EIGHT

Tip and I sat in my room after dinner that evening.

"So," the satyr said. "You and Brin, huh?"

I rolled my eyes at him. "What do you mean by that?"

"I don't know. Just that you guys seem to be really hitting it off."

"Tip, you've been with us a few days. I've known her twice as long as you. If you've got something to say, spit it out."

"It's all good. I don't...I mean...are you doing her?"

I shook my head. "Fucking Tip. It's none of your damn business if I were. You don't need to worry about it. We have other things to be thinking about right now."

"Yeah, yeah. You're right. But are you doing her?"

A soft knock at the door rescued me from the conversation. I got up and opened the door to find the gorgeous blue woman standing there.

"Come on in." I took a seat on the bed, gesturing toward the chair Tip wasn't sitting in. She sat down next to me on the bed and took one of my hands in hers.

Tip gave me a side-eye and I repeated in my mind several times. *Shut up. Don't ask. Don't say a word. Shut up...*

I spoke before he made things even more awkward.

"Brin, did you use a lot of magic earlier? I wasn't able to see what was going on with fighting Arinthalas like that."

"I used a fair amount," she said. "I did not drain my stores, but I did deplete them partially. Thus, this." She lifted our hands up to show me.

"Yeah, soak up as much magic as you can. We're going to need it. Which brings me to what we need to talk about. We need to go and find out what Arinthalas knows. The rumor about him having a connection with the umbrenix is obviously true. It's likely that he's the one who sent the shadows after Lucas and me and who's been having them hunt us in the last few days. Unless you know of another person with connections to umbrenix besides Aeyr."

"I do not know of anyone else. Since we know not where the Hungerer is, I cannot say if he is near. Arinthalas is the most likely culprit. However, if there is one who Aeyr entrusted to command the shadows, there might be others yet."

"Yeah," Tip said. "But if he's not the one who sent them after you and Lucas, he's still our best bet in knowing who did."

"Right," I agreed. "So, we need to get to him, and not when there are people around. Luckily, he doesn't want to make a scene, either, so he'll cooperate in meeting alone."

The satyr whistled. "That dude can swing a sword, though, am I right? Can you handle him, Gar?"

"I'll be fine. The problem is not only getting him without witnesses around, but when he doesn't have a bunch of the shadows with him, too. If people see us fighting, it may not be ideal for him, but for us, it'll be worse. I don't want the whole city mobbing us and killing us because we attacked their precious noble, so while he probably won't use the shadows if people are around, we'll end up on the losing end, one way or another."

Brin squeezed my hand, though I think it was involuntary. "We therefore must find a place where we can accost him out of the sight of the citizens of Greyveil. He lives on a small island off the coast. It is in the middle of the bay. We can search for a place on the mainland where we might be able to catch him unaware, without witnesses, but I believe the chances of interacting with him alone are better in his home."

"You want us to take a boat to his personal island, the place he lives and controls completely?" Tip asked.

"It is a suggestion."

I leaned my head back and looked at the ceiling. "I think I would have to agree. We got lucky we caught him without people around earlier, but it didn't last long, and he had umbrenix nearby. How many does he have? If we end up on his island, are we going to be swarmed by the things?"

"Perhaps we can scout the area before we commit?" Brin patted the hand she held with her other. "If we get close, even venture onto the island but not all the way to his home, I might be able to use my Lunar Light spell to detect the monsters. There may be more within the house, but some information is more valuable than no information."

"That's a good idea," I said. "Let's see if we can get hold of a boat. We can take a trip over to check it out and while we're out, we can try to find another alternative. I'm not so sure about going to his home, where he might have guards or traps or other defenses, if we don't have to."

"Could we not approach him in a public place and simply ask him if we could speak privately?"

I looked at the moonwisp. “Just go up to him and ask if we can chat?”

“Yes.”

“He took out a sword and tried to kill me while he sent umbrenix to kill you two.”

“To be fair, boss,” Tip said. “You did come at him pretty aggressively.”

I didn’t like the idea, but as I thought about it, there didn’t seem to be a lot of risk, not compared to attacking him when there might be people nearby.

“We can give it a try, I guess. So we’ve got three options. Talk to him in the street with people around, try to find a place where we can get him alone and beat answers out of him, or go to his home on his personal island that is probably infested with umbrenix and try to take him down there.”

Brin squeezed my hand again. “I would say that summarizes it nicely.”

Tip groaned.

“Okay,” I said. “That’s our rough plan. While we’re out tomorrow trying to work on those things, we need to check more shops and see if we can find Tip a magic weapon. I’d like it if you both had weapons that could hurt the umbrenix, but at least if Tip has one, you’ve still got your magic. If it comes down to a fight with Arinthalas and some of his shadows, we all need to be able to hurt them.”

There wasn’t much to talk about after that, so Tip left to go to his own room. Brin stayed, sitting on the bed with her hand in mine.

“What are your plans?” I asked.

“I will sleep.”

She was still holding my hand.

“Do you want to stay here tonight?”

"I would. It would be good to sleep next to you, with your skin touching mine so that I may gather more magic. When we confront Arinthalas, I would have as much magical power stored within me as possible."

I gave her a crooked smile. "That sounds like a good idea to me."

"Yes, to me, too."

There was something simple about going to sleep next to Brinawynn. Simple and precious. The woman had an amazing body, she was as gorgeous as any woman I'd ever seen, and her blue skin only multiplied that. I wanted her, and badly. Yet I didn't try anything, didn't push her, and satisfied myself with being with her, feeling her warmth next to me.

I know, it sounds like bullshit. But it isn't. My presence was soothing to her, and not only because it helped her regain a little magic after years of being drained of most of her power. She had put her trust in me, as a companion and someone who comforted her, made her feel safer. Quite a feat for a badass mage woman who could use a sword like she did.

Contemplating all that, how could I try to strain the boundaries? How could I risk pushing her away, making someone who felt safe to her suddenly unsafe? Nope. I wanted her, desired to do more than holding hands and kissing her, but I was going to make damn sure it was something she wanted before we broached the subject, even if we'd already crossed that particular line. Most of the people I'd known in my life would call me a pussy for that. Tell me no real man wouldn't press for what she obviously wanted anyway. They could all fuck themselves. Brin was not a piece of meat—or piece of ass—and I wasn't some dominating asshole. If that made me weak, so be it. Let someone say it to my face.

We slept, and only slept, and surprisingly, I woke up refreshed and ready to do what we needed to get done. When the muted sun coming through the cracks in the window shutters woke me, I kissed the sleeping moonwisp on the cheek, stroked her hair back out of her face, and extricated myself from her embrace.

After she roused and we met Tip for breakfast, we headed out into the city. We had things to do.

The mist seemed to allow more sunlight through than the day before. Thinking back, it had to have. That sunbeam coming through the window must have been a fluke thing. Maybe some kind of omen? I wasn't sure if those were a thing in this world, but I'd take it as a good sign.

"How'd you sleep?" I asked.

"Great," Tip said. "I'm still not used to sleeping in beds. I've always slept under a bush or in an alley somewhere. I could get used to soft surfaces like these beds."

I traded looks with Brin. She was thinking the same thing as me. The inn's beds were pretty uncomfortable. Hard, scratchy, straw-filled mattresses that had dips and lumps in them. It kind of made me feel bad for Tip and the life he'd led up until now. Until he opened his mouth again.

"Now if I could only find someone who would fuck me in that bed, things would be perfect."

*Oh, Tip.*

Brin answered my question, helping me forget what the satyr had just said. "I slept well. I feel energized. My magic has mostly recovered from my use yesterday. Thank you." She squeezed my hand, which was held in mine.

"You're welcome. So, I think it's probably best for us to search out the other shops and market stalls we haven't been to yet to see if we can find magic weapons. Preferably ones we can afford. While we're doing that, we can search for other places where we might be able to lure Arinthalas to so we can ambush him. If we have enough time left, we'll see if we can take a boat ride to scope out the island."

"That is reasonable," Brin said. "Do not forget we will try to speak with Arinthalas if we see him."

"Yeah. Sure, that too." I didn't really see us doing that. The man attacked me on sight, even if Tip said I was rude to him. It's not like he'd forget that we tried to kill each other.

That started me thinking. *Tried* to kill each other. I couldn't get it out of my mind that he'd come out ahead in all our exchanges. Without the umbrenix, he'd cut me, even if barely. I hardly needed Brin to heal it, though she did as soon as she saw the small wound. I never put a mark on him. I wasn't one to let mistakes get into my head, but I also couldn't underestimate the elf. If we attacked him at his home, on his own turf, what advantages would he have? We'd have to be careful, and I'd have to keep going over every bit of our fight to analyze his style. When we met again, I needed to be able to kill him. Or at least incapacitate him so I could ask any questions he wouldn't answer before we started to fight.

I had no doubt it would take me beating him, maybe torturing him after I'd defeated him, to get the answers I wanted. That was fine with me. This fucker was the one person who could tell me where Lucas was. I was not going to pass up that opportunity.

# CHAPTER THIRTY-NINE

We scoured the city, going to every shop we hadn't already been through, looking for something that would enable us—and by us, I mean Tip—to harm the umbrenix. It was a simple desire: any weapon that had been infused with the power to do magical damage would apparently work on the monsters.

"Nope." We were at the last seller of weapons and equipment Brin knew of in the city. Patar Anak was a sturdy dog beastkin, a solidly built man with several scars visible, including one on the side of his face that had taken part of one ear and continued down onto his cheek. "Good luck finding an enchanted weapon anywhere in the city. The mist lurkers have been active lately and with some of the reports of the shadow men from around Edgewood, folks buy any weapons like that as soon as they're for sale. Which they aren't, most times. They're rare enough without all these troubles. I have a list of people waiting for anything I can get my hands on."

"Well, shit," I said after we left Patar's shop, the Edge of

Danger. "I guess that means we won't be finding you anything magical, Tip. Not here, anyway. Sorry, buddy."

"If only my goddess weren't missing," Brin said. "Before she disappeared, and her magic with her, I could enchant a well-made weapon to increase its damage magically."

"Wait. What? You never told me you could do that."

"I *could* do that. Before. I no longer can. I have not the magic for it."

Tip scoffed. "Psht. Why don't you and Gar spend a whole day in your room and he can put his...magic in you. He can fill you up and then you can do it. Enchant the weapon, I mean. Well, the other *do it*, too."

I raised my hand to smack the satyr, but Brin answered him verbally.

"I cannot. It's true that Gar can help me to recover my mana faster than would otherwise occur, but that is not the issue. One must understand the difference between magic as an entire entity and mana or magical power as a fuel source.

"Take a campfire as an example. The fire burns hot and does work, that of heating all around it and providing light. In order for it to create the heat, however, it must have fuel to burn. If you do not put wood or coal into it, it cannot last. If, however, the fire has already gone out, you can pile wood on top of it for hours and it will never generate heat because there is not the flame to consume the fuel and do the work.

"So, too, my metaphorical wood pile is low. I am not capable of using the magics I managed before because I have not the ability to hold or channel that much magical fuel, or mana. To continue with the metaphor, my wood bin is now so small, I cannot hold more than a few logs. While it is advantageous for me to have more mana because I recover it so slowly now, I can only perform the most basic of spells, which is why I am trying to regain the items the goblins took from me. With those, I can use some of the magic I have lost because the item does most of the work, fueled by less mana than what I would need to cast it without the item."

I nodded at her explanation. "That makes sense, but if a particular spell takes too much mana or magical ability to cast, how can you still cast it with the items?"

"The items act as a catalyst of sorts, allowing me to utilize the spells they were created for with less mana. I spent years acquiring those items and it grieves me that they were stolen. I had a fraction of the power I used to possess, but at least it was something. I feel useless since I have been without them."

I squeezed Brin's hand. "You're not useless. You've gotten a few items back and you're very good with the sword. Plus, you know more than we do about everything in this world. I'd have never gotten this far without your help."

The blue woman gave me a small smile, though I could tell she still felt bad about losing most of her potency. I could understand. If I suddenly couldn't walk or use one of my arms, I'd feel the same way.

We were not done with disappointment for the day, however. During our time finding all the shops that eventually ended up doing nothing for us, we hadn't seen even one white hair of Arinthalas. We even made some offhand inquiries, usually together with our direct inquiries about Lucas, but we got no information about either. We weren't sure if the elf stayed on his island and had his people take care of things on the mainland or if we had unlucky timing. Either way, it was three strikes: no word on Lucas, no information on Arinthalas, and no magical weapons.

We dragged ourselves back to the inn and essentially repeated the night before. Eating, listening for information —and coming up empty—then Brin and me settling in together to get some sleep. I spent an hour attuning to my siangham, practice I desperately needed. I still couldn't do anything significant with it, though I did feel a stronger familiarity with the item. Brin encouraged me, telling me it would be worth it once I encountered a breakthrough. I just had to keep at it.

We kissed and cuddled, but that was it as far as doing anything intimate. Her mana replenished, and I fell asleep holding the gorgeous moonwisp. Not bad at all, though of course I did think about many delicious things we *could* do. In good time, I thought.

First thing the next morning, we headed to the dock area. We did a sweep, including where we'd seen Arinthalas before, hoping to find him there, but had no luck again.

"We need to get a boat," I said. "The only thing we have left to do is to go near the island so you can look for umbrenix, Brin."

"I am sure I can find someone who will rent us a boat," Brin told me.

"Actually rent it or have us pay them to pilot it? It won't look good circling around Arinthalas's island, searching for things, with someone else there. We could probably get a rowboat, but that's kind of a long way to row. Won't it look strange?"

"There is no need for that. I am accomplished at sailing."

"You are?"

"I am. We will convince a boat owner to rent his craft to us and I will pilot it."

Tip and I traded looks. Damn, Brin was full of pleasant surprises.

We did find an old man who was willing to let our beautiful companion take his boat out. I chalked it up to not only people being more trusting in this world but also that when the enticing moonwisp fluttered her eyelashes at the man, he nearly forgot his name. It was nice to know that some things about this world were the same as mine. A hot woman could basically get anything she wanted. She paid him in advance for renting the small watercraft for an entire day, to be returned midmorning the next day. It wasn't cheap, which was a concern because our supply of coin was evaporating more quickly than was comfortable, but it was a necessary expense.

We lucked out—for a change—and the bay was relatively calm. The little sailboat we were in wasn't going to break any speed records, but we moved much faster than we would have in a rowboat.

"I didn't realize it was so far," I said as we glided along. It dawned on me when we'd gotten to what seemed like the only spot within a hundred miles that wasn't socked in completely with fog. From a cliff on the northern part of the bay earlier, I could see for miles across the water, but I still didn't see Arinthalas's island. Come to find out that it was quite a distance away. Like the distance to Catalina Island from the Los Angeles coast.

"It is a fair distance," Brin said.

When we finally reached the island, which I'd been watching gradually get bigger, I wasn't too impressed. Arinthalas's manor house was basically a big tower with a cluster of outbuildings scattered around it. There was no wall or battlements, only the residence.

The island itself was barely larger than the estate, mostly rocky coast and a forest that had been carved up severely to build the structures. A legitimate dock, suitable for small boats like the one we were in, sat on a flat stretch of stone, two other vessels bobbing alongside it.

I didn't see any people.

"Can either of you two see anyone?" I asked.

"I've been looking, but nope," Tip said.

Brin shook her head. "I do not. Are you confident in the practice you have had on our trip here, Gar?"

"Yeah, I'm good."

"Then please take the tiller while I use my Lunar Light spell from the bracelet to search for anything or anyone hidden. Such as the umbrenix."

I took control of the boat and Brin braced herself along the side. She didn't do anything overtly to show that she'd cast the Lunar Light spell, but her eyes narrowed and she swung her head methodically, searching the island as I brought us around it.

We circled Arinthalas's home three times. Brin searched with her magic, while Tip and I looked for places to sneak up on the manor house and tower. As I aimed the boat back toward the mainland, we discussed what we'd seen.

"I saw only three of the shadows," she said. "I cannot be sure there are not more within the structures, but I feel that they would be outside, though that is purely assumption. I don't know much about the shadow people. The spell does not sense people or things inside a building, so I don't know how many there are within. Arinthalas, no doubt, but as to servants, guards, or others, I am unsure."

"We found some spots that could be good for sneaking

into the manor," I told her. "We'll probably want to go in at night, though that won't make us harder to see for the umbrenix. I'm assuming they have good dark vision?"

"I would expect, though I have never seen or heard anything conclusive that states as much."

"Okay, so the island is easy to get onto, the manor easy to infiltrate, and you only saw three of the umbrenix. It sounds like that's our best shot. None of the other options worked out. What do you say we eat an early dinner, get a little rest, then hit the island tonight? I'm sick of waiting."

# CHAPTER FORTY

If the misty streets of Greyveil were spooky and ominous in the daytime and early morning, they were doubly so at night. There were still plenty of patrons left in the common room as we passed through, though far fewer people on the streets. The fog created glowing orbs around the oil lamps on poles that attempted to light the streets, only succeeding in making targets for us to aim for as we walked toward where we'd docked the boat.

Brin used her Lunar Light spell to navigate easily through the mist, holding my hand the entire time to mitigate the magic she used. Using her light spell to create a globe of illumination would only call attention to us.

"Are you sure you should be using magic right now?" I asked. "We're probably going to need every drop of mana you have when we end up fighting."

"Holding your hand, I lose little overall," she told me. "We should be able to replace the deficit, if any, before we strike at the home of Arinthalas."

We made it to the boat without being spotted. At least, I

thought so. No one called out and, as far as I knew, there was no one around us for most of the trip. Brin had assured me that she could see right through the obscuring fog with her spell active, so I trusted that we remained unnoticed.

"Am I the only one who feels like we might get killed at any second by a werewolf or one of the mist monsters from the forest?" Tip asked, saying aloud exactly what I'd been thinking. It was eerie walking through the mist, like an old horror movie.

"The city's protections are adequate to keep the monsters from stalking the streets," Brin said. "There are guards, but more importantly, there are magical wards against creatures."

I swung my head, though it didn't do anything to help me see in the fog. "Do they work on the umbrenix?"

Brin stopped. "I...don't know. I am sure Arinthalas knows of the wards. If he is clever, he would have made sure they cannot block his minions. We were within the city limits when he commanded them to attack us, after all, though near the edge."

Great. So we couldn't be attacked by anything *except* for the ones most likely to attack us.

"Fear not," she continued as she started walking again. "With my vision magically enhanced, I will see the creatures before they can surprise us."

I shared a look with Tip. I trusted Brin, but what she said hadn't made me feel much better.

We arrived at the boat and set sail. Though they didn't seem to affect the preternatural fog, gentle winds still blew in the middle of the night. Enough to sail, thankfully. After Brin assured us she could see well enough to navigate the craft, we headed for the island.

The trip seemed to take many times longer than earlier in the day, but we finally reached a small side dock we'd found during our search in the daylight. We moored the boat and gathered on the small dock. I knelt, searching the darkness, the weathered wooden plank hard under my knee.

"At least the mist is less here," I whispered, not wanting to interrupt the silence. The soft lapping of waves against the dock, our boat, and the shore seemed loud and subdued at the same time. "How is your mana, Brin?"

"It is nearly what it was when we left the inn. Perhaps we should wait here, our hands entwined, as I recover it."

I caught Tip rolling his eyes. *Well, just wait, buddy.*

I pulled Brin to me and kissed her. She made a little squeak at first, but then relaxed in my arms and kissed me back. I couldn't get enough of her lips and lingered, reveling in the feel of her skin on mine, our tongues tickling each other's. I finally pulled away, solely because it was ridiculous for us to make out at the gate to our enemy's home.

"Did that do it?"

"What?" The moonwisp was a little breathless. "Oh. The magic. Yes, it replenished me to a level that is more than when we left our inn. Thank you. That was fine thinking."

I grinned at her. "I figured that would be faster. And nicer."

"Ahem. Yes. Nice." Her eyes were locked on mine, almost glowing in the moonlight. I stared back.

Tip cleared his throat softly.

"Right," I said. "Can you find any umbrenix for us, Brin?"

"I shall do my best."

I was regretting that we hadn't been able to find anything for Tip to use that could hurt the umbrenix. I almost offered him my siangham to use, but Brin had already told me that though it was made of magical materials, it wasn't magic itself—not enchanted—so it couldn't harm the shadows. Me being able to hurt them was because of that explanation she and Qamara had given, that I didn't have magic for the shadows to use against me, but it was still a little fuzzy. It all boiled down to the siangham doing no good in Tip's hands. Besides, he was still shit with close-quarters combat.

He was going to have to tag along and try to stay out of the way of the shadows. I just hoped he'd be able to help with Arinthalas himself, if necessary. Or any non-umbrenix minions.

We found the first of the shadow men not too far away. It was standing there, almost like it was sleeping on its feet. Brin pointed it out and I tried my best to sneak up on it.

The umbrenix didn't really have faces, but something about the way the monster was positioned, I thought maybe its senses were directed away from me. I hoped to hell I was right because I was not some super-ninja who could move without sound and all that stuff. I stalked slowly toward it, but I didn't have any illusions I'd get all the way to the point where I could kill it before it knew I was there.

It was no surprise when, maybe two or three paces from the thing, its head snapped to me and it raised its shadowy claws to slash. By that time, though, I was close enough.

I lunged, twisting to evade the claws that were still coming up, and rammed my siangham into its head. I let my momentum take me past it and I rotated to punch my knife through the area where eyes would be in a human. After all I'd been through so far, the resistance when I stabbed or cut the monsters gave me the willies. It wasn't as much as a regular body, but it wasn't what one would think of a monster made completely of shadow, either. Creepy. Slimy. Unnatural.

The umbrenix twitched as it fell to the ground. I waited, crouched over it, to see if it would move again. Also to figure out if it had somehow called another of its kind to us. After more than a minute with nothing happening, I waved for Brin and Tip to join me.

"You're sure you've never heard anything about whether or not the shadows can communicate without sound, or on some higher frequency or something? They can't let other umbrenix or Arinthalas know they're being attacked?"

"I have never heard of such," Brin whispered. "No one knows how they communicate, whether it be telepathically—if they even have brains—magically, or in some other way. I'm sorry."

"Someone is really going to need to study these things. I don't like not knowing if one has sounded some kind of alarm."

She took my hand, after I sheathed my knife. I didn't like being restricted like that in case we were attacked, but it was important that we keep her magic level as high as possible. She was going to be using her Lunar Light spell until we got to a place that was better lit, like inside one of the buildings.

We found three more umbrenix before we got to the first structure. I did my best to kill them before they sounded an alarm or escaped to report, but the last one made my heart drop to my feet.

I'd tried to sneak up on it like I had the others, but it detected me sooner than I liked. That meant it was prepared for battle.

I'd noticed that the ones I'd fought had varying levels of skill in combat, just like people. It was my luck this one was more skilled than the others. It was still primarily an offensive fighter, with little thought to defense, but its attacks were more precise and slightly faster than the others.

With my weapons and my abilities, it wasn't a true threat by itself, but it apparently realized after a few exchanges that it wasn't going to kill me.

So it ran.

It surprised me enough that I didn't react in time to catch it. In an open run—or glide, or whatever the hell the things did—I couldn't match it. I drew back my knife to throw it.

Several shapes that glinted in the moonlight shot toward the umbrenix, nailing it in the back and legs. The attack interrupted whatever form of locomotion the thing used and allowed me to catch up. I rammed both weapons into its back and head repeatedly until it stopped moving.

Brin and Tip caught up. I was breathing heavily from my sprint.

"What was that?" I panted.

"Water Spike. It uses more mana than I would like, but I saw no choice."

"Good call. We can't let them report. We don't know how many other shadows there are or what else Arinthalas has here by way of defense. We've already seen more than you detected when we looked earlier."

Brin's face dropped, like I'd chastised her for doing something wrong.

"No," I said. "I didn't mean that as an accusation. You

told us there might be some in the buildings when we were scoping the place out. It's not your fault. You're doing great. Thanks for the save. There was no way I was going to catch that thing." I put my hand on her cheek. "You probably used a lot of your mana on that, huh?"

"I did. Perhaps we—"

I interrupted her with a kiss. Yeah, I know. Not the time, right? Wrong. She needed some of her magic power back. I had a way to give that to her. Simple.

Plus, I really did like to kiss her.

Brin continued to search for umbrenix but didn't find any others. As one, the three of us flitted across a courtyard and to the largest of the buildings. Within, lamplight illuminated the windows, promising us encounters with creatures other than the shadow men.

"Are you both ready?" I asked. "There may be people in there besides Arinthalas. You'll get a chance to use those weapons now."

Tip nodded. Brin squeezed my hand.

The door we found was unlocked. We opened it and passed through.

The hallway we entered was what I would have expected of a power-hungry, politically minded elf lord. Wood paneling, thick carpet running down the center, tapestries and small pieces of sculpture sitting on shelves on the walls, and light provided by oil lamps, made me wonder how extravagant the rest of the house was.

"Where to?" I asked. Both Tip and Brin shrugged. "Okay, we'll wing it."

We ghosted through hallways, taking doors when we thought they might lead somewhere, moving toward the center of the structure—as close as we could tell—because I figured that was where Arinthalas would be.

In more than half an hour of searching, we saw only one other person. A woman with livery similar to what the driver of the carriage had worn. Blue and black with some kind of symbol on the chest that looked like squiggles. The sheets and blankets she carried dropped to the floor and she let out a strangled cry when she saw us.

"We're not going to hurt you," I told her. "Not unless you attack us. Where is Arinthalas?"

It took Brin asking her the same question multiple times before she answered.

"In the trophy room. Ahead, third door on the left, down the hall to the double doors."

"Thank you," I told her. I picked up what she'd been carrying and handed them back to her. "You should stay out of the area of the trophy room."

She nodded silently, clasping the disheveled linens to her chest.

Her directions were accurate and we soon found ourselves at the double doors. I wasn't sure how I felt about not meeting any other resistance. It only meant I expected to be met by guards, umbrenix, Arinthalas himself, and defensive measures in the room ahead of us.

"Anything you can suggest?" I asked my companions. "It's probably a trap, or at least a big group of enemies."

"The longer we debate, the more time they will have to prepare," Brin said. She held her sword at the ready, but I was more concerned about how much magic she'd used already.

"Fair enough. Be careful, especially with umbrenix. Tip, if you can use your bow, that's the best thing. Just don't shoot us in the ass. Arrows only in the bad guys, okay?"

"Sure. I'll shoot them in the ass." He chuckled weakly.

“I’d prefer the head or heart or throat, but yeah, you’ve got the idea. Let’s do this.”

I prepared to kick the door open, but paused. I figured I might as well check the lock. The handle turned and the latch clicked. Huh. It was unlocked. With one more look at my friends, I threw the doors open and darted inside.

# CHAPTER FORTY-ONE

There were no arrows or fireballs or even multitudes of troops waiting for us as we entered the room. The trophy room looked more like a museum. Shelves, free-standing cases with glass tops, and items displayed proudly in glass-fronted cabinets dominated the room. There were no trophies as I was used to seeing them. No figurines on bases like a sports award. Instead, some few familiar items and many other unfamiliar ones dominated the space. Many pieces stood displayed, easily visible with the room lit brightly by braziers and lamps. There must have been hundreds of different items.

An analog clock, a wireless phone, an early tablet, and more exotic things like black powder firearms were mixed with alien-looking objects that I doubted came from Earth. They called this dude Arinthalas the Collector. The name seemed appropriate.

The man himself stood near a large fireplace across the room, a curious smile on his face. He looked the same as when I'd seen him before, but now that neither of us were moving, I caught more details. The long white hair shone in the firelight, gathered back behind his sharply pointed elven ears. He looked to be dressed for a formal ball, with a white shirt of soft cloth underneath a heavy jacket that, while formal, had the style of armor. It even had semi-stiff shoulder pads of cloth that wouldn't do much against a sword but cut a striking figure. An elaborate brooch, a torque, bracelets, and rings on his fingers all glittered, some even glowing faintly. The man's narrow, sharp-chinned face oozed arrogance.

I wanted to punch him in the face repeatedly, just because.

But I had a lot of other reasons to want to attack Arinthalas, not the least of which was wanting to know where Lucas was.

"Where is my friend?" I growled.

"Tch, tch, tch. Do they have no manners in the world from which you come? That is no way to start a conversation."

I put aside my anger for a moment to scan the room again, more carefully this time. I didn't see any other people. With how brightly lit the space was, I was certain there were no umbrenix hiding nearby as well.

I scowled at him. "I'm not here for a social visit. You know where I'm from. Your creatures took my friend, too. Where is he?"

He waved an elegant, manicured hand in the air. He even had ruffles at his wrist. "I know nothing of your world, except for the trinkets I collect from it. There are many my shadows hunt in. I don't know which you come from and I do not care to find out."

"My friend. He's got dark skin, wearing clothes like my pants here. He was taken by your umbrenix. Where is he?"

"If he was taken, then he's dead."

"I was taken also, yet here I am."

"Alas, yes. No matter. I'll take care of that little problem shortly. You have caused me some amount of irritation. Do you know how hard it is to get more umbrenix from the master? How *do* you kill them anyway? Their skills are formidable and it takes potent magic to harm them."

"The same way I'm going to kill you. Good old-fashioned ass-kicking."

The white-haired elf chuckled. "Oh, how droll. You will find that I am not such as the shadows are. I am, simply put, too much for you to handle." He sighed. "If it is proof that you want, I am not averse to providing you an education. We have crossed weapons once already. Please do try to make it more interesting this time. If I am going to waste precious moments dealing with you rabble, at least provide me with some engaging training or entertainment."

The man lifted a familiar sword from a table next to him and withdrew the weapon from the scabbard. The same gently curved blade, reflecting the firelight.

He darted forward, several steps ahead of me. I drew my knife and siangham, figuring they would be better against his sword than fighting empty-handed. It was a toss-up. Both my weapons were short, not ideal against a sword. He'd moved so quickly that neither Brin nor Tip had been able to target him with spell or arrow until I was too close and they lost the opportunity.

Arinthalas started with a lunging thrust that he morphed into an upward slash and then a horizontal cut from my right to left, followed by a diagonal slash downward from left to right.

Of course, each of his movements were reactions to my own response, after the first one. As the thrust came in, I took half a step to the right and tapped the sword off its trajectory with my siangham. For the upward slash I pivoted to my left and bashed his blade to the side with my knife, which was sitting along my forearm as I held it in a reverse grip. The horizontal cut I slammed downward with my knife while pivoting back with my right foot and simultaneously thrusting in with the tip of my siangham at the elf's head.

He tilted his head just enough that my strike missed him and as he continued with his diagonal slash, I shifted my hips to swivel my body, spun the siangham into a reverse grip, and blocked the blow with the length of the weapon braced against my forearm. I wasn't sure it was going to take the punishment, though Brin had assured me the magical materials were tough. Happily, she was right and the sword skittered off the siangham's length and past any part of my body it could cut.

As the sword went wide, I swiveled my hips again and stabbed backhanded with my left hand holding my knife.

Arinthalas brought up his shoulders and arms while stepping back with his left foot, his blade blocking my knife. He smoothly turned the motion into a horizontal slash from my right to my left, which I met with both my weapons, crossed in their reverse grip configuration while moving my right foot toward his blade to maintain my stable stance.

My body was in a perfect position, so I fired off a side kick with my left foot, but the elf backstepped away from it. He slid his sword away from where my weapons held it in check and lashed out at my kicking leg, but was too slow to catch it before I brought my limb back.

Arinthalas nodded his head, humming at himself.

"You fight well. One would almost think your resemblance to the hero Kael the Blur was not only coincidence."

I didn't answer, having no desire to banter with him. If he wanted to chat about Lucas and where he was, that was one thing, but I wasn't about to trade compliments with him.

A twang sounded in the room and Arinthalas brought his sword across his body, cutting an arrow out of the air. I glanced over at Tip, pulling another shaft from his quiver and looking frustrated.

Arinthalas narrowed his eyes for a moment, almost like he was in pain. I wondered what he was doing, but then it became all too clear. Three umbrenix glided into the room from somewhere. It looked like they materialized from the shadows in the very corners of the room.

They headed straight for my friends. The motherfucker knew they couldn't do much against them, with Brin watching her magic use and Tip without magical weapons. The moonwisp made the motion I'd come to recognize as her Push spell, basically thrusting her palm out as if she was pressing on them physically. It sent the shadows spinning back, but as soon as the effect passed, they continued toward the two.

The elf had his haughty smile plastered on his face. He knew what I was thinking, trying to decide if I could help them. If I did, he'd come after me while my back was turned. I couldn't do that. They were going to have to handle themselves for the time being. I growled and flipped my knife in my hand so I held it in a standard grip.

I guess Arinthalas took that as a sign because he charged in again. This time, he didn't try fancy attacks, but stuck to basics. He lunged in, his front foot stomping the ground as he delivered three lightning-fast downward diagonal strikes, coming at me from my left to my right twice and then from my right to my left before blending his attack into a straight vertical attack down at my head.

I stepped back with my right foot and brought my siangham up diagonally, braced on my forearm. The sword deflected off and Arinthalas brought it up and down again so quickly I could barely follow it with my eyes. I flipped my grip on my knife and redirected it with a clang off my inward parry.

The sword swept around and came down again, this time in a downward cut from my right to my left. I torqued my hips and brought the siangham up again for an outward and upward diagonal block.

Again, the elf brought the sword down in the vertical strike. This time, I pivoted, whipping my right foot in toward my opponent's body. With both weapons along my forearms, I pushed the sword outward. The move didn't need much force, since the blade was cutting downward and only needed a nudge.

I was now inside Arinthalas's guard and took advantage of it. Leaving my knife still in contact with the sword, a maneuver called checking, I straightened my right arm to deliver a backhand jab with the point of my siangham.

The elf's reflexes were good and he jerked both arms toward his right, parrying my blow. I hadn't expected it to land, though I knew staying inside his guard would pay off. He flicked the sword around and using mostly his wrists, cut at me horizontally, coming from directly in front of me with the way I was standing.

I brought both of my weapons up to block the attack, giving myself room in case he tried to twist or do something clever with his blade. My siangham and knife were vertical and stopped the attack immediately. Leaving the knife to check the sword, I snapped out a fast and brutal back elbow into Arinthalas's face. I heard his nose crunch and he stumbled back a step.

Just enough distance for my next move.

I cocked my hip and fired off a strong side kick with my right foot, landing my heel and the edge of my foot onto his belly. With a huff of breath, he left the ground and slammed into one of his display cases several feet away. The entire thing exploded in a shower of glass. The elf rolled away, recovering his feet more quickly than I thought he could. Impressive, I had to admit.

I set my guard, ready to continue, but then spotted some items that had fallen from the case. Most didn't draw my attention at all, but one did. A Hamilton Khaki Field Mechanical Watch. With a leather band. The same worn leather band I'd seen for years.

Lucas's watch.

"Nooooo!" I screamed. "You motherfucker. I'm going to—"

Brin yelled in frustration and pain as one of the umbrenix slashed her with some of the spikes along its arm. I shifted my eyes from Arinthalas—still slightly dazed—to my friends. Two of the shadows were going after Brin, one of which had injured her, and the other was chasing Tip.

Fuck! I had to help my friends. Sure, I'd spent the last several years of my life trying to keep myself from getting involved with other peoples' problems, but those two were my friends. If I didn't step in, those shadow monsters would kill them. I knew the elf would come after me, but if I was quick, maybe I could keep from getting a sword in the back.

I sprinted toward Brin.

# CHAPTER FORTY-TWO

The first umbrenix was easy. It was right next to Brin, the one that had hurt her, and it had its attention solely on her. I reached it at a run and slammed into it, causing it to twist. Before we crashed onto the floor, I punched my siangham into it and slashed its throat with the knife, still in a reverse grip. It didn't get up when I did.

Tip, the little scamp, managed to shoot an arrow as he ran away from the other umbrenix, though Arinthalas batted that one away with his sword as well. Rex hissed at the umbrenix and darted in, feinting attacks, but the lizard seemed to know he couldn't harm the shadow. I was impressed he was not hiding somewhere.

The elf reached me before I had recovered my balance fully and slashed at me. I twisted away from the attack, then battered the second one away, but he got me with the third attempt, cutting a long slash on my left arm. It didn't cause me any immediate weakness, so I didn't think he'd cut anything too important, but I was now bleeding. The clock was ticking. I couldn't lose blood for long before it slowed me down.

Brin used her Push spell again and both Arinthalas and the other umbrenix near her were knocked back. She drew her sword. I wasn't too thrilled about that because it meant she was thinking of attacking the elf. She was good with that sword, but he would take her apart. I had to get my slow ass back in the fight.

Tip had circled around and come near enough that the shadow running him down was close to me. I leaped at it, slashing with my knife and my siangham. It moved efficiently, evading my blows. From the time I'd come over to fight the shadows, the battle had moved from technical and classical fighting to downright brawling. Even Arinthalas's slashes at me were now sloppy and inefficient, though at least one had obviously been effective.

It was the same with me. I continued to throw my weapons out, scrambling to get a piece of the monster before the elf recovered from his knockback. Frustrated, I dove at the umbrenix and slammed it to the ground, much like its earlier companion. The difference was that now I was not as controlled. Lacking precision, I decided on quantity.

Using both weapons, I went sewing machine on its ass. I punctured parts of its body as fast as I could, hoping to hit something vital. It squirmed, trying to slash me with its claws, and we were still rolling from my body slam, so it was the best I could do. It caught me with a few of those spike things lining its body, but the wounds weren't too serious. I got a few good shots to its head and it suddenly stopped moving. Good enough for me.

I rolled to my feet, but not fast enough. One of Arinthalas's slashes caught me on the hip, opening up another cut. It was also shallow, but it still let my blood leave my body.

Not good.

Luckily for me, the last umbrenix trusted in its master's skills. It went after Brin and I came up behind it and slashed its throat with my knife while punching my siangham into its back repeatedly. I slammed the point of the knife into its head, finishing it off.

Almost out of my field of vision, Brin's blade went for the elf. He disdainfully smacked it away with his own and counterattacked, almost lazily. Brin dove for the ground, rolled, and came to her feet several paces away, having evaded his strike. I took her example and shoulder-rolled away from the shadow I'd just killed just as Arinthalas swung at me again. This time I dodged the cut.

All three umbrenix were gone. If Arinthalas had more, I assumed he would have already called them, so it was now three against one. In our favor, for once.

Brin and Tip—who now had his sword in his hand—bravely went after the elf. I couldn't let my friends fight him alone. They wouldn't last half a minute. Cursing the stinging hip and the other bleeding injuries, I charged in with flurries from my knife and siangham. I shifted both to standard grips, thrusting and slashing.

But the elf was an experienced fighter and he knew he was out of range of my short weapons. Instead, he deflected the attacks of my friends and lashed out to keep them at a distance without putting himself in danger of the other being able to strike him.

By the time I was close enough to threaten Arinthalas, he'd moved himself around another display case and then toward a wall, where he couldn't be completely surrounded by us. He lifted up a hand and I realized that I hadn't seen whatever magic he had yet in the fight. My heart dropped at unknown things he would do.

From his upraised hand, a wave of water formed. Not a small wave, but one at least six feet wide and more than that tall. It shot out full force, as if teleported instantly from a stormy ocean. Coming straight for us.

The water picked my friends up and threw them across the room, slamming them into a wall. For me, the effect was...surprising.

I'd expected to be thrown across the room, too, but the water splashed against me and seemed to go right through me. Mostly. It barely pushed me back half a step and then it was gone, passed by me. I grinned. I don't know what had happened, but I suppose I was a lucky son of a bitch, at least at that precise moment.

Arinthalas didn't view it that way. His white eyebrows shot up his forehead and his eyes grew wide.

I didn't have time to gape, or gloat, still losing blood. I lunged in, daring the elf to attack me. With the shorter weapons, it was more effective to close the distance in defense than to try to enter his guard while his sword was waiting. I was in luck, because Arinthalas seemed to be in shock from his attack not working on me. His blade licked out with testing slashes. It was far from the calculated, aggressive attacks of earlier.

Disjointed slashes from several different directions, individual cuts strung together rather than the smooth, flowing attacks of earlier came at me. Each attack I parried or evaded, waiting for the one that would give me the opening I needed. I had to do it quickly. I was already feeling weaker, slower, and when he regained his senses completely, shit was going to go down.

A thrust came and I parried it with my knife while spinning off to my right to stab at his head with my siangham. He got his sword up in time to deflect it and tried to slide his blade down to cut my hand, but I brought the knife up to redirect his strike in turn. The knife had a hand guard; the siangham did not.

A swirling figure eight pattern with the elf's blade forced me back, slapping at his sword with my weapons and backstepping to gain some room. I managed to push his blade with both my weapons and spin around to his side, but he was regaining his fluidity and becoming more efficient, his shock at the earlier magic fading. He stepped back and his sword remained at a steady guard position. Damn it. I'd squandered the time I'd had.

The arrogant smile came back and Arinthalas looked at me like I was something lesser. A servant, at most. More like some kind of animal that needed slaughtering. Or something he needed to scrape off his boot.

"It was enjoyable as long as it lasted," he said. I didn't mention his busted nose and he didn't mention the cuts he gave me. "Alas, I have more important things to do than to tarry here with you. It is too bad I couldn't spend the time to kill you cleanly without help, but such is the way of things. Enjoy your death. It's a shame I cannot drain your energy for the master."

Arinthalas put his hand up, like he'd done earlier when he'd conjured that wave. I thought for a moment he was going to try the same thing again.

Nothing happened.

The smile dropped off the elf's face and first confusion, then horror replaced it. I took the opportunity, closing the distance and slapping his sword aside and down with my knife so powerfully it almost left his hand. At the same time, I punched my siangham into his chest, then savagely cut his hand as I brought the knife around again. The sword did drop from his grip this time. I lunged, slamming him against the wall, keeping my eyes locked on him as his life drained away.

"How?" he asked in a weak voice. "My magic. It takes hold of another's magic and uses it against them. You..."

"I don't *have* any magic, you asshole." I shifted the weapon in his chest, opening the wound more. In a few seconds, he slumped and I was holding his entire weight up.

"Magic. Psht."

I let his body drop to the ground and slumped myself. I had to lean against the wall to keep from falling down.

Then I remembered Brin and Tip. I spun to find them both kneeling by the wall they'd smacked into. They didn't seem too damaged.

"Are you two okay?"

Brin raised a hand and Tip gave me a tired thumbs-up. I let out a breath.

"I think it's done," I said. "I wasn't able to get any information out of him other than that bit about 'the master.' I guess what we thought was right. He's working for Aeyr. *Was* working for Aeyr."

"I am sorry," Brin said, levering herself to her feet with a groan. "We have failed in our stated goal. I'm sure we can find someone who knows something about your friend, Gar."

"Yeah," Tip added. "We're with you, man. Whatever you need. We'll find him."

"Oh." I shuffled over to the case I'd knocked Arinthalas into earlier and fished around among the items and broken glass there. I finally found what I was looking for and held it up.

Lucas's watch.

It was definitely his. Not only did I recognize every nick and scratch and worn spot on the leather band, but when I turned it over, there was what I was afraid I'd find. The inscription. *The only thing necessary for the triumph of evil is for good men to do nothing.* His mother had gotten the old watch inscribed for Lucas's dad before he went overseas for the war.

I let out a huge sigh and suddenly felt like I was ninety-eight years old. My knees gave out and I dropped to the floor. Weakness infused my entire body and I suddenly didn't care if I was going to die in the next few minutes from blood loss.

"I will heal your wounds, Gar," Brin told me. She looked down at the watch with curiosity, but put a hand on my arm. A sudden surge of cooling energy ran through me. "I have not the power at the moment to heal you completely, but I have closed your cuts so you will not longer lose blood." She stepped around to look me in the eye. "Gar? Are you well?"

I held up the watch. Her eyes went from the one I wore on my wrist to the one in my hand. Her eyebrows drew down and she opened her mouth to ask, but then I saw the light in her eyes.

"Oh. Oh, no. I'm so sorry. It doesn't necessarily mean—"

"It does, Brin. There's no way they would have gotten this from him unless they killed him. Arinthalas is the Collector, right? He takes the things of the ones his minions kill. I was too late. Most likely, I arrived too late to begin with. He was probably gone before I'd even gotten here. I've always known it was a possibility, that he was killed and drained immediately like they tried to do to me. I just didn't..."

Brin wrapped her arms around me and pulled me closer. This wasn't the close interaction we engaged in so she could replenish her magic. This was one hundred percent her trying to soothe me. I let her wrap me up in her embrace as I remembered my best friend. And the assholes who killed him.

I'm not sure how long we stayed in the trophy room of Arinthalas the Collector, Brin holding me and whispering words I don't remember to soothe me. When we finally left, I only remembered pieces of the boat ride back to the mainland and traveling through the city streets as daylight broke over the misty city. Such as it was.

I do remember Brin bringing me food, feeding it to me, and snuggling with me as I slept for I don't know how long. It's all a blur until finally, suddenly, I regained my senses. Turning to the gorgeous blue woman lying next to me, I kissed her forehead and got out of bed.

"What will you do?" she asked.

I turned to see her green eyes locked on mine. "I need to go pee."

She chuckled.

"How long have I been out of it?" I said.

"About two days. Your body seems to have finally succumbed to the strain of coming to this world and all that's happened since. That, and...what happened."

I frowned. "Yeah. I'm sorry. I didn't even know I could sleep that long."

"You didn't. You got up for a few minutes at a time. To eat, to go to the privy. Then you went back to sleep."

"Thank you for helping me."

"Of course. We are connected. I would not leave you of my own will, Garfield Hailey. Know that."

I forced a smile. It barely took. "I do. Thank you. We should talk with Tip, figure out what we're going to do."

"Yes. He has been worried about you. He will be happy you are well."

I didn't think I'd go so far as to call myself well, but I got her meaning. "We should probably do something. I want to find out more about Aeyr, and how to get to him to kill him. We also need to find your goddess and restore your magic. Any ideas on where to go, what to do?"

She hesitated. It was probably me talking so easily about killing what amounted to a demigod. "I do not. Qamara told us that she saw one of my items in Forge-haven. Perhaps we could start there. It is a large city and there may be information that could help us decide where to go next."

"Oh! Items. We should have looted Arinthalas and his place. There might have been something in that trophy room that was valuable."

Brin laughed. "Tip said the same thing. We took a number of things, both from the room, from his nearby study, and off Arinthalas himself. Did you know that the spell he cast, the one to create that wave, was from this?" She held up her hand and a gorgeous ring gleamed on her middle finger. Waves and foam in what looked like blue-tinted gold stood out in relief on the ring's surface. There was even a hole through which I could see Brin's skin, nearly a perfect match for the blue waves and contrasting with the white metallic foam. "It is called, simply, the Wave Ring. I had one before. Not this one, but the same type."

"That reminds me. Why didn't it work on me? For that matter, he tried something there, at the end. He said that his magic allowed him to use other people's magic against them. He tried to use it on me and nothing happened. I'm assuming it's because I don't have magic."

"Yes. I believe your assumption is correct. By the same token, that is most likely why the wave had little effect. We have already explained how magic works in the world. It interacts with one's own magic and produces the results from that interaction. Without your own magic, the wave had nothing to harness, nothing to fix upon."

"Right. I remember. Qamara said that it won't make me immune, but it'll most likely minimize the effects, right? Ha! That arrogant bastard. He was good with a sword, but he always had that ace up his sleeve. He thought that in a pinch, he could just make me hurt myself. I'm glad I killed that asshole.

"So what else did we get? Any magic weapons for you or for Tip?"

"Sadly, no. We do have quite a sum of money as well as jewelry and other items we can sell to get more. I think, for at least the time being, we have solved our monetary concerns."

"Nice. Okay, so I guess we'll talk with Tip and see if he agrees to head to Forgehaven, wherever that is. See if we can find another one of your items and try to get some info that'll point us which way to go. Sounds about as good a plan as any."

"I will go fetch him, and his little companion. I believe that Rex is also anxious and he will be happy to see you as well."

"Yeah. Great. I can't wait."

Brin's musical laugh filtered back to me from the hallway as she headed to Tip's room. I took a long breath, then let it out in a sigh.

I looked to the ceiling. "Lucas, buddy. I wish I could have been faster. I'll get those fuckers, though. I won't stop until I burn all this shit down. I hope you're happy and resting up, my friend. Keep an eye out. I think you're going to enjoy the mayhem I cause."

# CHAPTER
# FORTY-THREE

Tip and Rex seemed happy I was back on my feet again. The little furcan skittered around excitedly, running circles around me, and Tip had his infectious smile on display. He joked around like it was no big deal, but Brin had already told me how worried he'd been. Traces of it lingered in his eyes even now. After petting the reptile for almost half an hour, we left him in Tip's room to go eat dinner in the common room.

I wasn't much in the mood for other people, but it was a nice meal and we took the opportunity to discuss what we'd do. The satyr literally didn't care, so what Brin and I had already talked about ended up being the plan. We'd head toward Forgehaven to try to find one of her items stolen by the goblins and then we'd decide what to do from there.

After dinner, Tip went to his room and I headed to mine. Brin walked alongside me, her hand in mine, like always. When we got to my door, I opened it and turned to face the moonwisp.

"Thank you for watching over me the last couple of days. Sorry to be such a problem."

"You're welcome," she said, "and you were no bother. I understand."

I looked into her gorgeous green eyes, thinking I wanted to kiss her. The curious look on her face stopped me. *What was that about?*

"Why are we standing in the hallway?" she asked.

"Um...I don't know. Do you want to come in?"

She laughed and I tried to figure out what I'd said that was funny. She squeezed my hand. "I understand. I failed to tell you and you did not notice."

"Notice what?"

"I gave up my room when we returned to the inn. With the money we have from Arinthalas and his items, it's no issue, but still it seemed wasteful to pay for three rooms when we use only two. I spent every moment in attendance over you."

"Oh," I said. "Oh!"

"You did not notice my things in your room earlier. I can see if there is another one available and—"

"No. I'm sorry, like you said, I didn't notice. I'm still a little out of things. A lot on my mind. Come on in. To *our* room."

We entered and settled on the bed, sitting side by side. Our hands were still clasped.

It was awkward. I didn't really feel like conversation, all that had happened too new. I tried to dredge up something to say, but failed spectacularly. We sat like that, silently for a time. My palms started feeling clammy.

"Your magic," I said abruptly. "How's your magic doing?"

"I have spent a lot of time snuggled against you and

holding your hand," Brin said. "I easily replaced the magic I used in the fight with Arinthalas."

"That's good."

"Thank you."

"You're welcome."

"While we speak on the subject, I wondered..."

I turned my head to look at her. We'd been sitting side-by-side and mostly staring at the wall. "You wondered what?"

She shifted on the bed so her body was turned more toward me. Not squarely, but she didn't need to turn her head all the way like I had. I mirrored her to face her more fully as well.

Brin took a breath, then spoke quickly. "Do you find my form pleasing?"

I blinked. "Your form? Are you asking if I like how you look, your body?"

"Yes." She chewed on her bottom lip so cutely, I had to keep myself from pulling her in for a kiss so I could answer her.

"I love how you look. Your face, your hair, and your exquisite body."

"Truly?"

"Of course. I mean, look in the mirror. You are gorgeous and fantastic and so..."

"So...?"

"So sexy."

Her blue cheeks darkened. "Thank you. I have been thinking that maybe we are not taking full advantage of your ability to help me recover my mana."

My lips raised in a slight smile. It felt like I hadn't done that in a very long time. It almost felt like a betrayal of Lucas's memories. It slid downward. She noticed.

"What is wrong?"

"Sorry. I was just thinking about Lucas. You were saying about your magic?"

"It would seem to follow that if holding hands with you helps me to regain some mana and kissing or snuggling you with more skin contact helps me regain more, then there may be a way to increase the rate I recover even more."

The smile pushed its way back. She was actually going where I'd hoped when she started. I made a show of putting on a pensive look and even scratched my chin. "That sounds reasonable. What do you have in mind?"

She blushed more deeply. "I have no definite—"

Though her shyness was adorable, sitting there and watching her, being so close, I had to let her off the hook. I leaned in and kissed her deeply, more so than the other times we'd kissed. In all those instances, I'd held back, not wanting to push her, but now, I let myself *feel* what I would do, rather than to *think* about it. She responded with a more passionate kiss than she'd ever given me.

Fleeting thoughts of what we'd been through, of what had happened, and how I was not in a great place mentally and emotionally flickered through my mind. I pushed them away and focused on the comfort of the moonwisp's lips and tongue engaging so enjoyably with mine.

I broke the kiss. "Brin, can I suggest we do a little more than hold hands, snuggle, and kiss? I would really like to explore your fantastic body, if that's okay with you. Even if you don't need the mana right now."

She nodded, keeping her eyes on mine. "Yes. That would be a good experiment."

"Is that what you want, an experiment?"

She was biting that bottom lip again. "No. To be honest, I have wanted more, Gar. I am inexperienced in such things, but I know that people feel pleasure with each other and I would like that with you."

"I would love that," I said. I put my empty hand on her bare leg, just above her knee. "How about I start with something I think you'll like and you let me know if it's too much? We'll find out together about this magic stuff and in the meantime, we can feel that pleasure you're talking about."

"Yes. I would like that."

"Me, too."

I put my hand on her cheek, stroking it with my thumb. Down to her chin and then back up to her lips, I grazed her so lightly, I barely felt the contact. She put her hand up and mirrored me. When her fingers brushed my lips, I kissed them, then took one into my mouth and sucked it softly.

Her breathing changed, speeding up and growing shallower. I smiled.

I went to her lips, but engaged only briefly before I kissed down her neck, then back up along her jaw line to her ears. She hummed as I kissed, nipped at her, and dragged my tongue across her soft blue skin.

As I worked on her with my mouth, I released her hand and brought mine up to her arm. She was toned, though not extremely muscular, and her skin was silky smooth. I stroked her upper arm and shoulder, feeling goosebumps rise at my touch. I shifted to kiss down her collarbone and over to the other shoulder and took part of her skin into my teeth.

"Uhhhhhn."

I smiled into her shoulder. "You like that?"

"I do."

"Not uncomfortable?"

"No." Her voice was dreamy, like she was going into a trance.

I kissed across her upper chest, exposed down to just above her areolae. I dragged my tongue across, dipping it into the exquisite cleavage she so kindly provided for me.

"Uhhhhhhhhhn."

She rolled her neck, even reaching up to massage the base and the trapezius muscle.

"Let's get in a better position," I said, kissing her on the mouth. "Sitting here half sideways is going to make our necks sore." I pulled my shirt off and tossed it on the floor, then slid up to the head of the bed and put my back against the wall, sitting with my legs spread. "Come over here. There's something I think you would enjoy."

She crawled toward me, but I turned her around so her back was against my chest, facing the same way as I was, sitting in between my legs. I wrapped my arms around her and hugged her.

"Mmmm. I think I do like this. The feel of your skin on me and being nestled against you like this is very comfortable."

I kissed the back of her neck. "I'm glad. Here's another cool thing about it." I turned her head so I could kiss the side of her neck, then brought it back and positioned her mouth so I could kiss her, both of our necks craning at a soft angle.

There was something very sensuous about kissing like this and it was having an effect. I wriggled to settle in, my lower parts expanding and firming already. With her self-proclaimed inexperience, I wasn't sure if she picked up on it, but she squirmed in the most delicious way, making herself more comfortable and making me a lot more uncomfortable, but in a good way.

I ran both hands down her arms, then back up. When I moved them inward, over her shoulders and across her upper chest, she sighed loudly. I could feel tension in the air, and in her. That anticipatory pressure when someone is closing in on a location you know you'll enjoy being fondled.

I dipped a finger into her cleavage, soft as a butterfly's wings.

"Huuuuhhhhhh."

I nibbled an ear and whispered. "Does that feel good?"

"Mmmm. Yes."

"More?"

"Mmmm-hmmm."

I pulled her ear with my teeth and slipped the finger down farther, burying it between her breasts.

I could picture the sight. I'd spent a fair amount of time inspecting her chest, though hopefully slyly enough she hadn't noticed, and the thought that I was finally touching them swirled energy through my torso and shot it directly to my groin.

As I kissed her neck and shoulder, I added another finger, then two, pressing it under her tight top until I could feel the small bumps on her areola and the larger shape of her nipple. It stood out proudly, pressing against the cloth, a firm little nub that felt absolutely perfect.

"Uhhhhhnnnnggg."

I bit her neck and she exhaled forcefully.

My other hand went into play, dipping under her clothing to pinch her other nipple softly.

"Ooooooh. Gar."

"Can I take your top off?"

"Yes."

I kissed the side of her face and hastily undid the straps

on her corset-like top. Once I'd loosened it, I pulled the clothing down, exposing both her firm breasts and more of her back. Leaning around, I kissed her again, my hands roaming to cup both her tits. She wriggled, dragging her back across my chest. I was heating up, some perspiration coating my chest, so instead of her skin dragging across me, it glided.

It felt so fucking good.

I resisted the shouting in my mind to pull on her nipples, to grab her tits hard, to take her right then and there. I breathed out, calmed myself, and traced the areolae by feel while kissing up her neck from the side. She turned her head and our lips met in a kiss as I continued to slowly and softly explore the full size and shape of her fantastic breasts.

Her nipples became rock hard and she moaned into my mouth, wriggling and gyrating her hips. I'm not sure if she understood what that did to my dick, which at this point was diamond-hard, but I wasn't about to complain. She broke away from my lips to take in a full breath and to treat me to an audible appreciation for what I was doing.

"Oooooh. Oh. Oh."

My right hand ran down her breast and to her belly, circling her navel under the bunched clothing there while my other was still busy lightly tweaking her nipple. Her motions increased, pressing harder against me and thrusting in reverse.

The longer skirt part of her ensemble came free when I loosened a few straps holding it tight to her waist. I pulled it off her and tossed it onto a nearby chair. The rest of her outfit, the miniskirt and corset part, slid easily down her hips and thighs and joined the other clothing on the furniture.

With her clad only in tiny panties, I slipped a finger under the cloth and dragged my finger along the edge while my other massaged her nipple.

All her motions stopped. Even her breathing. I wasn't sure if it was a bad thing or a good one. I took a chance that I understood what was happening.

I pushed the finger farther under the cloth until I reached a moist, warm nub of skin just above an opening. A slit.

"Oh! Uhnnnnnnggggg. Oh, oh. Oooooh."

She put her hands on her chest, smashing my hand onto her and squashing her breasts. She thrust her hips, pushing against my finger, moaning.

"More?" I asked.

"More!"

Kissing up her neck, I plunged my finger down farther. A waft of strong scent, like a cool breeze across a field of wild grass, caressed my face and nose, making my head spin. Her hairless, wet skin gave easily to my finger, letting it slide inside the slit and down to where it was even hotter and wetter. She moaned and hummed as I crooked my finger and inserted it into her.

"Ooooooh!"

Her body trembled and suddenly my finger was drenched with hot, creamy fluid.

*Damn! Already?*

Brin turned her head and kissed me hard. She bit down on my lip as her body jerked and she arched her back. In another moment, she tore her lips from me and froze again, all her muscles tight.

"Unnnnnnnggggg."

When her body relaxed, she slumped against me, aside

from a few small thrusts. My finger was still in her and every time I wiggled it, she moaned again.

"Brin?" I said.

"Mmmmm. Yes?"

"Can I taste you?"

Her breath hitched. "Taste...me?"

"Yes. Like what I'm doing now"—I wiggled my finger in her—"except with my tongue."

Her body tremored. "Your tongue?"

"Yes. If you'll let me."

She paused for long enough that I wasn't sure she'd let me. Then she turned her head to kiss me again. "Yes, but only if you show me how to do the same to you."

A dribble of pre-cum oozed its way out of my dick.

"You've got a deal."

# CHAPTER
# FORTY-FOUR

I squeezed out from behind Brinawynn and put my feet on the floor, taking my first frontal look at her nearly bare body.

*God, she's hot.*

"How could you even have asked me if I liked your body?" I asked. "Look at you. You're perfect."

She put one foot on the floor to come to me.

"No. Lie back."

Her eyes widened, then a slow smile appeared on her face. Brin slid her body down and lay back. Her slender form curled into an S shape, her toned and perfectly shaped legs curving up to her hips with her torso cocked slightly to accentuate her sumptuous hourglass waist. Her breasts, still substantial as they fought gravity, called to me, but not quite as much as the dark-spotted red panties she still wore. The darker cloth at the junction between her legs told me how much she'd enjoyed what we had just done.

I started at her feet, kissing her instep and dragging my lips and tongue up her left leg, from the shin to the calf, and along the side of her knee as her body wriggled.

"Mmmmm. What are you doing, Gar?"

"Do you like how that feels?"

"Yes."

"That's what I'm doing."

"Mmmmm."

I crossed over to her right leg and kissed up her thigh, taking some of her flesh into my teeth and pressing down.

"Oooh."

Up along the side, then over toward her inner thigh, my mouth kissed, licked, and nipped at her. When I reached her panties, I skipped over them to kiss up her belly, moving upward. I didn't abandon her lower body completely, though. My hand traced the same route, except on her left thigh instead of the right as my mouth teased her upper abs and reached the lower part of her breasts.

The same time my tongue traveled up the side of her breast and around to the center, my hand softly stroked her inner thigh, all the way up to where her panties were soaked.

"Oh."

I flicked her nipple with my tongue and dragged my finger across her wet underwear.

"Uhhhhhhnnn."

My head tilted so our eyes met and I pressed down on the wet cloth, rubbing it against her wet skin.

"Huhhhn. Huh-huh-huh."

I smiled and took her nipple into my mouth, sucking softly. My fingers stroked the front of her panties, up along the length of them, as her hips thrust forward and her breathing got heavier.

"Gar...I've never felt...aaahhhhh."

The moisture at my fingertips increased. She was *so* sensitive.

I slipped my hand under her panties, from the top this time, and felt her soaking wet skin. Her scent grew stronger, up to where I was thumb-wrestling her nipple with my tongue. Her aroma made my mouth water.

"Huh-huh-huh...ooooooh. Yes, yes." She thrust harder pushing, grinding her lips into my hand. I crooked my finger into her slit yet again and her back arched. When I added a little pressure on her clit with my thumb, her whole body tensed.

"Oh-oh-oh-oh. Unnnnngggghhhhh."

I brought my hand up and put my finger in my mouth.

"Mmm. You taste really good," I told her. I waited for a few seconds to see if she wanted a taste, and her slitted eyes rolled to me as her lips pursed. She didn't say anything about it. I didn't want to make her feel awkward, so I let it go. There was one more thing I wanted to do.

With a little nibble on her nipple, I moved up to kiss her. I made it short, since she was still panting, and I turned around to kiss down her body. When I got to her waist, I grabbed the edges of her panties and pulled them down and off, giving me the first look I'd had at her uncovered pussy.

It was a perfect flower, her bald lips plump and soaking wet, her creamy nectar slowly dribbling down her slit. The lips were a little darker than her skin, just shy of a blueberry color, matching her areolae perfectly. I took one more look up at her beautiful face as she continued to suck in breaths, her amazing green eyes trying hard to focus on me, and I dove in.

She was driving me crazy, so I didn't prolong things. I licked straight up her slit, from bottom to top, letting the tip of my tongue spread her inner lips the slightest amount.

"Oh! Huh-huh-huh. Your tongue is so soft and... uhhhhnnngggg."

She slammed the back of her head into the pillow, no longer watching what I was doing. A sound grumbled in her chest and her body tremored, jumping under my tongue. It was so fucking hot, I felt another dribble of pre-cum exit my dick.

Of course, her scent was stronger down there, and her taste more concentrated. I sucked her lips into my mouth and squeezed them with my tongue as Brin ground her hips into me. I put my hands on her tight ass and pulled her, ramming my tongue down deep into her.

"Uh-huh-uh-huh-uh-huh."

Then I moved up to the nub of her clit, teasing it out of its protective hood. I pressed directly on it with my tongue and put a finger into her.

Her body went wild. She bucked and moaned, thrashing not only up and down but back and forth. I put a hand on one of her breasts and squeezed hard, then pulled on a nipple.

"Gar. Oh-oh-oh. I've never...aaaahhhhhh. Huh-uh-huh-uh."

The inside of her canal tensed, massaging my finger as the little jerking motions of her body increased in frequency, almost like contractions. She put a hand over mine on top of her breast and dragged air from the room into her lungs.

I rode the tremors, reveling in them and the way she was reacting. Pushed my finger a little bit deeper, and crooked it. Finally, I took her clit into my mouth, sucking on it and pressing down lightly on it with my lips.

"Yes-yes-yes. It's going to happen again. I'm going to....unnnnnghhhhh. Oh-oh-oh. Ooooooh!"

All of Brin's lower body left the bed, her form becoming deliciously rigid. She contracted around my finger and more of her juices flooded out. I licked them up, slurping them down as she finally relaxed and sunk into the bed, panting.

She was a trooper, though, Brin was. It only took a couple of minutes for her to regain her breath. By that time, I'd moved up so I could kiss her, strands of her wet hair plastering against her face and mine. She looked at me, energy cracking in her eyes.

"Oooh, what is that taste?"

I ran my tongue across her lips and back around the bottom lip as well. "That's you. Your nectar. Your juices."

"Mmmm."

"You like it?"

She was already flushed from exertion, but her face grew to an even darker blue. "Is that...okay?"

I laughed and kissed her. "It is. I think you taste fantastic. I think you agree, and it turns me on."

She smiled and flicked her tongue out to lick the tip of my nose. "I do agree. Gar, show me how to make you feel like you just made me feel." It wasn't a question, but a command.

"Yes, ma'am."

She looked at me strangely and I wondered if "ma'am" was a thing in this world. At the moment, I didn't really give a shit.

She rolled me onto my back on the bed and got up. Standing there, looking over my body like I had with hers, she let loose a little growl in her chest that made my dick jump. Or, at least it tried to, still in the constraints of my pants and underwear.

She remedied that immediately, unhooking and unzipping my pants to pull them down, underwear included. Brin stood back and inspected my shaft from afar, hard, standing at attention and ready for *her attention*.

"I take it into my mouth like a banana?" she asked. "Or do I lick the length of it?"

"Yes," I panted in anticipation. "Whatever you think will feel best for me. Why don't you try what you're thinking and then we can go from there?"

"Mmmm."

Honestly, after what we'd just been through, and looking at the super-hot moonwisp standing above me, if she did anything short of punching me in the nuts, she would make me come. I was already so close. Another little pearl of pre-cum formed at the tip of my shaft. Her eyes locked onto it.

"You make slippery juices, too?"

"For you, Brin? Definitely."

"Mmmmm."

She moved onto the bed, taking my cock in her hand, and pulled it gently toward her, flicking her tongue out to lick the tip of my dick. My eyes crossed as her smooth flesh dragged across my sensitive skin.

She smacked her lips. "Mmmmm. I have not tasted that before. Salty, but pleasant. You have more of this?"

*Oh my God*. My shaft twitched violently and she made a startled sound. "Yes, a lot. You can coax it out."

Her hand grazed my frenulum and it pulled a sound from me.

"Uh-uhnnnnng."

She smiled, then rubbed me softly. Her dry hand dragged a little bit, but she was smart. She noticed—probably not the least of which because I winced a little—and she reached down to between her legs, where the residual juices still coated her skin. She brought her hand back up with more than should have been down there. She must be making more. The thought sucked out another bit of precum.

With her hand lubricated, she stroked my cock, surprisingly gentle but with just enough pressure to drag moans from me.

"God, that feels good, Brin. Uhhhnnnn."

She stopped and I looked up to find her with a quizzical expression on her face.

"Brin?"

"Thinking. Would it feel good for you if..."

Her eyes flicked from my cock, still in her hand, down to her own chest.

*Oh God, oh god. Did she just figure out on her own that...*

She pulled me by my legs so I was at the edge of the bed, then dropped my feet to the floor. Getting on her knees, she leaned in and put my dick in between her luscious tits. The warm, soft flesh surrounding my shaft made my head spin.

"Oooooohh."

Then, apparently by instinct, she moved her torso up and down, dragging my dick in between her tits. Up and down, up and down, she started jacking me off with her fantastic breasts, wet with perspiration and some of her own juices that she'd smeared on my dick. After four or five strokes, she brought her head down and put her mouth around my glans, swirling her tongue around it and applying the slightest amount of suction. Then it was back to rubbing her tits against me, pressing on them from the outside to increase the friction.

By now, my eyes had crossed and I gave up trying to watch her, though it was one of the single most erotic things I'd ever seen in person. The spectacularly beautiful and sexy blue woman continued to service my cock with her chest, stopping occasionally to put me in her mouth.

Honestly, I lasted a lot longer than I thought I would. I did everything I could to make it stretch on for longer, clenching and holding and trying to keep from exploding. Every second, it got harder to achieve.

After about the fourth cycle of her taking me into her mouth, she did something with her lips and tongue that touched a bunch of nerves at a time. Her chest still pressing into my legs and balls helped it along.

"God, Brin, I'm going to come."

She pulled my dick out of her mouth with a pop and squeezed my shaft with one hand, swirling it around. All the cum I'd built up from the frustrating snuggling and kissing rocketed out in thick, warm strands, splashing on her chest. A bit even reached her chin. My body convulsed and my hips pumped without my permission, my balls churning out all the precious sperm I had in me.

When I was done, and my dick stopped twitching, I looked at Brin, still on her knees and with a wry smile on her face. White strands of cum slid down between her amazing tits. She scooped a bit up with her finger and brought it to her mouth. She licked her lips.

"Maybe next time I should let you do that in my mouth," she said.

I chuckled weakly, still trying to catch my breath. "It would be less messy."

"Yes, it would."

She leaned over and took my cock in her mouth, sucking off the residual. I'd given it everything I had, though, so my shaft was rapidly softening. I actually felt like I was going to go right to sleep.

"Lie back. I will clean myself up and we will sleep, skin to skin."

"That sounds nice," I said, and wriggled back up so I was lying completely on the bed. "Sorry about the mess."

A few minutes later, the dream of a woman was snuggled against me in all her naked glory.

"That did some interesting things for my magic," she whispered, and kissed me softly. "We'll talk about it when we wake up and are on our way to Forgehaven."

# THANK YOU FOR READING WEAPONSMASTER 1!

I hope you enjoyed the book. Book 2 is already written and will be out soon, if it's not already out by the time you read this.

Want to know how you can support my writing so I can keep putting out more books? It's simple, let others know you like my stories, especially through leaving a review or posting about them. I also have a Patreon that you can join if you want to get early access to chapters for new books, see what's going on with cover art and upcoming series, want to take part in helping me to decide which way a story goes, or you just want to buy me a cup of coffee (which is the fuel that runs the entire process!). You can check it out here: patreon.com/PhilAerix

Also, if you want to get a similar standalone story for free, I've written Elf Queen just for you. You can pick it up by going to my website (https://philaerix.com/) and clicking on the button next to the cover.

Fan of Harem Stories?

If you want to find more harem stories, or just hang out with those who appreciate them, check out the Dukes of Harem, Harem Gamelit Monster Girl Fiction , Harem Lit Readers, and Harem Lit groups on Facebook!

~

Book 2 is already up for preorder, though it will be launched much earlier than the preorder date listed. If you want to check it out, here's the cover and the link to the book.

Https://www.amazon.com/dp/B0CD1NHN8H

**Want to always know when the next book comes out...and get another full-length novel for free?**

Join my newsletter to get the news on what's coming next and you'll also get Elf Queen for free.

Go to philaerix.com and click on the cover to join!

# Also by Phil Aerix

Elf Queen

Aycrishi Sodality Series:

AS1 - Priestess (also on audio)

AS2 - Warrior (also on audio)

AS3 - Vagabond (also on audio)

AS4 - Princess (also on audio)

AS5 - Rebel (audio coming soon)

AS6 - Paragon (audio coming soon)

# ABOUT THE AUTHOR

PHIL AERIX

I'm Phil Aerix and I write fantastical stories with some heat.

I like tales about regular guys who through some twist of fate meet beautiful, sexy women of all kinds who may need some help, a little attention, or someone to go into battle beside. Elves, faeries, beastkin, monster girls, I love them all, and I love writing about them.

You can catch up with me via e-mail at Phil@philaerix.com or on Facebook (https://www.facebook.com/PhilAerixAuthor). I love getting questions or just chatting about the genre. I hope to see you around the block. Or in some harem-centric world, whichever is easiest and the most fun.

https://philaerix.com/
Phil@philaerix.com

Printed in Dunstable, United Kingdom

72346683R10221